The Alluring House on the Corner
a tale of secrets, lies, and twisted family values

By: Lona Wilson

A standalone romance with a guaranteed HEA ending.

This is a work of fiction. Names, characters, businesses, places, events and incidents are either the products of the author's imagination or used in a fictitious manner. Any resemblance to actual people, living or dead, or events is coincidental or fictionalized. No part of this publication may be reproduced, distributed, or transmitted in any form or by any means, including photocopying, recording, or other electronic or mechanical methods, without the prior written permission of the publisher, except in the case of brief quotations embodied in critical reviews and certain other noncommercial uses permitted by copyright law. © 2021 by Lona Wilson. All rights reserved.

Dedicated to Cheryl Shibley Farrer, in memory of her father,

The Reverend Richard L. M. Shibley, January 9, 1925 – February 4, 2017

and their struggles with Alzheimer's

and

To my father, Robert W. Barto July 22, 1915 – February 17, 1982

and his struggles with Multiple Sclerosis

Chapter 1

"Is it really necessary to display that horrible picture next to your bed?" Dori cluck-clucked as she wiggled her cane toward the picture.

Maddie bit her lower lip to maintain control as every muscle in her body stiffened. "He was my husband, Mother, and I loved him."

"You should never have married him. First thing he does is dump you and go off on some ship."

Snapping the top sheet over her bed she fought back the urge to engage her mother in the same old argument.

"You heard me! Right, Madeline? Off he goes, leaving you all alone. I knew he would do that to you. Haven't I always told you, all your life…"

Maddie tuned out the admonition that 'no one would ever love you as much as your mother' as she tucked the sheets under the mattress. But it wasn't working. Dori said it again, and a third time. So not true, so not true!

Covering the pillows with their cases, "It was a different kind of love, Mother."

"*Real* love is love, Madeline. If he had *really* loved you he would have stayed home with you. I knew all along he was just using you…"

Closing off her mind she finished making her bed, taking a quick glance at Marc's handsome face, smiling back at her as he always had. The long, loud, audible sigh from the doorway was just another way her mother expressed her indignation. "You never learned to listen to me, Madeline…"

Her mother talked about love as if she had ever had any to dispense. What a joke. Her mother was probably one of the few persons on earth who didn't have a single breath of love in her body. It was a useless argument. Pushing past her mother, "I'll come and change your sheets after I get this load into the washing machine."

Heading down the hallway ahead of her mother she could hear her, still clacking and sighing.

Dori was agitated, as usual. Her daughter was rude. She wasn't listening to a word she said. Why didn't her daughter take her advice? She'd been giving her excellent guidance all her life, and she constantly rebelled. If she'd been more like her brother she wouldn't have needed so much discipline, but there had to be something wrong with her head to make her so disobedient all the time. She had been, without a doubt, the most rebellious child ever born. She excelled at meanness, always doing things she knew would upset her. The only way to get any peace was to pull her over her knee and swat her with a large wooden spoon. Then off to her room. Silence. Blessed silence. She slapped the tip of her cane against the wall. SMACK. Maddie was 41 for crying out loud, and she hadn't learned a single thing about how people betray and use you. SMACK. "I want some green pea soup."

The screech was always like fingernails on a chalk board. Maddie cringed.

Pushing her hands deep into the washing machine she shoved the sheets down, her knuckles pushing against the bottom of the tub. With a sigh she lowered her head and closed her eyes. Take a deep breath, Maddie, a very deep breath.

"They don't make it anymore, Mother. I've told you that before." She threw a soap capsule into the washing machine, pushing the buttons to get it started. The water hissed as the cycle began and she could almost smell the suds. "Name something else and I'll make it for you," she brushed past her mother again as she walked into the kitchen, picking up dishes her mother had left on the table and putting them into the sink full of water.

"I know we have some in the pantry, Madeline."

Lifting her hands out of the soapy water she turned, picking up the edge of her apron to wipe her hands dry.

There was her mother, in her usual stance, leaning against the doorway, cane in hand, lifting it up and down in a swinging motion. What a sight. All Maddie saw was a ratty old crow who kept coming at her, who hadn't bothered to comb her hair or get out of her faded pajamas. The shock of white that surrounded her mother's irritated face occasionally resembled a halo, which was the antithesis of who she was, but this morning it resembled pictures she had seen of Phyllis Diller. It amused her. If the lighting were right her hair would actually seem to glow. But this morning it looked like she'd stuck her finger in a light socket instead. Maybe if she weren't so tired she would have smiled at the sight.

"I've told you before, several times, it's not available, not even on Amazon."

"Well check the pantry. We had cans and cans of it." Madeline wanted to reach up and plug her ears from the high pitched, demanding voice.

Still clutching her apron with her fists, she mentally counted to three and lowered her voice. Patience, Maddie, patience. She's still your mother. She can't help it. She's been this way from the moment you popped out of the womb. Maybe even from conception. "You ate them all, Mother."

"Don't call me Mother. I've told you to call me Mom. How often do I have to tell you that?" The pitch was rising. Replying wouldn't help. Dori knew Maddie lied to her about everything. She was trying to get even for having to come take care of her.

But Maddie didn't know how bad she hurt with the Multiple Sclerosis. And she wasn't about to tell her, either. It was fun to crack the cane and scream. It was all she had left to do, after all.

"I'll check the pantry," Maddie said, taking the few small steps to open the door.

She moved some cans around, knowing full well there was no green pea soup in the mix. The screeching didn't stop, "Green pea soup and grilled cheese sandwich. I supposed you're going to tell me next that they stopped making cheese. Anything to get out of making me lunch."

Through the crack of the door, she could see her mother's rage increasing, her hands raising and falling in agitation, the cane lifting to the ceiling then cracking down on the floor again, her face turning redder and redder, "We have split pea soup. Will that do?" and didn't she look like the Wicked Witch of the West in the Wizard of Oz?

"NO, Madeline. Why are you so dense?"

Putting both hands on one of the shelves she took several quick breaths. Maddie had kept those shelves perfectly organized. Soups in one section, pasta on another, rice up there, and all the little jars of sauces, herbs and spices across on a turntable. She had to keep calm. Escape was out of the question. There was no way she could pack up and leave. A daughter's duty was to take care of her mother, right? Just as she had been taken care of until she married that "awful, horrible man." True? How could she leave her mother that way? Getting her own apartment after college, and a teaching job. Horrible occupation. It was disgusting. Wasn't it? And getting married! She deserved what happened to her. Her mother had certainly made that clear.

"It's either split pea, or" she shuffled cans around, "chicken noodle, vegetable beef, or tomato."

She heard the crack of the cane against the refrigerator.

"Tomato," and make it quick. "With a grilled cheese sandwich. Two slabs of cheese. White bread. And DON'T

BURN IT," she pointed the cane toward the pantry door, wiggling it in her furor, then turned and left the room.

From the street he thought the house was lovely. Yeah, it was a silly word to use to describe a house, but for some strange reason it suited it to a tee. For just about two years he had wandered down past this house on his daily power walk. This house itself never changed. Not one iota. Other houses left stuff out on the lawn, or kids were playing catch. A man would come out of another house to walk the dog, or a woman was out doing some weeding. Washing cars and taking mail out of the mailbox were all things he saw routinely. But never at the house on the corner. Only one thing seemed to change, actually, but it didn't involve the house itself. While he'd seen a professional group taking care of the yard they could have been hired to mow and weed because the house was empty. They did a good job. Flowers beds had blooming flowers, even in the middle of August. The only one he could identify was black-eyed-Susan. His mother had made sure they were planted on their estate along with a few hundred other posies he had no clue about. Rounding the corner there was a tree on the driveway side of the house. It was some kind of willow tree, loaded with bird feeders. And it was those bird feeders that piqued his interest. Squirrels were always present, and he'd seen many different birds as he passed by on his daily walk. The flash of red always meant a cardinal was busy pulling sunflower seeds out of one of the feeders. Blue jays would swoop in and grab a peanut, shooting back into the sky with their reward. Slowing his pace, he could tell there were several peanut shells at the base of the tree, so it wasn't just seed being offered to nature's wildlife. Over the months he'd found it so fascinating he would turn down the music and slow his pace just to observe. He'd seen starlings, goldfinches, crows, red-winged blackbirds, and lots of little guys he couldn't identify. They zoomed, flitted, soared, and flapped as they made their way to and from the feeders and birdbath. Maybe he should buy a book of Virginia birds. It was a thought. Going past this house was almost like a tiny nature walk interrupted by an asphalt street. There were homes on both sides of the street, of course, of various sizes, designs, and colors, spaced nicely and well cared for but none of them held the mystery of the house on the corner. It was a one-story mixture of tan and brown brick face, and always quiet. There was a large, covered front porch, as well as a smaller one on the side. Chairs were visible but never seemed to change their positions. The only defect was a cracked driveway that was always empty. The most likely clue that someone did live in the house came on trash day. His walk was always spoiled if the trash cans were lined up on the street, waiting for pickup, since they usually smelled, *badly*, as he walked past them. Even with the lids down they stank. There was always a trash can out at that house on trash day. Passing cars spewing exhaust fumes didn't help. Ken had absolutely no idea why this particular house struck him the way it did. But, as usual, after slowing down to see what new pleasures might await him in passing, he sighed, turned up the volume on his Sirius music, and picked up the pace to continue his power walk. Still, he couldn't get that corner house out of his mind. There was something odd about it. Turning down the volume he thought it might help if he carefully looked at all the houses on his walk. Pulling the earbuds out he glanced left then right as he trudged down the street. He needed to look for specific things to see what was missing or had been added to the house on the corner. Shutters? No, they didn't matter. Some had the blue circle of a Ring doorbell and others didn't. It wasn't the color of the door either. He was always amazed when he saw a white house with a green door. Why would they do that? There were some ugly painted doors now that he was checking them out. That wouldn't have escaped his attention for sure though. He had been paying attention to the house on the corner. He'd look for blue lighted doorbells on his next walk, but he didn't think anything about security was the reason. Check that. Houses with those double front doors. He just knew they would be easy to kick in. One good boot and those locks would separate instantly. Landscaping wasn't it. Well, Ken thought. Tomorrow was another day. Maybe if he changed the time of his walk it would make a difference. Sun and shadows would be different. Surely someone lived there. Those peanuts weren't dropping out of the sky! The trash can didn't roll down to the end of the driveway all by itself. Good idea. Someone had to come out of that house at least once a day to take care of all those critters. He would adjust his walk daily until he figured it out and could stop obsessing about it. Unless, of course, the landscaping people were filling them.

She smiled. He was walking down the street. It was his usual power walk, heel down on one foot before the toe left the asphalt on the other, but it seemed he slowed down a bit to watch a squirrel rush to the peanut feeder. Arms swinging, with metronomic precision, sweat was obvious on both his face and t-shirt, even from her viewpoint. He was rather good-looking, she thought. Tall, very well built. That was obvious from the shorts and t-shirt that barely covered his torso, those nice strong shoulders and slim, trim waist. The word 'yummy' shot through her mind, and she had to shake it off. His hair was dark brown, streaked with gray, a lazy strand drooping down his forehead, with droplets of sweat running down his face. Leaning forward as far as she could she watched him pick up his pace and disappear around the next corner. She'd noticed him about two years ago, wondering who he was. Rain, sleet, or snow he would walk by her house at the same basic time every day. She wondered if he was sick and needed to walk for exercise. But he sure didn't look sick. Marathoner? Did they even do walking marathons? Could be military physical fitness stuff. She'd love to know who he was. She sighed, then backed away from the window to finish washing up the pots and pans from her dinner. She didn't even have to look at her watch… 4 P.M. Dinner was over, and she could relax. For some reason, her mother had gotten into the habit of an early dinner. "I used to get up early, so I went to bed early, so I ate early, so just shut up and follow my hours," she would say to Maddie, at least once a week. Shrugging her shoulders, she was glad her mother really did go to bed early. It gave her time to sit outside and watch her critters. She was getting older, her mother was getting older, and she would have loved continuing her prior life if her mother hadn't gotten so sick she needed a caretaker. She was the only one who could fill that role. Her brother was living in Chicago. There was no way he could resettle in Virginia Beach, and besides, she had no idea who he was anymore. So here she was, a widow at the ripe old age of 41, caring for a mother who never cared for her.

Making sure everything in the kitchen was clean and organized per her mother's demands she turned off the light and with a glass of water in her hand walked out the back door and settled into her folding rocking chair to watch the backyard birds, squirrels, and bunnies. She sat down quietly, seeing two baby bunnies eating on grass. Hopping from one blade to another their little white, snowball tails were the cutest thing ever. Even when she walked out into the yard to fill feeders the bunnies would just watch her carefully but never move. The squirrels would pick up a peanut, then sit up on their hind legs and nibble at it. Peanut shells would fly in tiny chewed off pieces, then back to the pile to grab another one. It was a wonderful respite from the doldrums of her daily grind. Placing her water glass on the table beside her chair she leaned back and closed her eyes, listening to the twitter of birds and the clucking of squirrels. Who was he? She had pondered that for the past two years. Every day was the same and always at about the same time. His six-foot frame was slim and well-built without being bulky. In both summer and winter, he wore a white t-shirt and navy-blue lightweight shorts. Winter weather hadn't seemed to affect him. Always the same color clothing. Year around. Did he wash them every day? Did he have several sets? How could he not be affected by the cold weather? On some days it was below freezing, and there he went, at 4 P.M. Like a robot. She snickered. That fit perfectly. Someone had built a robot and it walked around at the same time every day to make sure the oil was circulating in its frame! That would account for the time she was coming back from her neighbor's, and he walked right in front of her – eyes straight ahead, arms bent and moving in time, left, right, left, right. She waved and said, "good afternoon," and he ignored her completely. Okay, nothing really new about that these days. She certainly wasn't someone who would grab a second glance from a man. But that closeup look, she reached out and took a sip of water, had confirmed her earlier description of him. She put her head back against the pillow on the chair. "Why, oh, Why," she whispered. How had it all come to this? She knew from birth she wasn't wanted. At least not by her mother. Her daddy? That was different. She adored him, and just thinking about him brought tears to her eyes. The loud CAW, CAW, CAW, of several crows snapped her out of her thoughts. The crows were angry. Sipping her water she watched carefully, not moving. With a slight sneer she realized the crows sounded just like her mother. Maybe they took lessons from her. The sound of a barking dog caused further warnings from the crows, but the ruckus soon subsided as the dog, probably being walked by its owner, moved past their territory.

Maybe he was a Navy Seal. That would account for all that cold and hot weather walking. She'd seen groups of Navy Seals, in the middle of January, running down the beaches in their Speedo's and jumping into the Atlantic Ocean. It never ceased to amaze her.

Smiling she watched as a squirrel tentatively made its way up the steps and stopped to stare at her. "You looking for some free dinner?" she stopped rocking. The squirrel was a bit skittish, moving side to side with sharp, quick movements. "If you don't mind I'll get up and go inside and bring out a few peanuts," she stood slowly, watching the squirrel scoot backwards as she headed into the house.

It was still there, its eyes watching her return, tail flicking madly, "You remind me of my mother and her cane," as she tossed a peanut toward the squirrel. Deftly moving side to side, it made it to the nut. Picking it up it examined it, then tossed it back down. "Not good enough for you, huh?" She tossed another one down. This nut was apparently acceptable, so off it ran, nut safely in its mouth. "Why is one good peanut not alright and another one is?" she pocketed the three remaining peanuts. It made her wonder since both peanuts seemed to be perfectly fine. Maybe they could smell something. But the squirrel never answered her and was, in fact, racing down the fence with its prize in its mouth. It was curious, but dusk was now upon her with the usual drop in temperature, and she could use a good night's sleep.

Her eyes scanned the street as she slowly washed the pots and pans from dinner. She'd been disappointed for a couple of weeks now. Mr. Walk Around the Block hadn't been around, and it was starting to worry her. Why would it worry her? Why did she care if he hadn't been around? Maybe he found a new route. He probably got tired of the old route after two years and wanted some change. Maybe he'd gone on a vacation. But it would be a long vacation! It wasn't the first time he had disappeared for a week or two, or even three. But it was only recently that she had really begun to notice him. Well, to be truthful, she had to admit, she made it a point to be standing at the window as long as possible around the time he normally passed by the house. She liked seeing his fine features passing by as she cleaned up the dinner plates. Her hands rested in the dishwater as she gazed left and right, but he was nowhere in sight. Letting go of the breath she'd been holding in, she finished rinsing the pots and pans and dried off her hands. She'd stalled as long as she could.

"What were you looking at out that window?"

"Nothing, Moth…Mom. Just watching the squirrel running up and down the tree."

"Seemed a mighty long time to just be watching one squirrel, your head bobbing left and right like you was watching a tennis match!"

"There was more than one squirrel," she lied.

Dori snorted, but said no more, just picked up the cane she'd been tapping on the floor, and turning, "Can't imagine looking at squirrels could be all that exciting," she left the kitchen shaking her head.

Sitting down in one of the kitchen chairs Maddie massaged her forehead with her fingers. Something had to change. Here she was as good as a servant in her mother's home. It was hard to believe it was now fifteen years since she'd married Mark, and twelve since he died. The squadron wives had stood by her. Her good friends and fellow teachers were a constant source of comfort. She had managed to make a life, continuing to teach at the same school where friends of hers had introduced her to him. She felt a tear trickle down her cheek. Now she was 41 and stuck in limbo. One day was pretty much like the rest of them and it bothered her that she never had any excitement to look forward to anymore. It was just her mother, badgering her day in and day out, and tons of work. Her mother didn't lift a finger now – it was always one excuse after another, and *all* were, she would never hesitate to point out, because of the Multiple Sclerosis. She had the symptoms well memorized. Her mother didn't realize that Maddie saw she could walk just fine, without the cane. Maddie always left her bedroom door open in case her mother needed help during the night. She often watched her get out of bed and walk down to the kitchen for something. No cane. But then again, she didn't need the cane when she was swirling it around as she walked either. It had to be nothing but a prop, meant to keep Maddie off center. She sighed. She desperately needed to get away, even for just an evening. Elle called several times a month to see how she was doing. That's what best friends did, and Maddie needed an evening out with her bestie. Or something! Any *mention* of wanting to go out for an evening was met with guilt trips, handed out like candy - 'I'm your mother, and you owe me.' 'Labor was horrible with you. Your brother was so easy.' 'All you've ever done was get into trouble.' But she never got an answer when she asked what that trouble was. The spankings, though. She remembered all those.

His plan hadn't been working at all. He'd shifted his walk routine to pass the house on the corner at various times. He even walked early in the morning, just as dawn broke, but nothing. He had to admit he was enjoying the smell of fresh air, the left-over smell of mown grass, the absence of any sounds. No cars passing, no children laughing at play, just the sounds of birds waking up in preparation for the never-ending search for food. The air was calm and the temperatures much more pleasant although the humidity could use a good kick in the pants. Each day he was adding 15 minutes to his start time. That came with increased noise, sprinklers hissing, a few cars passing, and the occasional *BANG* of a huge trash truck picking up a massive commercial container and dumping the contents into the belly of the beast. He figured fourteen possible hours in a day, with 15-minute increments, gave him 56 opportunities to see who lived there. He hated to admit he was becoming obsessed with the idea of that house, but he wasn't harming anyone, and it was really a pleasant game to play. Really, that was all it was! He had to figure out what it was about that house that seemed so different from every other house he walked past. Good chance it was some old geezer living there, maybe all by himself, likely old because there was never a dog barking in the back yard.

It was the 8:15 walk when it hit him. He had started making mental notes of all the houses on his walk. Doors were opening and occupants were retrieving their morning paper. Dogs were being let out in back yards to bark and do their business. Garage doors were grinding their way to the top, and blinds were being lifted...*blinds were being lifted*! That was it! The blinds on the house on the corner were *never* lifted. Four in the afternoon and all the blinds were always down. He sped up and stopped at the corner. The front of the house was silent. All the blinds were down. Slowly continuing he saw that the side had one large picture window, probably in the kitchen. It was the only one without an obvious blind, but he couldn't see into it either. He saw no light inside. No movement. Maybe it was similar to cars with the darkened windows. You could see out, but no one could see in. Probably an illusion since it was so early. No one was likely in the room to be seen. Total privacy? Hiding? Obviously, he was going to have to walk past that window after dark to see if there was any light on the other side! Now he was determined. Someone lived there. Someone fed all those critters. He simply couldn't rest until the game ended.

It was the day before trash day. Just one more thing to have to do each week. Making the usual round of the waste baskets – somehow her mother managed to fill up every one of them, every week – all three bedrooms and bathrooms, kitchen, family room, laundry room, and dining room. Absolutely amazing. It was easy enough to take the plastic liner out, but it took time to put a new one in. "What's your hurry?" her mother poked her head into the master bathroom. "I will have more before the day is over." And even if she didn't she'd wad up some paper or something to make sure they were full again.

"I know you will," she set the basket back down, "but I need to get as much done as I can. I still have to drag that pine tree out to the street." That had been an emotional day. She had let it grow to see if she could identify it, and when she figured out it was a white pine she knew it would get far too large for where it was planted. Having grown about seven feet in less than a year she asked her yard man to kindly cut it down.

"Why do you have to drag it out? Why didn't the man who cut it down drag it out?" her cane was tapping, tap, tap, until Maddie stood up and glared at her. "Don't you glare at me young lady. I can still put you over my knee," the tip of the cane threatening to stab her in the chest.

"The man cut the tree down," she edged past her mother, pushing the cane down and away, "after the trash truck had already gone last week. I didn't want it out on the street for seven days." Picking up a towel her mother had dropped on the floor, "What would you like for lunch?"

"HA, like you care what I want to eat. Just pick any old can of something."

I can do that, Maddie thought. Chicken Noodle.

As her mother ate, Maddie finished picking up the trash. "I'll take this out and then drag the tree out," she watched as her mother slurped soup. Getting no reaction, she headed outside. The tree had been placed against the back fence. The needles had already begun to turn brown, but there was still a strong odor of that wonderful pine scent, and it saddened her for a moment. A white pine. Unfortunately, an 80-foot-tall tree wasn't practical, so it had to go. She regretted having to end its life, but it had been a volunteer, likely donated by a passing bird.

There was just enough room to turn it around to pull it out to the street from its base. It was heavy, but doable. The past few years had shown her she could do a lot more than she ever thought possible. When Mark died she had a house to take care of. No more apartment living where all the infrastructure problems were handled by someone else. So, she had learned some basic plumbing when the toilet quit working. Her dad, thank God, had seen to it that she knew how to use a hammer, screwdriver, saw, and more. "You're going to need these skills all your life, Maddie," he had said. She missed his wonderful presence every day of her life. Pulling on the end of the tree the scraping sound of the pine needles against the dirt made her wonder if a lot of pine needles were being left behind. She hoped not. That would be another job, raking them up. Lost in thought, she had never been able to figure out why her dad married her mother. They were total opposites. In every way. As far as she knew maybe they weren't even married. They'd never celebrated an anniversary, that was for sure.

Lugging the tree to the gate she opened it and began the pull it down the side of the garage, walking backwards to drag it to the driveway. Stopping at the front of the garage for a moment to catch her breath, she lowered the trunk, and shook her arms for a moment. Fifteen feet to go, she bent to grab the trunk again.

"Can I help you with that?"

Chapter 2

She jumped six feet into the air and screamed. Seriously, it had to be at least six feet. It felt like six feet. Landing on her toes she jerked backwards and turned, her face ashen in fear and her hands shaking. Seeing a pair of shoes and bare legs she fought to catch her breath. She reached up, putting her hand on her chest, gasping, "You scared me to death." Her eyes moved swiftly from the bare legs, to shorts and t-shirt, and a face.

"I'm so very sorry," he backed up, hands outstretched, palms our, in obvious apology. "I truly am. I just thought you could use some help with that tree."

Oh, my God, it was him. It was Mr. Walk Around the Block. She fought to calm down, fear turning to astonishment. He was so much better looking close up, face to face. His eyes were like saucers in their alarm, but so blue she could only think of films she had seen of the Maldives. Or Angelina Jolie. It was impossible not to stare. Suddenly speechless, and transfixed by his eyes, she cocked her head and dropped her arm to her side.

"You're Mr. Walk Around the Block," she uttered. Oh, God, had she said that out loud?

"Who?"

Swallowing, she looked down at the ground. "Sorry, it's just that I've seen you walking by on several occasions."

"Ah," he smiled. "Yes. I walk every day unless there's a thunderstorm." WOW! What was he looking at? She was nervous but trying hard to calm down. And lovely!

"You've changed your time, then."

She spoke so softly he barely heard her.

"Only temporarily. It was, ah," think fast Ken, "very hot during the afternoons, so I moved the time up a bit."

"More than a bit, but I understand. It does get hot. Even late morning and it's already stifling."

"I'm Ken. Ken Avery. I live down the street a-ways." He didn't want to offer his hand in case she objected. Better to keep some distance for the time being.

Goodness, he was handsome. And here she was in her tacky shorts and stained t-shirt, hair a mess, sweating from dragging the tree… "I'm Maddie…. Davis."

Taking a small step forward he lowered his hands to his side, "Nice to meet you, Maddie" He was both bemused and fascinated by the woman standing in front of him. Of all the women he had ever known he couldn't think of one that would have been caught dead dragging a tree out to the street. Maybe he'd been moving in the wrong circles. Well, clearly he *had* been walking in the wrong circles. He hadn't dated many women in his life, but the few he had dated spent more time in the beauty shop than in the kitchen. His mother would have been horrified at what was going through his mind at that moment.

"Can I help you with the tree?"

"I can manage, thanks."

"I can see you can manage, but I'd like to help." In more ways than one, maybe? For someone who looked a bit like a waif, she was gorgeous. He could tell she liked what she was seeing. Her hazel eyes were fixed on him but without the usual coyness and flirting. No eyelids fluttering. No sexy grin, and she turned down his first offer to help with the tree.

"Well, alright. If you drag it out I'll open the garage door and get the branch cutter and start cutting limbs off."

"I can help with that, too, if you don't mind." Anything to keep looking at her.

"I don't want to interfere with your walk."

"Trust me. I'll enjoy the respite. Walks can get very boring at times. I play music and listen to the radio, but some days are just boring."

Maddie paused, her eyes narrowing, "I waved at you once, but you ignored me."

"Are you serious?" He felt she looked a bit offended by the memory.

"Yes. I was coming back across the street from my neighbor's, and you walked right in front of me. Like two feet away. I waved and said, 'good afternoon' but you just stared straight ahead and ignored me. You didn't even turn your head."

He reached up and scratched his jaw, "I sometimes get in a zone, deep in thought, and often wonder how I did the entire walk without remembering a single thing about it."

"Like driving to the store and not remembering any of the turns. Sort of on instinct." She nodded in understanding.

"Exactly. And I wouldn't have heard you speak with the earbuds in my ears. I do apologize. I'm usually the friendly sort with all my neighbors."

Maddie simply nodded. "Let me get the clippers."

He watched as she walked to the garage and entered the code to open the door. Slowly backing up with the tree he kept his eyes on her. For some reason he couldn't explain, he couldn't stop watching. There were two garage doors and only one opened. Seeing a tan Toyota, he wondered if the other door hid a car. Or maybe her husband was at work and that side was empty. He wondered about that. If her husband was home wouldn't he be the one dragging the tree out to the street? As he reached the asphalt, and turned the tree against the curbing, Maddie returned with a rachet looper, but she stopped a good ten feet before reaching him.

"What are you looking at?" he smiled as she stood, silently watching something in a bush.

"Well," she crooked her finger for him to approach, "There are two Monarch butterflies zipping around the butterfly bush, and" she leaned in, "several bees, too."

"A fan of nature," he smiled. Standing next to her seemed so, so nice. Here he was, in a driveway, talking to a woman named Maddie, who's clothing was simple and well-worn, with not one drop of makeup on her face, shoulder-length dark brown hair that showed a bit of soft curl on the ends, and she was, well, simply lovely. That word was like a loop in his head.

He stared, more at her than the bees and butterflies. It was all so natural, so pleasant.

She turned from the bush, "Thanks for the help. I just need to trim off the branches," she lifted the looper, "so the city will pick it all up tomorrow."

"Let me," he reached over, and as he touched her hand to take the looper she dropped it, jumped back, and shook her hand.

"I just got stung by a bee," she said, looking at her hand, left, right, over, under, "but I don't see a stinger."

He started to reach for her hand to check it out but thought better of it. "No stinger? Are you allergic?"

"Ah, no. I'm not allergic, but I don't see a stinger."

"Maybe it almost stung you, but you moved so fast it didn't pierce the skin."

"Yeah, maybe, but it sure had the zing to it. I'll check it later to make sure nothing is swollen."

"Good idea." Bending down he picked up the looper and headed toward the tree. As he cut, Maddie took the branch and made a pile for pickup. In just a few minutes the job was done.

"Thank you," Maddie made sure to memorize his features as he handed the looper back to her. She wanted to be able to put his gorgeous face in her mind every time he walked by the house. If only she could have snuck the phone out of her pocket and taken a picture of him, "Maybe I'll see you on your walk again."

"I'll make sure to wave and smile. I'll even take the ear buds out when I pass," he laughed. He wasn't about to make the same mistake again.

"You best get going. It's already 90 degrees out here. Do you need water or anything?"

"No, I'm fine," he started backing up, "I'll see you again, I hope." It was killing him, and he had to ask, "and maybe meet your husband?"

Her expression changed. She stilled, and he watched as she seemed to be debating something. Her eyes had suddenly lost their sparkle like a cloud moving over the sun to dull the day. "I'm a widow," she shifted her feet.

"I'm so sorry," he blurted out and watched as she raised her hand and waved, then turned and walked back into the garage, closing the door.

"Who was that man? I saw you out there all smiling and cozy with him? You find another loser to latch onto or something?"

"He's a neighbor, just walking by and saw me dragging the tree. He offered to help. Nothing wrong with that," she felt her breathing pick up just a little bit as she flashed a picture of him in her memory. She had to get over that. It was one thing to look and another to let her mind think stupid things about him. He could well be married. Rats! She realized she hadn't looked for a ring. Closing her eyes and tuning out her mother, who was still ranting about men, she tried to see his hand. Was there a glint from the sun? He'd grabbed the looper with his right hand. Rats! She'd try to pay attention when he walked by another time. Speaking of which. No wonder he asked about meeting her husband. She was still wearing her wedding band. He probably saw it. Maybe it was time to put it into her jewelry box.

"…love you as much as your mother, and you know I've told you that and you never listen to what I say. You married that man who up and dumped you…"

Same old lines. Her mother had no idea what a wonderful husband Mark had been. They were so much in love, and when he died...such painful memories. Never again. So, who was this Ken? A sudden shift in her mind? How does that happen? Still... He looked to be in his mid-forties, so why was he home every day and taking walks around the block. Maybe he worked from home? Or maybe he worked a midnight shift? He did sort of come and go. She'd see him for weeks at a time and then not again for several weeks. Weird. Maybe he travelled a lot for his job, like a traveling salesman? STOP THINKING ABOUT HIM! Gosh, he really was the type of man worthy of a second glance. Or third glance. He had a beautiful, deep voice, and eyes of blue that made her want to swim in them. Hmm. That was stupid. She always talked to everyone walking a dog, or baby. It was natural and she knew them all by their first names. The dogs, too. But this Ken – he was different. He seemed to be pulling at her for some reason. Maybe it was time she figured out if she could BE pulled.

"...are you making for dinner?"

"What?"

"What are you making for our dinner, Maddie? Honestly," the cane went into motion, making circles in front of her face.

"Shrimp Creole."

A couple of 'cluck-clucks' and "well, get on with it then."

The air conditioning felt so good when he finished his walk. July and August in Virginia Beach were always hot and humid. It wasn't unusual for temperatures to soar well into the 90's and the heat index to go over 100. Walking earlier in the day seemed to be a good idea after all. At least he wasn't soaking wet. He'd really enjoyed helping Maddie with the tree. Serendipity? Retrieving a pitcher of cold water from his refrigerator he poured a glass and guzzled it, all the while speculating on what might be going on in the house on the corner. Did she live alone? Big house for one person, but she could have lived there with a husband – the one who had died. He placed the empty glass on the counter to reuse for the entire day, then headed to the bathroom for a shower. His sister would have been proud of him, helping out a neighbor like he'd done. They had been raised with specific goals in life. Never do something you can pay someone else to do. Or, better said, never get dirt under your fingernails. Trish, at one time, had even let her fingernails grow to over an inch in length, proving that she couldn't possibly stoop to the level of menial labor. Not a chip off the old fingernail paint, ever. Servants galore were there for that sort of thing. He snorted out a laugh. Those inch long nails were long gone with two children and a husband slamming her feet down to the real earth. But he smiled knowing that Trish was happier than he had ever seen her. The kids were teenagers, well behaved and a credit to a strong set of parents. Living on the Eastern Shore had given the kids opportunities not often available to most American children. As a Federal Wildlife Officer, Paul, and by extension, Trish, had used every opportunity to teach their kids about nature, conservation, and how to enjoy the beauty that was the Eastern Shore. Camping, hiking, fishing, boating – all were part of their everyday lives. The most fun Ken ever had was watching his sister pick up all the doggie doo-doo in the back yard. He wished he had a picture. He couldn't help but smirk. If their mother hadn't already died she would have fallen down dead on the grass had she seen her daughter scooping up poop! Whoever said a leopard can't change its spots wasn't around to see Trish fall head over heels in love with Paul. Little by little her fingernails got shorter, and her clothing got more casual. Paul would take her hiking, camping, and fishing. Seeing his sister with dirty, tousled hair, and a huge smile on her face after a weekend of camping was a sure sign she was going to do just fine in life. At the same time his own brothers were a bit more, well, hmm...stuffy was a fair word to use. Reed for sure was stuffy, two years older and lived at the ocean front. He was a high-priced attorney, married to an upper-crust woman who was every bit the image of their mother. Society and all that. Drew was next by one year and lived in Suffolk. He owned a peanut farm, of all things, and loved it. He wasn't so much stuffy as alienated. He'd have to go visit him one of these days.

   Turning on the shower he waited until it was hot enough then stepped in. She mentioned her last name was Davis. A widow. That complicated things. If she'd said her husband would be home at six for dinner he could have waved goodbye, and just waved at each passing in the future. If she was outside, of course. Or he could change his route. He could also get called back into action, too, and that would remove him from the scene for four to six weeks, or even longer. He never knew. He was on what could be called a "go team" and that meant being on an airplane within 24 hours and onsite within 48. Completely lathering his body, head to toe, he leaned his head against the tile. Oh, God, this was not good. His thoughts were totally not good. He shouldn't be thinking about her. Never in his life had he given much thought to any woman. He felt the water go colder as he stood lost in the visions dancing across his mind like little fireflies, flitting and dancing, each a different image of her in a different pose. With a deep intake of breath, he turned off the shower and grabbed the warm towel. He'd spent his entire life with one objective – to help humanity and be happy doing it. It had worked for all his adult life. No woman had ever really come close to making him want anything more than what he had. The last thing he wanted was a society girl who gave him daily reminders of his mother. Most women he met seemed to be shallow or clingy, or wanted to snatch him up because of his rank and job in the Navy. It was hard to keep himself low-key when he went to mandatory military events like those held in the officer's clubs or homes of senior officers. There were always daughters of Admirals or co-workers who would make it a point to slide up next to him, their eyelashes fluttering. Most were divorced and on the hunt. Ugh. No thanks. And now, at his age he was finally free to do anything he wanted to do – no strings attached to anyone, and only his volunteer work, which he could quit at any time, could get in the way. Now to figure out how to keep it that way. He was comfortable living alone. He loved being able to travel at the drop of a hat without anyone getting upset or angry that he wouldn't be home for dinner that night. If he didn't do his laundry it didn't matter. No one ever came to his home. He'd heard over, and over that a man's home was his castle, and that's exactly what Ken thought about his home. Yes, his home, decorated for a man. No frilly curtains. He could put his stuff anywhere he wanted to without getting glaring looks from a woman. He could dry his hands on the guest towels in the bathroom because he never had any guests. He really liked the house, a gift from his father when both he and Trish had made the gut-wrenching decision to move their dad into a nursing home. Alzheimer's was relenting. His father could only tell him, in one of his lucid moments, that he'd put Ken's name on the deed. "Reed is wealthy enough to keep his wife happy," his dad had said. "Don't know about Drew except he's happy, I guess. Has that peanut farm, you know," he'd scratched his head. "And Trish is well situated. You just came out of the Navy and never had a home. Now you have a home."

Both Trish and Ken, and a few nursing aides, had been caring for his dad until it was obvious he needed more specialized attention than they could provide on their own.

Ken's eyes scanned the kitchen. He really loved this house. It was a one story, much like Maddie's, and he'd inherited it fully furnished. When his dad sold the big mansion, after too many years of living alone in five-thousand square feet, he used the profits wisely. Besides buying the smaller home he had saved enough money for years of care at a top-notch facility. Maybe his father was a smart businessman, true enough, but he hadn't really been a father to any of them. What he had provided for materially he had taken away emotionally. Fifteen hours a day working tended to do that to children. Tomorrow he would go visit his dad. He no longer recognized Ken, but Ken wanted to show up every now and then to make sure he was being properly cared for.

She'd found herself wondering what time Ken might walk by today. As a result, she kept manufacturing reasons to be at the kitchen sink, looking out the window. She'd managed three visits to the window before her mother plunked her butt down at the kitchen table. Quickly going to the fridge, she pulled out various veggies and took them to the sink to chop.

"What are you doing?"

"Preparing dinner, Mother. Lots of good veggies."

"Is that *all*?"

"With chicken."

Dori didn't move so after dragging out the chopping as long as possible she was stuck with actually making some kind of dinner that used chicken and veggies. Finally tossing it into the oven with a can of soup and milk over it, "It's an experiment, Mother."

Her eyes opened wide, and she half stood up, "You're going to experiment on me?"

"On both of us, Mother." With her back turned toward her mother she had to smile at the gasp she heard.

In the end the meal had turned out rather well. Her mother made no comment at all, so that was a sign that it wasn't all that bad. But Dori would never give her the satisfaction of complimenting her on her cooking. Amazing.

Her phone rang just as dinner ended. Putting the dishes down on the counter top she took her phone out of her pocket. It was Elle calling. Oh, lordie! She had made so many promises to her and broken every one of them but now, suddenly, she was in a mood to strike out and have a bit of fun. Anything to get away for a couple of hours. Hearing her mother push back her chair she answered the phone.

"Elle! How are you?"

"Missing my Bestie. Joan and I were just talking about going out for a bit, and you simply have to come with us. It's been way too long, Maddie. Summer is almost over, and we'll be back teaching and not have the time for all this fun."

Maddie listened, all the while watching her mother make faces at her, while spinning her cane. This was *not* going to go well with her mother dearest.

"I'd love to come. I need to take a break. Where shall I meet you?"

"Beachside Social at 7!"

"I'll be there. It will be so good to see you guys again."

"You aren't going out are you? You can't you know."

"Yes, Mother, I'm going out to meet Elle and a couple other friends. I taught school with them, and they stood by me when Mark was killed."

"What about ME?" she screamed. "Didn't I stand by you, too when that jerk got killed? How can you leave me alone?"

Exasperated, "I've been stuck in this house for months, except for grocery shopping, and it ends tonight. I will have a life outside this house." Where had all that come from? She never thought she'd talk like that to her mother. "I've watched you get up at night and walk down the hall without that cane. Most nights you go to bed and stay there. And just as a matter of fact," she took in a deep breath and faced her mother, "you most certainly did *not* stand by me when Mark died. You skipped the funeral and memorial service."

"I had other things to do right then! The world doesn't stop every time somebody dies you know."

Maddie's mouth dropped in shock. Gasping, "Is that so? Well, then, alright. Consider that I just died, and your world can just keep on spinning, so whether or not I'm in this house shouldn't matter."

"Well, it DOES matter, miss smarty-pants. I'm your mother and you owe me. How dare you go out and leave me alone."

"You have a choice, Mother. If you EVER talk to me like that again I'll go back to my own house, which I still own. I can have the tenants leave at any time. Then you will be alone, every single day, to cook for yourself, take out the trash, do the dishes and vacuum the floor. And laundry. You can do that, too. I'm tired of being a slave." What in the world had come over her? One phone call from a friend, she guessed. A friend she had ignored for almost a year because of her mother. And somewhere, deep in the back of her mind, a guy who intrigued her. Her past life ended today. Oh, dear Lord, somehow that burden was easing. She felt her eyes mist but recovered quickly as her mother droned on.

"You always were a smart-mouthed little snot. Always causing trouble and needing a heavy hand to control you. So, GO. Go have your fun. Just hope I don't have a heart attack, or seizure, or fall or something while you're gone. That would show you up for sure."

"You have your phone, Mother. Use it if you fall, or feel dizzy, or your arm starts hurting."

Slamming the cane down on the table, "You'll be sorry. Everything I've ever given you, all your life, the money I've spent on you for clothing and food."

"Not gonna guilt me anymore, Mother. As I recall you did all that for Dan as well, and you never took a switch to his sweet butt... he knew he was the guilty party and just stood by while you whipped me so hard I couldn't sit down... he knew I would never rat him out... and I don't see Dan here fixing your dinner."

"Men don't do that sort of thing. It's a woman's job to take care of her parents when they get old and sickly."

"Get used to it, Mother. I'll leave at six and be at the ocean front. I'll have my cell phone, but if you call me it better be because you've just called rescue. If you cry wolf I absolutely guarantee you I'll move out tomorrow." She was shocked at the words coming out of her mouth. But it was refreshing to finally stand up for herself. "Now, I'm going to change my clothes when I get the dishes done and go out for an evening with my friends."

Maddie couldn't understand why the cane didn't snap in two. Her mother was literally slamming it against the wall with force. And, oh, geeze, glancing out the window, there he was, walking by. He looked up and waved and frantic to wave back she splashed water all over the window. His smile. Oh, lordie, she could look at that smile all night long. Maybe he was the reason she decided to go out with her friends? Now that was an interesting thought. If he wasn't married maybe he'd ask her out for coffee sometime. Or maybe she could offer him coffee on the porch. Forget him meeting her mother. That would be a bad idea, or more likely, disastrous. And then he was gone around the corner. She sighed, finished the dishes, and headed for the shower.

His walk would be abbreviated, but he was back to the 4 P.M. time. He didn't want to take his usual long walk because he was going to see his father, but he couldn't do that without seeing if Maddie might be outside, or at least at the window. His thoughts were so centered he'd forgotten to turn on the music, and before he realized it he was at her corner, now passing her house again. Yes, it did make a difference when all the blinds were down. Like some serious privacy concerns. Could she be hiding from something? Couldn't be avoiding the sun. No, not likely. She had spent time outside with it beating down on her. She said she'd waved at him once before while coming back across the street from a neighbors, but for the life of him he couldn't remember anything about it. Not only could it have been weeks, or even months ago, but he had no idea *which* neighbor. He wanted – no he needed to find out more about her. Mysterious, yet she had said she was a widow. She could have said her husband was at work. It had taken her a few seconds to give him that information, like she wasn't sure she could trust him with it. Maybe if he had told her he was a retired Naval Officer? Might have made a difference. For sure he wouldn't have shared that he was a naval flight surgeon. It never ceased to amaze him. Say those three words and everyone in the room suddenly surrounded him with medical problems. It had gotten so bad that he would just tell everyone he worked in Intelligence. All he had to do was say he couldn't talk about his job, and that would end any further questioning. Maybe next time he saw her outside he could tell her that. Maybe it would put her a bit at ease. She might be thinking he was a serial killer or something. A woman alone couldn't be too careful. He looked up at her window – the only window that didn't have a blind. He could see a figure standing there, so he waved, and watched as she waved back. Was that good, or bad? Probably not good.

A quick shower and off to see his dad. He was sleeping and Ken didn't want to disturb him. It was clear to him, however, that he was being well cared for by the nurses and staff. He'd come back again in a day or so.

Chapter 3

She took her time driving to the oceanfront. It would be nice to see Elle again, but it was hard to trust her. Their history was not pretty. Rather, Elle's wasn't, and Maddie was not a fan of Elle's lifestyle. But Elle had steadfastly stood by her side when Mark was killed and slowly helped her through the major grief cycles. She was an odd woman, fiercely loyal to her teacher friends, but not her own husband and kids. She was seven years younger than Maddie and already had a child when they first met. They'd become close friends when Elle began teaching at Corporate Landing School. Where had all those years gone? But Elle had so many faults that some couldn't be easily overlooked. Some, in fact, made her stomach turn. She was two different people, really. Elle had her sweet, caring side, and her wild side, and maybe she was schizophrenic. Maddie had often wondered about that. She grabbed the steering wheel, remembering the time she paid Elle's fine to keep her out of jail. The judge had told her to get professional help. Elle couldn't even explain why she shoplifted. She brushed it off and promised to never do it again. She begged Maddie to keep her secret, and Maddie had reluctantly agreed. It didn't make sense though. She could well afford to buy anything she wanted. Dick made good money and loved her. She was a good mother to her son, and he was growing up to be a fine young man. But it didn't stop with shoplifting. That's what gave her shivers, just thinking about it. Who *was* this woman? It stunned her the time that Mark was on exercises and Elle called her and begged her for the use of her house for a rendezvous with a lover. That was so shocking Maddie could barely answer. It was a good thing Elle was asking by phone. Finding out that she was cheating on her husband was too much. She refused to let Elle use her home. There was simply no way she was going to go shopping or something, for a couple of hours, just to give Elle time to spend in a bed at her home with some random guy...

She just couldn't summon any real closeness with Elle anymore. She cared about her, enough to go to lunch with her, but she'd never really be able to trust her again. Anyway, this was a great excuse to start spreading her wings again. Whether or not it was this Ken's doing she wasn't sure, but it was nice to be on her own again, even for an hour or two. Mark had been gone twelve years, and as much as she still missed him she was beginning to think she could have another life where someone cared as much about her as she did about him.

Elle was waiting outside the door to the club as Maddie approached.

"Joan is in getting us a table. It's so good to see you again Maddie. How have you been doing?"

Managing a wry grin, "You've met my mother. That should answer all your questions."

"Oh, my. You're still taking care of her then?"

"Things are going to change after tonight." Walking to the back of the restaurant Joan greeted her with a huge hug. "You look fantastic, Maddie. It's been forever!"

"She was just telling me about how she's taking care of her mother," Elle pointed out, as they all sat down.

"It seems like years since you left your job to do that," Joan signaled for a waiter.

"It has been years! You both know I taught for seven years after Mark died, but then Mom told me she had multiple sclerosis and needed me to help care for her. I moved in with her and tried to teach for another three years, but it was exhausting. So, I left my job to help her. Idiot that I was I believed she was in horrible shape with the MS."

Eyes bugging out, "She doesn't have MS?" Elle gasped.

"Oh, yes. She does. But it's a slow kind apparently and she gets around just fine. For five years now I've done all the shopping and house stuff and just tonight," she pointed to Elle, "your phone call struck a nerve. I told her I wasn't going to be her slave any longer and she could start taking care of herself."

"I can just see Dori's face now?" mused Elle

"Actually, you'd hear her cane. I think she pretends it's like a whip, she keeps pointing it at me and banging it against walls, and tap, tap, tapping it. Makes me nuts."

"I only remember seeing Dori once, so I don't know much about her," Joan stopped as the waiter arrived. "I'll have the Cosmo, please."

Both Elle and Maddie followed suit. Joan turned back to Maddie. "Was she like that when you were growing up?"

Maddie snorted. "She was worse. Old age has slowed her down and I'm too big now to put over her knee and beat the living.... well, I couldn't sit down for a bit."

"I am so sorry," Joan put her hand over her mouth. "I can't even imagine…"

Maddie shrugged her shoulders. "It was always something my brother did that I got blamed for. If he hit a baseball through the front window, and I was playing with dolls in the back yard, I was the guilty party and got the paddle. When he was younger he would snicker at me for not ratting him out, but he and I both knew Mother would never believe me, so there was no point. It was obvious my mother enjoyed beating me, and when I got to the point that I refused to cry she would double down."

"Didn't you tell me once," Elle broke in, "that your brother lived in Chicago?"

"Yup. Completely out of touch. Mother moved back here after Daddy died. Dan was old enough to stay in Chicago."

The drinks arrived and they tapped their glasses together in a toast to promise to get together more often, then sipped.

"Love the cranberry!" Elle smiled.

Reminiscing over the next two hours was like a breath of fresh air. Maddie sipped her drink slowly, knowing she had to drive home. The same couldn't be said of Elle, so it appeared to her that not much had changed in Elle's life. Her "how's the family" question was met with a good report. Her son was doing well, and her husband was still working at the same job. But Maddie knew there was more to the story. She was glad Joan was there or Elle would have been bending her ear about the latest escapade. Elle would never quit until she was caught. It was what it was. Joan on the other hand had a solid marriage and three children. Maddie noted that Joan had only had one drink, like her, while Elle had three. And more to the point, as Joan finished her drink she bid them goodbye, as she had to get home.

"I'm right behind you, Joan. We need to get together again soon," Maddie stood. "We need to let Elle get home before she has to call a cab."

All three laughed. "Well," Elle said, "since I don't see any handsome guys in here tonight, I guess I'll head on home, too."

Maddie swallowed, wondering if Joan knew Elle's habits. Since she didn't flinch she either knew or thought it was Elle cracking a joke. They all promised to meet again around Christmas, for lunch.

That could have gone worse, for sure, Maddie thought. Making sure to stay within the speed limit she drove down I-264 and headed home. It was only 8:30 P.M. so it wasn't like she's stayed out all night, yet that couple hours of freedom since backing out of the driveway was like a shot of fresh air. Even better neither one of them asked if she was seeing anyone. They just assumed she was consumed with taking care of her mother. She wasn't seeing anyone anyway. But she wanted to. Her eyes had scanned the bar just in case, maybe, he'd be there, too? Silly woman.

She was still up! Maddie wasn't surprised, somehow.

"So, are you done having fun?"

"It was nice, Mother. They are both very good friends of mine and I've ignored them for too long."

"You don't need any friends. You have enough to do here to keep you occupied."

"Nope. Not gonna happen. I told you earlier if you give me a problem because I go out to meet friends for lunch or dinner, or even if I start dating someone," OH, wouldn't that be nice! "I'll simply move out."

"I'll kill myself."

AH, the ultimate guilt trip. This was a new one. She'd never tossed that one out, and since the cane was circling it was an obvious ploy, "Well, you know, ultimately there's nothing I can do to stop you. I can't watch you 24/7 because I have to shop for groceries and sleep. So, if you decide to do it then I won't be able to call rescue for you."

BANG!

Maddie actually jumped, then glared at her mother. "One more, Mother, and I'm gone."

She watched her mother back up a step, then start crying. Oh, goodie. Guilt trip number two. "But I need you Maddie. I can't do all of this stuff myself anymore."

"We can find you a nursing home then and sell this house."

The shock on her mother's face was worth every word she had just said. "Yes, Mother. There are several nursing homes. I'll start checking them out tomorrow."

After several moments of silence, and standing stock still, her mother finally softened her facial features. "Okay, then. You can go out and have fun. Just stay and help me." Maddie had to bite her tongue to keep from asking her mother to say 'PLEASE'! But she had pushed her further than she thought she could. And it felt good.

"I'll stay for now and we'll see how it goes, Mother. Believe me, though, when I say I won't forget any of this. I know you're suffering, and I do want to help you, but you're going to have to help yourself as best you can as well. You can't just sit back, moan and groan, and not at least try to help yourself."

Dori nodded. Maddie watched as she left the room, cane in hand but not rotating, tapping, or banging. How in the world had she found the courage to confront her mother? Yes, she did need help. Yes, there were things Dori couldn't do anymore and did need someone there, whether she hired out or Maddie stayed. Maddie made a promise to herself. She would help but her mother would have to do what she was able to do. Maddie knew her weak points with the MS. It was hard for her mother to walk. She was tired a lot, and her limbs were weaker than they'd ever been. Tingling and numbness were persistent. Her vision, especially in one eye, was "smeary" as her mother described it. She also would experience dizziness every now and then, ergo she used the cane. Hmm – she HAD the cane. She didn't necessarily use it as intended. Regardless, she had been properly diagnosed and did need help for her physical illness. It was the mental stuff that Maddie had to get past, and she swore she would not put up with all the guilt being thrown at her.

It was late and her mother had apparently settled down. Her bedroom door was closed. With a quick shower Maddie fell into bed, both exhausted and exhilarated.

The next several days were pretty much like all the others except her mother had managed to calm down. Her speech was softer, and Maddie appreciated not having to listen to the screeching. Even the tapping had ceased. Maybe this could become doable. If she took time off now and then, to do some fun things, or even just shop for an hour without needing anything… but she was disappointed. She hadn't seen Ken walk by and she was definitely watching for him. He'd said he was changing his hours, yet he'd been there at 4 the last time she'd seen him. Maybe he was coming earlier since it was so hot out. That's what he'd said. So, okay. She'd change her hours for feeding then. And, naturally, it would take her much longer to do all that feeder filling and changing the water in the bird bath. She might even pull a weed or two from the flower bed. She only used sunflower seed, so those didn't make weeds. They made sunflowers. They didn't grow very tall though, and she finally realized it was because they were growing under the shade of a willow tree. Well, duh! They are sunflowers, which means they need SUN! Didn't stop other weeds from finding their way into the beds though. She had already done her morning feeder rounds, but, heck, another check on them wouldn't hurt. In fact, she'd go out every hour. It wasn't like she was stalking him. He was just a nice guy… handsome… sexy even… and she enjoyed the thought of finding out more about him.

8:00. 9:00. She was just about to give up on the 10:00 outing when she saw a figure coming around the corner. It was Ken. Her heart actually fluttered, but what if he was married? Obviously, it was time to find out. Lifting her hand in a wave she turned off the water, having refilled that poor birdbath some ten times now. Willow trees could always use a bit of overflowing water anyway. It wasn't wasted water at all.

Ken pulled the earbuds out and left them dangling on his chest. He broke into a huge smile as he walked towards her. She got more beautiful every time he saw her, and it was making him nervous. Was it possible to start an honest to goodness relationship at his age? It seemed totally ridiculous. He wasn't really sure how to start even, never having had anything more than a few dates with any one woman. He wasn't being stubborn all his life, he just never found anyone that interested him. Until now. He couldn't help himself.

"Hey Maddie! Feeding the critters for the day?"

OH, that smile and those ocean blue eyes, "Yup. Sometimes the squirrels figure out how to be squatters on the feeders, so I have to keep inventing ways to outwit them."

"You can outwit a squirrel?"

"Let's just say we challenge each other on a daily basis."

He laughed. A wonderful, deep, natural laugh. She couldn't remember when she'd last heard a laugh like that.

Taking the bottom of his shirt he lifted it to wipe his brow, "Is this your normal feeding time then?" It would be nice to know when to be sure to be walking by.

Her heart spiked at the sight of his bare midriff. Swallowing hard and tearing her eyes away, "I usually get out here at dawn, and then as needed," she was almost stuttering, "when a feeder gets empty, or water is gone from the bath…" where was she going with this? "Sometimes the mallards eat dirt then take a drink and the water is so muddy…"

He was walking across the grass, approaching her. Calm down, Maddie, calm down. He just wants to say hi.

"So, what can you tell me about birds and squirrels? I know nothing about wildlife. My sister does though. She lives on the Eastern Shore and her husband is one of the conservation officers."

"That must be hugely interesting. I've been over there a couple times to visit the parks during a bald eagle release, but that was a long time ago. It's beautiful over there."

"I have to admit I haven't visited my sister in quite a while. I need to do that."

"Just one sister?" Those blue eyes were going to be the death of her. And that lock of hair that kept falling down on his forehead, no matter how many times he pushed it back.

He ran his hand back through his hair. It didn't help.

"No, I have two brothers, one here in Virginia Beach and one in Suffolk. How 'bout you?"

Suffolk! She flinched. Mark was buried there. God, she still missed him. Shaking her head back to the present, "One brother in Chicago. Haven't seen him in twenty-five years."

"I'm sorry," his face had fallen. He noticed the flash of sadness but wasn't sure what had caused it. Obviously, if she hadn't seen her brother in twenty-five years there was something that happened a long time ago.

"No big deal," she continued. "When my father died I was 16 and Dan was 20. Mother hightailed it back to Virginia Beach as fast as she could pack up the house. I was forced to come with her. Dan was old enough, and going to Loyola, so he stayed behind."

"I was fourteen when my mother died. I understand."

"Oh, WOW! That's so young. At least I had my dad a little longer. He was my everything. He believed a girl should learn the same things as a boy, so I had screwdrivers in my hand when I was five and could change a tire at ten."

"Ah, the perfect formula for an independent woman." He grinned.

"Could have been, I guess, but my mother didn't teach me anything."

"Seriously?"

"Long story. Maybe another time." Looking down she scraped her toe against a weed, trying to dig it out with her shoe.

"Where's your mother now?" Maybe he needed to drop that line of questioning, but something made Maddie the way she was, and he wanted to know everything he could.

"In there," she pointed back toward the house. "She has Multiple Sclerosis."

Ken nodded, then lowered his eyes. He couldn't miss the look on Maddie's face. It had gone empty. She was a caregiver. But if her mother never taught her anything it went deeper than just being faced with caregiver problems. "Looks like we have mother issues in common," was all he could think to say. But he knew there was a lot more to her story and he would eventually hear it, he hoped. But now seemed a good time to change the subject.

She beat him to it. "So, do you work from home?"

"No. I'm retired Navy. Gave them the best 21 years of my life."

"What did you do?"

He hesitated. Her mother had MS. That meant questions. He didn't know her well enough. Not yet anyway. "Most of the time I was in intelligence." His usual lie when he wasn't sure of how someone would react.

She merely nodded in acknowledgment. "I used to teach school. Before Mother got diagnosed... but hey, this is all interrupting your walk, and I don't want to do that." God knows she didn't want to do anything that would cause that beautiful body to get flabby. Whoa!

"It is getting warmer," he wiped his brow again, "but are you ever available for coffee, or even lunch?"

Her heart skipped a beat. "I'd like that," was all she could say. She fought to keep her face from showing too much excitement.

"Super." Holding up his phone, "If you'll give me your number, I'll call you to set something up."

He typed as she recited her number, then he held out his hand. Taking it, she felt that same buzz she'd felt when she thought she'd been stung by a bee. Looking up at him she saw he had felt the same thing. "Goodness, static electricity in all this humidity."

He laughed, pocketed his phone, put the earbuds back in and waved as he headed toward the street. Yes, he'd felt that buzz, too, and it scared him. But not enough to stop him from calling her for that cup of coffee.

Her mother was actually standing at the stove stirring some soup. "I saw you out there, you know, talking to that same man that dragged the tree out for you."

"Yes, Mother. His name is Ken. He lives down the street. He was asking about the squirrels and birds."

"You seemed mighty cozy with him."

"We were just talking." Now the time for the test. "He said he might call me and take me out for coffee or lunch some time."

The spoon froze in the pan. "Another man in your life? Like it wasn't enough that one dumped you?"

"Say another word about it and I'll start packing."

Her mother gave her a quick glance, then continued to stir the soup. "And if he asks me, Mother, I'll go out with him. The only men I've spoken to in years have been store clerks and really old men out walking their dogs."

He was in deep now. He'd made the offer and she didn't turn him down. So much for thinking it might be a way to not think about her anymore. She lived with her mother, and it seems there was something going on that wasn't good. While Maddie had smiled a couple of times she didn't seem happy. He'd spent enough time in his profession to be able to read pain, fear, and hopelessness in both patient and family. It was the worst part of his job, and even now, with his volunteering, he hadn't escaped completely.

Maddie would be interesting to talk to, of that he was certain. She hadn't really reacted when he told her he was retired Navy. Asking what he did was a natural question and there were no follow-up questions from her. That meant his little white lie worked. It likely didn't surprise her since the entire local area was loaded with retired military officers. He was curious to find out how her husband had died. It was a natural curiosity to a doctor.

He finished his walk and headed toward the shower but not before he called her. Coffee at 10 A. M. tomorrow was a go.

Chapter 4

She was waiting in the driveway when he pulled up. Unusual, but he was sure it had something to do with her mother. She could be sleeping. Maddie didn't even give him a change to get out and open the car door for her. As she settled into her seat and pulled the door closed behind her, "Good morning," her smile lit up his day.

"Good morning to you!" She was wearing a soft pink pullover top and gray shorts. "You look lovely this fine day."

She checked out his polo shirt and tan slacks, "And you clean up well, too," her laugh filled the car. Oh, how she wanted to tell him he looked way better half naked! "I heard that line in a movie once and it seemed to fit," she gave him a wide smile.

Backing out of the driveway, "I thought we'd go to the Village Inn Restaurant up at Town Center. It won't be crowded at this time of the morning. Breakfast crowd gone and lunch groups not there yet."

"Sounds perfect."

It was a short drive and as he parked, "Now, don't go racing out, please. Allow me the honor of opening the door for you."

"Okay," she actually had to fight the urge to open the door herself.

Feeling his hand on her back as he guided her into the restaurant gave her a sudden sense of comfort that had been missing in her life for years. She was pleased to see there weren't a lot of people near where they were seated. Village Inn Restaurants tended to be huge rooms with a ton of seating, both booth and table. There was no particular ambiance other than televisions stuck high up in the corners of the room. Looking over the menus, "What would you like?" he pointed the menu towards her.

"I have to confess I had breakfast at 5 this morning, but a cinnamon bun and coffee would be great." He doubled the order to include himself.

As the server left with their order, Maddie folded her hands on the table, then began rubbing her fingers. "I, ah, hate to have to ask this," those blue eyes were locked on hers, "but I'm assuming you aren't married."

He broke into a smile, reached over, and put a hand over hers. "Nope. Never have been."

"Really? Never?"

"Really, never!"

Cocking her head, "I'm surprised. I really am. I would think you had your choice of any number of beautiful women."

"I did," he patted her hand and brought it back to pick up his water glass. Taking a sip, "My life has been somewhat complicated. My dad was a bank president and very wealthy. We lived in a house big enough to be called a castle – well, at least to children. We had all sorts of maids and servants. My mother was ultra, and I do mean ultra, status driven. It wasn't enough to beat the Jones', she had to crush them. I can't remember ever once seeing her without every single hair in place, dressed in a dress or suit or ensemble of one famous designed or another. Makeup was always totally perfect. Her expectations for all of us kids was literally over the top. We were sent to the best private schools, had private tutors and our own personal servant to make sure we were dressed appropriately. That wasn't too bad for us boys, but my sister! Holy cow. From the moment she was born she was outfitted with the best *designer*" he emphasized, "dresses. A baby in a designer dress. Can you imagine?" Maddie's mouth dropped open and her face crunched up in disbelief. "Of course, she outgrew those dresses in just weeks and a new bunch would arrive." He paused when the server arrived with their food.

"And your father allowed that?"

"He worked long hours and didn't pay a lot of attention to us kids. He figured he was the provider, and she was the stay-at-home mom."

"It's hard to envision a baby in a designer dress," looking down to put cream in her coffee.

"I have pictures. She'd be horrified," he laughed. "When Mom died Trish was 13 and had been a proper young lady all her life. She had these real long finger nails. They terrified all us boys. She could scratch like a tiger, and we had more than one bloody face to show for it. We called her Queen Wannabee, and she hated it. But she took after Mom. Until she met Paul!"

"Is Paul her husband?" She took a bite out of her cinnamon bun, made a humming noise, and swallowed. "This is really good, Ken!"

He watched her face as she ate. She seemed so relaxed. There was nothing tense about her. and she was actually eating food – not some poached egg white with spinach in it.

"Hmm, OH, yes, Paul is her husband." Pay attention to the questions, Ken or she'll think you're sorry you brought her here.

"I think the minute she met him she reinvented herself for him. He's an outdoorsman and always was. That was the farthest thing from Trish's mind. All of a sudden she's wearing jeans and t-shirts and trimming her nails. Absolutely amazing. Thank goodness she got past all the hype our mother pounded into her."

"What about you? What hype did you have to endure?" She finished her bun and was now twirling the coffee cup in her hands.

He leaned back into the booth and sighed. "We…all three of us boys… were only ever introduced to proper girls and ladies, from the moment we were born. Birthday parties were only for the elite, and those were the little girls that came to our house for cake and candles! Even as I got older that tape my mother had stuck in my brain kept playing and the few times I dated it was always some society woman."

"No one ever tweaked your fancy?"

"Not even close," he grinned. "Most of them were hugely over-indulged and very high-maintenance. Two dates and I found an excuse to never call again."

Squinting, "I don't feel I've ever been over-indulged, but I'm not sure what it means to be high-maintenance to a man."

He burst out laughing, "Trust me, Maddie. You are *not* high-maintenance."

"Well, you tell me if I get that way."

He laughed again, "I promise. You don't seem like the demanding type at all." And he knew that would never happen with her. "So, you take care of your mother?"

"Ya know, now that you talk about high-maintenance, that would apply to my mother. She's very demanding and I'm fairly sure she would have aborted me if today's world was allowing it back then."

"You're kidding."

"No. She was okay with Dan, but not me. It's a really long story. Depresses me."

"Then we'll save that for another day. Cat or dog?"

"Huh?"

"Do you prefer cats or dogs?"

"Dogs, I think. If nothing else they force you to take a walk!!!" She laughed.

"True enough. I prefer dogs, too. Favorite television programs?"

"Science and Smithsonian. Some cooking, and an occasional movie. I don't get to watch a lot of television though. You?"

"Like you, I don't get to watch a lot, but I enjoy an occasional football game, some medical programs," That slipped out, quick, charge forward, "forensics. I love forensics."

"YES! I watch those at night. Incredible what forensics can do these days. Between DNA and cameras everywhere you almost can't get away with crime anymore!"

Finishing his coffee and roll and placing the cup back on the table, "This has been a very nice morning for me, Maddie. I don't want to keep you away from your mother for too long, but maybe we can do it again, or have lunch, or even dinner?"

Shyly, she nodded. "I'd like that. My mother can still take care of herself for the most part. I told her I can't just be a prisoner when she can walk and even cook a bit. She dresses herself, showers, and just needs a cane," for more than walking, she thought, but no need to go into that now.

"Oh," his face winced, "I need to mention one more thing, just in case I vanish for a bit."

"I have noticed times when you didn't seem to be walking," she lifted her eyebrows in interest.

What an interesting thing for her to admit to, that she was aware of his walking routine. It gave him a warm feeling for some reason. "I do occasionally get called back into service for special operations. They can last for just a few days or five or six weeks. It's always a fast recall. I have to be on a plane within 24 hours."

"I had no idea the Navy could recall you after you retired."

"They sure can, forever! But from what I understand they don't recall people after they turn 65. Anyway, they do have that power."

"WOW! That sounds like an NTSB go team for an aircraft accident."

"Hmm. Well, yes. Very similar. But I don't want you to worry. I'll try to let you know, or I'll try to call you while I'm gone, but I can't guarantee either."

Signaling for the bill, he could see the disappointment in her face.

"Alright," she said softly. "I appreciate you telling me that, so I don't worry…too much."

Standing he took her hand to help her out of the booth. A warm, comfortable hand. Nice. Very nice. Smooth, too. He certainly didn't do a lot of manual labor with hands that soft.

Taking a slightly different route back to Maddie's he slowed down and stopped in front of a house. "This is where I live," he pointed to the house. "My father gave it to me when I retired. He'd been living in it for a few years."

She turned her head to where he was pointing. "I go past here all the time. Another nice one-story home. I thought you said your father lived in a mansion?"

"Oh, he did, but a few years ago he decided to downsize so he found this house and bought it. He was diagnosed with Alzheimer's about a year before I retired, and Trish managed to come down and take care of him and I helped when I retired. Eventually it got to the point that he had to be placed in a home. So, I took over the house. Made sense to all of us."

"Where's your dad now?"

Pulling away and heading for her house, "He's at Our Lady of Perpetual Help, on Princess Anne Road."

"I know exactly where that is."

"Do you see him often?"

"Not as often as I should. I need to do something about that."

She nodded.

Pulling into her driveway she paused. Smiling back at her he got out and opened her car door.

"I figured with all that high society training you had as a child I'd better let you open my door."

He chuckled.

Taking his hand, "Thank you so much for breakfast. I enjoyed our conversation." And, she thought, I really enjoyed looking at you for an hour. Not long enough, that was for sure.

"The nice thing is I think there is a lot more conversation we can share," he winked. "Think about what your favorite song is and why. We can discuss that next time."

"But I have more than one!"

"Then rank them. It will give you something to think about."

"I can do that. Okay, but you have to do the same thing."

"I will."

He lived only a few blocks down from Maddie's house so was home in a flash. He was beginning to doubt his sanity. It was really stupid to have some mystery house lead to a coffee date. He most assuredly was not in the market for any relationships. The few he had tried, in his youth, just left him cold. They were all daughters of his mother's society friends, and a stuffier, more self-centered group would be hard to find. They would go from being made up like a model to acting like a street walker once he found himself alone with them. Was it possible he had stumbled upon a woman who could manage to take away his life-long aversion to relationships? It seemed to be heading in that direction. He needed that conversation they'd just had. He'd set it up as a test – a quick, easy to get out of test. If she passed he would likely ask her out again, for a real date. If she failed all he had to do was change his route and she would think he had been recalled for one of his missions. He'd wondered if she would turn out to be ditzy, or unable to hold an intelligent discussion. Would he see the usual signs of a clingy woman, flirting with him, and making not-so-subtle moves? What would her clothing be like? Low cut blouse, leaving nothing to the imagination? Short skirt riding up as he drove her to and from the restaurant? And the one that would turn him off immediately – fluttering fake eye lashes – would he see those? He shuddered at the thought. And none of that had happened today. She was delightful. Maybe even enchanting. She was down to earth, conservative, caring for her mother and all the wildlife surrounding her. But there was a sadness, too. She hadn't said more about her mother and there was obviously something going on there. He was curious as to her husband's death, but he'd wait for her to share it. He shrugged his shoulders and exhaled a large breath of air as he parked his car in the garage. The door banged closed just as his phone rang.

"I saw you staring out the window, Mother. Are you spying on me?"

"Nonsense. I just happened to be standing here when that man pulled up into the drive."

"His name is Ken, and we went to breakfast, just as I told you before I left."

"Another man, Madeline? Will you never stop? One already left you high and dry and then got himself killed. What do you know about this one?"

Maddie had to bite her cheek to the point she could taste blood. At this rate she wasn't going to last a week in this house. She would never be able to make her mother understand that twelve years had shot through the universe since Mark had been killed.

"He's retired. He's nice. I enjoyed having a mature conversation with someone my own age."

"Retired, huh? From what?"

"The Navy."

"Oh, my GOD!" Splashing her hands in the water she pulled the plug and grabbed several sheets of paper towel off the roll to dry her hands. Picking up her cane from the counter top she shuffled out of the room.

Dropping her purse onto the kitchen table Maddie sat there, staring at the wall. This really had to stop. One minute she felt a new sense of purpose and then she walked into her mother's house. Thinking about Ken made her smile. Her mother was determined to ruin it, and Maddie was just as determined to see Ken again. His story fascinated her. Born into great wealth, never having to lift a finger, yet look what he managed to do with his life. She should never have given up her teaching job. Suddenly a little light bulb lit up her mind. She could still teach. Maybe not full time, but enough to get away from her mother for a few hours here and there. She could be a substitute teacher. Or, if that didn't work, she could just volunteer some hours with the local school system. She remembered her school was always looking for help with paperwork, computer entries, attendance records, and answering telephones. Joan and Elle would be able to find out for her. She'd have to invest in a new wardrobe, but it would be worth it.

She felt bad, though, for sluffing off any real information about her mother. While Ken had shed a lot on how he grew up she was only able to blurt out a sentence about her mother. How do you explain how many times you were whipped?

Fine. She'd figure something out. Walking to the sink she saw her mother had made a lunch for herself and all the dishes were waiting to be put in the dishwasher. The sink was full of the suds that hadn't gone down the drain with the water. A pile of wadded up paper towels were on the counter, right where her mother had pitched them just moments ago. It was two steps to the trash can. Typical of her mother. Do only what was absolutely necessary. Checking the laundry room was no different. Clothes were still piled high in the baskets. Time to get tough. She put her own clothes in to wash and left her mothers in the basket. She could almost hear the screeching now. By the time she finished her chores it was time for dinner. Maddie decided to do leftovers, since there were quite a few in the fridge. She reheated the chicken breasts in a soup sauce, the green beans in a small pan, and added some water to the mashed potatoes and microwaved them.

"Leftovers again, Maddie?"

"Would you rather I throw them away?"

"You never cook a meal from scratch anymore."

Oh, good grief. "Eat or don't eat Mother. Makes no difference to me." She was being baited, and she knew it. Her mother knew very well that in order to get leftovers you had to have cooked something that had enough to be saved. Or something like that!! Eating quickly, she took her plate to the sink hoping Ken might walk by, but either he didn't, or she had missed him. She was tired enough after finishing the dishes that she just wanted to sit out on the back porch and watch the wildlife. It wasn't long before she was lost in thought. In all her life she had never had a lot of friends. She was 16 when she was ripped from Chicago, and the friends she had there soon faded into the background. Her sophomore year was at one high school, and then her mother moved into a different "school zone" and she was forced to do her senior year at yet another school. She was old enough now that her mother didn't put her over a knee for a good spanking. It became more emotional than physical. Dori never attended anything that Maddie was interested in and didn't bother to go to her graduation. Maddie realized, too late, that she probably had made a mistake going to ODU for college. Not the college, but the fact that she continued to live at home. The "why are you studying that stuff," and "what slug of a man are you dating," comments never really stopped. She finally moved out when she got the job teaching. Her teaching friends had introduced her to Mark at a party. And the rest was history… a short history, but history none-the-less. Squadron wives had helped her get through the first year of grief, but then their husbands were slowly transferred, and they moved away. Only Elle and Joan still stood by her. She needed to start being a true friend to them again.

Maddie awoke suddenly and realized it was now quite dark outside. "Oh, I fell asleep," she muttered. Looking at her watch she was stunned to see it was after 9 P.M. She stood and stretched and picked up the water glass to go back inside. Hopefully she'd be able to get back to sleep. It was most unlike her to fall asleep like that.

Two days went by without any word from Ken. She spent part of every waking hour both days standing by the window and watching for him. Maybe she'd upset him somehow. She went over and over everything that had been done and said when he took her for coffee and couldn't think of a single thing that might have made him turn away from her. It was an empty feeling in the pit of her stomach. How odd that after only a couple of times being around him she should be acting like a teenager, thinking about him, picturing herself on a real date with him. When she couldn't stand it any longer she remembered that he had called her. That meant she still had his number in her recent phone numbers. Maybe she could call him and apologize for whatever she had said or done. She was so nervous. She'd left the phone in her bedroom. Retrieving it she opened it to find she had a message. *Oh, Good Grief!* It was from Ken.

Maddie, I tried to call but it went to your voice mail. I have to leave for one of those recalls I told you about. Please don't worry. I'll try to call if we get to an area that has cell service. Keep thinking about what your favorite song is.

She let out a huge sigh of relief and was surprised to find a tear flowing down her cheek. Ken was alright, she knew, and it wasn't something she had done or said. That was such a good feeling to know he'd called her. Looking at the date stamp she realized it was the night she'd fallen asleep on the back porch and had left her phone in her room. Effective immediately that phone would be in her pocket at all times. If he called again she didn't want to miss his call. She felt like humming for the first time in years. She'd think of something.

Chapter 5

Haiti... Hot, Humid, and Hell. There were no other words for the devastation he found himself confronting. First it was the earthquake, just offshore. Then the downpour. The mudslides had ruined so many lives. Rain from a passing hurricane that barely grazed them had caused the mudslides, burying homes and businesses. No one could ever imagine such horror, even when it was graphically displayed on the Weather Channel. You had to smell it. Almost taste it. Bodies were still being pulled out by rescue workers, and others with broken arms, head injuries, and internal bleeding were being brought into the hospital one after another. The stench of rotting bodies, combined with the smell of mud, was overwhelming. Rescue teams, most masked and some wearing hazard suits, were still trying to find anyone alive, but it had been three days and getting hopeless. Dogs sniffed the earth searching for any sign of life. He was one of six surgeons whose job was the internal injuries, and he was immediately put to work on a man who had a fence picket going through his midsection, front to back. And he was still talking. Ultimately, Ken had been able to pull the stake out, shocked that there had been no serious internal injuries and only minor bleeding. Ken could only shake his head at how lucky the guy was. He owed his life to the rescue team that brought him in without trying to remove the stake. It kept the bleeding to a minimum and ultimately made it possible to save his life. There were so many patients that day he hadn't realized he'd not eaten for almost sixteen hours when they advised him there were no more patients waiting for him. Other surgeons had arrived to take over the load.

"Don't let that fool you, Ken," his friend, Jerry, Senior Medical Officer, remarked. "There will be more tomorrow and for the next week or so. Well, until they decide no one could possibly be alive under all that rubble and they shift from rescue to recovery."

"I'll be good as new after a few hours' sleep," he assured Jerry. "Where are we billeted?"

"Hotel down the street. They're expecting you. They do have good food there for all of us so be sure to take advantage while it's there. I did hear that the Red Cross expects more planes first thing tomorrow. They're at the same hotel. Go get some sleep."

"Thanks, Jerry. See you tomorrow."

Shaking his head, he made his way toward the hotel. Would Haiti ever start planting trees to keep the mudslides from displacing and killing thousands of people in Haiti? Maybe no one ever learned from their prior mistakes anymore. Haiti seemed to be located in a perpetual zone of destruction, the bullseye for hurricanes and earthquakes. He was exhausted by the time he got to the hotel but grateful to know that they had his room ready, and food would be brought up shortly. Dragging his suitcase to his door, and sliding the card into the slot, "Why Doctor Avery, what a surprise to see you here."

Oh, NO! He knew that voice. Much worse, he knew the smell of that perfume she wore. Was it really perfume? Maybe she made it herself? Turning, he watched as she approached him, nurse Nancy, one of the banes of his existence. "Nancy, how are you doing?" She must have just applied that perfume, made from a combination of human sweat, rotten food, and tobacco. Maybe too much chemistry in nursing school?

"I'm fine, Dr. Avery. How have you been doing since retirement?"

"Keeping very busy. This is probably my last rotation with Doctors World Wide. My father has Alzheimer's and I need to stay close to him." Right now, he would say anything to have her vanish.

"I'm sorry to hear that. I was hoping that maybe we could get a drink or something for old time's sake."

"I'm wiped out, Nancy, and haven't eaten since yesterday... ah!" He heard the clanking of wheels in need of some oil, "Here comes my dinner now. Nice seeing you again." He opened the door and entered before the waiter arrived, then quickly closed the door after them. Nancy! Of all the nurses in the entire world... Oh this was not going to happen again. Tipping the waiter, he undressed and sat down to eat. Food first. He was starving and thank goodness it smelled of a wonderful meatloaf with gravy, potatoes, green beans, and that welcome aroma of coffee. He put the cup of steaming coffee up to his nose to replace the mental memory of that perfume. Then he dove in, eating every bite. He sat back, satisfied that he had arrived safely, had complete success in the OR, and now had eaten a very good dinner. The doctors and nurses who were part of Doctors World Wide weren't paid much for the jobs they did. It was more of a volunteer job, but he was happy to be involved. His plate clean he needed to make two phone calls. Moving over to the overstuffed chair he put his feet up. The first call was to Jerry.

"Everything alright at the hotel?" Jerry sounded concerned that one of his doctors might have been having a problem with the hotel.

"Sort of. The hotel is fine, but I need you to do me a favor, Jer."

"Name it."

"Do you remember a nurse on the Ike named Nancy Lewis."

"Ah, yeah. Don't tell me she's here."

"She's here."

There was a long pause on the phone. *"You know that's not my fault. Head nurse brings in all the nurses she thinks we need."*

"Figures. Who schedules when and who they work with in the OR?"

"I can handle that where she's concerned. I know you talked to me once before about how she couldn't keep her hands to herself in the OR."

"She couldn't hand me anything without touching my arm. She's outstanding at her job, but I've heard rumors that I wasn't the only doctor she tried her tricks on. Anything you can do will be a big help. She caught me in the hall when I was about to open my door. I know she would have done her best to follow me in, but I got lucky, and the food arrived at the same time. She asked me out for a drink later. I don't need this kind of aggravation."

"Got it. I'll talk to Chelsea and see what we can do."

"Thanks, Jer. I appreciate it."

"NO problem. Now get some sleep."

Now to make a quick call to Maddie to make sure she knew he was out of town. Her phone rang six times, and he was just about to hang up when she answered.

"Ken. How are you doing? I did finally get your message that you had to go out of town again."

"Yes. I think I can make a few calls from here. Not sure how long I'll be, but no longer than necessary."

"I miss seeing you walking past the house. I look out of habit now."

He smiled. He was surprised that one sentence could mean so much to him. He wasn't used to being missed by anyone. Certainly not his brothers. His sister might have thought about him now and then, but even she never sent him any care packages. Odd that all that just occurred to him only now. *"I miss walking past your house every day, especially when you're outside."* He could almost hear her smiling.

"I just hope you're safe."

"I am. Not to worry. I just wanted to hear your voice."

"I like hearing yours, too."

"Is your mother alright?"

"Alright isn't the word I'd use, but she's holding her own."

"Is that who I hear in the background."

"She wants to know who I'm talking to, and I'll just tell her my friend, Ken. But she won't like that."

Ken rubbed his forehead. He was tired and didn't want to say anything negative about her mother over the phone. Stuff like that had to be said while you were watching the face of the person you were talking to. You had to be able to read their expressions... did they agree or disagree with what you were saying? *"Well, I'm sure you can handle it. I don't want to be the start of anything though."*

"That will never happen. I'm finally tired of her bullying me and making me feel guilty all the time. I want to take my life back, and plan to do just that."

"Good to hear," and it really was, he thought.

"Guess I'd better let you go. Call me when you can."

"I will. Hopefully I won't be stuck here too long."

"I hope that, too. Sleep well."

"You, too. Good night, Maddie."

"'Nite, Ken."

He felt better talking to her. Now he knew she missed him. It just felt good. A quick shower in a few minutes, a good night's sleep, back to the operating room, and with luck, no nurse Nancy.

She felt warm all over when she hung up the phone. It had been a short conversation, but it meant the world to her. To have someone think about her enough to call her was totally foreign. And she could handle a lot more of those. Even though Elle called her every couple of months she could never be sure there wasn't an ulterior motive involved. She grinned. There was no way she'd call Ken, not knowing what he was doing at any given moment, but she would be sure to have her phone in her pocket at all times, and by her bed overnight.

"What are you smiling about, Madeline?"

"Ken just called me to say goodnight."

"Seriously! You trying to get another man in your life? Once wasn't enough to teach you a lesson?"

"No, Mother. Once wasn't enough it seems." Turning she looked her mother straight in the eye, "And I'll see him as often as he asks me out, and I'll talk to him every time he calls."

Dori turned to walk away, "Idiot…"

"Oh, and Mother. You might want to do your laundry. I think there are at least three loads in there that are all yours." She watched as her mother turned and saw the look of death. The look that Maddie always saw as that heavy paddle came out and she was grabbed by the neck and thrown down across her mother's lap. But this time she stared her mother down. "I'll go grocery shopping tomorrow, Mother, so if you want anything be sure to write it down on the shopping list on the fridge." It was now after 9. Grabbing her book, she walked down the hallway and closed her bedroom door behind her. She knew if her mother had a serious problem overnight she'd screech to high heaven and wake up the devil in the process.

A warm shower and plop into bed with her book, but she just didn't have the focus to read. All she could think about was Ken. Did she think she could ever be important enough to him, or any guy for that matter? She was dowdy, and maybe just a tad overweight. She knew she still had all the right curves in all the right places, but maybe they were a bit curvier now. Maybe she should start a little exercise program and lose a few pounds. Not a lot, but a few. Maybe stop at a store that sold nice clothing and get a couple pairs of shorts or slacks, and a few new blouses. She'd start on a plan tomorrow. Maybe eventually she could join Ken on his walks. That would be awesome. If he didn't walk too fast they could even talk about all sorts of stuff. Her book lay folded on her lap and with her head back on the pillow she fell asleep thinking about all the things she could do to make herself more attractive.

Ken woke with a start. Glancing at his watch and shaking his head to figure out where he was, he noticed it was after 11 P.M. He'd fallen asleep in the chair just after hanging up from his call to Maddie. He'd been dreaming and he couldn't remember the dream. It was frustrating him because he knew, somehow, that Maddie was in it. He didn't sense that it was a bad dream, or one that upset him. At least not in a bad way. In fact, he was beginning to realize that she was upsetting him in a good way. He never woke up thinking about a woman, and at his age he shouldn't be doing it now. He was too old to begin any kind of permanent relationship. And marriage? The only example that popped into his mind was his own mother, ruling the house, setting them all up for the 'right' person to marry. Holy smokes, if his mother had been around to see her daughter get married to a "tree hugger" she would have exploded. Which made him realize that his sister, was married to Paul now for, dang, twenty-one years, if his mental calculations were right. She was 24 when they eloped, much to their father's chagrin. Ken had thought it was the biggest hoot of his entire life to hear about that. He was in medical school and found out about it after the event. Just thinking about it made him laugh. And happy? Oh, they were still very much in love. So, maybe it could happen. Sort of?
 Putting his phone on charge he glanced around the room. Basic nice, with a comfy chair and simple desk, and one king size bed. It was well made and the color combinations in the room were soothing. Four pictures of ocean views graced the walls. Walking into the bath he liked that the shower wasn't one of those dinky jobs. No tub, but that was fine with him. He ached for a shower and welcomed the warm stream of water,

soothing his sore muscles. It had been a few months since he'd had to stand that long in an operating theater. As he dried off he thought about Maddie. As he crawled under the covers his last thought was about Maddie.

"You have four in line for your surgery, Ken." Jerry looked him over. "You look like you slept well enough."

"I did, for sure." Carefully washing his hands and arms in preparation for surgery "It's a nice hotel. Even the free breakfast bar was good. But I'm wondering when *you* sleep. You're here when I arrive and still here when I leave."

Jerry just gave him a sheepish grin. "Hasn't anyone told you? I sleep while you're in surgery!"

"Yeah, right. Sure, you do. Best you start taking your own advice, my man."

"I'm a micromanager, you know that."

"True. But that hotel is nice, and the food is good. You should partake of it!"

Jerry smiled. "Only the best for our surgeons. Don't worry. I'll be fine. You have a ruptured spleen, one guy with abdominal bleeding, a pneumothorax, and the last would be a woman with a piece of rebar through her leg. Hopefully Max will arrive soon and can take one of them off your list. Take the abdominal first."

Ken nodded. "Line them up. Who's the anesthesiologist?"

"Edwards."

"Good man. Thanks."

"And I took care of that other problem."

"Triple thanks," he looked Jerry in the eye. "I like working for you," he grinned a wolfish grin.

"Uh, huh. You'll change your mind if I find a fifth patient for you today."

Ken shook his head and laughed, making his way into the first operating room.

Another long day, but only the first four patients with no additions. And no nurse Nancy. He owed Jerry a steak dinner sometime. Hot and sweaty he appreciated the coolness of the hotel air conditioning, even if it was being run by a generator. He was anxious to get back and call Maddie again. But his timing was horrible.

"Dr. Avery, we meet again. How lucky for me."

Cringing inside, "Excuse me, Nancy?" He closed his eyes in a moment of frustration, his hands fisting as he lowered his arms to his side.

"I was hoping we could have that drink together."

Had she been waiting for him? He looked over her head to where she had come from, and it was just a bunch of chairs around a television set. Could she be wearing less clothing? It would have taken some effort. A low-cut blouse hid nothing about her cleavage, and her skirt barely covered her butt. He didn't want to think about whether or not she was even wearing panties. Oh, Geeze, Ken, clear your mind. Concentrate on that horrible smell she squirts on her body.

"I'm afraid that's impossible. I'm having dinner with other doctors in half an hour, and I need to freshen up first." It was a lie, but a necessary one.

"I don't mind eating with them, too, you know. I know all of them."

Clenching his jaw, "We'll be talking about my cases today, and since you weren't involved in any of those cases it would be a HIPAA violation for you to be present."

"I got stuck with Dr. Gardano. He's such a stick."

"Why do you say that?" Narrowing his eyes, he was growing impatient with nurse Nancy.

"He actually brought his wife with him. Who *does* that? To a disaster zone!"

"Well, obviously Dr. Gardano does. And since his wife is a first-class nurse, it makes perfect sense. Now, I really have to go get ready. You have a nice evening."

Reaching the elevator, he pushed the button but wasn't fast enough. She stopped the door before it closed and climbed in with him.

"I'm on your floor you know." She managed to brush his arm with hers.

"No, I didn't know." He shifted left.

"I mean, we could have that drink after you get back from dinner." She was looking up at him with hope in her eyes. Her hand reached out and brushed the back of his. He lifted his arm to his chest.

"Ah, I'm only going to say this once, Nancy. I don't drink and I don't date, and I don't have random hookups with anyone. So please don't continue to ask me, alright?" Great! Next she's going to tell me she's right next door to me.

"You have no idea what you're missing," she blurted out, her eyes shooting arrows at him as the elevator doors opened. She stomped out ahead of him. His mouth dropped open. He knew his jaw was going to hit the floor. What in the world was she thinking? This was so incredibly inappropriate that something had to be done. It wasn't that doctors and nurses didn't "hook up" all the time, but this one was a bit over the norm for sure. But he was also worried that any official action he might take could end up with her going off the charts. She could easily get angry enough to start stalking him, especially if it cost her her job. She wouldn't have a problem finding out where he lived. He followed slowly, watching as she headed toward the end of the hallway, swiped her card, walked in, and slammed the door. He'd have to talk to Jerry again. Were there any "single" doctors there besides him? Maybe a little hint in the right ear might get her on to someone else who might be interested in spending time with her. Just a slight hint that she was looking for some fun was all it would take for the right single doctor to find her as his assistant. The rest would take care of itself.

Turning around he went back down to the front desk to see if it was possible to get a different room on a different floor! But no such luck. Well, at least she was several doors away, and he needed to call Jerry again.

"Jer! We need to double down on Nancy."

"Uh Oh, what happened?"

Describing the event he'd just gone through, *"Do we have any single doctors on the team?"*

Jerry chuckled. *"There are three, actually."*

Ken breathed a heavy sigh of relief. *"Any of them known for playing the field?"*

"Yup. Duane Gooding is all about that."

"Never heard of him, but can you put a bug in his ear?"

Jerry laughed. *"Oh, this is so good. I love a good set-up. This guy is young, energetic, and has chased more than one nurse or female doc. He's also very good looking. The perfect man for this job. I suspect all I have to do is put her on his team and the rest will be instant history."*

"Man, I owe you two steak dinners. When are you coming to Virginia Beach?"

"You'd have to include my wife on those free dinners!"

"Done. My extreme pleasure. Get Nancy off my back, almost literally, and I'll even put you up in my house. Might even let you meet a woman I find very interesting."

There was silence on the phone line.

"You still there, Jer?"

"Ah, yeah – I'm just processing what you said. I've known you your whole Naval career and never heard you say anything even close to that. Hmm."

"Well, nothing is really happening yet, but she interests me. A widow and as down to earth as they come."

"Then I'll make sure Donna and I come down for that dinner!"

Showering and ordering dinner he sat down to call Maddie.

Maddie enjoyed hearing from him almost every day during the next week. It felt good to have someone caring enough about her to call and see how she was doing. They didn't talk long. She was aware he had been recalled for something important and she didn't want him to get himself in any kind of trouble if he called her too often or they spoke too long. She was never one for long telephone conversations anyway. It was enough to hear his voice. Time did seem to drag though. Her mother had gone relatively silent, so maybe all her promises to leave were having some reasonable results. It was rather nice to not hear that cane constantly banging around and the shrieking had subsided a bit. Yet, for some reason, it made Maddie nervous. She had to stay on her toes. Her mother wouldn't dare do anything with Mark's picture, would she? Maddie kept close tabs on it.

August was close to ending. When her phone rang she thought it would be Ken, but it was Elle.

"You promised one more lunch before school starts. Labor Day is almost upon us, then back to school we go."
"How about tomorrow then? The ocean front has calmed down now that school has started almost everywhere but Virginia Beach. Same place?"

They agreed. Something was up, though. There was no mention of Joan and Elle sounded nervous. School would be in full swing shortly. Maddie had a sinking feeling in the pit of her stomach. She spent the rest of the day trying to figure out what Elle was up to now. The choices were endless. Elle's history was not the best. She was an outstanding teacher and well thought of in that regard, but her personal life, as Maddie knew only too well, was a complete mess. What would cause someone to steal and cheat? She had to have grown up in that environment. And she had a sneaking suspicion that Elle had deliberately not invited Joan. That meant she had something to confess. Not good.

She had to change clothing. Not knowing what Elle wanted Maddie decided to put on her yellow dress. It was simple enough and the only nice thing she had. A few flowers on the bodice accented the primarily soft yellow color of the dress.

She found Elle sitting at the very back booth. "Hi, Elle. How are you doing?" Maddie sat down across from her. The waitress appeared as Elle began to answer, putting water down in front of them and promising to return in a few minutes for their order. Maddie noted that Elle was squirming a bit, and her head was down.

"What's up, Elle?"

Elle still hadn't looked up, and her hands, resting on the table, were shaking.

"Elle!"

Maddie sat back silently and waited. When she saw tears starting down Elle's face she knew it wasn't good.

"Elle... just tell me what's happening."

Inhaling a large breath, "I was arrested again for shoplifting."

Maddie sat forward, taking one of Elle's hands. "NO!" By the way she said it and the look on her face Maddie knew this was a more serious charge.

Elle nodded yes. When the waitress appeared they both quickly ordered BLTs just to get an order in and have the waitress leave.

"Talk to me, Elle. It sounds more serious than the last time."

"It's a second offense, petit larceny, and could mean jail time. School hasn't started yet so I don't have any money yet... and... Maddie, this one could mean jail time."

Maddie froze. Jail time! Her stomach twisted into a huge knot. It was all she could do to control her question. "Tell me more."

"It was a Fitbit. I had an associate get it for me and she was so busy she said I could pay for it up front when I checked out all the other stuff in my basket. I managed to pick up a couple of empty boxes before checking out and hid it between the two of them, and I used self-check-out. It was more than $150 and they caught me going out the door. The cops came and they even showed me the videos. All around the store, Maddie. They saw me pick up a box, then another box, and put the Fitbit in between them so it looked like I was just getting a couple of empty boxes. It was all there on video, right up to me paying for everything else, and looking guilty at the register. It was so obvious."

"What kind of fine are we talking about?"

It could be up to twelve months in jail and/or a maximum fine of $2500.00. I can't afford an attorney, Maddie, and it would mean Dick would find out. I'd lose my job...."

Maddie sat back, trying not to show her disgust.

"Maddie, I've sought free help from a psychologist. She's going to go to court with me and try to help, but I'll still need money for a fine. I'll pay you back every cent, like the last time. I'm getting help, Maddie, I really need to understand why I do this. I've had three sessions with her."

"When's your court date?"

"Next week."

"Oh, Elle." She kept her voice low, "Why do you do this? You have such a wonderful husband and a great kid."

Elle managed to hold her emotions together long enough for the waitress to place their sandwiches on the table. Her head was down, and she was covering her eyes with her hands.

"That's fine," Maddie said to the waitress.

When the waitress was far enough away, "Elle. Why?"

"I don't know," she whispered. "I honestly don't know. You're right ya know. I have a wonderful husband and great kid." Tears were streaming down her face.

"Maddie, I know this is hard for you. I understand, I really do. I also know if I were to get caught a third time it would be considered a felony and up to five years in prison. PRISON, Maddie. It would destroy all our lives – my husband, my son... I'm begging."

"If I help you how do I know you won't do it again, Elle? This is the second time. I'm going to tell you right now I'll be just like Judge White when you were arrested for shoplifting the first time. He gave you a little slap on the wrist. This is twice. You don't get a third time. Do you understand me?"

Elle nodded.

"So, you're talking about a possible $2500 to be on the safe side then, and even at that hoping you don't get sent to jail?"

Elle took a tissue out of her purse and began to wipe her eyes. "Yes."

Maddy was beside herself. The conflict was almost more than she could bear. Unfortunately, there was one thing Maddy was sure of. If she didn't help Elle the end would be so much worse. "Alright. You can follow me to the bank after we eat. Obviously this is the last time because next time I won't have to get involved. You'll be in prison. And I hate to bring it up, Elle, but you need to stop running around on Dick. It would be different if you were single and some kind of swinger, but you have a family, and I don't want to see it destroyed."

"I promise, Maddie. I swear. No more messing around. The psychologist is helping me with that too. No more one-night stands. No more anything. I'll pay you back every cent. It just might take me a few months though."

I'm going to get you the $2500.00. I want you to call me after the court hearing and tell me what the fine was. Then return any money you didn't need. From there I'll figure out how much you'll pay me each month. That makes it just difficult enough for you to remember the reason why you owe me. Every dollar you have to give to me is one you can't spend on yourself."

Elle nodded.

They ate their sandwiches in silence. Maddie was angry enough to scream, but she also could easily afford to help Elle, and for sure didn't want to see her go to jail, or worse, have to tell Dick about her situation.

Following Maddie to her bank she waited in the parking lot until Maddie returned and handed her the money. With tears in her eyes Elle thanked her and promised she would turn her life around.

"I hope so, Elle," Maddie said softly. "You and Dick should take a nice vacation during Christmas or New Years. Reconnect. I know you love him, and he adores you. If you need to keep seeing the psychologist, then do it. You have the rest of your life to make up for all this. Realize what you'd lose if it happens again. I'm only a phone call away and I love you dearly, but you need to earn my respect again, okay?"

"Thank you," she whispered. "I won't let you down, Maddie."

"I'll count on it. Now go do what you have to do and then move forward."

Maddie watched as Elle put her car in gear and headed down the street. She wondered if she'd ever hear from her again. And she couldn't help but wonder if she'd get paid back. The first time Elle had repaid her. Time would tell. She was glad she had plenty of money. She kept her mouth shut about it but when Mark died he had a gigantic insurance policy that set her up for life. On top of it he'd taken out mortgage insurance. The house they were living in was instantly paid for. She would never have to struggle again. She had no idea what her mother's Last Will and Testament said, and she didn't want to know or care. Dori could leave it all to Dan or whatever the witches group was she probably belonged to secretly!

A tough day and she got home a bit later than she expected. Her mother was doing laundry! Well, *that* was a shock. Maddie busied herself with making spaghetti and opening a jar of sauce to heat. She'd pour out just enough for her mother. She wasn't hungry.

"I thought you might be home," Dori walked through the door and plopped down on a chair. "I heard the pantry door open and close. So, are you home for dinner?"

"No, I ate a large lunch, but I'm making you some spaghetti.

"With garlic bread, toasted, I hope."

"I can do that."

"Good. Makes a difference, you know."

"Yes, Mother, I do know."

"And don't forget the parmesan cheese."

"I won't."

"I'll go back and struggle with getting the clothes out of the washing machine and into the dryer."

Maddie started pouring sauce from the jar into the pan, almost dropping it. Catching it just in time she sighed. Her mother was never going to leave her alone for a minute. Suffering in detail is what her mother was up to now. Maybe Ken had the right idea. Ear Buds. Stick them in your ear, turn on your music on the phone, and tune out everything her mother said. Hmm... Ken, wonder where he is right now.

Chapter 6

With Ken gone the week just seemed to drag. When her phone rang just after finishing with the dishes she assumed it was Elle. She really didn't want to talk to her, and more to the point she couldn't get over her anger. She was trying to understand, but it was difficult. Sometimes it was just too much information. She managed to get her hands dry enough to pick up the phone. It was Ken. WHEW! Close call on not answering.

"Ken, Hi! How are you doing today?"
"Much better," he sounded happy to her.
"It sounds like you had a good day then."
"Sure did. I'm home!"
"REALLY!" Oh, geeze, nothing like acting like a teenager with run amok hormones!
He chuckled. *"So, have you eaten dinner yet?"*
"Actually, I didn't eat dinner. I had lunch with Elle which meant I wasn't hungry when I fed Mother."
"That's all done?"

"Yes, sure is."

"Why don't you come over for some pizza? Maybe you'll be hungry by the time it gets here."

"I can do that!" She was so excited she was almost jumping up and down. Be cool, Maddie, be really cool. *"In about 15 minutes?"*

"Perfect. I'll order a pizza. How do you like it?"

"Most any kind of meat, or supreme."

"Done. See you soon."

He hoped he wasn't making a mistake having her come to his house instead of taking her out to a restaurant. But it was a little late to get ready for something that might be considered a real date. Real dates scared him anyway. He was very much interested in Maddie. He liked what he saw and so far she seemed like a smart and caring woman. Having mixed feelings was making him nervous.

She wasn't sure what to expect when she arrived. He opened the door and took her hand, leading her into the entryway. She set her keys and purse down on the small table to the left.

Seeing her in the yellow dress she hadn't changed since lunch, "You look lovely. I like the dress."

She thanked him, letting him lead her into the home.

"There used to be a living room and den, but the previous owner took out the wall and made it one huge den. I like it much better this way. Who uses a living room anymore?"

Laughing, "My mother has one and it just is there. Never been used that I can remember. Just has furniture in it that no one ever sits in."

"Exactly. Across the hall I turned the dining room into an office. I guess dining rooms have their place, and this could become that again easily."

"One, two, three, four, five, six, two-drawer filing cabinets lined up with a board on top. That's some desk you have. Nice that you left a space between two of them so you could sit down." She snickered.

"Hey, be nice. It was cheap and it's functional."

Touching his arm, "I completely agree. I'm teasing you."

"I'll get even."

The doorbell rang and Ken moved to get the pizza. Maddie continued to look at the rest of the office space. A nice chair on rollers. Desk had all the necessary toys like a computer, stapler, printer, three-hole punch, router, Scotch Tape dispenser, and a bowl of paperclips. All were neatly arranged. As she began looking at the pictures on the wall she heard him clear his throat.

"Is it always this neat?" He almost panicked, remembering he had documents on the wall declaring that he was a physician, and there were pictures of him in surgical gear. The second she left the house tonight those would be changed out for others. He was thankful he hadn't taken too long with the pizza. Thank the gods she hadn't turned around toward that wall.

"It is," he smiled. "Unless I'm working there. Then all bets are off. Come on, let's eat in the kitchen."

"You updated the kitchen!"

"No, Dad did when he first moved here. You have to remember we always had servants doing everything. There was always room in the old house for live-in maids and such but that couldn't apply here. I suppose he could have redone the room over the garage and made it into some kind of maid quarters, but it doesn't have plumbing and it would have been outrageously expensive to redo it. The chef never lived in our old place, so Dad just paid him extra to drive the extra distance to come and fix his meals for him. He'd come on Sunday's and prepare a weeks' worth of dinners, stick them in the freezer and Dad would just reheat them. It surprised me to learn that Dad actually learned how to fix himself some cereal in the morning and a sandwich for lunch. Or he would go to one of the places like Pancake House." Opening the box, "Have at it. Four meats and extra cheese. What would you like to drink?"

"Water is fine."

"Water it is then." He brought out two bottles from the fridge. "Want a glass?"

"No, the bottle is fine, thanks."

"I don't really cook much. Microwave mostly. But I think the kitchen's well done."

"It's actually Perfect. I do like it. It's bright and modern, but without that 'stainless-steel' look."

"Not a fan of stainless, huh?"

"No. Also, I don't think I would have ever thought of using a pale rose color for the walls."

"Dad had a decorator, of course. He wasn't big on having to do a lot of cleanup and maintenance so he went with the solid surface counter tops, and they are white so he could repaint the walls if he got tired of the rose color. Decorator convinced him it would be a way to change out things like chair coverings and towels. As if he really cared about chair coverings and towels!" Folding the pizza he stuck it into his mouth, then grabbed a napkin to catch the dribbling sauce at the corner of his mouth.

Maddie found herself so focused on the dribbling sauce that she momentarily lost her train of thought.

Lowering the napkin, and swallowing, he tapped a finger on the table and pointed to her slice of pizza. "Eat woman. It's getting cold." She saw the corners of his lips curl up.

Picking up her knife and fork, "Oh, it smells so good."

Ken put his hand up to his mouth to suppress a small laugh, but she caught him.

"What?"

"Not a fan of the fold and eat method, huh?"

Her fork and knife, held just above the slice, "Never tried it, actually."

"Let me show you how then."

Lowering her utensils, she watched him pick up another slice, deftly fold the two sides together, and looking over at her, "Okay, now you try it."

Grabbing from the end crust she started to lift the slice, but to her chagrin several pieces of the sausage fell off and onto the plate. She dropped it back down.

"Thumb and fingers on the end crust," he demonstrated, "then lift the pointy end up with the forefinger of your other hand," he showed, "and using your thumb and other fingers of that hand gently fold toward the center."

Concentrating on all those finger movements, she managed to follow his lead and successfully fold the slice.

"Now you just stick it in your mouth," he laughed, "keeping both hands on it so it doesn't open up."

She succeeded, and the smile on his face was beautiful. "However," she picked up the knife and fork, "this is way easier!"

"You did well, though!" His eyes were jovial. "Sometimes it's fun to try a different way of doing things."

"I like that."

"Alright, Maddie, what's your favorite song?"

She gulped, then coughed. "Not fair to ask me questions when my mouth is full."

"Huh?"

She giggled.

"I think you mean it's not fair of you to answer when your mouth is full."

They both burst out laughing.

He wiped his mouth with the napkin. "At this rate we'll never get through all this pizza."

"You *will* have extras. No question about it."

"Don't change the subject! Favorite song!"

Maddie sat back, suddenly somber. Ken noticed that the light had gone out of her eyes. He stopped eating and kept silent while she looked down, then back up at him. Folding her hands together in her lap and looking down at them, "I don't think you will have heard of it."

"I can always check it out on YouTube."

She nodded. Lifting her eyes to watch his face, "It's a haunting song, with eerie words."

Whoa! Ken went instantly on alert. There was just the barest hitch in his shoulders. He'd never heard those words used to describe a song before. He sat silently, his brow furled, not wanting to interrupt her thought process.

"It's Quentin's Theme, from Dark Shadows." Her eyes had locked on his.

"Theme music then? What is Dark Shadows?"

"There are words. It's from an old television show about a vampire."

Vampire? That made him curious, and he responded, maybe a bit too quickly. "I've never heard of it, but I'll look it up." She said Dark Shadows, haunting, and eerie. That sounded strange for a favorite song. Quentin, remember that name. Maybe he needed to take a step or two back. Learn a little bit more about her.

"What's *your* favorite song then?" Maddie took a sip of her water while she waited for his answer. Putting his elbow on the table he rested his chin on his fist. Apparently she didn't want to go into detail about her song. Okay, he could go with a change of subject for the time being.

Pushing his chair back, he brought his left ankle up to rest on his right thigh. "I wondered about that while I was gone. I can't come up with any special song. I do like classical and country music. Those sound at odds with each other, but I only like the old country music, not the new stuff."

"Never had a girlfriend that you had a special song to dance to? I know officers in the Navy always have tons of official functions they have to go to… with their wives and girlfriends."

Where was she going with this? That slight pause before she added the wives and girlfriends part? Glancing away from her, "Oh, goodness. I can't even remember when I last danced. And no. I never dated anyone long enough to get to the 'our song' stage."

"Oh, I'm sorry. Assumptions I guess. Well, Mark and I never had an 'our song' either, really." Oddly, it was true. She and Mark never had 'their song.' She sighed, her eyes drifting down to the pizza. "One of these large slices is all I can eat," she glanced up at him carefully. He seemed to have lost some of his enthusiasm. Maybe he was just tired. "I also like to listen to classical music. My favorite composer is Hayden, ah, Joseph Hayden. For some reason his music is soothing."

Ken nodded, "You sure you don't want any more pizza?" He felt it would be awkward at this point to correct her assumptions about his dating and dancing. She was making him somewhat nervous with those kinds of questions anyway.

"No thanks, I'm full." It was a fair clue that the night was over.

"Want some to take home?"

"No, you keep it. Preheat the oven to 375. Put some foil on the bottom of a baking sheet and heat that in the oven for 2-3 minutes. Then put the pizza on the foil and heat for ten minutes. It will taste like you just got it."

"Good to know. Thanks." Folding the top of the box back over the pizza he stood, picked it up and placed it on the counter. "I'll find a container to put it in later. More water?"

"I'm fine. I should head home before Mother goes off the grid again. I really enjoyed the pizza and am so glad you're home safely."

"I'm probably going to go see my dad tomorrow, but I'll give you a call." He followed her to the front door.

"I'd like that, and thanks again for the pizza. Enjoy the leftovers."

"I'll do that," he promised

Closing the door, he couldn't get to his computer fast enough. Dark Shadows. A Search shows it was some old show theme. On television, like a soap opera, from 1966 to 1971 – Goodness. Neither of them had even been born then. She didn't say she'd seen the show, though it was possible it was in syndication, or on one of the streaming networks. That wasn't what mattered though. It was the song that she was talking about, and she'd said 'it has words'. Searching for Dark Shadows Theme song he listened to it on YouTube. Yes, it was eerie and haunting. But there were no words. He wracked his brain.... She had said someone's name. Quentin! Quentin's Theme from Dark Shadows. Searching for Quentin's Theme, there it was: The Original Music - Shadows of the Night (Quentin's Theme). Pen in hand he began writing down the lyrics. His hand came to a stop after the third line. Hearing the voice of David Selby, reading the lyrics, blew him away. He was stunned. He listened to it no less than five times, then began writing. He noticed a version sung by Andy Williams, and listened to that as well, but much preferred the Selby. It was most assuredly haunting. Searching on lyrics he found them and printed the page out to study later. That helped. He couldn't write fast enough just listening. He wished now he had asked her how *long* it had been her favorite song. And then he wondered – was it truly a *favorite* song? Favorite songs usually brought back good memories and smiles. She wasn't smiling. Maybe it was a song of torment, one that she was driven to listen to as if saying a prayer. He felt fairly sure it was about losing her father but could also be about her husband. Or both. Unusual for it to be a favorite song though. Haunting and eerie was what she had said, yet the lyrics seem to speak of death or loss. Could it be a wish for death? He was puzzled. He felt sweat on his brow and quickly wiped his face with his handkerchief. This was not a phone conversation topic, that was for sure. He'd have to be very careful how he brought that subject up again. Picking up the sheet of paper he moved to his easy chair in the family room and tried to let everything gel in his mind. Darn, he wished he knew when she first heard the song. Pulling his cell phone out he tried to see if he could download it, but that version wasn't on iTunes. He fell asleep in his chair thinking that this wasn't the romantic kind of favorite song most women would choose. Not the 'Can't Help Falling in Love with You', or 'When I Said I Do'....

It seemed strange to her that the evening had suddenly landed with a dull thud. She hadn't expected that. She was so excited to see him again. He had to have been very tired from all the work and travel. It was extremely odd that he'd really never done much dating. At least that's what he was telling her. Hard to believe. He was *so* handsome. And her faux-pas about her assumption that he had dated a lot and danced was rather unforgiveable. Maybe that's where he took umbrage. It seemed really odd to her that a man that good looking had kept himself a basic bachelor. She doubted he was gay, but that was certainly something to think about. It just seemed that one minute he was hot and the next he was cold. She certainly preferred the hot!

    She began humming the tune. Like now, she was driving her car when she first heard that song. 1998 and she would never forget it. It was exactly two years since her father had died and she thought it was spooky when it first came on, with all the outer space music or something. Then a man started to say the words and she had to pull over to listen. Bawling until she could barely catch her breath, by the time it ended she would have given anything to be hauled up into the sky to be with her daddy. She was eighteen, having been dragged away from all her friends in Chicago, to live in a city that wasn't friendly to her at all, with a mother that hated her. At least the whippings had stopped. Maddie did her level best to stay as far away from her mother as possible. She was forced to live at home while attending Old Dominion University. "Not enough money for anything else," her mother had said. In hind sight that was not such a good choice. Living at home that is. Dear old Dori continued to harass her and watch her every move, criticizing most of them. She couldn't wait to get her degree, find an apartment, move out, and start her teaching career. And it had gone well. Then she was introduced to Mark, and they married in 2006. She had his love for three years when the Navy chaplain and a female Naval officer arrived at her door. Even now she felt the energy of her life draining out of her, and now that Ken had made her remember the song… it was going to be a very difficult night. If only he'd forgotten about naming a favorite song. But at least she hadn't lied and made up something stupid. She was happy that he was going to spend the next day with his father. She would have sold her soul to be able to visit hers. At least she wouldn't have to pin herself to the kitchen window, or run in and out with multiple bird feedings, trying to catch him. She was feeling alone again. It was nice having those few weeks with Ken. Maybe she needed to reach out to others again, somehow. Until this second she hadn't realized how lonely and alone she had been for the past several years. The ringing of her cell phone jarred her out of the memories. Picking up her phone off the car seat it was Elle.

"Hey Elle."
"You sound sad, Maddie."
"No, just tired. She lied. *Pulling into my driveway now and can't wait to hit the pillow."* Maybe it was just a half-truth.
"I just wanted you to know that everything is over, and I'll keep my promise to you. I thank God you're in my life, and I'll pray for you."
"What happened then?"
"It was Judge White again. He really blasted me, but my psychologist was very convincing. She only talked about the shoplifting part, of course, but in the end he gave me a one-thousand-dollar fine and no jail time, but he guaranteed me if I ever showed up again I'd go to prison."

Maddie actually felt her eyes misting.
"I'll get your money back to you tomorrow."
Doing some quick math on her cell, *"Wait until the first payment, when you'll give me the $1500, plus your monthly $88.00 payment. That will be due the first week in October. Then $88.00 a month for one year."*
"Thank you, Maddie. I'll get that started next month with my first teaching check. Sleep well."
"You, too."
God let her live up to her promises.
She was grateful her mother wasn't at the door waiting to give her some form of grief for leaving her alone for a couple of hours. Sleep was going to be hard enough as it was.

He'd told Maddie he was going to visit his father, so he was going to do just that. Emotionally he'd never felt so confused. What to make of Maddie and her song? While she had mentioned that it had to do with a vampire he hadn't really made the connection. Hmm. Vampires were really not dead folks. They just woke up every now and then for blood and turning regular people into vampires. Right? Could she be a lover of the occult or something? Did that go with vampires?

More googling. Not occult. That wasn't vampires. That was magic and card reading. Back to vampires. Dead and alive at the same time. Somehow they transcend life in a powerful way. Seen as handsome, strong, independent, sexy. There were a lot of words to describe a vampire that didn't have to do with blood sucking! If she viewed the vampire as either her father or husband, then maybe she heard herself being called to him. His brain was fried, and he was getting more confused than ever. He doubted he'd ever be able to come up with a way to talk to her about something that seemed so deep. Right now, he was just feeling numb. He was back to being his normal self. But that brief stint into what he thought could have been....

"Your dad is up and active this morning, Dr. Avery. He ate a very good breakfast."

"Thanks, Anne."

Heading down to the room he prayed his father would recognize him this time. His memory was so selective.

Knocking gently on the door he cracked it open and peeked in. He could see his dad sitting in an easy chair, a blue blanket covering his lap and legs. He wore a checkered shirt, neatly buttoned. Entering slowly, he tapped lightly on the door again, but his dad just stared straight ahead. Television wasn't on. Approaching he could tell his dad was getting excellent care. They had no idea he would be coming for a visit, yet his dad was dressed in clean clothing, his face was shaved, and his hair was trimmed and clean. It was a good place for his dad.

"Hi, pops."

Turning his head, Martin looked up at Ken. "Are you my new nurse?"

It was an instant stab to his heart. He winced and closed his eyes, gathering the patience he knew he needed.

Pulling up a folding chair he sat down at a slight angle from his father, "No, I'm not a nurse, I'm your son, Dad." Leaning forward he put his elbows on his thighs and looked at his dad.

"You just missed Grace. She was here for quite a while. You should meet her sometime, she's such a lovely woman."

Ken felt his eyes misting. Grace was his mother, gone for so many years now.

"She was an angel you know. Wonderful wife."

"Yes, Dad. I do remember her."

"You call me Dad. I'm not a dad. Not yet anyway."

Ken took in a deep breath. He was a doctor. He was trained to be stoic for families, and now he was one of them. There was no doctor that could give him any hope. His dad was going faster than he was prepared for.

"Can I get you some fruit, Mr. Avery," he replied to his father.

"You are a nice, respectful man. You just missed Grace; you know. I'm really sorry. But she'll be back tomorrow, and you can come and meet her then."

"I'd love to meet her. She sounds lovely."

"Oh, yes."

"Would you like me to read to you?"

"No. I'm fine."

"Can I take you outdoors for a while?"

Ken watched his father rub his hands over the blanket, as if to dry them, "No, I'm fine."

It was hard to sit there, but Ken sat back in the chair and after asking his dad if he could turn on the television they both watched the weather channel for a while.

"Gonna storm, they say. Lots of thunder and lightning. You best make sure your sister is alright, Son."

Ken's head jerked up. His father was looking at him. "Don't worry Dad. You know I'll take good care of Trish." He needed to control his breathing and act normally.

"She has a fine family. When are you going to get a wife?"

Ken smiled and filled his dad in on a little of his struggles with feelings for Maddie.

"Don't lose time, Kenneth. Life is over so quickly. You think back to how fast you got to be retired from when you started college. POOF." His dad raised an arm and brought it down suddenly. "Over, just like that. Chop, Chop." He repeated the gesture.

Ken almost started to cry. One minute his father had no clue who he was and the next they were talking, Father to Son, like they had NEVER, EVER talked before. His dad had *never* delved into his personal life, and to do so now was, frankly, startling.

"Dad, you know I love you, don't you?"

"Yes, son, I do. And I've always loved you. I'm very tired now. Will you help me into my bed?"

Carefully helping his father, he leaned down and gave him a hug.

"You go now, Son, and give your sister and brothers my love. Get back with your brothers, Ken. They can come see me, too. I'd love to see them all again." Folding his hands over the blanket and closing his eyes, he drifted off to sleep. Ken watched for a few more minutes and then left, tears flowing down his cheeks. There was a lump in his throat he wasn't sure would ever go away, but his father had made it a point to suggest that he get back in touch with his brothers. Had they ever visited their father? He needed to find out and see if they would consider it. Yes, time was flying by. He needed more of it. He needed to figure out what to do about his brothers, his sister, Maddie, his life, his volunteer job. He had to make some kind of sense out of his fractured life. It was fine when he was a doctor. Everyone was young, everyone was busy, everyone had their own "thing" they were doing. But now life was getting toward that half-way mark and that shocked him. His father was only in his late 60's. Did he, himself, have only twenty years left? That scared him. He hadn't thought about death, dying, horrible endings like Alzheimer's or cancer, and if he wanted to live a nice life in the last half he needed to decide which way to go. What would it be like to mend the fences with his siblings? What would it be like to love Maddie for life? And then there was her mother. Reaching his car, he got in and started to head home. His first order of business, as best he could think at the moment, was to contact his siblings and see where they all stood with regard to him and their father.

Chapter 7

At least he'd sent her a message that he was going to the Eastern Shore to spend some time with his sister, and that would be followed by meetings with his brothers. She wasn't sure what to make of it though. It was a simple, 'I need to get my family situation in order' kind of message with no promise to call her, tell her when he might be back, or that he missed her. She guessed he didn't miss her. Maddie put the phone down on the counter and looked out the window, longingly. She noticed that the temperatures were beginning to fall, just a little, but it was nice to have days in the 70's and low 80's, instead of the ones that made you feel you were in a sauna. Labor Day was just around the corner. Just another day on the calendar for her. It used to be an exciting time. School would start the day after Labor Day, and she loved meeting her new students with a job that kept her on her toes at all times. Labor Day meant there would be tons of activity at the ocean front, but she had no intention of getting mixed up in it. Half the time it was so packed with people you couldn't even see the band that was playing. She'd hang the flag and that would be her acknowledgement of the holiday.

"What happened to your man friend, Madeline?" Her sneer was clear.

"He's at a family reunion, Mother." Well, it was the best she could come up with since he had said he needed to meet with his sister and brothers. Who knew what that would be about? At first it seemed hard to believe that Ken had been retired for something like two years and was just now seeing his brothers and sister? Well, yeah, she hadn't seen her brother in twenty some years, but that was totally different. She'd been ripped away from Chicago as a teen and he stayed behind, never once showing his face in Virginia Beach. If she tripped over him she wouldn't recognize him.

"See, just like I knew it would happen," jeering, "He's up and left you. Don't say I didn't tell you that was going to happen. Men are just like that. Even your father figured out a way to die and leave me. He did it deliberately. Never fails. They always figure out some way to do it." Cane up in the air, Cane down. "Never fails." She sat down in her chair, "Will you never get smart, Madeline? When's dinner?"

Trish was as beautiful as ever. Looking like the rag-a-muffin she had become he was overjoyed at the smile she gave him when he got out of the car.

"Oh, my god, you are so handsome still," her eyes were as big as saucers and her smile outdid the sun for its brightness. Grabbing onto him she held him in the biggest hug of his life. And it felt so good. When he backed away there were tears in her eyes. Kissing her cheek, he wiped the tears away with his thumbs. "Hey kiddo, how are you?"

"Two years, brother! It's been two years since I saw you, when we put Dad in the nursing home."

"I don't have any good excuses, Trish." Gently taking his arm, they began walking toward the house. "Every time I turned around I was called back into Doctors World Wide, spending weeks at a time in horrible conditions in some horrible locations."

"You could have called."

"Hmm. Couldn't the same be said about you, my dear sister?"

"Touché. Mea Culpa. Guilty as Charged…." She wiggled her eyebrows at him.

They both burst out laughing, with Trish giving him a good punch in the gut. "I'm sorry, Ken. I just get so busy, and you know how that goes. Two teenage boys are not something easy to manage sometimes. One wants to fish and the other wants to photograph nature. One goes here and the other goes there and Paul is up near Maryland or something arresting poachers."

"Did I come at a bad time. No one around, not even the dog."

"Paul and the boys are camping this week, so your timing is great for us to fill in the last couple of years." Motioning for him to sit down in the kitchen, "They took Radar with them. Coffee."

"Please. You look happy, Trish."

"When I'm not so tired I drop, I'm the happiest woman on earth, Ken. Just the other day I was looking at a picture of me when I was ten or eleven. Oh, the horror of it all."

Ken nodded in understanding.

Putting the coffee cups down and taking a seat across from him, she twirled her cup, "I was such a Diva. All those servants who knew what you needed before you even did. My clothes were always laid out in perfect symmetry. My hair was curled by a maid, and Mother! I shiver sometimes at some of the things she told us."

"I think, and I'll need to talk to Reed and Drew, but I think *three* of us managed to escape all that."

"But not Reed."

"Nope, not Reed." Ken tapped his fingers, rolling them over in order, lost in thought. The high-powered attorney was a mirror of their mother.

"So, what have you been up to, Ken, besides the Doctoring? I worry about you, living all by yourself now that you're retired. Still see your Navy friends?"

"Oh, no. And I don't miss most of them at all. I do see my old boss, Jerry. He was Chief of Surgery on more than one of my duty stations. He's retired and now runs Doctors World Wide."

She looked lovingly at him, "I'm glad you're staying in the area. When we put Dad in the nursing home I was surprised to find his house was in your name. I guess he knew Reed wouldn't want it, Drew is exactly where he wants to be, I'm fine, and you were leaving the Navy, so he figured you'd need a place to stay. He paid cash for it, too. And it was nice that you could stay there with him until the time came that he just had to be moved for his own safety."

"I had no idea he'd done that, but it was welcome. I would have had to find a place with no real idea of where to start. Bachelor quarters and ship's cabins are all I've ever known for years."

"I'm glad he took care of you." Sipping her coffee, "He had gotten better while I was checking on him every week. I think he was aware of how much he had missed of our growing up years, and I really think he regretted that Reed ended up in that same status push that our mom had lived."

"Good old Reed has his own mansion near the ocean. Dad's house would have been a tax burden or something. And Drew?" Ken chuckled. "Try dragging him out of that pile of peanuts."

For a few moments both were silent, thinking about the now and then.

Standing, she took her empty cup to the sink. "More coffee?"

"No, thanks. I don't drink a lot anymore, except when I'm in the field. Then I have to stay awake."

"I'm making a simple dinner. Just some chicken pot pie and even though it has a crust I'm also adding some homemade rolls."

Ken smiled. God he loved his sister so much it was almost too hard to put into words. She had found the perfect life with the perfect man. "You had me at chicken pot pie, Trish. Cook used to make it just for me, remember?"

"Yes, I do. I also remember that we all ate it at the little table in the kitchen, by ourselves, while Mother and Father ate in the dining room."

Ken inhaled sharply, then tapped his hand on the table. "Yup. Food and company were great. Situation, not normal."

Trish looked at her brother as she continued to check on the dinner. He was still one of the best-looking men on the planet and it wasn't natural for him to be alone. She hated the thought that he'd end up an old man, living in that house, with no one to hug or kiss during the day, and no one to keep him warm at night. He'd broken away from all the programming of their mother, so what was going on with him?

"So, Ken. Tell me why you aren't married?"

His eyes snapped to hers. Wasn't that taking a straight shot. "What?"

"Tell me why you aren't married. If you're gay, I couldn't care less and will support you to the ends of the earth…"

"Whoa, Sis. I'm not gay."

"Then what? Can't be Mom's ideas since you obviously broke away from all that by joining the Navy."

He was silent for a few moments. "Might as well get me another cup of coffee, Trish."

She obliged, setting it down in front of him and taking a seat in the chair closest to him.

"In a way it is Mother. She demanded, if you recall, that we only ever know high-society. I was only to associate with daughters of her social friend chart. Same with you. Birthday parties, Christmas, Valentine's Day, and heaven help us if we sent or got a valentine from anyone who wasn't on her chart. So those were the only groups we ever knew, the private school gang!" He gritted his teeth and his jaw moved back and forth.. "I dated a few and it was just awful. All they cared about was money. All of them dressed to the nines, faces full of makeup to the point that you had no idea what they *really* looked like. What ever happened to natural?" He glanced up at Trish admiring her fresh, clean, unpainted face. "Anyway, I take them out to dinner, and they eat a lettuce leaf with two one-inch cubes of watermelon or cucumber on it. OH, and for goodness sake don't even think of touching their hair."

Trish burst out laughing, shaking her head, and letting her long locks swirl left and right.

"I love that. Swishing your hair is beautiful," he smiled widely at her. "And I'll bet Paul does, too."

She grinned back. "Go on, Ken. So, there's been no one of interest?" She suspected Ken was visiting her for more than one reason. Maybe it was sisterly ESP or something, but Ken just wasn't one to visit anyone, at all. He'd been far too busy all his career, and now with the volunteering. They would call each other on their respective birthdays, on Christmas, and Thanksgiving. She had invited him over for Thanksgiving dinner twice, and he was always doing something else. Geeze, once he said he was somewhere in Africa. She sat there, silently waiting for him to talk. It was clear she was right when she watched him wring his hands and swallow hard.

"There could be, maybe. There's a woman down a few blocks that I met when walking." Going into detail about the house and the blinds, he shook his head, "It's strange. She's a widow. I haven't found out how her husband died. Right now, she's taking care of her mother, who has MS, but is a total witch. And she feeds all the birds and squirrels peanuts. Drew would like that! We've had coffee, and a pizza. That's all."

"Ken Avery!" She shifted her chair to be close enough to touch him. "It's about time. Tell me more."

"I really don't know much more. I've only really known her for about two weeks, Trish. Her father died when she was young., and he was her idol. Her brother lives in Chicago, and she hasn't seen him in something like 25 years. She's beautiful and down to earth, just like you, Trish. For some reason I was drawn to her the minute I saw her. She was dragging a tree down to the street and I asked her if I could help. She rather reminded me of you, dressed in an oversized t-shirt with a squirrel picture on it, and plain blue shorts. Totally utilitarian." He gave her a good poke in her arm.

"So, what do you think makes her different from anyone else you ever dated."

"Thing is, I never really dated much, but Mother planted this picture in my mind of a gorgeous woman, dressed in designer clothes, perfect makeup and hair, very sociable and a descendent of some grand and glorious lineage. And, truth be told, that's what I always seemed to date. And the date always seemed to disappoint me. I even wondered a time or two what they would look like without all the makeup. It could be a horror story to take one of them to bed and wake up the next morning to something ugly looking back at me!"

"You can't be serious, brother."

"Oh, but I can. Add their eating habits and it's almost not worth taking them to dinner. I get a steak dinner and they get sliced tomatoes on a lettuce leaf."

Trish cackled. "I can actually remember those days… before Paul."

"I'm sure you can," he laughed. "Point is, Maddie was exactly the opposite of all that, and it really surprised me. Her dark hair had been combed but nothing special. He skin was natural, and her eyes were Hazel. Lovely eyes. I think about her too much, and it's a bit hard for me to understand that. Never cared about any woman before, so why am I now? She is beautiful, she seems to be down to earth and is intelligent for sure. She just appeals to me."

"Sounds rather perfect. What's the problem then?"

"I asked her what her favorite song was and it's a bit scary to me." He pushed back his chair and crossed his left ankle over his right leg, folding the creases of his pants with his thumb and forefinger.

"Hello, earth to Ken. What's the song?"

Quirking his mouth, he reached into his wallet and took out the piece of paper with the lyrics on it. "I keep studying them and wonder what it's really saying."

She spent the next five minutes reading and rereading the words.

"Nope, Ken. I totally get this."

"Seriously?"

Nodding, "I'm going to make an assumption here, but I'm guessing that after she lost her husband she heard this song. It grabbed her at once. She's longing for her husband who is now a spirit. She desperately wants him back. On top of that her father has left her, too, and she's now dealing with two men she loved deeply, and both are spirits. Then," she paused, "and now she's taking care of a witch of a mother...Oh, Ken, I get this. This woman is so lonely it's breaking my heart. She wants to be back with both of them. OH, Ken, this is making me cry." Standing quickly, she grabbed a tissue and wiped her eyes. "I want to meet her. You said her name was Maddie? You go get her and bring her here."

He was absolutely speechless. His mind had gone blank. He couldn't believe it, but his sister was *still* crying. Getting up from his chair he walked over and pulled her into a hug. Looking into her eyes, "My gosh, Trish. Is it really that sad?"

She nodded. "You need to find out about her husband, and for goodness sake, Ken, don't base an entire relationship on one song! Especially one you don't know the reason for it."

Now that he thought about it all the conversations that he'd had with Maddie had been basically one-sided. She heard all about his family and more, and he only knew she was a widow, had a brother in Chicago, and a witch mother with MS. He needed a lot more information, an hoped it wouldn't' be too late after he got back. But he needed to get with both of his brothers first. He needed to know they were visiting their dad. Time was getting to be very important where Dad was concerned. Okay, he got it now.

"You been over to see Dad?"

"Changing the subject on me?"

"Yes, I am. It's important, too. I'll find out more about Maddie. I promise."

"Maddie... I like that name."

"Dad?"

"I'll go as soon as Paul and the boys get home to take care of the house. I've been horribly remiss, and I'm sorry for it. Dad wasn't much of a dad to us, but he's still Dad."

"Yeah, I agree." He filled her in on his visit with their dad. It wasn't pretty, and she hung her head in shame.

"The guys will be home Saturday. I'll go down on Sunday."

He'd gotten what he'd hoped for on the visit. A second opinion on that song was important to him and he knew the only one that would figure out if he was right or wrong it would be Trish. She had the world by the tail! Fresh thinking was always good. She didn't for a second see anything like ghost hunting or something. He needed to speed up his visits with his brothers and get back to Maddie.

Somehow time just flew. It was clear that Ken had distanced himself. For the life of her she couldn't imagine what had happened. Lately she just quit thinking about it for the most part. Her mother wasn't any nicer, the cane tapping continued, and one day segued seamlessly into the next. He hadn't sent her any text messages, and nothing showed up on her recent calls list. Since it had been something like ten days she had to give up any hope of having a nice guy in her life, even as just a friend.

With dinner over she was finishing up the dishes when the doorbell rang. She hated the solicitors that were forever ringing the bell, and she usually just waited for them to walk away. But this one wasn't walking away. The doorbell rang a second time, and a third.

"Answer the stupid door, Maddie, my ears are killing me with that dong, dong, dong."

Opening the door, Holy Cow, what was with this flood of handsome men all of a sudden? He was over six feet, light brown hair neatly combed. He bore a small mustache, which she didn't think looked good on him. He wore khaki slacks and a red polo shirt and seemed a bit familiar. Maybe one of the neighbors. People often looked different when they changed from the clothes they wore when walking the dog to what they would wear to a meeting or work. "Yes, what can I do for you?" she asked the stranger standing before her.

"Madeline?"

"Yes." Nice looking man, no clipboard that poll takers use, well dressed, she eyed him up and down. She couldn't remember any dog walker that sprouted a mustache.

"Madeline, it's me, Dan, your brother!"

She shot him a look of suspicion, then began to recognize him.

"What are you doing here?" She was so stunned she didn't know what to do.

"Can I come in?"

Slowly backing away she made room for him to come inside.

As he entered he looked around the room, almost analyzing it.

"Again, what are you doing here, Dan?" She found her hands were actually shaking.

"I haven't seen you in 25 years and thought I'd do something about it."

Was it the way he said it? Something was wrong. And then Dori walked into the room.

"Oh, Danny, thank God you've come. It's been just horrible with her," as she pointed the cane directly toward Maddie. "I'm being treated horribly. She tries to hide all the mean things she does to me."

"Mother, you called me and said you were dying, and you wanted to see me before you die. I expected to see you on your death bed."

"I was when I called you. It was hard to get a phone number for you, you know. I hear you're some famous voice person who is a millionaire talking into those video game things. I had to find out who your agent was and tell him I was dying to get your phone number. And she *is* killing me," she raised her cane and pointed it directly at Maddy. "Your very own sister. She's putting poison in my food I think."

"May I sit down, Madeline?" He looked at her and saw the face of shock. She nodded once, and he pulled out a chair at the kitchen table. "Sit down, Mother."

Madeline stood, ramrod straight, as if watching a horror movie that had her too frightened to move.

"You look alright to me, Mother." Dan watched her every move toward the table, eyeing her carefully as she sat down. He remembered his mother's disposition – oh how he remembered.

"She won't cook me the stuff I like. Says they don't make it anymore. And she's been seeing some man. She deserts me to go spend time with him. I have to make my own bed and do my own laundry. She just leaves it there in the basket and does her own…" up came the cane, smacking down on the table, causing Dan to flinch, "and, well, there are just tons of things."

Dan turned to look at Maddie, who by that time was standing there shivering, her arms folded defensively across her chest. She had never expected her mother would do something like this. To call her son, a son she hadn't bothered to contact in 25 years and haul him out of Chicago to level horrid accusations against her….

Standing, Dan took Maddie's hand and led her to a chair, whispering in her ear, "I'll get to the bottom of this, Maddie."

What choice did she have? She was about to pass out. She looked up at her brother. Yes, he was her brother, and a handsome guy. How odd. He'd be more handsome if he shaved off the mustache, but that was just her personal opinion. She's always told Mark that facial hair was grounds for divorce, and he would laugh. 'Navy doesn't allow it,' he would counter. Dan was about six feet tall, and obviously took care of himself. He wasn't muscular but had a trim body. His hair had more gray than brown in it. That didn't bode well for what her hair would look like in four years! Her eyes snapped back to him when she heard him scrape the chair on the floor before sitting down in it.

Dan listened to Dori for the next fifteen minutes, calmly analyzing her claims and cataloguing them in his mind for later verification. He knew instantly that there was way more to the story than what he was being told. He cringed at each crack of the cane on the table but managed to keep his emotions in check.

"What do you want me to do, Mother?"

"I want you to come and take care of me."

She had to be kidding. His mother hadn't changed one iota. While she had favored him over Maddie, he was ashamed to admit, he was amazed that she thought he could get one phone call, two decades later, and come be her caring son again. He looked at Maddie, sitting silently with not a single blink of an eye, staring into space. Sitting forward, it was clear what he had to do. He had been thinking of more than one scenario while he was on the plane. Was Maddie the problem or was it his mother. Now he knew which way he was going to take control.

"That's absolutely not possible, Mother. I can find a nice senior home for you to live in, or I can hire nurses to come and take care of you, but I can't leave Chicago."

"WHY NOT?" WHAP!

That was a hard one. He actually jumped a little but noticed that Maddie hadn't moved an iota. So, she's heard that noise before! She simply sat there, staring into space, but he felt she was watching, and listening.

"My job, my ex-wife, my son are all in Chicago, Mother. I can't leave them. And I can't move them here. You contact me after all these years and tell me you're dying. You tell me you want to see me one more time. Yet here I am, and you seem to be fine."

"I have multiple sclerosis, and I'm not fine."

"Yes, you told me that on the phone. You had MS and were on your dying bed."

"Well, it feels like that with her in this house."

That was it, Maddie jumped up. "I'm gone. I'll go pack and be out of here in less than an hour." Turning she started to walk out of the room.

"Maddie, stop. Please stop." It was a gentle command, which surprised her.

"No, Dan." She softened her voice, "I've told her more than once I'm tired of the lifetime of abuse. The only peace I've ever had in my life was with my husband before he died, and now a man I just met who made me smile for the first time in years. I'm done."

Maddie watched as Dan lifted a finger and gave her what seemed to be some kind of signal. She stayed standing, noticing that Dan gave her a subtle wink.

Turning back to Dori, "Okay, Mother. Since Maddy is leaving, first thing tomorrow I'll arrange for you to be put into a nursing home. I've already done a lot of research on your local homes," he lied, "and there are openings in most of them," he lied again. "Nurses and nurses' aides will be able to take care of you. They do have kitchens and cook for all the residents, but you won't have much choice of what to eat. It will be nutritious though." He kept talking, watching as his mother's face slowly drained of blood. "They'll also make you exercise every day, probably two or three times a day, to keep you as active as possible with your MS." He pushed his chair back and made like he was about to leave. "I'll leave now and can start on it immediately," he looked at his watch. "There's still time to get to one or two of them before the administrative offices close."

"You'd do that to me? Your own mother?" she screeched.

"Ah, Mother, I really don't remember much about you. You zipped out of Chicago practically the day after we laid Daddy to rest, dragging Maddie with you. But since I am your legal son I do have an obligation," he winked at Maddie again," to see to your care, and since I can afford one of the lesser nursing homes that's the best I can offer you right now. I can have it all set up and you moved in by the end of next week. Then you won't have to be abused by Maddie anymore."

Her face, now in a rage, Dori stood, and with a WHACK that almost broke the cane, left the room.

"She's gone to bed, Dan."

Leaning forward, and motioning for Maddie to return to her chair, he spoke softly as she sat down. "You do know that all that was just window dressing, right?"

Maddie's lips curled up just enough to show she knew. "I've done my research, too. It takes about six months to get anyone into those places. But it was a good story. Would you like a tour, so your mind is at ease? Can I get you something to eat or drink?"

"No, I'm fine. Trust me, I understand. It's clear that nothing has changed from our childhood."

Dan could see the pain in her eyes when she leveled them at him. "It's gotten worse, actually. The only real change is she can't put me over her knee anymore and hit me so hard with the paddle that I can't sit down."

Dan lowered his eyes and nodded. "Right now, Maddie, I'm tired from a long day, but I want to spend time with you. We need to find ourselves again, and if it's alright with you I'll go back to the hotel and rest. Maybe I can come back tomorrow, and we can sit on the porch, maybe when she's napping, and talk."

"I'd like that, Dan. I really would. And I have a fabulous back porch. I sit out there a lot," she gave him a wry grin.

Taking her hands, he stood and brought her to her feet. "Keep the faith. It will all work out." He then leaned in and kissed her cheek. "Nice to meet you again, Sister." He had his answer when he saw her tears start to form.

Dan decided to spend the next two days in town. He was totally enjoying his visit, dramatic as it was. Drama was his life after all. He did voice overs for multiple gaming companies and was an expert at doing various voice inflections. While it was costing him time from his extended family and job he was grateful to finally have a chance to see Maddie again. He owed her. He owed her big time, and now was the right time to try to make it right.

Returning the next day, he found Maddie making breakfast for Dori. When she offered him eggs and bacon he didn't refuse. He was, after all, still observing. It was clear Maddie was doing just fine. More than fine actually. He had to work hard to suppress smiling when all Dori did was give him an evil eye.

"Good morning, Mother."

She glared at him.

"I managed to find a place for you at one of the local homes. They have one small room available. It's a tiny room, but enough for a bed and one of your chairs. A small dresser. No cooking allowed, but they do all that and will do all your laundry. They are pretty good at taking care of people but sometimes they can't get to you fast enough when you have to use the bathroom. I told them I'd come back today and sign the papers to have you committed. Then we can move you in in a day or two."

Maddie turned her back to the table so Dori wouldn't see her grinning.

Shaking in rage, with sudden thoughts of lying in a bed in her own bowel movement, "How DARE you, Dori yelled. How DARE you come here and tell me you're putting me in a home."

"Mother, you really leave me no choice. The only other choice I have is to call the police and have Maddie arrested for trying to kill you. The detectives will come and analyze the situation. They'll talk to all the neighbors and anyone walking by to get an impression of how badly you're being treated. They'll search the entire house for signs of poison and blood, and they'll make you go get blood taken to test for various poisons like arsenic or ethylene glycol. They'll take Maddie out in handcuffs at once, of course, and then the cops will have social services come in and take care of you until we get other arrangements made. And social services has a few homes, but you and I know they aren't very nice. You leave me no choice, Mother. If Maddie is trying to kill you I have to either remove YOU from the situation or remove HER. So, it's either nursing home for you, or cops for her. Tell me what you want."

Obviously in a panic mode, "I want YOU to stay here and care for me."

"Not going to happen, Mother. Tell me now which way you want me to go. Nursing home or cops?"

He watched as tears fell down his mother's cheeks, but he had to keep his resolve. She had to be given time to think about what he just said, and at that moment in time Maddie placed his breakfast in front of him, along with a cup of coffee.

"Thank you, Maddie. This looks great," he looked up at her with a wink.

He picked up his fork, diving into his meal, side-eyeing his mother as she picked up her napkin to wipe her tears off her face.

"Can Maddie stay?"

Swallowing, he glanced up, placing his fork back down on the plate. "Excuse me? You want her to stay when she's trying to kill you?" He faked total shock.

"Well," Dori spoke so softly it was hard for Dan to hear her, "maybe she's not really trying to kill me."

"You lied to me?" Dan faked horror, his mouth a gaping hole and his eyes open as far as he could make them open.

Dori bent her head. "I might have exaggerated things a bit."

"Really Mother? You dragged me down here on a whim? I don't know what to say. Let me think." He pretended to be deep in thought as he lifted his coffee cup and drank. "I guess it would depend," he slowly wiped his mouth with a napkin, "on whether or not Maddie even wants to stay, Mother. Seems to me if you are making all those accusations to me, and they aren't true, then it's Maddie that's being abused. Maybe she doesn't want to be abused anymore." He lowered his hand and napkin to the table.

The room grew silent. No one moved. Finally, Dori shifted in her chair, her head dropping to her chest. She folded her hands on her lap. Dan would have sworn her face had suddenly sagged, probably showing her surrender from her true self. "Okay."

"Okay what?" Dan picked up his fork and began eating again. He had to do something to keep from laughing.

"Okay. I'll do my own laundry and make my own bed and exercise and be nice."

"Hmm. What do you mean by 'be nice'?"

"I'll stop yelling. She can go out sometimes."

"What do you think about all that, Maddie?" Dan asked.

Eyes blazing, Maddie looked directly at her mother. "She has to stop with the cane stuff. She doesn't need it to walk and all she does is slam it about, hitting walls and tables trying to scare me. She needs to let me have time to myself, to go out with friends and not complain if Ken should ever return. He's very nice, by the way," she looked over at Dan, smiling.

"Mother?"

Taking her cane, she slid it across the table to Dan. "Alright. I'll try very hard to do all that. You can put the cane in the garage until I really need it."

"Maddie," Dan looked at her.

"If she keeps her promises I'll stay."

"Alright, Mother. Maddie will stay, but she's going to keep in constant touch with me. We'll talk on the phone at least once a week, and even video each other on Facetime, so if you start acting up again I can just come down and sign the papers and get you into the home. Do you understand me, Mother?"

She nodded.

"Good. Now Maddie and I are going to go out and she's going to show me a bit of Virginia Beach for the next couple of hours. I assume you'll be alright."

"You two go and catch up. I'll take care of the dishes."

Chapter 8

Reed was hard to reach by phone. He was one busy attorney apparently, taking on only the highest profile cases for only the highest profile clients. Even his wife flitted around town with the upper class. Lunches at the golf club. Parties for the governor when he was in town. Didn't take any effort to find all that out, between news stories and information he could get online. It took him three days to get Reed to agree to a meeting, and then it was on a Saturday a couple weeks into September. Time was getting short for his dad. He could feel it.. Seems his brother's Sundays and Wednesdays were golf days. Tuesdays were court. The rest of the week he was knee deep in consult with clients. Ken knew that being a doctor was stressful and time consuming, but it seemed a lawyer had it twice as bad – that is if he wanted to remain part of the upper crust. They agreed to meet for dinner at Steinhilber's Restaurant. Seems that was the only time Reed could make it, and he knew the owner, so he got a reservation in an instant. It was considered a five-star restaurant, naturally. Entering, Ken spotted not only Reed, but his wife as well. That wasn't expected at all. While Ken was dressed in a pair of slacks, he had decided, thank goodness, to at least wear a shirt and blazer. His brother was in a suit and tie, and Ruth was in a stunning lavender, designer dress with matching jacket. Ken could spot designer anything from a mile away. He felt rather underdressed without a tie, but it was what it was. Reed should have told him it was a refined location. Quirking an eyebrow, he shook his brother's hand and nodded as he was introduced to Ruth. They'd been married a long time, but Ken had no clue as to how long. Reed made it a point to let Ken know his wife was a descendant of one of the Virginia Beach founders, someone named Adam Keeling. It made Ken instantly wonder why there were no children to carry on this important heritage. He mentally shrugged his shoulders. It was none of his business. Maybe she couldn't have children. Just looking at Reed it was hard to believe he was his brother. He was the clone of his mother, and there was no doubt about it.

"I took the liberty of ordering all of us a steak dinner. I hope that's alright. Ruth and I have a charity event to attend in an hour."

"No problem," Ken answered. He couldn't help but wonder why he wasn't surprised. "I haven't seen you for quite some time and thought I would touch base. Wondering if you've seen Dad, or Drew." Glancing over at Ruth the look on her face was one of distaste. He could actually hear a tiny 'cluck, cluck' coming from her mouth. Wow. Reed didn't even look at her, just unfolded his napkin. "Haven't seen Drew for years," He snapped his napkin down onto his lap. "He's not really a social kind of fellow. He married rather, ah, out of our status. I'd imagine Dad isn't happy about that." Ken watched as Ruth nodded forcefully.

"Dad doesn't know, Reed. He's in a long-term care home with Alzheimer's. He wants to see both you and Drew before his mind is gone. It's bad now but soon it will be gone, and he won't know any of us anymore." Now Ruth's eyes were rolling. So much animation and not a word out of her mouth yet. And he wanted to slap those rolling eyes right down her face where they belonged.

"Hmm. Well, that's probably for the best. Not like he was around when we were growing up. Mom did everything. Taught us properly while all he did was work. Don't remember him ever going to any of our events or throwing a baseball, football, or basketball with any of us. Do you remember anything like that?"

"No," Ken had to admit. "I don't."

"Hard to take time out of my life to go see someone who won't know who I am, then, isn't it?"

"I guess so, but he is our father." He felt he should probably watch what he said. Or he could express his opinion about who he was sitting in front of, then get up and leave in disgust.

A waiter arrived with their meals. They all began to eat. "So, you still in the Navy?" Reed stuck a piece of steak in his mouth.

Seems like the topic of their father was over. "Retired. Doing some work with Doctors World Wide"

"Married?" So much for any interest in his humanitarian work.

"No, still very much single. Living in the house Dad moved to after Mom died."

"I didn't know that, but I'm glad I don't have to deal with it when he dies." Ruth nodded, again, in agreement. "I'm the oldest so all that estate stuff would have landed on me. Nice to know there isn't really an estate now."

Ken was shocked but managed to hide it. "Well, Dad had a few million as we were growing up. He never remarried after Mom died. That leaves the four of us." Suddenly, Ruth's eyes bugged out, and Reed's knife froze in his hand. "Using it all up for that nursing home, I'd imagine."

At that point Ken had no intention of letting them know that the nursing home was being paid by an insurance policy. Nope! "Most likely. I guess I should make sure it's being paid monthly. He had some gigantic medical bills for the past three or four years, so all that money might be gone now. It's possible we would all have to chip in and pay the nursing home bill every month. It's something like fifteen grand a month."

He had to bite his tongue to keep from laughing as Ruth gasped and her face went white. He was sure that just the thought of giving up one of her orders for a fifteen-thousand-dollar pair of pajamas would crush her.

Quickly finishing their dinner, Reed signaled for the check. "Gotta say, it's been nice to see you again, Ken. You should get yourself a good job at one of the hospitals. Ruth knows a few single ladies of the proper lineage and could fix you up easily. Really lovely women, every one of them."

"Appreciate the thought, but I'm very happy just the way I am, Reed. If you change your mind about seeing Dad, he's in the Our Lady of Perpetual Help, on Princess Anne Road."

"I'll consider it if I ever find a tiny break in my busy schedule. Maybe you and I can have lunch together some time."

"Sounds good," in your dreams, brother dear.

Reed escorted his wife out, leaving an ample amount of money on the table to cover the meal and a huge tip. Ken calmly finished his meal, then left, laughing at the most incredible display of highbrow behavior he'd ever seen. He'd met the occasional ridiculously arrogant anesthesiologists and cardiologists in his time, but his brother had them all beat by a mile. And another thing was abundantly clear. Ruth wore the pants in that house. It was no wonder there were no children. She wasn't just an ice cube; she was the Arctic Circle. He doubted Reed had ever even seen her naked!

If his dad asked, Ken would have to tell him that Reed would try to come over but was a very busy lawyer. He's just leave it at that.

Next stop would be Drew. That one would be much better, he felt sure of it. He looked forward to the forty-minute drive to Suffolk.

"We have a couple hours, Maddie. Tell me about your life since leaving Chicago." Maddie had driven Dan down to Little Island Park in Sandbridge. Removing their shoes, they decided to walk in the wet sand and just talk. Hearing the splashing ocean waves, this early in the day, with no one else around made for a very pleasant walk. They strolled slowly.

Maddie smiled. "My high school years were miserable. Two different schools, no real chance to make friends. But I persevered and managed to get to ODU to get my degree. Started teaching and met my husband." Taking her time as they walked she filled him in on all the pain of losing him, and the years since. She told him how she ended up living with their mother. Finally, she reached over and took his arm. "Enough about me for now. Tell me about yourself."

"I used to teach, too. Interesting that we both ended up in teaching when our parents weren't in that field at all. I was married, had a son, then ended up getting divorced. That's a long story, but it involves the fact that I got a great job she didn't appreciate after a year or so. My son is now 16, living with his mother. We get along well enough."

"What did you teach?"

"My school had a public speaking course and they asked me to teach it. I resisted at first, I'm not exactly a public speaker, but in the end they managed to talk me into it. Turns out it was the best thing that ever happened to me. One of my student's fathers heard me working with his son on one of the lessons and told me I was a natural to do voice over work. I had no idea what it was, but he took me to a studio that next weekend and introduced me to some guys who create video games. I was given an audition and all at once I was doing different voices for several characters in their games. It exploded from there and now I do voice overs for the games and movies, commercials, and narrations all over the place. I'm betting you've heard me and didn't even know it. Making mega bucks. Love every minute of it."

"But your wife didn't?"

"No. At first she thought it was great, and loved the money, but I was doing a ton of traveling. I'd be in Las Vegas, Los Angeles, New York, even England and Canada. While I was zipping all over the globe my wife found someone else who paid attention to her. It was a friendly divorce. She was right.

Our son... your nephew... Andy, is a fine young man. Sara has done a wonderful job with him. Believe it or not, she's dating a really nice guy, and we'll all get together for Christmas dinner. He's an engineer who stays home," he grinned.

"You're happy?"

"Very!" He squeezed her hand. They were walking back toward her car. "I guess we should head back. Don't want our mother to think we've deserted her. It will be interesting to see how she behaves for the next couple days. I also need to contact my boss and let him know what's going on and when to expect me back."

"Are you staying then?"

"I'll stay for a couple days. We have a lot more to talk about, Maddie."

"Well, why don't you come over for dinner tomorrow. We eat at 4. I know it's early…"

"It's fine! I don't have a time to eat. I eat when I can. Work often keeps me in front of a microphone for hours. I eat at 2 in the afternoon, and I eat at 10 at night."

"Great. We can eat with Mother, then, if you like, we can go sit on the back porch and talk. All the birds and squirrels will be there."

"Perfect. I'll come over about 1 and I'll just observe Mother. If necessary I'll reinforce, in subtle ways, that I'm not kidding, but I do think we have her scared enough that she'll start behaving."

"It would be heaven!"

He hadn't seen Drew in years, and there he stood, a fit man for sure, wearing worn and torn dungarees and a faded t-shirt, with holes at the underarms. Ken had to chuckle. Clean shaven, his brother's curly hair was turning gray at about the same rate as his own. Thinking back a few days… well, darn if Reed wasn't dyeing his hair. Had to be. Not a strand of gray in those very dark brown locks. He slapped his thigh at the thought.

"What's that slapping about," Drew looked down at Ken's leg.

"I just realized that you and I are graying at about the same rate. I saw Reed and his hair is as black as the day he was born."

"You kidding me?"

"Nope. He's dyeing it. And I'd bet the money in my wallet that Ruth is dyeing hers, too!"

"Well, dang. Just like Mom."

They both continued to snicker as Drew led Ken out to one of the fields.

"Looks like a bunch of weeds to me," said Ken. "You sure these are peanuts?"

Drew laughed, reached down, and pulled up on one of the plants. Sure enough, there were peanuts, like roots. "We're just about to start our harvesting. You can see the plant tops are dry and brown now. We pull them up with a huge machine, which turns them over. A few days later another machine pulls off the peanuts, leaving the leaves on the ground as nutrients."

Taking the plant from his brother, "I never really thought about how peanuts are grown."

"There are four varieties. Virginia, runners, Spanish, and Valencias. Betcha didn't know that!"

"You'd be right. Which are these?" He rolled a peanut between his thumb and index finger.

"Virginia. They are considered the gourmet peanut... the Cadillac of them all. They have larger kernels and are what you get when you go to a baseball game."

"Peanut butter?"

"Oh, no. These are premium and are for snacking, not making peanut butter."

"You love it, don't you?"

"Never been happier, Ken. This is a perfect life. We just plant and harvest and sell. Left over rejects, too small or broken, go into large bags to be sold for critter food. It's a simple life, but I wouldn't trade it for anything."

"And you're married. Trish told me she's perfect for you."

"I have a wonderful wife and two great kids and got away from everything Mother ever tried to teach us. Like I said, we live a simple life."

"I know what you mean. Seeing Reed, the other day... He didn't escape."

"So, I've heard. Come on up to the house and meet the family."

Wearing a plain cotton dress almost completely covered by a huge red apron, Tessa was waiting on the porch with her hands in the apron pockets. She reached out to Ken with open arms. "My wife's a hugger," as Ken was pulled into her arms.

Ken liked what he saw. She was of average height, with olive skin, and curly, light brown hair cut close to the scalp, also showing streaks of gray. Another woman, he thought, that didn't have time for makeup. Her face was radiant.

"I'm so glad to meet one of Drew's brothers. He's told me quite a bit about you being in the Navy and a doctor. Come in, come in. I have a lunch ready and lots of coffee or beer. This is just fantastic." She opened the screen door and ushered him into the kitchen.

An ordinary kitchen, but very functional. The appliances were basic, and had been there for a while, but were clean and, as far as Ken could tell, in perfect working order. The walls were painted blue with a strip of kitchen fruit wall paper running around the top of the walls. One wall had gigantic wooden utensils hanging down, spoon and fork. As many countries as Ken had been in he'd never seen anything like those before. Other kitchen tools hung from hooks on the wall, close to the stove, and the refrigerator was slammed with artwork done by the kids. A simple, gray vinyl floor completed the room.

Drew just smiled and Ken knew that this was what Tessa was like all the time.

"I was a bit surprised," he followed Tessa, "when I heard Drew got married. Thought he'd be a vagabond all his life. Reed would be Mother's clone, I'd be in the middle, and Drew would be the black sheep."

"Wouldn't work, Ken. I'm the kid in the middle. You're the baby."

"Not true! Trish is the baby."

Drew slapped his leg and laughed. "Yup, that's right. Little miss prissy who managed to escape, too. We really need to go visit her up there on that Eastern Shore. You seen her recently, Ken?"

"Just a couple weeks ago and she and Tessa would get along like sisters. Very much alike."

"Sad that this many years have gone by, and Tessa and Trish have only spoken over the phone. Mostly about Dad. I'd be in the field and Tessa would take down the message about how he was doin'"

"You need to remedy that then, Drew. Neither Trish nor Tessa has a problem sticking their hands in the dirt."

"Well, you know how I wound up with Tessa, don't you?"

"No. Just heard you were married. I was overseas at the time."

Tessa walked up next to him and put her arm around his waist. "Tessa used to work for me, way back when I first started. She helped with harvest, along with several other part-time workers. Course once you pay them they're off and running to the nearest saloon, and Tessa here got in a tussle with another worker from another field. Ended up arrested, she did. Suffolk cops called me, and I bailed her out. Hadn't really noticed her before that, but sure did notice her afterwards." He winked at her, and she smiled brightly. "She's given me two awesome sons, too. Roddy is 13 and Sonny is 11. Both are scrappers, but good boys. I'm a lucky man," he leaned over and kissed Tessa on the cheek.

"Okay, y'all sit down now and eat. Make yourselves sandwiches. What can I get you to drink, Ken?"

"Water is fine, Tessa. Thanks."

At Drew's request Ken filled him in on the life he had led as a Naval doctor, and what he was doing since he retired. He was aware that Drew knew their dad was in a nursing home because Trish had given him a head's up. They had kept in touch a time or two, and neither of them had any idea where Reed was. And, just as stubbornly, neither of them were interested in finding him. It really wouldn't have been that hard, Ken knew, to find one of Virginia Beach's most prominent attorneys. Trish never got news from the Tidewater/Hampton Roads area, and Drew never read a newspaper in his life, so that played into their not knowing much about him.

"So, you actually went and saw Reed, huh?" Drew's mouth quirked up at the corner, his eyebrows raised in interest. He was chewing on a dead stem he'd picked up off the ground.

"Sure did."

"Come on, brother. Give it up."

Ken took a bite out of his sandwich and finally gulped his food down.

"I don't know. Hard to talk down about the man, but he's just like Mother was. Well… let me correct that a bit, cause maybe he's not. I think his wife, Ruth's her name, dresses him. Totally rules him. When I told him about Dad his responses were, ah, neutral? Maybe more like disinterest? He said that Dad hadn't spent any time with us as kids, so he didn't see any particular reason to give up any of his valuable time to go visit him. Ruth was in total agreement with him. It was almost like she was kicking him under the table."

He heard Tessa gasp. "Oh, my god. His own father." She was shaking her head.

"He always was a pansy," Drew's lip curled up on one side. "Mother had him brainwashed, so it stands to reason his wife would, too. But tell me, Ken. What does his wife look like?" His mouth formed a sneer.

"DREW AVERY," Tessa snapped at him. "You be a gentleman now. No trash talking about another man's wife, no matter who she is."

Drew just cocked his head and smiled. "Gotta try, hon. Maybe Roddy can look her up online," he ducked as she threw a sponge at him, chuckling. Ken just smiled a knowing smile at him. "Let me just say, remember Mother!"

"Oh, God!" He shook his head at the memory. "Speaking of which, you never married?"

"Eat your sandwich, Drew," Tessa interrupted. "Don't want to throw it out for the rats to git."

He picked up half, pointing it toward Ken, "So?"

"No. Never married. It always seemed the women I met were like Mother. All made up, fancy, and hanging on me. Hated it. I gotta tell you there was one woman – I kid you not – thought she'd be a good date. When I picked her up I almost went into shock! Dressed to the nines in some expensive outfit. Too much perfume, hair all styled on top of her head, and sprayed like concrete. And makeup? I swear she used an entire tube of lipstick there was so much on her face. Made her lips look twice as big. Just horrible. There I was, dressed in jeans and pullover taking a date out for pizza who looked like she was ready to walk down some runway."

"UGH," Drew wiped his mouth, "Did you take her for the pizza?"

"Yes. She didn't seem the least bit surprised either. Like maybe she dresses like that for all her normal dates. Sure never asked her out again."

"You needa find someone, Ken," opined Tessa. "You're what they call 'HOT' in the world I live in. Got lots of friends that I could set you up with, too."

Ken laughed. Tessa was adorable. "Tessa, my only regret was not finding you before Drew did." He raised his glass of water and saluted her with it. "But to tell you the truth, there is a lady in Virginia Beach that seems to have grabbed my attention, much to my surprise."

"Oh, Hello!" Drew sat upright, instantly on alert. "Go on."

Ken filled them in on his meeting Maddie, and how she was caring for her mother. "I found her interesting. She's not like any other woman I've met, except maybe now," he pointed to Tessa, "She's a lot like Tessa there."

Tessa's face turned into one huge grin, and she stood straight and tall. "Yeah? I want to meet her."

"Might happen. I think about her a lot, but she's stuck taking care of her mother. Still…"

"What still?" Tessa poked him in the shoulder, gently.

"I'm a bit old to be getting married. Set in my ways, I guess. And I travel with Doctors World Wide…and then there's Dad."

"You hearing this brother of yours, Drew?"

"Yup. I'm listening." Folding his arms and crossing his legs, "You want to live alone for the next 40 or 50 years?" Drew stared at him.

"Trust me, I keep thinking about that. I've never thought about any other woman as much."

"You best keep taking her out and see if it works" Drew's face was serious. "From what you've told me she might be just what you need."

Ken sighed. "Yeah, there's a good chance you're right. The bad part is I told her I worked in intelligence. She doesn't know I'm a doctor. With her mother sick I was afraid I'd get bombarded with questions and requests for help, like I always do when people find out I'm a physician. So, I always make up a story to keep them from bugging me."

"He's right." Tessa said. "You can straighten out that stuff about lying. The sooner the better though. She'll understand if you tell it right."

"You afraid to think about living with someone?" Drew grimaced.

Ken hesitated. "I don't think so. I'm really not sure. I always had to share quarters on ships, so it's not like I haven't had someone around me all the time. And of course, I couldn't go off and do things just because I wanted to. Navy kinda frowns on that sort of behavior, and a lot of women do, too. Don't want someone crying because I'm off to another Doctors World Wide location. It just seems like it might be a lot of work, balancing all that stuff. Dangling a relationship with my interests seems daunting. On the other hand, I also think it might be nice to have a woman around. Home cooked meals would be nice." His impish grin was obvious.

"HA! Lemme tell you brother. Nothing beats curling up at night with the love of your life," his eyes softened as he looked at Tessa. "I wake up in the morning and watch her sleeping," he jerked his head up toward her, "and wonder how I ever got along without her. When I'm sad, or stressed, she folds me into her arms and doesn't even have to talk. I know she's on my team, and no matter what happens she has my back. Can't beat that brother. Course she gave me two little hellions that I have to yank back to reality every now and then," he laughed, his eyes bright with pride, "but I can forgive her for that," he ducked as another sponge came hurling at him.

Ken smiled. "Alright, I'll see what I can do." Finishing his sandwich, he moved the plate back from the edge of the table.

Drew reached over and patted him on the back. "Come on and git down to earth with us family black sheeps. It's way more fun. Roll in the mud with us and forgit the glitter."

Ken burst out laughing. "I've never been one for the glitter. Operating on people – well, there isn't much glitter, just shiny red blood."

"EW!" Drew put his hand up to cover his eyes.

"You get used to it, Drew, very quickly." Putting his elbows on the table, "Getting serious, though, you know Dad's in a nursing home."

"Yes. I did help Trish with some of that planning and all before you got retired and moved in with him."

"He's rather worse. At first he told me Mom had just left, that I missed seeing her. Then a bit later he recognized me completely, and hoped he'd get to see you, Reed, and Trish."

"We'll git over there this weekend," Tessa spoke up, then walked over and stood next to Drew. "We'll be going into harvest in a few days or a week, so now's the right time. Right, Drew?"

"Right, Tessa." Ken was seized with emotion as he watched looks that Drew gave to Tessa. It was just pure, unadulterated devotion to her. Every fiber of Drew's being gathered momentum and life from her. And she adored him as well. They weren't putting on an act for him. They were simply two of the most genuine people he'd ever met. It darn near made him want to buy a peanut farm and move to Suffolk. Seeing the two of them together, "You two would like Maddie, I think. I haven't been very nice to her this past couple of weeks. Haven't called or messaged her at all. Told her I had family to mend and that was the last she heard from me. Might have tossed out the baby with the bath water."

Tessa's mouth grew firm. "You got some heavy-duty cow-towing to do, so you best start tonight."

"Will tomorrow do?"

She harrumphed but gave him the okay. "You figure it all out tonight then and go git her tomorrow."

Ken couldn't help but smile.

Drew stood, "Come on out to the barn. Kids might be back." He gave Tessa a quick kiss on the cheek. "We can go up to the loft and you can look out and see most of my land."

After thanking Tessa for the lunch and welcoming, he followed Drew out the door. His brother was right about the land. As far as he could see there were peanut plants growing. "Is that all you grow?" Ken was mesmerized.

"We alternate fields with cotton. You can't see that part from here. Next year all this will be cotton and the other fields will be peanuts."

Looking out over the fields, "Maddie buys peanuts and feeds them to the birds and squirrels. Says it's the only true comfort she gets with her mother screaming at her all the time. She feeds them twice a day."

"Well, I can fix her up with peanuts for life. Just go and marry her. Free peanuts for life."

"She'd be in heaven!" Ken chuckled. "We'll just see how it goes first."

"Tell her to plant her own peanuts. It's fun. There's a lot of stuff online about doing it, but all she really needs to do is sink a raw peanut into the dirt and watch it grow."

"Really?"

"Yup. But not an eating peanut. Use one of those that comes for critter food. Once they're roasted the jigs up."

Just as they were leaving the barn both boys rode up on their bikes. "Hey Dad," the older one said.

"Ken, this is Roddy. He's 13, and that one over there next to him is Sonny who's 11. Boys I like you to meet your Uncle Ken."

"WOW," Roddy jumped off his bike and offered his hand. "You're the doctor who was in the Navy, right?"

"Sure am. Glad to finally get a chance to meet you boys."

Sonny had joined his brother and offered his hand as well.

"I'd like to be a doctor," Sonny said, shyly.

"Takes a lot of work, but from what your dad says about you I think you'd make a great doctor. He's very proud of both of you young men." He noticed both boys suddenly stand up straighter and grin. "Study up on the sciences and medicine, and then you'll get a good idea of whether or not you want to follow that path."

Roddy was smiling at his brother with a look of pride.

"What about you Roddy?"

"I'm thinking I'd like to take over the farm. I love these peanuts and cotton. Love running the equipment and bagging everything. Can't say I won't change my mind, but this is where I'm happy."

Could a man have better sons? Ken couldn't see how.

"If you have any questions as you study medicine you just let me know, Sonny. I'll be seeing a lot more of you two now that I'm retired."

Drew walked him to his car. "Real glad you came, Brother. Let this be the first of many trips out here. We might be in the boonies, but we're still friendly," he grinned, shook Ken's hand, and said, "We will visit Dad on Saturday. Count on it."

His timing wasn't the best on the drive home. He got stuck for a bridge lift at the High Rise, but he finally made it. He felt at ease for the first time in several days. Drew was rock solid, and his wife was no shrinking violet. He knew he'd be spending a lot of time with that family, and just the thought of the peace and quiet that he had experienced looking out over those fields of peanuts surprised him. There were times in life where you actually stopped to wonder what you were doing and where were you really headed! It was already his dinner time, so he would forego the walk for today and start again tomorrow. He would try to time it exactly right, catching her as she brought seed out for the birds. He needed to come up with a sincere apology for ignoring her so long. That would be his challenge for the night, and one he took seriously.

Chapter 9

Maddie felt like she'd been walking on eggs the entire morning, waiting for her mother to blow up about something, or that she might go out into the garage and retrieved that horrible cane. But there hadn't been a single BAM all morning. She'd walked into the kitchen and found her mother cooking herself an egg. Maddie controlled her excitement with a "Good morning, Mother."

"Good morning, Madeline. Would you like some eggs?"

"No thanks, I'll just have some coffee." Her mother was dressed in a pair of slacks and a soft pink blouse that accented the color of her pure white hair. More to the point, her hair was combed.

The entire morning had stayed calm and quiet. But Maddie found it hard to relax. She likened it to someone running from the law, making you look over your shoulder to see if they were gaining on you. It was that kind of apprehension that any second a brick would fall on her head. She couldn't wait for Dan to get there.

Arriving at 1 P.M., as promised, he was pleased to see that nothing had been broken since he last left. Maddie was calm.

Their mother wasn't in evidence, so he asked the usual generic, "How's it been going?"

"So far, so good. She made her own breakfast, cleaned up her own dishes. I think she's taking a nap now. I would have thought it would take less energy to do that work than all the prior yelling and cane banging, but I guess not. She does seem to be walking slower though. Honestly, Dan, I don't mind helping her. It was just the incessant noise and screeching that was making me insane."

"Why don't we go outside and talk until it's time for you to worry about dinner."

"It's just going to be spaghetti. I wanted to keep it easy, not knowing what to expect exactly." Motioning for him to follow she led him out to the back porch and two lawn chairs. "I love sitting out here in the rain. Even the worst storm leaves me just a tiny corner to sit in and not get soaked. It's fun watching the squirrels grabbing a peanut, then shaking water off to eat it. I've watched birds hang on under the squirrel baffles to keep dry. Wildlife is amazing. I should have asked if you would like a cup of coffee or something."

"I'm fine, Maddie. It's nice out here."

"My little slice of heaven, I guess."

Reaching over he patted her hand. "Maddie, I have often thought about you and how I treated you when we were children."

She stilled but kept her eyes on the birdfeeders.

"I am so ashamed. I was so jealous of your relationship with Dad. You were his little piece of sunshine, and he spent more time with you than with me." Dan rested his head back on the top of the chair and looked upward. "The first couple of times you did something bad, and got whipped, I thought it was fantastic. You had messed up and were getting whipped. A few tears and Mother would let you go. Then I got the idea that if I messed things up I could wrangle it so you would catch the blame. And it worked."

"Dan, you don't have to explain. We were children. I didn't understand why you were being so mean, and I figured it was just all because of Mother."

"Shh, please Maddie. Let me go on. I've agonized over this for years."

"Okay," she glanced over at him, then they both laid their heads back on the chair, not looking at each other.

"I came up with all kinds of ideas to get you in trouble. I used to spray the spoon and forks with water after you had dried them and put them away and Mother would think you had been too lazy to dry them. When you'd finish your breakfast and went to get ready for school I'd spill some of your cereal to make it look like you did it… and I'd spill out all the milk, so you'd get blamed for it… and…"

"Enough, Dan. Honestly," she whispered. "I remember it all."

He caught his breath. "After a while I started to realize that Mother, even if she saw me messing up, would grab you for the spanking. And you *never* gave me up or said anything. You took the paddling, cried and she'd let you go. Then something odd happened. You started to refuse to cry, and I watched, scared to death, as she started beating you with a vengeance. You were either going to cry or she would beat you until her arm was hurting so much she had to let you go. By then you were hurt so badly you couldn't even sit down. I'll never forget that. So, I started trying to behave, but I was a boy and boys always do something stupid. You kept getting beaten and I was so scared I was next I never said anything. I should have told Dad. Maddie, I am so very sorry," he was choking, and she looked at him and saw tears streaming down his face.

"Dan, I…"

Taking her hand and looking straight into her eyes, "Can you ever forgive me, Maddie? Please, please forgive me. I was so scared."

She was silent for several minutes. Then she exhaled a small breath and grinned a small grin. "Up until you walked into this house I hoped to never see you again. You caused me so much pain and I never understood it. I was six years old, and you were ten. It makes sense now that you tell me about Dad. But when you came in that door, the other night, and I thought you were both going to crucify me again I was terrified. My life was becoming one disaster after another, and I've never been able to understand why. I'm not a bad person. I had a wonderful husband and a terrific life until he was killed. Then Mother cons me into moving in with her and I find, after leaving a good job, that she's putting me on for the most part. Just more of her inhumane treatment of me. There has to be something wrong in her head, like part of her brain is missing or something." She sighed and threw her legs out in front of her. Shrugging, "I do understand, Dan. And maybe you've saved me from any future torment from her."

"I certainly hope so." He took her chin in his hand and turned her head toward him, "and I think I was quite masterful at it."

She concurred with a smile.

They lazed on the porch for another hour, sharing stories and events until they heard noise inside the house. "Sounds like she's up," Dan noted.

"Time for me to cook anyway," so they got up and went into the house.

Dan sat at the table and watched as his sister began the preparations for dinner. Their mother was actually setting the table.

"Tell me about your job, Dan." She placed his plate and utensils down in front of him.

He was surprised. She was sounding as sane and as nice as anyone else on earth. Her voice was smooth, her words were clear, and there was no anger in her speech or fire shooting from her eyes. He caught a stunned look from Maddie. Dan couldn't remember a single time in his life when he had heard his mother speaking in that same tone of voice. It was always shrieking, screaming, yelling, so it caught him off guard.

Clearing his throat, he started to tell her about his job and how much fun it was to do different voices for different characters.

Putting the last fork down she sat across from him, quizzing him about her grandchild, and what he was going to do from this point on in his life. He talked to her at length about Andy and how well he was doing. She nodded with interest and asked more questions until Maddy suggested everyone wash up for dinner.

"Oh, that smells so good, Maddie! Makes me extra hungry." He stood to pick up the bowl of spaghetti and meat balls to take it to the table. When Dori got up to take the garlic loaf out of the oven Dan and Maddie looked at each other with their eyes wide open. Both smiled, just a tiny bit.

Maddie filled the water glasses and the three of them sat down to eat. Dan decided to preside at the head of the table, laughingly asking for each plate so he could dish up some of the meal to each of them. Dori picked up the loaf of garlic bread, already sliced, and passed it around. Each of them ate several forkfuls of spaghetti before Dan turned to his mother.

"What do the doctors say about your MS, Mom?" He knew that calling her "mom" would please her. There was no need to awaken a shrilling banshee.

Dori paused. "I have some vision problems, and my arms and legs tingle. I'm tired all the time and sometimes I stumble. It scares me." She looked down at her plate, "Doctor wants me to do as much as possible without a cane or wheelchair. I'm weak. It seems to be going faster than I want to think about."

"What can I do for you?"

"Nothing, Dan. I should never have called you like I did. Just fear I guess. I could use a ton of energy, but that won't happen." She actually smiled a bit, then twisted more spaghetti onto her fork. Lifting it to her mouth it was clear she had problems moving her hands. She managed, but it wasn't easy. It gave Maddie pause to watch her slow-motion progress. Maybe her mother was really sick, but it had all been hidden behind banging canes and screeching. She'd taken her mother to the doctor many times but had never gone into the room with them. That would stop now. She was going to be present to hear what the doctor had to say. She was just going to have to toughen up and help her mother as best she could until it became obvious she needed more help than she could provide as a sole caregiver. If her mother went back to her old ways after Dan left, the threat to put her in a nursing home would become real. She wasn't going to put up with that anymore. Maybe, just maybe though, things would now be better, and she'd have some breathing room.

Finishing with dinner Maddie wanted to show Dan the whole house while Dori promised to do the dishes. Dan and Maggie shared another look of astonishment, but she quickly led him out of the kitchen before Dori changed her mind.

"I sure hope she stays like that," Maddie pointed out where the bathroom was, moving on to the three bedrooms. "This is my bedroom."

"Still with lavender walls, huh? I remember that's what you had in Chicago."

"I'm surprised you remember."

"Oh, Maddie. I remember a lot."

Guiding him across the hall, "This is Mother's. It's the master with its own bath. She has always managed to keep it neat. I change the sheets because it really is hard for her to do, but other than that she does the rest."

Dan nodded. "White walls and white furniture. Interesting."

"Stark. I agree. Last we have a small third bedroom. Just big enough for a double bed and a dresser. But it's never used. If we had known you were coming you could have stayed in here."

"Better I was in the hotel. Easier for me to do a little work and keep in contact with my boss."

"All that's left to see is the family room and dining room, which you've seen as you walked through to get to the back yard."

"It's all nice, Maddie, and you're doing a great job. Just know if things return to what she was like, one call, and I'll take care of things."

Putting her arm around his waist she hugged him. "I'm so glad you came. I've wondered about you but didn't think you'd want to hear from me. This has made such a difference."

He kissed her on the cheek.

"Are you going back tomorrow?"

"Yes. It's a later flight, so I'll spend the morning trying to find a gift for Andy."

"Come over here about ten and I'll be your guide to Target, Walmart, and anywhere else you want to go."

"That would be wonderful, Maddie."

Arriving back to the kitchen, Dori had finished the dishes and was wiping down the table.

"Good job, Mom," Maddie said, using the word 'mom' and not feeling forced to do so.

Dori smiled. "Are you leaving now Dan?"

"I'll be back tomorrow morning. Maddie is going to take me shopping so I can get a gift for Andy. Then I'll be going back to Chicago, but I'm only a phone call away. Maddie has all my numbers and she promised to give them to you when I leave."

"Thank you. Both of you." She looked down.

"Don't worry, Mom. We'll take good care of you. I'll stick around here for a while tonight so we can get to know each other better."

Dori sat stoically. She wished she could explain to them how much she really hurt. It wasn't just a little tingling in her arms and legs, it was almost crippling. She gritted her teeth and plowed through doing dishes or her laundry. She was weak, and her eyes often betrayed her when she wanted to see things up close. It was hard to backtrack with Maddie. She'd been a lousy mother to her, and she knew it. She felt she had to keep up the façade for some ridiculous reason, and now Dan had called her on all of it. She'd struggle through as long as she could.

Ken was anxious to see Maddie again. He needed to apologize to her in so many different ways. He realized he'd basically pushed her out the door the night she came over for pizza. Then he barely let her know that he was visiting his father the next day. Why would she think it would take him the whole day to do that? Then he wanted to mend his family relationships. That would never have taken another week or so. Well, maybe it would have but he didn't bother to let her know anything about what he was doing. The weather was starting to be cooler, with nice breezes to make walking a pleasure. He felt ashamed of the way he had ignored her, basically cutting off all communication. She hadn't tried to call him or text him either. He could understand that now. She felt his cold shoulder to her core, he was sure of it. He needed to see her, face to face, to offer her an apology, and ask her out for a real date. With luck she'd be outside feeding birds, or at worst he'd see her waving at him from the window. The house looked the same as he approached, with the blinds all down and shade taking over the front porch, but he came to a stop as he rounded the corner. There was a car in the driveway. It wasn't hers. He was floored. He walked slowly past the window, carefully looking into it, hoping to see a waving hand. There was nothing. The car was a white Toyota with Virginia plates. Could she be having someone over for dinner? He could feel his blood going cold. Maybe it was just some tradesman fixing something. Or maybe it was one of those friends of hers from school. It could be someone there to see her mother, even. Maybe therapy or something. He needed to calm his heart rate down several notches. Picking up his pace he didn't want neighbors that might be watching to get suspicious. With a dog he could have stood there for several minutes, but not just to stare all by himself. He finished his walk. Tomorrow would be another day. Once home he wanted to go back in the worst way. He needed to see who's car it was. What if he got into his own car, parked down the street a ways and watched? No, that was stalking. Why was he even *thinking* things like that? Calm down, Ken. Stop pacing. Turning on the television he munched on pretzels and waited for his TV dinner to heat up. He was going to have to learn to cook more than TV dinners. Maybe he should rehire his dad's old chef to come and fix him some good freezer meals. Not a bad idea, actually. He was deflecting and he knew it. Truth was he was now scared that he had botched up any opportunity he might have to try to find out more about Maddie. That soccer ball in the middle of his stomach felt like it would explode at any moment and double him over. He kept thinking that maybe she was seeing someone else. He'd been a card-carrying fool and it astonished him that he felt just a flash of panic. He'd try again tomorrow. That was the best he could come up with for the moment.

    He'd barely slept a wink worrying about Maddie. Then he would worry about his father, and then back to anxiety over Maddie. He finally gave up and dragged his weary bones into a hot shower.
    Ken doubted Maddie would be entertaining anyone during the morning hours. She'd be too busy taking care of the house and her mother. He'd do his walks at twelve, two, four, and six. He wouldn't do the whole walk, just enough to get past her house and back. As he neared the corner on the first walk of his day he felt a car pass him from behind. It turned the corner then pulled into Maddie's driveway. Ken slowed down and watched as a man got out, rang the doorbell, and waited. Ken quickly raced over the cross road to remain hidden from Maddie's view. It was only a moment before Maddie came out and was helped into the car. Managing to sneak behind a tree trunk he watched as they drove off, almost right past him. His heart sank. The skin on his face went slack. He actually felt a pain in his gut. She's seeing someone else. They're off to a nice lunch somewhere. He recalled the guy was about their age, well dressed in slacks and short sleeved shirt. Maddie was wearing that same yellow dress she'd worn to the pizza dinner

with him. He really liked that dress. It fit her perfectly, showed off her curves and long legs, and the color went well with her dark hair. Putting his forehead against the tree trunk he waited until the car disappeared. Such was life when you screwed things up badly. He wished he knew who it was. Maybe it would just be temporary. All he could do was walk by every day and see if the car kept coming back. But he wasn't about to stalk her. He'd messed up. It was all on him. It would be best to keep walking, just like he always had, and take each day at a time, just in case the guy never came back. Yes, good plan.

Chapter 10

Three weeks with no word from Ken - like a shooting star - a long flash, then gone. She missed him, though. She hated to admit it, but every time she thought about those blue eyes she felt warm all over. Weird. Dan had been gone for several days and she missed him, too. What an amazing visit it had been. Someone she thought she'd never see again and even beyond that, someone she had resented from childhood, had managed to worm his way back into her heart. Her brother's love was a powerful motivator that kept her spirits up. She knew all she had to do was pick up her phone and call him if she needed any encouragement. She had someone to talk to now besides Elle or Joan. Then her thoughts always shifted to Ken, and she'd watch out the window to see if he was still doing his walks. Either he had stopped, was out of town, or she was simply missing him when he passed by. With a sigh she folded the laundry and reminded herself that at least her mother was being more rational and cooperative. Not much else changed in her daily routines anymore, but they were more peaceful. As always, the best part of her day was feeding the critters, then sitting on one of the porches and watching them dive in from every direction.

Opening the garage door, she was surprised at how dark it had gotten. Black clouds were looming and moving in from the west. Quickly filling the feeders under the tree, she filled a scoop with sunflower seed and started filling the feeder hanging from the kitchen porch ceiling. With the feeder under the crook of her arm she began emptying the scoop of its seed when a crack of thunder so loud made her jump. Cursing as seed scattered all over the tiled decking, she sat down in a chair as lightning snapped close by. "DAMITOL," she yelled, angry that so much seed had been spilled. Now the squirrels would be drawn to all of it, and they always made a mess of things. Rain was pouring down, the seed was wet, her mood was dark, and she sat back to catch her breath. Thankfully, the door to the kitchen was open so she didn't have to get wet going back in through the garage. The downside was that now rain was peppering the inside of the garage! She was about to stand to go into the house and close the garage door from inside, when she saw a figure appear. "Oh, my God, Ken!" She yelled at the top of her voice. "GET UP HERE."

He was moving quickly, soaked from head to toe, his arm above his head trying to protect himself from the pelting rain.

"KEN," she yelled again, spilling the contents from the birdfeeder, now upside down in her arm, onto the tile. But this time he heard her and looked up. She motioned for him to get up onto the porch.

"Oh, Ken, you are soaked. Sit down. You'll get killed out there with all this lightning."

"I got caught. That storm was sudden. Thought I could make it home," he was wiping rain off his arms and face with his hands, "Guess I was wrong. Knew better than to try to stand under an oak tree!" Just as he reached down and scrunched up the front of his shirt to squeeze it dry another bolt of lightning flashed at the same time a clap of thunder made both of them jump.

"Geeze," Ken sat down. "Where did that come from?"

Setting the birdfeeder down on the small table, "What a mess. I'll be tracking sunflower seed into the house for days now."

Ken glanced down and shook his head. "Won't the squirrels and birds just get it all?"

"What they'll do is come up on the porch and sit here and eat the seeds alright. Then they leave the hulls behind. Little pieces of hull, all over the place, and much harder to clean up. I'll have to use a leaf blower when they dry." Sitting down on the edge of the second chair, she turned to look at Ken.

"Long time no see," she couldn't resist a bit of rancor. "Maybe what I should do is just start feeding sunflower kernels or chips. More expensive but less mess."

"Maddie, I…"

Her eyes glaring, "Give me your shirt, Ken. The rain isn't slowing down any and it's going to be raining for a while. I'll throw it into the dryer and get you a towel."

"I'll be alright…"

Standing up she motioned for him impatiently to take it off and give it to her. He complied.

"I'll get you a couple of towels," she walked into the house, making sure to close the garage door on her way to the dryer. She was almost dizzy from looking at his bare chest. She had tried not to stare - perfect shoulders, perfect arm muscles, perfect amount of hair…. Ah, yeah. Perfect. She groaned.

She knew she shouldn't have snapped at him, but it just came out of her mouth. On one hand she felt bad, and on the other she felt he deserved a zinger. Still, she knew she wasn't a nasty person. Quite the opposite, actually. So why now? Throwing the shirt into the dryer she grabbed two towels from the cabinet and headed back outside. She needed to make light of the situation and counter her meanness. Handing him the towels, "I'd ask for your shorts to dry but don't think the neighbors would appreciate the display."

With the towels at his face his motion stopped. Slowly pulling down the towel to reveal those blue eyes, staring up at her, then his mouth, he was grinning. "Ah, but what would you think?"

She turned almost purple. Then, in a split second, her lips curled up, she looked him in the eye, "Might prove interesting at that." For crying out loud, Maddie, *shut up!*

Still drying off he patted the chair next to him. "Sit, Maddie. I owe you a couple thousand apologies."

"It won't take long for your shirt to dry…" Did she want to hear what he had to say? Maybe he was going to tell her he was seeing someone else and that he should have been upfront with her. Maybe…

"Maddie" he interrupted her thoughts, "Well, there are a couple of things, actually. I really did go see my two brothers and sister. And my dad, of course. Some of it was good, and some not so good. It took longer than I expected, but I let you down horribly in all the confusion. I have no excuse for not calling or texting you." Taking the driest towel, he started to rub his hair to keep the water from dripping down his face. She wasn't looking at him, just staring at the rain, coming down so hard it made it difficult to see cars passing by.

"How is your dad?" Her voice was soft, and it was hard to hear her in the driving rain. Rain could be very noisy and distracting, he thought. Or, under a tin roof… he crumpled the towels onto his lap.

"Not well. He didn't know me at first. Thought Mom had been there, then later he knew me. He's tired, and weak. It's not fair. He wasn't much of a father to us, growing up, but he did support us, gave us everything materially, but in the end he's still my father. I hate seeing him die like that." He bowed his head and massaged the towels. "How's your mother?"

Turning to look at him, oh my gosh, his hair was all mussed up like he'd just gotten out of bed. Her heart skipped a beat. All she wanted to do was reach up and run her fingers through every single strand of it. And then…get a grip, Maggie, she bit her lip, "Much better in a funny way. Seems she called my brother, Dan, in Chicago. Told him I was poisoning her, or something, and she was on her deathbed, and she wanted to see him again after some twenty-five years or whatever. So, he comes rushing down to see her before she dies, and WALLA, there she is, screaming and yelling and banging her cane, just like always."

"Your brother was here?" His heart suddenly soared. The car... the man... that was her brother! Not another man she was dating. Her *brother*!

"Hadn't seen him since leaving Chicago. Didn't even recognize him." She paused in reflection. "He's a good-looking guy though. And thank God, he's not one to make rash assumptions."

"What happened?" He knew if he felt his pulse he'd find his heart rate going crazy. It was her *brother*! He turned his chair to face her.

She shifted in her chair. Their knees were almost touching. "I guess when he was on the airplane he figured out that there was probably two things possible. I really *was* murdering her, and she *was* on her deathbed, *or* she was the mother he knew from his youth. He remembered the beatings I got. But he didn't know anything else about me, my husband, or why I was in my mother's house. Smart man. I have to give it to him. He came here without any preconceived notions. He told me that Mother just sounded too "alive" when she called him. It made him suspicious. It also didn't make sense that I would try to kill her. Can I get you some water or something?"

He laughed. "No thanks, I seem to have it all over me."

Quickly looking him up and down she again turned red, then laughed with him. "True."

"Is your brother still here?"

"No, he went back to Chicago. I am so glad he came. He's a super guy. Does voice overs for commercials and stuff. Anyway, he's one clever guy. Told Mother that since I was trying to kill her he would put her in a nursing home by the end of the week. Made it seem hugely real to her, too. Scared her big time. Gave her two choices, nursing home, or start being nicer to me. He really scared her. Stood up and said he was going to go sign the commitment papers. She panicked."

"I don't think he could do that to her, though, legally."

"Oh, he knew that, but he was counting on her *not* knowing that."

"And it worked?"

"Totally. She agreed to be nice, and so far she has been. We did talk about her MS, and we all agreed she should do what she could to help herself. She's been doing her laundry and helps with dishes. I think she hurts worse than she's letting on, but she's so terrified now that we'll stick her in some horrible nursing home that she's soldiering on. I see her wince in pain, sometimes. I'll be going in with her the next time she sees the doctor."

"Is she taking any medicines?"

"I've seen the label on one called Gabapentin. I've looked it up online and it seems to be a medicine for the neurological pain, or neuropathy. She said she has a lot of tingling of her hands and feet and maybe even her legs. It's hard to pin her down about stuff like that, which is probably why she never wants me to go into the room with her when she sees the doctor. But from now on I'll go in, regardless."

"I think she can refuse to let you go in with her."

"I'll just tell her I'm going to call Dan and start the process to commit her to a nursing home."

"Ah, blackmail?"

"Perhaps, but it's the only way we know to make sure she's being cared for properly. I know she beat me most of my life, and I know she hates me and wishes I'd never been born, but the fact is still I'm all she has unless we throw her to the wolves. There's no way Dan can move here, and he shouldn't have to do so. It's enough that he holds the brick over her head. He calls her every Saturday to see how she's doing. She knows he's just a plane ticket away from doing her in, as it were."

"No other meds?"

"I'm not sure. She gets them in the mail and has a screaming fit, even now, if I try to open them."

Ken nodded. His surgery specialties didn't include anything having to do with MS. That was the province of neurologists, and apparently she was being seen by one.

"This is a small porch, and the rain is angling into us. You want to go to the back porch? It's much larger and the rain only hits the edges of it."

"Sure, no problem." Finally, he thought, a chance to see the inside of this house on the corner. The house he's been curious about since he first walked past it. "I assume we get there by going through the house."

Giving him the 'what, are you stupid? look' she opened the door and hooked her finger for him to follow.

Take it all in, Ken told himself. Concentrate. She was talking… "Mother must be asleep…" the kitchen was neat. He could hear the dryer spinning in a side room. Everything seemed to have a place in the room. No sink full of dishes. They crossed over into an obvious family room with a couch, two matching chairs, television, end tables, and all were arranged for best television viewing. The blinds were down. He couldn't help it, "May I ask why all the blinds are down in the house?"

She stopped. "Yes, actually. Mother's eyes bother her with the MS. Sometimes she has trouble seeing and the bright sunlight hurts. I could open and close them according to where the sun is in the sky, and I used to do that, but it got to be just one more thing I had to do, several times a day. It took time and energy from other things. The only one I refuse to put a blind on is the one in the kitchen. I look out of it constantly to watch birds, see what the weather is doing, see when the garbage has been collected so I can go get the can back from the street, see when the paper and mail have been delivered…"

He started laughing. "Got it. Your window to the world."

Her mouth dropped open, "Exactly. That's exactly right." Turning away from him she continued to the back porch. Ken followed. She looked as good from the back as she did from the front, and he pinched his leg to keep from thinking about it.

"Raining back here, too," he joked.

"That really happened to one of the teachers I used to work with. He was in the back yard playing with his daughter when it suddenly started raining. He rushed her inside then made a bee-line for his front door, knowing he'd left the top down on his convertible. He gets outside and it hasn't rained a drop. Not one single drop. So, he walks down the driveway enough to be able to see over his house and it's still raining in his back yard. Never did touch the car. True story."

"Those are the stories you wish you had on video tape."

Scanning the yard, "Four crows in that tree next door. They have good cover there. All the bushes are loaded with birds cowering from the rain. Squirrels will be the first ones out after the rain stops, and bunnies won't be out until later this afternoon."

"Sounds like you've been observing for a long time."

"I could probably write a book, but I'm sure they've all been written already. The most interesting time is spring. That's when birds chase each other for territory. Grackles will chase crows relentlessly, and just as vigorously crows will chase hawks. And squirrels? It's like musical chairs. It gets funny. I can have 30 peanuts on the ground. A squirrel shows up to eat. A second squirrel shows up and it's off to the races. While those two are gone and remember there was plenty of nuts for both of them, here come the crows and blue jays, and the peanuts disappear before the first squirrel gets back. And it happens every day."

"I'd love to watch something like that going on."

"You'd have to come back and sit for an hour after each feeding."

"I can do that."

Her head snapped to look at him. Was he joking? He seemed serious.

"I told you I was sorry, Maddie, and it won't happen again if you let me back into your life."

Suddenly she could hardly breathe. Ken didn't move, waiting, waiting…

"I'd like that," she said.

Just as Ken reached over to take her hand the door opened.

"Why are you out here with a naked man, Madeline?"

"Oh, lordie, the nasties were back,." She shrugged her shoulders.

"Answer me, Madeline," Dori screeched.

Slowly turning her head, "Mother this is Ken. His shirt got soaked in the rain and it's in the dryer. Otherwise, we are both fully dressed."

"Honestly! Today's children are disgusting," as she slammed the door.

Maddie tapped her fingers on the armrests. "I think you might have been upset about the song."

"What?"

"Dark Shadows. Yes, it's a depressing song. It speaks to me. There are times I want to see my father again. And Mark. But it's not a sinister song, really, Ken."

"I have to admit I did wonder about it when I read the lyrics and listened to the recording on YouTube."

"Thought as much. Thought I might not see you again."

"I'm ashamed to admit that the same thing crossed my mind, too. You scared me a little bit. It's strange that when I talked to Trish about it, she said the same thing you just did."

"Trish."

"My sister, Patricia. We call her Trish."

"Oh, yes. Sorry. I forgot. You saw your brothers, too, you said."

"Sure did. Both of them. In a nutshell my older brother Reed and his wife are too far up on the social ladder to be bothered with the likes of us, or our father for that matter."

"You're kidding?" Now she placed her hand over his and be damned if her mother was peeking out some keyhole.

"Nope. Lost forever to us folks in low places. And then there's Drew. Talk about what Reed, and especially Ruth would consider as a very low place! Drew has a peanut farm in Suffolk. And more down to earth people you couldn't find. You and Tessa would be a dream team and add my sister Trish and the men in our family would run for cover. Oh," he winked at her, "Drew says you should plant your own peanuts. I'd love to take you out and show you how easy it is! A fun thing to do anyway."

Maddie couldn't help bursting a hearty laugh. Just the thought of knowing two people like he just described would be enormous fun. She used to have fun. She could again. Growing peanuts did sound like it might be interesting.

"Good thing one is on the Eastern Shore and the other is in Suffolk then," she observed.

"With you right in the middle," he squeezed her hand. "And while I'm sitting here chattering on about my past, I just want to set you straight on one thing, for the record."

"Okay."

"I'm actually a retired Navy Captain. Never was enlisted. Don't know why I feel the need to make sure you know that because now that I'm retired it really doesn't matter."

Her hand stopped moving for just a split second. "My husband was a Navy pilot. He…"

The door slammed open again, "When's dinner, Madeline? I need you to stop messing around and get in here and feed me."

"I'll be right there, Mother."

"See to it. And here's that man's shirt. Dry. Disgusting." Throwing the t-shirt out it landed on the deck between them.

Moving forward in her chair, "Another time, perhaps?" She hoped, reaching down she picked up the shirt, handing it to Ken. "At least the rain has stopped."

Rising from his chair, he smiled gently, drew the tips of his fingers softly down her cheek, and lifted her chin. Gazing into her eyes, "You really have no idea how beautiful you are, do you?" Tapping her chin with his thumb, "I'll leave by the gate," he turned, pulled the shirt over his head, and walked away.

Strolling into the kitchen Maddie brought her cell phone to her ear. Her mother was in the kitchen, so timing was everything.

"Dan, how are you? Oh, good to hear everything is going well."

She noticed out of her side vision that her mother was suddenly alert.

"I can understand how busy you are, but remember what we said about you signing those papers down here?"

"Yes, that would be great. You can come down in six days. This time I'll have the guest room ready for you. Easier to pack things… yes… okay… I'll talk to you when you're done with that voice over job. Love you, too. Goodbye." She had seen Dori's hand reaching out to take the phone to talk to Dan, but she ignored it as if she hadn't seen it. Oddly enough Dori hadn't started screaming to be able to talk to him. Hmm.

"What did he say."

"If I don't call him back in the next week he'll fly back down to sign all those papers."

She knew better than to ask. And Maddie felt like patting herself on the back for the fake phone call. She probably should call him, for real, later, and make sure he knew to play the game.

"Oh, Mother, I do need to mention that Ken is back in my life, and I plan to see him every now and then. Maybe lunches, maybe dinners. But you need to respect that if you want me to stay."

Dori nodded.

"I'll get dinner going now."

Chapter 11

What a nice way to spend an afternoon. Ken was elated. His shorts were still wet and uncomfortable, but he didn't mind. It was worth it. He couldn't have planned meeting her like that no matter how hard he tried. Zeus and his angry display of thunder and lightning must have coordinated the entire event. He wondered how she had handled her mother, who might have reverted to the bad behavior. There was so much to think about now. He could have spit when her mother opened the door, just as she mentioned her husband. Now he knew his name was Mark. Mark Davis. It sounded familiar, but he'd met so many different men in the Navy, many of them pilots on the several ships they both served on, and it was a very common name. It was also possible, of course, that Maddie went back to her maiden name. She loved her father. It was a possibility. His time with her today had been interesting. She surprised him with the bit of teasing over his shorts. He saw the look on her face as she tried not to look at his bare chest. He worked hard to be physically fit and appreciated the look on her face. It was clear to him that he was giving very serious thought to some kind of commitment. After all this time? Could he give up his entire freedom, or even part of it? This was a subject that he'd never considered, ever. He certainly wasn't a player, but he'd done just fine in the single life. It occurred to him he might be putting the emphasis on the wrong syllable. Subconsciously his associations with women were the kind his mother would have chosen, and because he wasn't brainwashed like Reed, he passed over every one of them. He'd never actually dated anyone like Maddie before. Sure, he'd had his one-night stands in the past, but they were few and far between, and not a single one of them meant anything to him. Maddie didn't seem to be the clingy type, that was for sure. She never called him during all his absences. He'd dated one or two women in his past that would burn up his phone for days until he made it clear to them he wasn't interested. It was shocking how possessive a woman could get after just one dinner date. He absolutely needed to get to know Maddie better. He wanted another "back yard" session with her but without Dori slamming doors again.

He slept well but dreamed about her. A good dream. He would delay his walk until about the same time and maybe she'd be out with the critters. He'd love another back yard session. That was nice, but it could be nicer touring the yard without any rain.

He got his wish. She was waving at him from the window, and he watched her move toward the door.

"Hey," she walked toward him as he stood under the tree. "Nice to see you all dry."

He laughed. "Nice to see you, too." He moved towards her.

"I made a fake phone call to Dan last night and got Mother back in line. Told her if she wasn't nice to you I'd have to have Dan come down."

They both leaned against the tree trunk as he reached out and took her hand. Their eyes locked on each other.

"I don't want to mess with your exercise, but if you want to sit on the back porch…"

"Thought you'd never ask."

"Mother just went in to take a nap so it will be a couple of hours before she's up wanting her dinner."

They walked silently through the house and out the back door.

"Looks better in the sunshine," he commented. "All the bird houses and decorations are fantastic. Can we walk around the yard?"

Leading him down from the deck, "Every flower and bush is bird, butterfly, and bee friendly. I have parsley growing for the Black Swallowtail butterflies, milkweed for the Monarchs. There are butterfly bushes, and black-eyed-Susans. Did have some mint, but it was too invasive, so I ripped it all out."

"You have bird houses on every other fence post."

"For bluebirds. Some house wrens take them over, but there's enough for everyone. The feeder over there," she pointed, "is for mealworms only."

He was impressed. The yard was well managed and probably very interesting all day long.

Returning to the chairs on the deck, "I can sit here, quietly, after putting down peanuts for the birds, and in one half hour see squirrels, rabbits, crows, cardinals, blue jays, butterflies, bees, pigeons, grackles…the list goes on and on."

She was so animated as she spoke about her small nature habitat. Her face lit up like the sun.

"I can see why you love it. Under the circumstances it helps keep you from sadness." He didn't want to use the word "depressed", but he figured she used her landscape as an escape.

She smiled. "Oh, I get depressed," she hadn't missed that reference as she narrowed her eyes. "I just refuse to give in to it. I look at my yard and critters, and smell the gardenias, and with what my life has been like so far I know only too well how limited my time is here on earth. I love this planet. I study a rose, or smell a gardenia, and wonder how I could ever leave any of it. I watch a butterfly flitting over a bush, and I cry, because I'll miss all the beauty of earth and I can't get enough of it. I focus on a worm, crawling over the concrete and I pick it up and put it into the dirt, in the shade. It's life. I'm surrounded by it. I don't want it to go away. I don't want to leave my planet. I've had too much of that in my life, and it hurts. So, I don't focus on the death. I focus on the life." She stopped and took a deep breath. "That's not *always* true, of course." She smacked her lips, flatlining them, then continued. "If I hear Quentin's Theme it all comes back to me, and I go have a good cry in the bathtub. Used to cry myself to sleep, but I've gotten past that."

"Does it happen often? The crying?"

"Not so much now. I think, honestly, having Dan come down and reconnecting with him has made a huge difference in my life. I feel hopeful that things are improving, despite Mother's MS."

"I can be here for you, too, you know."

"I'm counting on it."

God, he wanted to pull her up into his arms and kiss her. He had to settle for taking her hand and holding on to it, caressing it with his thumb, looking at her with desire. The breeze was blowing strands of her hair here and there and she was gorgeous. She squeezed his hand back and the only thing stopping him from pulling her out of that chair was the fear that her mother would kick the door open.

"Your mother…"

"She beat me as a child." Her lips trembled and her eyes filled with water. Scooting his chair closer to her, "We can go look at flowers, Maddie. You don't have to go back to that time."

"No. I want you to know. It's important I think."

He nodded. Both of them leaned back, facing upward toward the sky. It seemed easier for Maddie to talk, in a stream of consciousness flow. Ken was not about to interrupt.

"As far back as I can remember she would grab me and beat me over her lap. She'd seize whatever was handy. Usually, it was a big wooden spoon. I never really knew what I'd done wrong, at least not at first. As I got a little older I noticed that if Dan messed up then I got the beating. It never made any sense to me, but she'd hit me until I cried and then she'd let me go. It was obvious Dan was her little boy and could do no wrong. And just as obvious I watched him deliberately do something that would get me spanked. He'd pour my brand of cereal on the table or mess up my bed after I'd made it. Lots of little things, and I always got the spoon. Daddy had no clue, of course, and for some reason I thought it was normal. Eventually I started to get defiant and refused to cry. That only led to much worse beatings – to the point that I couldn't sit down. It kept up until I was too old to put over her knee. Then she found other little ways to punish me like making my favorite dessert but not letting me have any. Stuff like that. I couldn't get out of that house fast enough, but she forced me to stay there while I went to college to save money. I doubt that now. I'm sure she just wanted the control. Anyway, that's the story of my life until I graduated and got the job teaching school. I just seemed to go from one bad life to another. I was happy for a little while, though, with Mark!" Sitting up straight and turning toward him, "There you have it, my life in a nutshell." She smiled, a forced smile.

No, Maddie, that's not your whole life in a nutshell, he thought. But we'll let it go at that for now. "And she still finds ways to terrorize you, like the screaming and the cane."

"Yeah, but she's much better now since Dan came. She does regress though, like yesterday. It's like a switch goes off in her head and she goes nasty again. But all I have to do is "pretend call" Dan and she straightens out."

Just then there was a crash sound coming from the house. Both Maddie and Ken raced inside. They found Dori on the floor, crying. "I can't get up," she whispered through her tears.

"Oh, my God. Ken, help me lift her."

Ken reached down and picked her up as if she was a small child. "She doesn't weigh very much, Maddie."

"Put her on the couch, please."

Gently placing her down on the couch, he backed up to let Maddie move in next to her.

"Do you want me to call an ambulance?" she asked her mother.

"No. I'm just weak. It's hard to walk. I knew it was going to happen. Doctor told me so last month. I've been able to…to…I guess I need my cane back now."

"I think it's worse than that, but I'll take you to see the doctor tomorrow. I'll call him now."

As she left the room to find her cell phone Ken looked down at a woman, deeply saddened by what had happened.

"Can I get you something to drink?" he suddenly realized he had no idea what her last name was. Maddie had never mentioned it, and while Maddie used the last name of Davis, that could be her married name. He had no clue and was shocked that he'd never asked.

"No, thank you though. You're very kind."

Handing her a tissue, he felt driven to take her blood pressure and heart rate and all the other things doctors did to decide the level of wellness. But he didn't dare. Maddie would have been suspicious, and rightly so. He'd been a fool to keep his real occupation from her for so long. Now he was afraid if he told her she'd give him a well-earned slap in the face, and he'd never see or hear from her again. He knew he didn't want that to happen. He couldn't make it obvious that he had medical training in front of her mother. Dori would have had a field day with that lie and confession.

Maddie returned, "We have an appointment tomorrow, Mother."

"Will she be able to walk?"

"We have a lightweight portable wheelchair in the back bedroom. I can handle it easily. But thank you."

"It makes me think I need to go visit my father again."

"Yes, Ken. Please don't let these moments pass. You don't have to worry about taking time off work anymore. Your time is your own. You and your siblings should be spending as much of it as possible with your dad."

"Can I help you with anything else?"

"No. I really appreciate it. We'll be fine and the doctor will tell us what to do next. I'll walk you out."

Reaching the door, he took both of Maddie's hands, pulling her in to give her a kiss on the cheek. He stood back for a second, then pulled her back in for a hug. "Call me if you need anything. I'll be with my dad."

"Thanks for the hug. Haven't had one of those since Dan left."

His hands froze for just a moment then gently moved up to frame her face. Bending down, her soft, warm gaze met his as he gently kissed her. Wiping a lone tear off her cheek with his thumb he smiled, then turned and quietly walked out the door.

Finishing his walk, he was lost in thought. Well, that was all very interesting. He certainly never would have guessed that he'd end up kissing her, although he was glad he did. It startled him that she had returned the kiss. And the tear of emotion nearly undid him. He'd had to leave quickly.

Maddie stood by the door, watching him take the few steps to the street, then finally disappearing from her view. He'd kissed her, and she liked it. She had kissed him back, and it shocked her. Yes, a shock. Like when that bee got her when they were dragging the tree down the driveway. He'd taken her completely by surprise but the feel of his arms around her – WOW – she wanted him back. She wanted to feel that "zing" again! She wanted to feel her blood warming within her body. Hearing her mother coughing broke her reverie. With a huge sigh she returned to see how she was doing.

"How are you now, Mother?"

"I think I can walk if you'll get me the cane."

"Are you sure?" She hadn't seen the fall so couldn't judge how unsteady she might have been.

"Yes. I think my toe just stubbed or something. The cane will help."

"No slamming or banging it around?"

"No. I need it to walk, Madeline."

Nodding, Maddie went into the garage and retrieved the cane, praying her mother was not going to start using it as a weapon again.

Handing it to Dori she watched as she scooted up to the edge of the couch then gently stood with the aid of the cane. "Is there any dinner?" She asked acidly. "I mean you were so busy with that man I wasn't sure you cooked today."

"That was Ken, Mother, and if he hadn't been here to pick you up and gently place you on the couch I would have had to call rescue and you'd be in the hospital now, so you might want to consider that for any future falls you might take." Maddie could not help a small display of anger towards her mother and as she watched her sit down in the kitchen, Maddie glared at her, "And for the record, he kissed me, and I plan to see him again, so unless you want to end up in the hospital or a nursing home you'd best control your mouth about him."

Dori looked at her in shock but managed to keep silent.

"Dinner is hamburger soup and garlic bread. I'll serve you now."

Slowly eating her soup, Dori didn't look up, "What time do we see the doctor?"

"Eight O'clock. He has a full day so wants to see you before his first scheduled patient. It's huge of him to do that for you."

"Yes. It is. I'll be ready."

It seemed to be the story of his life. No sooner did he make plans to do one thing when Jerry was on the phone calling him to duty. Alabama – Tornado touchdown, near Birmingham, several killed, many injured. Grabbing his to-go bag he sent a quick text to Maddie to let her know he'd be out of town again for an unknown amount of time. While he knew he would be doing life-saving work it was beginning to frustrate him that he had too much going on in his life right now to be leaving town again so soon. He needed to see his father. He wanted to get back to Maddie, badly. He wanted to kiss her again, and not just a brief brush of the lips. He needed to know her response to a more romantic kiss. He was past worrying about his bachelorhood now. He could envision a life with Maddie. He was kicking himself for lying to her about his occupation. This was not good.

Arriving at near midnight, Jerry met him at the hospital. Portions of it had been destroyed by the tornado.

"We'll put you online tomorrow, Ken. I have all the operating rooms going right now, so you can relax for a bit."

"Okay. Ah, listen Jer. I think after this round I'm going to have to back off for a while. My dad's getting in really rough shape, and I need to be there for him."

"I'm truly sorry to hear that, Ken. As much as I like having you on the team it's not a problem to give you a bye so you can be with him. We can even cut you loose early. We have more injured coming in, but it doesn't seem to be as bad as Haiti."

"That's good news. I appreciate it. I'll see you early tomorrow then."

Jer gave him a rough salute.

Finding his quarters, he flopped down on the bed and made a call to Maddie.

"Hi, Ken. I got your message. Thanks so much for letting me know."

"How are you doing with your mother? Gosh, it seems like I just left your house. I'm so sorry to be calling you so late."

"It's fine. I'm often up at this hour either worrying or reading. Maybe even watching some television."

Pushing himself up to lean against the headboard, *"So, your mom sees the doctor tomorrow?"*

"Yes, 8:00. I'll go in with her now. I need answers."

"Yes, you do. I wish I could be there to help you."

"You helped me a lot today. I was thankful you were here when she fell."

"I want to see you again," he spoke so softly she felt goosebumps on her arms.

"I want to see you again, too."

"I'll try to call you every night, but don't worry if I don't. For sure I'll let you know when I'm home."
"The sooner the better."
"I certainly agree with that," he sighed.
"You take care, Ken."
"Let me know how it goes tomorrow, even by text."
"I will."
"Goodnight, Maddie."
"Goodnight, Ken."

He slept soundly, dreaming of all the things he wanted to do with Maddie. In more ways than one.

He only had four surgeries the next day and they were fairly short ones as surgeries go. Deep lacerations that had to be checked out thoroughly, another collapsed lung – all relatively minor for a change.

"No more surgeries for you today, Ken. I might have a van arriving shortly with medical equipment and supplies. If you could stay and help unload it that would be great. Won't take long."

"Do you ever stop working, Jer? I swear you're here 24/7."

"Not quite that bad…." He reached down to answer his phone which was buzzing.

"Van's here with the supplies." Jerry headed toward the rear of the building where the van was parked.

The driver and an assistant unlocked the rear door of the van and hopped in, moving boxes forward. "Bandages, syringes, gloves, masks, soap…" Pulling boxes down to take into the hospital they were suddenly surrounded by a gang of men, all wearing stocking masks, and waving guns.

"Drugs. Give us the drugs," one screamed. "Now or die." Three of them waved guns around, pointing them at the four men who stood in shock, holding boxes.

"No drugs here," Jerry shouted. "Just bandages and soap."

"I said," the front man put a gun to Jerry's head, "GIVE US THE DRUGS."

"I SWEAR, man," Jerry looked straight ahead, afraid to move an inch, "there really are no drugs. You can open all the boxes and see…"

The driver of the van suddenly dropped his box, causing one of the bandits to fire his gun. As fast as the sound of the bullet travelled the masked men all turned and bolted, as a second shot was heard.

And Ken fell to the ground, wounded.

"KEN! Oh, my god, Ken! You," Jerry pointed to the driver, "go inside and get help." The driver took off for the door to the hospital, followed by his assistant.

Bending down he saw blood coming from Ken's chest. He was still breathing, but it was shallow, and he was turning white, going into shock. It was only moments for the hospital doors to open and a gurney was ready to rush Ken into an operating room.

Jerry paced. One hour. Two hours. He couldn't bring himself to go into the operating room for fear he'd collapse. He'd done a thousand surgeries in his career and never felt panic. Now he was in a state of full-blown panic. Ken was his best friend. Literally his best friend. Why hadn't he thought about security. It was just supplies. No drugs. But why hadn't he taken into consideration that someone might not realize that and try to rob them. It was all so sudden. Thank the gods one of the surgical teams was between patients at the time of the shooting. Now police were everywhere, taking notes, asking questions, waiting to see how the surgery went. It was pure torture. It was also an eye opener. As many family members as he had spoken to – he never really understood the depth of their agony until now. He knew Ken was shot in the right chest and not far from the heart, but he hadn't been able to get his gown off to see exactly where the wound was. All he remembered was seeing the blood oozing all over his gown and Ken's face going white. Ken was alive going into surgery. He had to hold on to that. What was HAPPENING in that room?

Finally sitting down, he put his head in his hands, listening to the drone of the police officers who stood waiting with him. They were seasoned police officers. He could tell by their detached stories about the damage to the city, their chatter about their families or other cases they were working. This was just one more story they had to follow up on in order to get to work solving the case. Odd that he was getting such a totally different perspective on something he had been involved in multiple times, but from the surgeon's point of view. Now he knew three sides to that horrible coin, the surgeon's cool, detached, unflappable demeanor as he or she orchestrated another hopefully successful surgery, the police officers detachment of just another routine shooting, and the excruciating pain of marking time in a surgical waiting room. Then, with a puff of sound, the door opened, and Walt came through, heading directly for Jerry.

All Jerry could do was stand and look at him, clearly worried.

"He's gonna be fine, Jerry. We took a metal-density bullet out of him, just behind the wall of the right pulmonary artery and close to the bronchus. No real damage."

The police officers had joined them and were taking notes.

"Thank God, Walt. Wonderful job. Prognosis?"

"I think a few days of monitoring. His vital signs are good. He's on fluids now, and meds for the pain and to prevent infection of course." Turning to the police officers, "And we have the bullet for you."

"When can we see him for a statement?"

"He's in recovery now but I think maybe early tomorrow?"

They nodded. "We'll be back then for his statement."

As they left, Walt turned to Jerry, motioning for him to sit down.

"Listen, Jerry, I know we'd normally keep Ken here and do all the monitoring, but we're woefully short of beds. What about flying him over to Jacksonville Naval Hospital for follow-up?"

Jerry tapped his finger to his lips in thought. "Hmm, I have a better idea. He's from Virginia Beach and if we send him to Portsmouth Naval he'll be close to home and family support. Plus, his dad is in a nursing home with Alzheimer's and from what I understand he's getting close to the end. It's a little further but worth it. We'd end up flying him from Jacksonville to Norfolk anyway after recovery, so might as well get him up there now."

"I'll get a chopper ready to go tomorrow, after the cops are done with him."

Jerry nodded, following Walt out the door with a handshake. "Walt, thanks for sticking with us on this one." He was exhausted and close to tears, but he needed to go see Ken before trying to get some sleep.

"My pleasure, Jerry. I'm just thankful he'll be fine."

It was a short walk to the recovery room and the nurse gave him a gentle smile when he entered.

"He's doing well, Dr. Hepler. Coming out of the anesthesia normally."

Jerry breathed a sigh of relief seeing his friend lying there, breathing normally, with just an IV line attached. He hadn't needed any special tubes for any other reason, and that was the best outcome he could have hoped for.

"Thanks, Val. I'll be back in the morning to see him off to Portsmouth Naval. He'll recover there."

"I'll take good care of him until then."

Jerry didn't sleep well that night, abbreviated as it had been. All the emotions refused to calm down enough to allow his mind to grow silent. What a marathon it had been. He knew that in the future any deliveries would be guarded. This had been so stupid. It was just gloves and gowns and bandages. No drugs would ever come in a van like that. He could only hope that the description he had given to the police would help, but he didn't see how. They were all hooded, all the same size guys, so many guns were pointed in their faces that all they could focus on was the guns. Just another random shooting in a world so used to it that, unless you were related to the victim, you just shrugged your shoulders and got on with your day.

Chapter 12

The chopper ride back to Portsmouth was totally uneventful. He felt fairly good for a man who'd been shot, but he had needed rest and care to be sure no infections took over. The anesthetic always took time to fully leave the body, so it had helped him sleep. Every four-hour interruptions for blood work, blood pressure, heart rate, oxygen level, made him realize that hospital stays were not very restful when all was said and done. But he'd zonked right back out again after each and every interruption. He might had even slept right through a few?. Now that he was awake he found the food was rather good – but he knew he was comparing it to his random microwave boxed stuff.

Suddenly he realized he hadn't talked to Maddie in what, WHAT? – he's just missed one night, right? Yes, just last night. Was it just last night? What day was it anyway? Sitting up as best he could he scanned the table next to him. Water, urinal, tray with toothbrush and stuff… he refocused on the rest of the room, rotating his head to see if his duffle bag was there. The room was empty. He had no idea where his phone was. In fact, he had no idea where any of his stuff was. He needed to at least borrow a phone to get a message to Maddie.

A nurse's, maybe. No, not good. The caller ID would be a woman's name and that could spell disaster. A male nurse? Possible, with the right up-front explanation to Maddie of why he wasn't on his own phone. And there was always a chance she would think it was SPAM and just delete it. Lined phones would show they were coming from the hospital. Doctors might have the DR in front of their caller name. He was flat out trapped.

The next nurse that walked into his room, "Any idea when I can get discharged?" he asked her.

"No, sir. I don't, but your doctor should be here shortly. If you'll lie back down I'll draw the blood, take your stats, and check your wound" Giving him a sly smile, "We don't trust the doctors to do it right."

He caught the twinkle in her eye, "You're probably right, too," he smiled back. "What's his or her name?" She was a competent nurse, for sure. Got the blood with hardly a prick to his arm.

"Dr. Anthony. Kyle Anthony."

"Thanks. How long have I been here?"

"You've been out of it for a couple of days."

"Seriously? Thought it was only one day."

"Nope. You slept through it all. Groaned once or twice when we came in for the stats every four hours, but other than that you slept like a lamb."

Scratching his head, this isn't good, he thought. "Okay, thanks. Do you know where my stuff might be? Did it come with me? I need my phone."

"I'll check with the charge nurse, Dr. Avery."

"'Preciate it."

Having made all her entries into his record, and making sure the IV's were working properly, she asked him to open his gown so she could check and redress the wound.

"Excellent," she said. "No signs of infection, stitches look good. Is there any pain?"

"Tender a bit but not pain."

Redressing his wound, she quietly left the room, leaving Ken in calculating mode. He didn't call Maddie the night he was shot; then he was airlifted the next day because they needed the bed, he apparently slept for a day, so he didn't call her that night, so he had missed two nights. He was sleepy and it was hard to calculate, but it seemed he had missed just two calls. That wasn't bad but now he was likely to miss more of them. It *was* only two, right? He shook his head, maybe it was three? He was surprised at how foggy his brain was.

"Dr. Avery, how are you feeling?"

"You must be Dr. Anthony!"

"Kyle."

"Ken."

They both grinned at each other. "How long do I have to stay here?"

"We'll see how the blood work goes, but maybe tomorrow. You had a rather nasty wound. Lucky you were taken into surgery immediately. All your numbers are starting to look good now though, and the nurse said the wound was healing beautifully."

"What was the end result?"

"It was a bullet taken from just behind the wall of the right pulmonary artery and close to the bronchus. No real damage to any organs, and all we really need to be concerned about is any possible infections."

"Well, that sounds good."

"From what Dr. Hepler explained you were very lucky. Seems there was a second shot that took a piece of ear out of the driver of the van."

"Oh, geeze, it was all so stupid. It was just routine supplies. No drugs."

Kyle nodded. "Jerry said it was six or seven men, all dressed in black hoods and masks and all with guns."

"And they'll never catch them either."

"They have the bullets, but you're right. Unlikely to find the guns that the bullets belong to."

"Did they send any of my stuff with me? I can't find my phone, or clothes."

"I'll check with the nurse. If there's anything I'll have her bring it in to you."

"Thanks."

"Get some rest now. If you're eating and eliminating well we can probably let you go tomorrow with a bottle of antibiotic pills. Your wound looked good yesterday, and Sandy just said it still looks great. Later we'll get you up and walking."

He woke up two hours later to find a bag on the chair next to his bed. Reaching over with his left arm he dragged it up and over to see what was in it. Apparently Jerry, or someone, had gone to his room and gotten his clothing, adding his cell phone and wallet to the top. WHEW! He breathed a huge sigh of relief. Now if it was charged….

Maddie was surprised to see her mother ready to go at 7:30, dressed and having eaten her breakfast cereal. Even the bowl and spoon had been placed in the dishwasher.

They were ushered into Doctor Foster's exam room and only had a five-minute wait.

"Ah, Mrs. Rogers. And who have we here?" he nodded toward Maddie.

Holding out her hand she shook the doctor's, "I'm Maddie, her daughter."

She stood behind Dori as the doctor checked her vision, walking, arm, and hand movements, and asked many questions. Anytime Dori was dishonest with the doctor, Maddie would shake her head so only the doctor could see that Dori wasn't being honest with him.

"And you've only fallen once?"

Dori nodded, and Maddie agreed.

"What you'll need to start doing, then, is to use your cane and walker so you don't fall again. Have you been taking all your medicines?"

Dori hung her head.

"Mrs. Rogers, it's critical that you take the meds. They'll be a tremendous help with your neuropathy, balance, movement, and vision problems. Promise me you'll take them every day."

Again, Dori nodded.

"Doctor," Maddie interrupted, "If you'll have your nurse print out a list of her medications, amounts, and how often, I'll make sure she takes them every day. I think she's been hiding some of them from me."

"Is that true, Mrs. Rogers?"

"Side effects."

"You really have to let them get adjusted to your body and it won't happen overnight. And I promise you the benefits are worth the few side effects. So, promise me you'll take them."

"Alright, I will."

"Good. I'll have the nurse print out the list for your daughter. I'm sure she can help you with them. Is it alright if I talk to your daughter privately about your MS?"

Dori's eyes shot up to look at him, but she gave her approval.

"I'm going to have the nurse take you down for some blood work. We haven't done that in quite a few months, so I'd like a reading. She'll stay with you until I'm done talking to your daughter."

Leading Dori out, the nurse closed the door.

Offering Maddie, a chair, "I had to ask her permission to be able to speak with you in depth."

"I understand."

"She's starting to fade, I fear. The medicines will help her, but she has lost some of the use of her legs. The neuropathy is worse. It's always frustrating for a doctor to try to help someone who won't take the medicines or do the exercises" he leaned forward in his chair, forearms on his thighs and rubbing his hands together, "but anything you can do will be a help to her." A tap on the door and a nurse came in with the paperwork for Maddie. "Here's the prescription list, Dr. Foster."

Handing it over to Maddie, "Do the best you can."

Maddie smiled. "What will the blood work tell you?"

"It's really a test to check for a substance called neurofilament light chain. That's a nerve protein that can be detected whenever nerve cells begin to die. If her numbers have gotten higher it will tell me her MS is advancing."

"You'll let me know?"

"Of course, and if you need more help just call again."

"Thank you, doctor. I appreciate you taking the time to see us before your regularly scheduled patients."

"My pleasure. I'm glad you called me."

Turning her phone back on when they got to the house Maddie saw there were still no calls or messages. She was getting depressed between the new prognosis possibility for her mother and her lack of phone calls or messages from Ken. Her mother was tired, so she helped her into her bedroom so she could nap. She had promised to send Ken a text message about her mother's doctor appointment, so she wrote out a short report and hit send. She noted it was delivered.

The next two days Maddie spent most of her time going over the medicine list the doctor had given her. She checked out every prescription online, noting what the major side effects were and how each drug was designed to help her mother's disease. She noted any possible interactions. There wasn't any alcohol in the house, so that wouldn't be a problem. No smoking either. With her mother's help she'd found all the drugs and lined them up in the kitchen.. Making out a chart, there wouldn't be any more mistakes. She now knew exactly what drug to give her mother and when to give it to her. She also started looking around the house checking for tripping hazards and anything blocking a possible pathway. She removed all scatter rugs and shifted some furniture slightly to make a bit more room for her mother to navigate to a chair. An accomplishment for sure, but now she was back to worrying about Ken.

It was hard to go to sleep that night. Ken must be in some secret location and unable or not allowed to make phone calls.

She just had to be patient. Still, it kept her awake and worrying. She was restless but managed to get a few hours' sleep. Struggling, she got out of bed and dressed to go see to her mother. She'd been quiet all night, but that didn't mean all was well.

She was grateful. She found her in the kitchen pouring herself some cereal. Her mother was trying hard to be nice. She hadn't slammed her cane on anything, much to Maddie's relief.

The morning hours seemed to pass agonizingly slow. While she knew it was silly she kept going to the window and looking out. Maybe he'd gotten home too late to call her. Even so, she was becoming obsessed with looking out the window. Again, gripping the edge of the sink, and leaning forward as far as she could see, she saw nothing outside but birds and squirrels.

As she put lunch down for her mother, her phone rang.

"I've been so worried, Ken," she blurted out.

"I'm fine. Good to hear your voice though. I'm sorry I was out of touch for two days."

"Any idea when you'll be home?"

"In the next few days, I think"

"I've missed you."

"Me, too. I saw your text about your mother's doctor appointment. What about details?"

She walked to the next room and spoke softly. *"She's worse than we thought. He's doing something 'light chain' to see about nerve cells dying. He gave me a list of her meds, so now I can be sure she's taking them."*

"It's a start then. Is she behaving though?"

"Yes. I think she knows she won't be ambulatory for much longer. I'll start the process to get her a nurse's aide to help her with bathing and all. She refuses to let me help her,"

"Try to get someone who can come and stay with her for 8-10 hours a day to give you a rest."

"It's expensive, but I'm lucky to be able to afford it. I'll need to see what's available and also check her finances. It will all work out."

"I know you can make it happen. I'll help when I get home."

"I look forward to it."

"I'll see you soon."

They both said goodbye.

"Your boyfriend?" Dori dropped her spoon into the soup.

"Yes, Mother. That was Ken just calling to see how you were doing."

"Not likely."

"Believe what you will. I'm going to go call Dan and let him know how it went at the doctors." She'd been a bit remiss on that. She'd been busy with the medicine research, but she also didn't want to tie up her phone in case Ken called. It would be hard to hang up on Dan to take a call from Ken.

While she was on the phone briefing Dan she heard her mother go into the family room and turn on the news. She rarely did that, but maybe she was hoping to overhear what she said to Dan. She'd be disappointed. It was just a routine call with the doctor update. Hanging up she walked past the family room to see if the dishes had been put in the dishwasher. She had to grin when her mother suddenly turned the volume up. She *had* been trying to overhear her speaking to Dan while pretending to watch the news! She couldn't help but roll her eyes. She heard the local weather report come on first and then,

"News on the home front. We've just learned that one of the local doctors who volunteers with Doctors World Wide was in Alabama helping those badly injured from the tornado when he and three others were attacked by a group of hooded and masked men trying to steal drugs. Dr. Kenneth Avery, a retired Navy surgeon and Captain is currently in Portsmouth Naval Hospital recovering from a gunshot wound. No further information is available at this time. Meanwhile the Norfolk City Council has voted….."

Maddie froze. Her mind screamed, what? WHAT? Putting the cup that was in her hand back onto the counter she stood up straight and found it hard to even breathe. It couldn't be Ken. She'd just talked to him half an hour ago. She had to be sure. Grabbing the back of a chair she turned it around and sat down, her hands shaking, her breathing shallow. They said Alabama. Was Ken in Alabama? But he was in intelligence. It has to be someone else with the same name, she decided. Yet the more she thought about it the more it was upsetting her. If she called the hospital she'd only get the same information she'd just heard on the television newscast. If she called Ken, and he had lied to her, he would only lie again. If he told her it really was him, that he didn't want to worry her, then he'd lied the first time, and, GEEZE, even right from the start if he was a doctor and not in intelligence. But he had told her he was a retired Navy captain. She felt the blood drain out of her head she was so upset. Covering her face with her hands she tried to make sense of something that didn't make any sense at all. There was only one way to find out.

"Mother, I need to run an important errand. I'll be back in an hour or so."

"Where are you going?"

"You have your phone. Call me if you seriously need me and I'll come right back." She walked out the garage door with Dori yelling after her. She knew if she told her mother she was going to the hospital her mother would go ape for many different reasons. No need to stir that up!

Walking into the hospital she was shaking like a spider web caught in a heavy wind. Checking in at the reception desk she was told the room number and where the elevator was located. She'd never been here. Despite being a Navy widow, it had always just been easier to see doctors closer to where she lived. And besides, she really didn't have but one primary care doctor and she only saw him once a year.

Finding the room, she heard voices, so she paused outside the door. Gathering her strength, she prayed that when she did go inside the man in the bed would not be Mr. Walk Around the Block. Leaning back against the wall she tried to control her breathing. It was only a moment before the door opened and a nurse could be heard, "Your dinner will be here around 5, Doctor Avery."

She heard him say "thank you," and it was Ken. She'd know that voice anywhere. Starting a turn to leave, tears beginning to cloud her eyes, the nurse saw her standing there and asked if she could help. Shaking her head, she told the nurse she was just here to visit with Dr. Avery for a few minutes. The nurse nodded and went on her way. Finding strength from some unknown source, Maddie opened the door and stepped inside.

Ken was sitting on the edge of the bed in one of those gorgeous blue patterned medical gowns they make everyone wear. His bare legs dangled down the side and as he squirmed she could see he was having trouble getting the tie of his gown to knot at the side.

Hearing a slight noise, he looked up. She was a vision. A dream. She took one step towards him, moving only her feet. Her eyes were empty, her arms dangling down her sides. Her vacant eyes just stared at him. There was no expression on her face. Nothing came out of her mouth – not a scream, not a word, nothing. It was the tear that jolted him out of his shock.

"Maddie!" he could see the set of her jaw and knew she was angry, then tears started to run down her cheeks.

"I just wanted to make sure you were alright," her voice was flat, the words almost catching in her throat. Turning she walked out of the room.

"MADDIE," he screamed. "*Please*, Maddie, come back!" Frantically he tried to get his feet to the floor. But. still hooked up to an IV and not having had any of his walking exercises, he fell to the floor, still screaming for Maddie. Laying there he felt tears welling up in his eyes, and it was not just the pain caused by his fall to the floor, but his fall from grace. Oh, my god, he thought. She knows who I am. She knows I've lied. "Maddie, please," his voice quivered. His IV line was wrapped around his hand, his gown open in the back as he lay on his side. His gut hurt. Everything hurt.

He heard footsteps and moved his eyes to see two nurses rushing to him. "Dr. Avery…." They bent down to help him back into bed. "What happened, Doctor?"

He could only shake his head as a stray tear ran down his face and into his ear as his head touched the pillow.

"I need to check your wound again, Doctor."

The first nurse skillfully checked the wound while the second made sure all his IV lines were untangled and still working correctly. "You're lucky you didn't pull this out," she pointed to the where the IV was still inserted in his arm. "I'll get Dr. Anthony," she put a bit more tape on his arm to add to the security of the line.

"No, I'm alright."

"His wound is okay. You didn't hurt your knee, arm, hand, or head in the fall, did you?"

"No. I just slid down the side of the bed."

"Dr. Avery, please! If you need to get up just ring for one of us. You have those yellow socks on for a reason, you know."

He nodded.

Placing the call button in his hand they left the room.

As much as Ken wanted to follow Maddie and try to explain, he knew it was useless. He was dead to her now. How had she found out? Jerry didn't even know her name so he couldn't have called her. Trish and Drew didn't know he was in the hospital. And even at that they only knew Maddie's first name. Suddenly he felt so empty he laid back down and curled up on the miserably uncomfortable bed. He couldn't even summon the energy to call her. An apology? Wouldn't work. He'd ripped her soul right out of her. He could see – no that was it – he couldn't see because her eyes were empty. And she said just that one sentence, coldly, quietly, in a monotone. Aside from that she hadn't made a single noise. She just turned her back on him and left. If only she had screamed or yelled or come over and hit him on the chest. Anything would have been better than the almost total silence. The look of absolute disappointment. Now, at long last, he knew how much he cared for her, and had hoped for a very serious relationship. Still, he thought, she wasn't entirely blameless. She'd kept a lot of her history from him. He knew absolutely nothing about her husband other than his first name and that he was a Navy pilot. While it wasn't an outright lie, it could be considered a lie of omission. Why was it such a secret? Tired, so tired. He rang for a pain pill. It was the only way he would be able to hide.

Hearing voices he woke up to a crowd around his bed. His whole family was staring at him, all anxious. Well, except for Reed, of course. He wasn't there. Pushing backwards to sit up, he grimaced at all of them. "I'm fine. I'm totally fine, guys! It's just a scratch."

"Yeah, right," snapped Drew. 'Just a little scratch, huh? Slept for days over a little scratch!"

"Something like that. How did you find out? The TV news?"

"Nope. None of us watch TV unless there's a hurricane or tornado, and we don't get Virginia Beach newspapers." Leaning down almost nose to nose, "Seems you have me listed as your next of kin, Dude, and I got this call from Dr. Hepler this morning. It took him awhile to get the info from his wife about who you had listed as your next of kin. They need to up their response time for notifications! Doc even apologized for being so totally disorganized. Well, no kidding! He said you were resting comfortably at Portsmouth Naval, so after several phone calls and major travelling time today, here we are. He thought maybe your family should know what was going on with their brother. Very considerate of him." Backing off in frustration, "He could only tell me you'd been shot and were here. Wasn't allowed to say more than that. You need to update that stuff so they can tell us something in detail."

"Yeah, I get it. Sorry, but he knew I was alright so it's not like you were being called in to watch me die or anything."

"We just talked to the doctor, by phone, Ken. He was already gone for the day. Nurse hooked us up. We watched the nurse check your wound, Dude, just before you woke up. That's not a little tiny scratch on your chest."

"And if it was you'd still be in Alabama," Trish added.

"Okay, okay. I'm lucky, and I'm fine now. Doc says I can go home tomorrow probably. So, chill, okay?" All he saw was a sea of sour faces. "Come on, keep up with me, okay?"

A tap on the door and a hospital aide brought in Ken's dinner, setting it on the table next to his bed, leaving without saying a word.

"Want us to feed you?" Trish asked. "Can you use your arm on that side?"

"I'm fine. I can eat just fine. I appreciate that you came but I need to eat and then go back to sleep."

"Don't mess with us," Drew demanded.

"It was close. I could have died. I didn't. I'm here. I'm fine, now let's not dwell on it. And please, if by some miracle you get to meet Maddie, make no mention of this to her."

"You saying this woman of yours doesn't know?" Tessa stood with her hands on her hips.

"She came here, knows I lied to her about what I do. She left."

"Well, that's sure not very friendly of her," she clucked.

"Yeah, end of story. I'm fine. The doctors here will tell you that."

"If you're really sure." Drew still didn't look convinced.

"Yes, I'm sure. I'll go home tomorrow and rest for a few more days. The only thing they worry about now is infection and I'll take some pills for ten days."

They visibly relaxed, but Trish couldn't help making one last pitch, "You need to *retire* retire. Just stay home and no more running around into disasters."

Ken just smiled at her, took her hand, and squeezing it, "I'm thinking about it, Trish. Maddie's mad at me now because I never told her I was a doctor, and I don't want her to know how bad the wound was, so mums the word."

"Alright. If we ever get to meet her, that is."

Ken was discharged the next day after the nurses made sure he could walk, did both bathroom duties, and ate well. They'd taken good care of him. He'd make sure the head nurse was aware of it. There was no need to have family members driving from Suffolk or the Eastern Shore to take him home, an UBER would be fine. He had no desire to do anything other than get more sleep. Just on the small chance that she might forgive him, eventually, he called her, and wasn't surprised when it went to voice mail.

"Maddie, I know you don't trust me anymore, and I understand that, but I'm begging you to let me give you my side of it. There's a valid reason. Sometimes when you do something, with a valid reason from the start it just gets to the point where it's hard to correct it. I was afraid I'd lose you if I confessed, and now I seem to have anyway. I can't really see why it matters whether or not I'm in intelligence or medicine. But to be fair you haven't been totally open with me either. I'm out of the hospital now---It was more a flesh wound and I'm fine. Anyway," he paused for several seconds, *"I'm sorry. Please call me or send me a message"*

Sadly, he realized that Maddie was just stubborn enough, and independent enough to just delete anything he tried to send to her. He was sure, by the look on her face when she left his hospital room, that she was in some kind of shock. No facial expressions, no life in her eyes. She wouldn't feel the deep anger or hurt until later, and he had no idea how much later. Now his father had to take priority. He felt fairly sure that his best course of action was to simply forget about Maddie.

Ken spent the next two weeks with his father, arriving at noon and leaving at six. His father either slept or didn't recognize him. Drew and Tessa came over from Suffolk to spend the weekend with Ken, Drew would take turns sitting with their dad. Tessa had never met him, and Drew felt she might be more comfortable doing some shopping again, as she had the earlier Saturday they'd come. There were more things she could get in Virginia Beach, than were available to her in Suffolk. Fabric was a biggie, as she made her own clothes.

Ken had talked to Jerry more than once, the driver of the van was alright, and yes, he was alright, too. Dr. Anthony had called telling him to return for a checkup and to get the stitches removed. And no, Ken was not allowed to remove the stitches himself. It was just one more thing he had to do.

Drew had just entered the room to give Ken time to get some rest and food when their dad stirred. Bringing his covered arm out and over the blanket, "You boys here to take me home?"

Ken signaled Drew, "No, Mr. Avery. We're just here to make sure you're comfortable."

"Oh, my mother was here just a bit ago for the same reason. You never met Grace, she's the best mom a guy could have."

"Your mother's name is Grace?" asked Ken.

"Beautiful name, isn't it. My dad couldn't come with her today, but he will tomorrow she said."

Ken saw Drew's quizzical facial expression, and leaned over to whisper, "I know. Grandma's name was Esther." Drew nodded in sudden understanding.

Turning to face his dad, "What is Grace doing these days?"

"She has the most beautiful garden. She brought me some flowers, but I guess they died. I don't see them anymore."

"Do you want us to go get you some flowers, Mr. Avery?"

"No, she'll bring me some when she comes back."

Drew took a few steps closer to the bed, "Are you comfortable …Mr. Avery?"

"Quite so, quite so."

"Can we get you anything?"

"No. I'll go back to sleep now," he closed his eyes.

"Mr. Avery?" Ken asked.

There was no response.

"He's in deep sleep, Drew, or whatever it is his brain does now."

"He used Mom's name for his mother." Ken could see Drew's eyes were filled with tears.

Ken closed his eyelids and sighed. Pulling the covers up to his dad's chin, "Alzheimer's works differently for different people. But most go back and forth from youthful memories to suddenly recognizing those standing next to the bed. I'm really glad you could come, Drew. I'll keep you posted. I know you have to get back to the farm. It's harvest time."

"Gotta neighbor helping out with that, kinda monitoring for me this weekend. It's basically the end of harvest season. Might get a tad more the last week in October and early November, but we usually are wrapped up by the end of October. He understands. I've done as much for him."

"Then Let's go home and order in some Chinese. Then you and Tessa can go home before it gets dark. The nurses will call if there's any dramatic change."

Tessa was waiting for them. Making sure everyone liked Chinese he ordered online. Tessa quickly set the table, having done her usual reconnaissance of the kitchen when she got there an hour ahead of them.

"No problem getting in, I gather," Ken asked Tessa with a knowing grin.

"Key code on the garage worked fine."

"Good. I'll freshen up and then we can all sit and talk."

"While you do that," Drew hitched up his pants, "I'll go get our stuff out of the bedroom and get it into the car."

"I already washed the sheets and put them back on the bed, Ken."

"Oh, Tessa, that wasn't necessary."

"Woman's work, Ken. I have the towels in the dryer and I'm fixin' to go fold them for you."

Ken just nodded once, then started shaking his head, "Thanks, Tessa. When you get tired of hanging around with my ugly brother, you can come live with me."

"Fat chance," was what they heard hollering from the hallway.

"You look tired," Tessa put her hand on Ken's arm.

"A bit. Hard to see Dad like that."

"Yeah, I get it. Where's that lady you talked to us about?"

"Maddie? Oh, I blew that, remember?" Retelling her the story about the doctor/intelligence lying, "she just turned and walked away. Not a word, Tessa. I was hooked up to those IV's and couldn't run after her. Sent her one phone message, but she hasn't replied. I don't expect her to."

Drew came into the kitchen carrying the food. "Caught the guy driving up. Paid for brother."

His lips curling up just a little, "Thanks, Drew. I owe ya."

Tessa didn't want to push Ken. He was tired and had said enough for her to know what the score was. Maybe she'd call him in a day or two and see how things were going with their dad and see if things had improved with Maddie. At least he would know someone cared.

Chapter 13

Was it Linus who lived under a dark cloud? Maddie was pretty sure she could "out cloud" him. Her life was just one downpour after another. Her clouds were the kind that whipped up the winds of destiny, destroying her spirit - maybe even her very soul. She was 41 and could only count three years of those as happy years. There were a few days when she could almost see the gold ring hanging from the carousal rafters, beckoning her to reach out and grab it. Last chance… then the merry-go-round sped up and threw her off her horse, just as she was reaching up…up…up.

A squirrel skittered up the steps and stopped in front of her. She took a peanut out of her pocket and tossed it. Squirrel and peanut were gone in a flash. Even the squirrel didn't want to eat in front of her. Here chimes hung silently above her head, lamenting the lack of even the smallest breeze on this blistering hot October afternoon. It was only 85 degrees but felt like 100 with the humidity high and no wind at all. Extremely unusual for this time of year. A few birds flew onto the feeders. At least something was alive. She replayed the scene at the hospital, over and over in her mind. She should have punched him. She should have screamed at him at least.

Running hadn't solved anything. She'd seen two nurses suddenly run past her and into his room. She didn't dare return to find out what it was about. She would have lost all her composure, and that was unthinkable. Never again. Mark's death was enough of that.

She'd saved Ken's message. She wondered what could be "valid" about lying about his job. Yet on the other hand what did it matter *what* his job had been in the Navy? Spook or Knife Wielder. If he felt he had to hide it he must have a very good reason and it was logical to assume that after that reason had vanished he might feel scared about revealing later how he had lied about it. It was the part about her not being open with him that struck her. He was right. She'd hidden information from him. While it wasn't a lie, she was careful not to explain how Mark died, and for the life of her she had no clue why she didn't want to share that with him. And *that* was a valid point on his part. She literally had no earthly reason to *not* tell him. Totally ridiculous. All she could imagine was that it was such a personally traumatic event that to verbalize it again would turn her into a sobbing mess. She could think about it, but not put it into words. Ken most certainly deserved better than that. Was she afraid if she opened herself up completely to him he might not be interested anymore? He knew Mark had died, and it wasn't like he was murdered or jumped off a bridge, but then Ken didn't know that did he? Maybe he was thinking she hadn't told him because it was suicide, or she murdered him. It was clear she hadn't been fair with him. He'd shared about all his non-girlfriends and why they remained in that category. He was honest about his upbringing, his mother's obsession with status, his father's penchant for working too hard and too long. He spoke about his sister and two brothers. Maggie threw another nut onto the porch and hoped the little squirrel would return. They always made her smile. Right now, she felt - trapped. There was her mother, getting weaker, faster. It scared her. It wouldn't be long before she was totally bedridden. The fingers on both of her hands were busy tapping on the armrests. How to solve all this? She had hoped, so hard, that maybe something would come of her relationship with Ken. It didn't matter to her what his job had been in the Navy. He wasn't doing it anymore. Except, she now knew, those so-called intelligence trips were really doing humanitarian work in some rather awful locations. She considered she actually would have been very proud of what he did, had she known. It didn't make sense, and she was tired of thinking about it. She hasn't seen him walking for almost a month. He hadn't called or texted after the day she ran from the hospital. It was obvious he wasn't going to chase her, that was patently plain. Maybe he was called out on another mission. Maybe this, maybe that! He had recovered, she knew that. He looked alright when she was at the hospital, and he said he was home, so enough was enough. Why, oh why, had she made it such a big deal?

Tomorrow she would have to call Dan and fill him in on their mother. She was going to hire a nurse's aide to help her. She knew he'd be happy to hear that. He'd been after her for the past three phone calls to get one, and if there was a money problem just let him know and he'd take care of it. A day worker would be such a blessing. It was time.

Maddie, Maddie, Maddie. Somehow he had to get her out of his mind. Is he being too critical of her? For sure he doesn't know the full story of her life because she hasn't wanted to share it with him. It wasn't fair, either. He'd given her plenty of time and chances to tell him about her marriage. Maybe it was another case of abuse – spousal abuse. Maybe he hit her, or psychologically belittled her. Maybe he cheated on her and the other woman's husband shot him to death. The mind can make up some scary stories when no facts can be found. On one hand he felt like he really should just back off and return to his bachelor life, while on the other hand he wanted to give love a chance. He'd never done that, and he thought…. thought what? Straddling a fence was not the way he'd done things in his life, and he hated being there right now. He's so lost he can't think straight, can't decide, can't figure it all out. She was beginning to make him nuts.

The next week was a blur. November winds were escorted by chilling temperatures and too many leaves on the ground. Some weird Canada wind sneaking down or something like that. He was glad to find that his father's room was warm. He didn't like the fact that all his dad did now was sleep. He was rarely awake and when his eyes opened he would be totally confused, unable to talk and didn't move very much. Ken knew the end was near and prayed that his father wasn't suffering. He'd lost his appetite and was increasingly weak. Lifting the blankets from his feet he noted that there was swelling in both his feet and ankles. It's time to call Trish, Drew, and Reed.

Trish and Drew were on their way. Ken had to leave a message for Reed. He could do no more. He pulled a chair up to his father's bed and held his hand. Even that was swollen. It was hard to keep the tears from falling, but maybe his dad could hear him if he spoke.

"Dad, it's Ken here. It makes me sad to see you so weak and tired. I'm a doctor, you know. I'm supposed to be able to help everyone get better, but sometimes God takes it out of our hands. I love you. I know you couldn't spend a lot of time with all us kids while we were growing up, but you worked hard to provide for us. We had everything a kid could ever want. Sometimes I think you worked extra hours, so you didn't have to come home. Can't know that for sure, of course, but Mother always had something social going on in the house. Even so, in the end you can know we all turned out well. I joined the Navy and retired as a Captain. I don't think you ever saw me in my unform, but I loved my job as a surgeon. And Reed? He's a lawyer and a fine one. Lives here in Virginia Beach and is married. Oh. I forgot to add, I'm not married but I did meet a fine lady. I kinda disappointed her a while ago. Not sure if she'll take me back, but if she does I'll likely ask her to marry me. You'd be proud of Reed though. He's one of those big, powerful attorneys. I think you'd get a big kick out of Drew. Owns a peanut farm of all things, but it's beautiful out there in Suffolk. His wife is amazing. Both are down to earth with two wonderful kids. I wish you could see how peanuts are grown, Dad. It was a real education. All that said, the best story is Trish. You should see her, married with two kids and living on the Eastern Shore. Flat out the best of the lot, Dad. She keeps me in line. You got four good ones, Dad, and we do owe you and Mother for making sure we stayed out of trouble and became good citizens...."

The door opened suddenly, and Drew and Tessa came in. "We raced here," Drew said.

Ken nodded. "I was just telling Dad here how he raised a fine family."

Walking up to the bed, Drew took his father's hand from Ken. "Hey pop. You remember I used to call you pop. I always liked that name for you. Gotta say me and my wife, Tessa here, are doin' just fine on a peanut farm. We're making good money and we love living in the country. So, I wanna thank you for everything you did for us."

Tessa was weeping. All of them sat down in the extra chairs that were provided by the nurses, Ken handing Tessa a box of tissues. Taking his phone out of his pocket he opened the app for the local classical music station and let it play. It would enable him to talk to Drew and Tessa without his father overhearing. He knew patients often overheard what was said in the operating room, under anesthesia, even while unconscious. He hoped his dad could hear them when they talked directly to him.

The soft music played as Ken turned to his brother and whispered softly, "His breathing is starting to change its pattern. You can see him breathing rapidly, then not breathing at all, even gasping. The end is near."

Just then Trish came through the door. "Paul couldn't get loose in time. He'll come when he's done with work."

Ken stood up and hugged her.

"The kids?"

With a friend's family. They're fine.

"Hi, Drew – Tessa. Are your boys here?"

"With friend's families, too."

"Ken?"

"He's fading fast, Trish. Please go hold his hand and talk to him. We all have."

Moving to the chair closest to her father she took his hand and began talking to him. Ken, Drew, and Tessa remained closer to the door, allowing Trish her private moment with their dad.

"Do you want me to get one of the nurses, or a doctor?" asked Drew.

"No, they know I'm a doctor. We'll let them know when it's over."

It was only half an hour before he took his last breath. There were tears on all of their faces as Ken rang the buzzer for the medical staff to enter.

The on-call doctor declared the time of death, shaking the hands of each of them while expressing his condolences. As many times as Ken had been present at situations identical to this one, where a patient died and he did the declaration, it never ceased to amaze him at the professional care given to the deceased. He'd watched nurses tenderly washing their bodies and carefully preparing them for the trip downstairs. He couldn't watch it this time.

Leading his family from the room, "Let's all go meet at my house. They'll take good care of him, and the funeral home will be here for him later this evening."

Driving home, his siblings following in their cars, he had to keep it together. While tears were streaming down his face he couldn't allow himself a full-blown bawling session, despite the need for one. Later, in the shower. He should have spent more time with his dad. He always had leave time in the Navy. He had no excuse. He just assumed his father was active and working hard, like always, and wouldn't even notice that he'd never come to visit. It wasn't like his dad contacted him either. But still...

Opening the garage door, the other two cars pulled into his driveway.

"I just talked to Paul," Trish closed the car door. "He's going to stay home, and the kids can come home to sleep if they want to. They'll come over as soon as we have the arrangements made."

"All of you are welcome to spend the night here. No need to drive all the way back. You're more than welcome to come to the funeral home with me tomorrow to make the arrangements, but I understand if you'd rather not. It won't be much since Dad had apparently taken care of all the necessary stuff. He showed me where all his papers were before... well, before."

Raising her hand, "I'd like to stay, Ken," Trish spoke lovingly, "and there is no way I'm going to have you go alone to the funeral home. I'll be at your side. We're family."

Drew looked at Tessa. "Well, it's a tossup, since we are only 30 minutes away, but yeah. I think we'll stay. Trish is right. We're family. Family does stuff together. The kids are happy to sleep over with their friends. I think they spend more time with them than they do with us anyway. We'll call Marie and make sure it's alright." Tessa pulled out her phone.

"I'll order some food," Ken dragged a menu out of a drawer. "What would all of you like?"

Going over the Domino's menu they chose three different pasta dishes to share. Adding some garlic bread twists, and cookie brownies for dessert, "Looks interesting" was all Tessa had to say.

"I have plenty of eggs, bread and bacon for breakfast. We can all eat lunch at a restaurant after we take care of the arrangements."

Trish looked over at her brother, "Sit, Ken. We all have puffy eyes and guilty feelings. It's normal and you know it. I think in the end he knew we all really loved him and were there for him."

"Yeah, all but good old Reed." His hand was on the table, his fingers scratching his palm.

"It is what it is, Ken." Taking her phone out of her back pocket again, "I'll call and leave a message for Reed that Dad has died. I'll tell him the obit will be in the paper and the Altmeyer Funeral Home web page. He won't be able to say we didn't let him know. Then the ball's in his court."

Tessa left the room, returning when she heard the doorbell. "I made up all the beds, Ken. Fresh towels in all the showers."

"Tessa, Tessa, Tessa! You didn't have to do that."

"Hadda be done you know. Drew's not gonna want to put his bare butt on any bare mattress."

Everyone burst out laughing.

"Thanks, Tessa."

"You're welcome, Ken."

And from Drew, emptying bags and setting everything out on the counter. "Okay you guys. Grab a plate and toe the line. I'll go first."

Tessa just shook her head. "Man's a food machine. Always starving."

It was always an eerie feeling walking into a funeral home, and for various reasons each of them had been there before when losing friends or co-workers. The somber atmosphere was like a cloak draped over all of them, holding them together. "So quiet," whispered Tessa. "And so cold," added Ken. The funeral assistant met them promptly and led them into a private conference room. The majority of the meeting was just making sure the paperwork was still correct.

"Do you wish to see the casket he ordered?"

They all looked at each other and nodded yes.

Ken swallowed hard as they were led to a beautiful walnut wood casket, with a high gloss stain and interior fabric of almond velvet. The assistant pointed out the spindled corners, locking mechanism solid walnut wood construction and other amenities. He was amazed to learn that his father had chosen a moderately priced casket when he could have well afforded a much more expensive one.

Looking around at the other caskets in the room Ken noticed that some were shaped differently and asked about it.

The attendant smiled. "The major difference is the container's shape. A coffin has six sides, and the top of the container is wider than the bottom. Basically, it's tapered to conform to the shape of a human's body. A casket is rectangular in shape. Also, the coffin has a removable lid while a casket's lid is hinged."

Standing next to one of the coffin's, "It looks like a Dracula bed, ah, coffin."

With a wide grin the attendant ran his hand over the coffin, "Precisely!"

With date and time settled they left for lunch before returning to their homes, each silent in his or her own way.

Death! It seemed to have consumed him lately. His father was at peace and suddenly he was thinking about Maddie's husband. If only she would share that with him, so he'd quit obsessing over it. It wasn't natural to be so preoccupied by an event which, in this time and place, likely had no bearing on anything having to do with Maddie. Or did it? Rain had started to hit his windshield just as he got home. Tossing his keys onto the kitchen counter he opened the back door to the covered back porch. A nice rain with no wind, coming straight down. He grabbed a lawn chair and sat down, closing his eyes to the pattering of the rain drops on the porch roof. Calming. He felt his shoulders relax and his head flop to the side…. Maddie, Maddie, I can't stop thinking about you. I want you with me.

As was usual there wasn't much new in her life. Maddie was still there for her mother but was glad there was a nurse there to take care of her for most of the day. She came at 10 and left at 8 and would also be available overnight when the need arose. As such Maddie had set up the extra bedroom for her use. Vanessa was wonderful with Dori, and the surprise was that Dori liked her. Dr. Foster had recommended her. Best of all she was a retired RN, and not just an aide she'd have to hire through an agency. It was nice to be able to go to the store, or just drive around, or have lunch with her school friends on weekends without having to worry about her mother. She would have loved the ability to go on dates with Ken, but, sighing heavily, that could never happen. She was as guilty as he was, and sometimes with total lack of conversation, things just go off the edge. She probably should have stayed by his bed and asked him why he lied. Too late now.

It was almost 8, so Maddie went back into the house to say goodnight to Vanessa. She was older than Maddie, maybe early 50's, with a heart of gold. She kept her blond hair short, and her slim and trim frame belied her strength. She could lift her mother with no problem. All she wore were scrub outfits. They were comfortable, she explained, and easy to clean if her charges got sick, or had accidents. She always carried a spare set in her car, just to be on the safe side. She was a widow, living alone, and therefore could easily spend the night if needed.

"How'd it go?"

"Your mom and I are getting along fine. I know sometimes, when people like me show up to care for them, it's like a rude awakening. They've managed to live in a certain state of denial, thinking they'll get better. And your mother is relatively young still. Sixty-Seven is not considered old anymore. It gets to be a double whammy. But we sat and read books together, played games, do puzzles, and watch television, as best she can with her vision being so bad. When she naps I take out my knitting and start clacking the needles. But so far she's cooperating and doing all I ask of her for exercise and food choices."

"I'm so glad we got you for her. It was getting beyond my control."

"Caregiving is not for the weak." She smiled at Maddie. "Sleep well and I'll be back at 10 tomorrow. Oh, one thing! I left your newspaper on the kitchen table. I guess all of us forgot to bring it in."

"Thanks. I appreciate it."

Following Vanessa out the door, Maddie looked around to be sure everything was in order. It was nautical twilight, that few moments between daylight and darkness when nature's sounds became muted for the night. Birds and squirrels had gone to bed. It was a time of calm each night, in many ways one of comfort. Glancing up at the sky she searched for Orion, her favorite constellation, and one of the harbingers of cooler weather approaching. Not yet. Not until mid-November, maybe another week or two. She kept hoping that Betelgeuse would go super nova while she was watching. Ya never knew about stuff like that! Could happen at any time. Noting that the bird bath was full of water she waved as Vanessa drove off, then went back inside.

Her nightly routine was to turn off all unnecessary lights and equipment, make sure all the doors were locked tightly and all the windows were down and locked. Satisfied, she went to check on her mother and found her sleeping. Wandering into the kitchen she made herself a cup of coffee, and spying the paper decided to flip through it. Maybe the Ask Amy column had some good advice for someone like her. She also enjoyed the Ask the Doctor… Yeah, sure! Glancing over the obituaries her eyes locked on a name. MARTIN ROBERT AVERY. Could that be Ken's father? She'd never heard his first name. She knew he had Alzheimer's but wasn't sure what his status was other than he was in a nursing home. Flipping through to the page of obituaries, there it was: Predeceased by wife Grace. Four children, Reed (Ruth), Drew (Tessa), Ken, and Patricia Sinclair (Paul), and four grandchildren. Memorial Service time and date were listed, as well as the location for the interment. Her hand went to her mouth, covering it in the sudden sadness. Ken must be devastated. He said he had lived with his father from the time he retired from the Navy until they had to place him in a home. Does every family have to suffer all the horrible ends of life? Alzheimer's, MS, Cancers, heart attacks… can't anyone get out of this life some normal kind of way, like falling asleep when you're 95 and not waking up? She took a deep breath and felt tears welling up in her eyes. No matter how upset she was about the intelligence/doctor thing her heart was breaking for Ken and his siblings. Standing, she took her full cup of coffee and dumped it down the drain. Could she sleep? She had no idea. Now thoughts of her mother were dancing through her head. The knowledge of how horrible it was going to get was upsetting her more than she would have thought possible. She was a horrible mother, but NO ONE deserved to die like that, in pain, in misery, unable to move, talk, eat, click the clicker to change the channel, or read a book. It was all gonna happen and she was going to have to watch the horror of it eating away at her mother. She rushed to the bathroom and poured a bath. The running water hid her sobbing. It scared her to death.

She hadn't heard from Ken in just over a month, but most of that was understandable since he would have been spending time with his father. Under better circumstances she would have been there for him, talked to him by phone, or kept up with text messages. Maybe she should have tried. He'd left the door open. Maybe she should have walked through it. Even sending him a simple message of condolences would have been a great idea. Why had it never occurred to her? Idiot! But she couldn't let it go. She had a black pair of slacks and a gray, sleeved shell. She would wear that with an overcoat and go to the funeral at least. She could stand way back so's not to be noticed, but she felt the pull to be there.

It was a short, simple service. Martin was at rest in the beautiful casket he had selected. A few of Martin's old buddies came to the viewing, which was followed by interment at Woodlawn. It was a small group with all four of the grandsons present. Only Reed and Ruth were missing. They were lucky to get a gorgeous day with moderate temperatures and a glowing sun. They couldn't have programmed it any better. Ken, Drew, and Paul sat stoically while Trish and Tessa cried softly. All four of the children behaved beautifully, a slight surprise since they had probably only seen their grandfather once if that. Ken had no idea.

The last thing to be done was for each of the siblings to stand by the casket and say a few words in private, laying a single dark crimson rose on top as a gesture of love. Trish was first, followed by Drew and lastly Ken. As he placed his rose on the casket the family gathered to walk together to the limo. Ken took Trish's hand as they started when something caught his attention. Off in the distance, maybe a hundred feet away, standing under a tree for shade... Maddie.

"Maddie!" Oh, God! Maddie!" He screamed and turning loose of Trish's hand he began to run towards her. Maddie had already turned and was walking away from him towards her own car. Leaving his family stunned he continued running until he caught up with her. She was crying. Ken was beside himself. Should he draw her into his arms? What should he say? Clearly she was there because she cared about him, right? He couldn't stand it anymore, "Oh, my god, Maddie, please don't leave. Give me a chance to explain. I am so sorry. Can you ever forgive me?"

His family held back watching to see if they would be needed or not. They weren't sure who she was but thought he had screamed the name Maddie. Trish held them all in a little group, "Give Ken a chance before we rush in and ruin everything." They all stood together, in silent agreement.

"Maddie, please. Give me a chance to explain. Please."

She nodded. Wiping away a tear, "I'm so sorry for your loss, Ken." Even with her eyes filled with tears she was the most gorgeous woman he'd ever seen, and he couldn't ignore his feelings for her any longer. Closing the gap between them he pulled her in for a hug. She accepted it, putting her head on his shoulder. "I'm so sorry, too, Ken. I'm as guilty as you are. Can you forgive me?"

When he lifted her chin and gave her a quick kiss his family knew they could approach, arriving in just a few seconds.

Through tears Maddie looked at them, "I'm so sorry for your loss." Ken just kept her tight to his chest with his arm around her waist. "Folks, if you haven't guessed, this is Maddie Davis."

Each of them moved forward and quietly introduced themselves, holding onto her hand for just a moment.

"Maddie," Ken began, "The limo is going to take us to my home. No one else will be there except us. Will you join us?"

She was starting to shake her head when Trish reached out and touched her arm, "Oh, please do, Maddie. All of us want to get to know you. Ken has told us so much about you and I know Tessa and I already think you'll fit right in with our fun ways. Please join us."

Several mumbles and head nods from the other families convinced her to say yes.

"Then, we'll see you at my house in just a few minutes, okay?"

"Okay." She managed a small smile.

Ken spent the limo ride home trying to remain calm. It was hard when he kept wavering between terror and excitement. He simply had to do everything right. He had to get her back in his life.

She wondered where Reed was when she got to the house and was seated at the kitchen table with all the rest of them gathered around. The kids were in a bedroom with television and games. There was food galore, all over the table and counters, and hot coffee was soon being distributed. A good hour was spent on small talk and memories of their dad, and as the day wore on things lightened up quite a bit. She found herself watching each member of his family and they interacted with each other, including her in the conversations as well. One thing was for sure. Those folks loved each other, very much. Both Trish and Tessa could talk you under the table and seemed more like sisters than in-laws. Coming from what was likely different backgrounds made it all the more special. Both Paul and Drew were good looking guys, again, in different ways. Paul was like a stately cop, yet it was easy to tell he was an outdoorsman with his dark tan and strong, muscular body. Both he and Drew were in great shape, but she could see the country-boy in Drew, too. She felt totally comfortable and didn't miss the fact that Ken never took his eyes off her.

"I hear you feed peanuts to the squirrels," Drew winked at her, leaning so far back in his chair she was sure he'd be on the floor with the slightest movement.

"Little critters think I'm a chef," she winked back.

Drew howled. Tessa smacked him gently with the back of her hand. That smack almost did him in as he swiveled in his chair to regain his balance, narrowing his eyes at his wife. "I'll fix ya up for life, little woman, if you marry this lug of a brother of mine."

"DREW AVERY, you shut your mouth you heathen. Don't you go embarrassing Maddie like that. Now *I'm* gonna give her peanuts for life and you ain't got nothin' to say about it. And there's no requirements to it, either!"

Drew just grinned.

Ken looked mortified.

Maddie just held up her hand. It was impulsive and she knew it was the only way she was going to be strong enough to say what she needed to say. They all turned toward her.

"I owe Ken an explanation about my husband's death. It's the elephant in the room. I can only think that I held back because it was the most traumatic time of my life and talking about it brought it all back to me. As a result, I could never find the words. But I'll find them now. That is, if it's alright. I can always wait til later to tell Ken privately."

The room went dead silent. She looked each one of them in the eyes, then, seeing no disagreement, took a deep breath.

Chapter 14

Maddie gave one final glance to Ken, then folded her hands on her lap.

"Mark was a pilot, flying the FA-18F Hornet. We got married in 2006. I didn't know his parents. They were unhappy that Mark and I had eloped, but Mark told them it was only because he had just gotten orders for California and we didn't want to be separated for two or three years, three thousand miles apart. We were transferred to Lemoore, California, and VFA-122. He did Skype and talk to his parents regularly, but I was usually in the background, pretty much at their doing. Two years later we were back at Oceana, and Mark was attached to VFA-103. Little did we know he would be heading out on the Ike in 2009, to the Persian Gulf and Enduring Freedom. We wrote, we texted, we videoed when possible. Then I had just gotten home from my teaching job when a car pulled into the driveway and a Navy Commander, and another woman officer told me…Ken had…" she swallowed and took in a short breath "died." Maddie paused, looking down long enough to gather her courage and keep the tears at bay. "I asked if he was shot down, and they said no, it was a landing accident." She gulped. "That was all they knew. Later I was told that both he and Mike, his back seater, ejected at a low altitude and had also died. Mark had told his parents, even before we were married, that he wanted to be buried at the Albert G. Horton cemetery in Suffolk, so the Navy airlifted his body back.." She paused, bowing her head, and breathing slowly. "I got letters from his Commanding Officer, and his roommate sent all of his personal belongings. It was shattering. Each item in the box…his wedding ring. I didn't know pilots took off their wedding rings when they flew. I had only met his parents very briefly through Skype. and they were destroyed. He was their only child. They came down from Baltimore for the funeral, upset that he wasn't being buried back at their home cemetery. It was tense."

Trish moved her chair closer to Maddie and placed a reassuring hand on her arm. "I'm so sorry, Maddie. I can't imagine…"

A sudden sharp, agonizing whisper interrupted, "Oh, no. Oh, my God." All heads snapped to Ken. His hands were shaking. He was leaning forward in his chair, his elbows on his knees, covering his face with his hands. Rubbing his forehead with his fingers, then running them through his hair, he repeated in a whisper, "Oh, dear God."

"What? Ken, what's wrong?" Trish let go of Maddie's arm to reach for Ken.

Finally lifting his head, he looked straight at Maddie, his face ashen, a flash of sadness clouding his eyes. "Oh, my God, Maddie, Mark died on my operating table."

Maddie went white. There was absolute dead silence in the room. No one moved an inch. A split-second later Maddie slid to the floor, unconscious.

"KEN," Tessa yelled at him as he sat frozen in his chair. Snapping out of it at the sound of his name he dropped to the floor to check on Maddie.

"She's breathing. She's just fainted. Did anyone see if she hit her head?"

"No," Drew slid down next to him, "She just glided down."

"She was in one of the soft chairs so that's good." Ken reached down to pick her up as Tessa stood up to make room for her on the couch. Carefully laying her down he sat down in the chair Drew brought to him. "Her pulse and breathing are normal. I think she'll come out of it quickly. It was just a shock."

"Ya think?" Drew exclaimed.

"Drew," Tessa gave him a good slug to his shoulder, "Button it. None of us was expecting this. Ken had no way of knowing. She never told him any of that stuff."

"Sorry, brother."

Ken nodded, just as Maddie started to stir. With a groan she opened her eyes, looking at everyone staring at her. "What?" she said trying to sit up.

"Stay down for a few minutes, Maddie," Ken gently lowered her shoulder back down. "You've had a shock… well… all of us have had a shock. I'll get you some water so you can sit up slowly."

"I'll get it," Paul headed for the kitchen,

Maddie's eyes were glazed over, and after several long breaths, "You were there, with Mark, when he died?"

"Yes, Maddie." Taking her hand, "He was still alive when they rescued him. I was the ship's surgeon on duty. We did everything we could to save him, but his injuries were just too severe."

"Did he say anything? What were his injuries?" She asked softly, looking straight into his eyes.

Ken knew he needed to tell her whatever she asked for. "No, Maddie. He never spoke. He was brought in unconscious, barely alive. His back was broken, Maddie, and his spinal cord was severed. He had severe head injuries when he went through the canopy. He died within minutes of arriving in the operating room. I won't tell you it was a blessing, Maddie, because I didn't know him, but he would have been a quadriplegic had he lived."

An agonizing sound came out of her throat, then Maddie started sobbing and shaking as Ken held on to both of her hands. "I'm so very, very sorry, Maddie."

Regaining some control, "Help me sit up, please, Ken." As he brought her to a sitting position Paul handed her the water. "Thank you, Paul."

"What about Mike?" She held the glass tightly with both hands wrapped around it, her hands shaking and water splashing over the edge of the glass.

Covering her hands with his, and helping her take a sip of the water, "He died instantly. He was almost lost at sea, but the helicopter found him and brought him back to the ship."

"Mark wasn't wearing his wedding ring?"

"Most pilots and crew take all rings off for safety reasons. They can get caught on equipment and rip a finger off, and it's also possible any number of things could cause the hand to be injured and the finger to swell, necessitating surgery or cutting the ring off. Medical staff could have removed it as they brought him into the operating room for surgery, too."

Maddie nodded. "I guess this can be a nice story for your family. Coincidence and all that. I'm so embarrassed – fainting and crying. It's been a long time, you know," half smiling in an attempt to alibi her passing out. Odd though, it was cathartic to have told the story. She felt a sense of freedom, even with the awkward display of fainting. As she struggled to stand, Tessa stood in front of her. "Can I tell you my story, Maddie? No one knows it but me and Drew there." She waved her hand towards Drew. "The family will keep my story to themselves, just like they will yours. You don't mind, do ya hon?" She looked lovingly at Drew.

"Nope, Tessa. It's your story to tell."

Maddie snuggled back down on the couch and Tessa took over the chair Ken had been seated in. With Ken sitting next to her, his arm around her shoulders, Maddie felt a bit stronger.

"Well, now, it's like this." She brushed off her hands as if there was flour all over them. "We all got something screwy in our pasts if we think long enough about it. I wasn't the nicest girl on the planet. Far from it. Left home young. Hung out with the guys if you know what I mean. Managed to get a job working on a peanut farm for, well, peanuts. Not much money that's for sure, but enough to have a bit of fun now and again. Did manage to skip the drugs though. But *so many* good-lookin' guys working on that farm, and when we got paid, off we go to the saloon. I had my own guy, for sure, and I go to the loo, and come back and some red-headed, ah," she swiveled her head making sure the kids hadn't come into the room, "bitch, is sitting on my man's lap, rubbin' him up and down. So, I rip her off his lap by the hair-do and I'm tossing her around," Tessa had her arms swinging in the same circular motion, "by her hair and she's just a-screamin', and a-yellin', and a-cussin'. Then the cops show up and I go to jail in handcuffs." Tessa snorts. "And my man? Well, that a-hole just went over and was dancin' with that bitch as I was being dragged out the door, just a-kickin' and making them cops work hard to get me to jail."

Maddie sat staring at her in amazement, her eyes popping open more with each new sentence. No one else is making any sounds as they seem equally as engrossed in her story.

"Well, I'm not sure who called Drew here, but lo and behold I'm let out of jail cause he bailed me out. Now why would he bail me out, I'm worrying. He says to me it's cause I work for him, and he takes care of his crew. So, I reach up and kiss him for it. Now he's all shocked and backin' away from me, and I say, 'That's okay, Mr. Avery, I'm just thankin' you.' Then he looks at me, like it's the first time he's really *seen* me. We was married a week later. True story. So there y'all."

Drew just sat there with the biggest ear to ear grin on his face. "Got me the best woman on the planet…" he looks over at Ken… "well for me, anyway!"

Maddie reached over and grabbed Tessa in a hug. "You are simply wonderful, Tessa. I'm gonna come out and see that peanut farm of yours!"

"Good. I'll give you your first bag of squirrel peanuts," she glared at Drew with a half-smile on her lips. Drew just chuckled.

The ice was broken. Everyone laughed.

Tessa stood up, "Well, since both Maggie and me have shared our darkest secrets, who's next?" She looked around the room. "What, no man got some kinda deep, dark secret? Buncha chickens."

"ME!" Shouted Trish. Waving her hands in the air. I'll tell my story. Sliding forward to the edge of her chair and stapling her fingers, "There I was, one of the Neptune Festival princesses, all dressed up like Mother taught me, in a gown and totally beautiful, well, by what her standards were anyway. The parade had ended, and I was getting off the float when my heel caught on something, and I was flying backwards. Landed in the arms of the handsomest guy ever. I mean, WHOA! My eyes bugged out when I saw that face. He lets me down easy and says, 'I'd marry you, but I don't think you'd like my job.' I'm standing there stupid, just staring at those gorgeous brown eyes, and ask him 'what job'. He looks down at me with those gorgeous chocolate eyes and says, 'I'm a Federal Wildlife Officer and you don't look like you'd fit in very well.'"

All eyes turned to Paul, who was smiling and nodding his head.

"What does a Wildlife Officer do? I ask"

"We spend a lot of time outdoors fishing and camping and getting our hands dirty, was his answer."

Paul sauntered over to stand next to his wife, "I gave her the simple version," he grinned.

Looking up at him, "So, I asked him why wouldn't I fit in very well? And he tells me my hair is too sprayed down, and for sure my fingernails didn't qualify me for that kind of life. Now, I'm here to tell you I couldn't take my eyes off this guy, so I tell him to take down my phone number and call me in three days. All this hair spray and inch long fingernail stuff are fake, I tell him, and I'll prove it to him. Three days later he calls, and by then I've had time to comb out my hair, cut off my fingernails, buy several pairs of blue jeans and plain old blouses and be ready for a date. We went fishing! Six months later we were married. Best fall ever!" Reaching up she took his hand and squeezed it. "God, I love this man!"

Everyone applauded.

"Hey Mom, we're hungry back there."

"Bring the guys out and have at it, Dale."

Pointing her finger at Maddie, with a smile, "And I want you and Ken to come over to the Eastern Shore. We can go camping."

Drew snickered. "I'm hungry. Gotta beat the kids to more food."

They were well into their second round of food when the doorbell rang.

Lifting a finger Ken indicated he would get it. Still with half a sandwich in his hand he headed to the door.

"REED?" he gasped, loud enough for the group behind him to hear.

Like a mosquito looking for blood, a form swished past Ken and landed squarely on Reed, almost toppling him over. As he staggered backwards he managed to keep his balance as Trish wrapped her legs around him and peppered him with kisses.

"Hello, Kiddo," he grinned, kissing her on the forehead.

Still holding his sandwich, Ken just stood there stunned.

"Thought I wasn't gonna come, didn't you?"

"True enough."

"Well, can I come in?"

"Oh, sure," moving aside.

Reed walked into the main room and stood quietly, eyeing each person, one by one. "Well, I recognize Drew and that's about all, I'm ashamed to say."

Trish came to his side and led him forward. "The lady in the chair is Tessa, Drew's wife. And on the couch is Maddie. She and Ken are dating." She hoped that was close enough without upsetting anyone. She wasn't sure they were dating but could hope they were. She really liked Maddie, both for her ability to overcome the trauma of her life and because she knew Ken loved her. That spoke volumes. "And this is my husband, Paul."

Reed shook hands with each of them in turn.

"Drew's two kids, and my two kids are back in the bedroom running video games!"

Reed grinned a knowing grin. "I guess all of you are wondering what's going on."

Ken spoke, "Ruth couldn't come?" He eyed Reed, a bit suspiciously.

"About that..." Reed rubbed the back of his neck and smiled. "Seems I wanted to come to my father's funeral." He turned to look at Ken, "Ever since we had that dinner I got to thinking, THAT WAS MY BROTHER I just had dinner with, and we treated him like some fly on the wall. My dear wife was even worse toward you, like you were a busboy interrupting her meal. I couldn't get that out of my mind. So, when Trish called me that Father had died, I read the obit and told Ruth I was coming to the funeral. It was a last-minute decision, sort of, but she pitched a holy fit. Seems we were supposed to go to some social thing, and quite frankly I'm more than a bit tired of her social things."

Ken pulled up a chair and offered it to Reed. He sat down. Seems the reception was taking on a lot of happenings, and as much as he was worried about Maddie, after her fainting spell, he was also shocked to see his brother arrive. But he kept his eyes on Maddie, as Reed began his tale.

"There I was, in my nice suit, and I just had told her the worst imaginable thing possible. I was going to put MY family ahead of HER social event. Really now, enough was enough. I went over to the desk, took out a copy of the prenup she signed when we got married, handed it to her, told her she could have the house in the Northern Neck on the Chesapeake Bay, and I wanted her gone and out of the house by the end of the day."

"Seriously?" gasped Trish.

"Yup! She left in a huff, and I called the bank, took her name off the accounts, closed out all the credit cards and will put my monster of a house up for sale soon. It's in my name only!"

Each person had a different look on their face. Trish was smiling, Drew was scratching his head, Tessa side-eyed him in disbelief, and Maddie just looked at Ken to see if she could figure it all out. Was this for real? Like Trish, Ken was smiling.

"Welcome back to the family, Brother," Ken leaned down to shake his hand, but Reed stood up and grabbed him in a manly hug. Trish joined them, and with a gentle nudge from Tessa, Drew got up and became the fourth in the huddle.

As they broke apart, "Well, that's why I'm late. I did stop at the cemetery and put flowers on Dad's grave."

"Won't she sue you for a pile of money," asked Tessa, clearly thinking about how swiftly he'd booted his wife out the door.

"Ironclad prenup. She comes from a great deal of wealth herself, so she'll just go back to her Daddy's money. If I had to guess she's already gotten all her clothing and jewelry out of the house, won't care a whit about the furniture, will ask me for the deed to the Northern Neck house, and be gone."

"WOW!" Maddie had finally managed to express herself. She was slowly regaining her strength, but still had questions, and still felt the residual shock of hearing that Ken had tried to save Mark. It was just too much to digest; her mind felt scrambled.

"Pity the Northern Neck," Reed surmised. "I doubt they're ready for that level of social life."

"After you sell," began Ken, "why don't you move in with me. I'll admit it's a small house, but maintenance is easy and it's convenient. You can move your office to the Town Center and go on from there."

"I'll certainly consider that, Ken. It sounds like a good plan. It will be a few weeks before I can get it all together, but I thank you for the offer."

"Then again, I might even be selling this house before long myself. You can buy it from me, switch out the furniture for what you like from your current house, and be all set to go."

Reed nodded. "I like that."

Maddie just sat there, almost in a panic. What? He was planning to sell? Where was he going to go? Had he just led her here to get her to tell her story out of his own curiosity? He'd kissed her at the cemetery! Was that all for show? Now that he'd heard her story and knew how Mark had died was he going to just move on? Was it a ploy of his...all that 'please forgive me' stuff to get her to agree to come here with everyone? His family was watching them. She felt a knot in the pit of her stomach and watched as Ken led Reed to the food-filled table and handed him a plate. They stood off in the corner, talking privately. She figured they were making arrangements for Reed to move in with him, or even buy the house already. She felt the knot grow heavier in her gut. No, no, no, this couldn't be happening. Had she and Ken grown that far apart so soon? She looked over at him, so animated with his brother, smiling and gesturing, his arms swinging and his head nodding. What were they taking about? He'd only glanced at her once, that she'd caught. She saw them both take seats at the table. Maybe they were planning the big bachelor party when Reed was free again. Snapping her head back she noticed Tessa watching her carefully.

"You okay, hon?"

Nodding, "I guess it's just been an overwhelming day."

"Well, that's for damn sure," was all Tessa could come up with.

After everyone took last dibs on the food, and the ladies helped put the leftovers in containers to either take home with them or leave in the fridge for Ken to munch on, they gathered their respective children and began leaving.

Walking up to Maddie, Tessa tapped her arm. "Now you listen up, Maddie. I don't think you have anything to worry about with Ken, there. We're all pretty sure he's head over heels; he just needs a jolt of something to recognize it. Meanwhile, if you've ever a mind, you just git on over to Suffolk and visit us on the farm. I know your momma is in a bad way, but if you need someone to talk to, that's where I am." Handing her a piece of paper, "Those are our phone numbers and address. Put them on that phone of yours."

Maddie broke into a smile, trying her best to hide the tears forming in her eyes. "I'll do that, and thanks so much Tessa."

"Now, I'll grab those youngins and we'll git on our way!"

It continued to be a struggle to hold back tears as Maddie said goodbye to Trish and her family, who also told her to stop over anytime. All that was left was Reed, and he and Ken were still sitting at the table, laughing,

"Thanks for everything, Ken," Maddie waved at him from the family room. She was holding on to her overcoat.

Ken jumped up. "Where did everyone go?" NO! He couldn't let her leave. Not now. It amazed him that everyone had vanished, but he couldn't let Maddie get away.

"Home. They all have a ways to drive and wanted to get home before dark. They waved at you, but you were so busy with Reed they didn't want to disturb you. They said to tell you thanks."

Taking her coat from her arm and hanging it up again, "I need you to stay. We need to talk."

"I, ah…"

"Hush. Reed said he's just leaving, too. He's curious if Ruth might have burned the house down or something."

"Seriously?"

"Hell hath no fury…" he turned to shake Reed's hand as he moved toward the door. "Okay, Reed. Keep in touch. And welcome back to the family."

"I'm glad to be back, and nice to meet you Maddie."

Maddie smiled as Reed walked out the door.

Turning, Ken quickly boxed Maddie in against the wall. "Who's watching your mom?"

"Vanessa."

"Who's Vanessa?"

"A retired nurse."

"Does she have to get home for any reason, I mean, what are her hours?"

"She comes at 10 and leaves at 9. She lives alone now."

"No pets?"

"Why all the questions Ken? I need to get home so she can leave."

"It's not 9 yet. Not even close."

Trying to duck under his arms, Ken just lowered them, still holding her captive.

"Call her and offer her double to stay the night, under the table. I'll pay."

"No, Ken, I…" He shut her up with a kiss, and one she would never forget. Practically sliding down the wall, she held on to Ken to keep from falling. Oh, good heavens, she could hardly breathe.

"Call her," he whispered in her ear. "Please."

"Ah, um," her mouth opened and closed, barely able to speak, she needed to slow her breathing. She opened her eyes, and they were so glassed over she could barely see Ken. A soft puff of air left her mouth as she worked to shake the cobwebs out of her brain. It took her a moment to calm her hands enough to pull her cell phone out of her pocket. She probably sounded like a drunk idiot, but Vanessa was more than happy to spend the night for double pay. In cash.

Ken took the phone out of her hand and started kissing her again, slowly, moving inch by inch. Her mouth, her cheeks, her neck, and she shivered as his lips moved downward…how had he opened her blouse without her knowing it? It was as if she was floating on the clouds, the heat of the sun pouring into her. His kisses were at the top of her bra and then the bra was free. She couldn't move, she couldn't even breathe, yet he held her against the wall so tightly – she thought for sure she would turn into a puddle and melt to the floor. "I want you, Maddie," he whispered in her ear. She groaned as his hand covered her breast. "So beautiful… I need you, Maddie," he spoke softly. Her blouse was coming off and he was backing her up, down a hallway, through a door, and as he laid her down on the bed, "I love you, Maddie. God in heaven, I love you."

"Ken…" she reached up for him. Every nerve came alive as she felt him gently baring her body, slowly kissing her, touching her, making her insane with need. Reaching for his clothes she helped as he shed them, and suddenly she was naked with Ken beside her. The ecstasy of his kisses and touch was so intense she could only want for more. She met each of his kisses with a hunger of her own. So many years had passed since a man had loved her, and a spark of fear flashed through her head. Could she be the woman he thought she was? It had been so long, but the ache was too intense. Nothing could stop her. "You are so gorgeous, so beautiful," his words were sweet and tender, taking her higher and higher. His kisses never stopped, and as they became one she arched into him, holding on to him, moving with him, speaking his name as she shuddered. At the same instant Ken groaned in his own release, falling gently down and to her side. "Oh, so incredible," was all he could say. His breathing was heavy, and he could feel his heart rapidly thumping in his chest. He was shocked to find himself pulling Maddie into his arms. Cuddling was never part of any sex he had had before. But he needed it now, felt content now, and didn't want it to ever end. She hadn't said a word, but she *had* responded to his love. It was a good sign. Gently touching her face, he was pleased to see that she was asleep. He gently pulled the covers over both of them, drifting off to dreamland, too.

Chapter 15

The sun, streaming in from the window, was bright when she wakened. For a moment she panicked, seeing nothing that she recognized. The sudden sensation that she wasn't alone in bed gave her a start, then she remembered. Squinting at the shimmering rainbow patterns in the glass, she knew it was Ken behind her. Slowly turning she was surprised to see him on his side, looking at her.

"Good morning," he reached up and pushed the stray hair from her face. "You are so beautiful, Maddie. You have me so tied up in knots I don't know if I'm coming or going half the time." He leaned down to kiss her.

"Good morning to you, too." She lifted a finger and began to draw a line on his chest. Focusing for a moment on a small section of his chest, "What's this? A new scar?" She gently drew a line down the scar with her fingernail. "It wasn't there when you took off your shirt during the rain storm. Is this where you got shot?"

"It's just a flesh wound, nothing major, like I said."

"They put you in the hospital for just a flesh wound?" She found that hard to believe. "The TV said you had a gunshot wound. This looks like a bit more than a flesh wound, Ken."

"Really, it's just a grazing wound. I'm fine. Totally fine Maddie. I just got scraped is all." He sure didn't want to bother her with the details, and it hadn't done any real harm. No point in making her worry unnecessarily. "They just wanted to make sure no infections set in because of the gun powder. Perfectly reasonable." Hopefully she didn't know a lot about gun powder and infections.

Maddie was sure it was more than that, but she let it go. She'd had such a wonderful night and that was the most important thing. Just looking into his eyes made her melt, and as if he could see it he began kissing her again, until she was begging for him to fill her one more time.

After both of them had showered, Ken promised her a good breakfast before she had to go relieve Vanessa. As she began dressing she couldn't stop thinking about the scar. It was upsetting her. It was too fresh and too large, so she was pretty sure it was more serious than he let on.

He'd made such gentle love to her she felt no pain, only a deep connection she never expected. He'd told her he loved her. Did that make her happy? Actually, yes it did, but only if he meant it. It wasn't unusual for a man to say whatever he felt he needed to say to get a woman into his bed. Ken didn't seem like that kind of man. At least she certainly hoped not. Finger combing her hair she walked out into the kitchen to find Ken sitting at the table, a cup of coffee in his hand for her.

Staring him straight in the eye, "I know what happened, I just don't know how it happened." She couldn't help the shy smile she gave him, her eyes downcast just a little. She wasn't embarrassed, but she had been completely caught off guard by the events of the last evening.

"We didn't use any protection, Ken."

He smiled and handed her the coffee. "It's easy. I was frantic to have you. I love you. And we wanted each other, or it wouldn't have happened. One word from you would have stopped me. And I knew from what you said you hadn't any time for romance. And I haven't been with anyone for, hmm... three years at least. As a physician I am tested regularly, too."

She considered what he had just told her. Ever since moving in with her mother her periods had been irregular, which she blamed on stress. It had been two years, at least, but her doctor had even thought she might be at the beginning of an early menopause since she'd gone through puberty at a very young age. Stress certainly wasn't helping, he had agreed, but he also told her that recent studies found that girls who began their periods before the age of 12 were 30% more likely to have an early menopause, between the ages of 40 and 44. It was possible, she guessed. She'd started at age ten. So maybe that's what was going on. She had just quit worrying about it. She considered asking Ken for his opinion, but he was a surgeon, not an OB/GYN, and likely wouldn't have any idea.

Maddie nodded. "Well, if it means anything I think maybe I love you, too."

"You think?"

"I'm fairly sure, but you don't know me well enough to tell me you love me, Ken. And really, I don't know you well enough either. It's hard... I'm so conflicted, but so drawn to you it makes me crazy. And obviously it doesn't take much for you to turn me into melted butter."

He had to grin at that. Melted butter was very good. Taking her free hand and holding it on his lap, "Maddie, my love, all I do is think about you. Day, night, hot weather, cold weather, rain, snow."

"We haven't had any snow, Ken."

"I would have been thinking of you when it came. Honest to God, Maddie, I'm as stunned by all this as you probably are. I never, ever thought I would fall in love, but every time I look at you I see something else that makes me care. You've taken on the responsibility for your mother, despite her bullying. You love animals, nature, the moon, and stars. You've a very forgiving nature, and not just me, but your mother and most especially your brother. And you're beautiful."

"Enough, already." She held up her hand. "I am what I am is all. And I'm definitely not beautiful. Plain Jane, that's me."

"Exactly, beautiful, gorgeous, no affectations, down to earth Maddie." Stroking her hand and looking down, "I'd ask you to move in with me if I thought you could. But I know your mother wants and needs you there."

Did she hear him right? He was actually asking her to move in with him? "Ken, I love that you want me to move in, but don't you think it's a bit sudden?"

"Nope. I knew you forgave me when you showed up at the funeral for Dad. My heart soared when I saw you standing there. Am I right?"

"Well, yes. I've missed you terribly. I make excuses to check the birds outside or look out the window. I felt so bad for being such a jerk. I mean, does it really matter if you're a doctor or a spy? And why did you do that anyway?" She turned her face up to look at him, wrinkling her brow.

"Doctors get tired of questions. I can be in a line at Walmart and if I were to mention I was a doctor I'd have five people start to ask me questions. It's worse at parties. They hound you with their ingrown toenails and creaky bones. Lawyers do it, too. They make up occupations to avoid legal questions. I asked Reed that last night when I told him about you, and he said absolutely. Lawyers can be good liars."

Her stomach growled as she laughed. "So, no more lies then?"

"No more lies, that's a promise. As of this moment the slate is clear."

"Okay."

"I do have eggs and toast."

"I'm starving."

He cooked while she watched, surprised at how organized he was while making eggs, toast, grits, and bacon all at the same time.

"I need to get home and pay Vanessa." She patted her full stomach. "That was very good. Thank you."

"Money's by your purse."

"No, Ken, I can pay her." Scrunching down her eyebrows in thought, "except I don't have that much cash on me right now."

"Money's by your purse, and so is a key to this house."

She sighed.

"Maggie, my love, last night was the best night of my 46 years. I want as many repeats as I can get until I can convince you to move in with me. I know you think it's too soon, but I want every chance I can get to know more about you and have you get to know me. Hire twenty-four-hour care for you mother. Move in with me. Get to know me better. I want you in my life, Maddie."

"Can we just take it one day at a time for a while?"

"As long as I see you every day," he looked at her in earnest... "Sure!"

"When I heard you tell Reed you'd sell him your house I thought you might be moving."

"Ask *me* to move in with *you* and see what happens."

"Oh, my gosh, can you even imagine what my mother would have to say about that? She'd buy an extra cane and start using them as drum sticks."

He rolled his eyes and smiled. "Can I see you tonight?"

"Let me see what's going on with Mother. I don't know how often Vanessa can stay overnight, but maybe she'd be willing more often than not. Mother does sleep a lot, but I really should try to eat most dinners with her."

"Call me, regardless, will you?"

"Yes." She leaned over and gave him a kiss. "I gotta go feed critters," she laughed.

Vanessa smiled a broad smile when Maddie handed her the money. "Mrs. Davis, this means so much to me. I'm trying to save up enough money to go spend time with my daughter and grandson in Hawaii. She's married to a man in the Navy and will be there for the next three years. When Dr. Foster heard about my wanting to go he gave you my name in case you were looking for a good nurse. I used to work with him. I have nothing at my condo to worry about. No kid left, no dogs or cats. So, I'm very grateful for the chance to stay over more often. I'll save every penny."

"Well, Vanessa, you've got yourself a deal! And call me Maddie. How did it go last night?"

"I left my door open, like you do, and the horn was right by her bed if she needed me, but she never used it once."

"She usually sleeps through the night, but I could never leave her alone."

"I completely understand. I know you told me I could use that spare room, but would it be alright if I bought over a few clothes, so I'd have a change the next day. The extra set of scrubs I keep in my car is rather an emergency sort of thing."

"Bring your whole wardrobe, Vanessa!"

They both smiled and hugged. Vanessa was maybe fifty-one or two? Maddie felt like she'd struck gold getting her to help. Even better, her mother seemed to like her. Odd, but very nice. Maddie now knew they could come to some kind of arrangement.

Walking into her mother's room she found her sitting up in her easy chair. "How are you feeling today, Mother?"

"Whersch Nessa?"

"She went home."

"Like her. Takes goosh care of me."

"Yes, she does. I'm glad you like her."

"Plays games, n does pusheles and keeps me occupied. You never did. Not once."

It was getting harder, and harder to understand the words her mother was saying, the slurring of her speech slowly becoming more pronounced. Biting her tongue, "I'm sorry. But I had an entire house to take care of if you think about it. All Vanessa has to do is stay and play games and do puzzles with you."

"Hrumph."

"What would you like for lunch?"

"Too early for lunch."

"Yes, I know, but do you have any requests?" Geeze, Maddie thought. Why does everything have to be so hard?

"If we still have any tuna schalad, a sammich."

"I just made it yesterday morning so there should be plenty."

"When Nesha back?"

"I'm not sure, but she'll be bringing back a lot of her clothing so she can be here all day and all night for you."

"Oh, really?" Her mother actually broke into a grin.

"Yes, really,"

"You gonna schtart running round, aren't you? Abanson me for some man."

"His name is Ken, Mother, and yes," she sighed, "I'll be spending more time with him."

Her mother just reached over to the nightstand and picked up a book to read. Maddie just shook her head. There was likely no way her mother could read anymore with her eyes the way they were, but there was no point in saying anything.

Starting a load of laundry and making sure there was tuna salad in the fridge, she went out to feed the birds. "I'm sorry I missed your feeding last night, guys. I'll make up for it right now. I know it's getting cold, and you need to get those peanuts stored." Looking up into the tree she saw one of the squirrels splayed around a branch, looking down at her. She felt bad that they'd gone to bed without their evening food. And people would think she was crazy if she said that out loud. She had barely made it back to the garage door when she saw squirrels coming across the street. There were enough peanuts on the ground and enough sunflower seed in the feeder for now.

The fish was frying for dinner when she heard the door opening. Vanessa had been given a key to use in case of an emergency, and now she walked into the house dragging a large suitcase. Maddie smiled, "there's plenty of fish and French fries to go around," she said over her shoulder.

"I'll just take you up on that, then."

"Excellent. Go ahead and put your suitcase away. Dinner will be ready shortly."

"First, I want to make a deal with you," Vanessa sat down.

"Sure."

"Ah, okay. Listen, my condo is paid for. My utilities are minimal, and HOA is paid for the year. I don't want you to worry that if you pay me my hourly rate I'll be gone in one month, heading for Hawaii. Anyway," she lowered her voice, "I really like you and your mother. I'm having a great time with her, as odd as that might sound." She stood and showed Maddie a piece of paper. "It took me some time to get back here. I figured all this out and this is a fair amount to pay me each month, give me one day off a week, and I'll just live here like I'm your aunt or something. It will be nice to have company, someone to eat dinner with and talk to. Very nice compromise for me."

Maddie looked down at the sheet and almost choked. "That's not nearly enough, Vanessa."

"Maddie," Vanessa looked down at her toes, "To be honest, you're mom isn't doing well. I don't expect to be here very long, and if we make this arrangement for payment it will get me where I want to go, and if you feel guilty about it then just add some kind of bonus at the end."

Maddie gulped, finding it hard to hold back the tears. "Vanessa…," She flipped the fish, "I can well afford your normal rates, but you'll see that in the bonus then."

"Good. Now, let me run this suitcase back to my room, and get the grand lady into the kitchen for dinner."

They were chattering like magpies when Vanessa wheeled her mother into the kitchen. It was like the weight of the earth had been taken off her shoulders. Vanessa had her mother laughing and talking fairly well, despite the setbacks caused by the MS. Slurring made it difficult to understand her at times, but Vanessa seemed to get it all with little trouble. Odd. She could speak well enough with Vanessa. When she had a problem lifting the spoon or fork to her face, Vanessa simply reached over and helped her. Maddie was almost in tears as she watched the seemingly natural friendship that had developed between Vanessa and her mother. At least as far as her mother was concerned she could relax. If only she could relax as easily thinking about Ken.

Vanessa moved her mother into the family room and turned on the television. Maddie picked up the plates and began loading the dishwasher when her phone rang.

"Hey."
"Hey, yourself, Ken," she spoke quietly.
"Can you come over tonight?"
"We just finished dinner, and Vanessa just took Mother into the family room. Let me see how it goes. This is her first day, full time, so I'll wait until she puts her to bed. That should be in about an hour."
"I've missed you all day."
She felt that warm glow of contentment at those words. *"I missed you, too. Can I call you back in an hour or so?"*
"Absolutely. I'll be here waiting."

In less than an hour Vanessa almost pushed her out the door.

"She's already asleep. You get out of here. I'll see you tomorrow morning. Then you can tell me about your young man!"

It was after dark when Maddie arrived at Ken's. "I hope I'm not assuming anything, but I brought a change of clothing."

Kissing her, "I asked you to move in, Maddie. Bring your whole wardrobe next time." He began kissing her in earnest. She could barely breathe. His kisses were like some kind of magic pill, reducing her to mush, willing to follow him anywhere. Pulling back, "I can't think straight when you're kissing me like that," at which point he began kissing her neck. Her purse fell off her shoulder, hitting the floor with a thud.

"Ken, I…"

"Hmm," as he continued to kiss her neck, his hands moving slowing up from her waist.

"Ahhh," how could he undress her so quickly. Oh, he was a doctor. But nurses did all that didn't they? Taking her hand he led her to the bedroom, quickly removing his t-shirt and sweat pants. He wanted to take his time with her, to show her how much he cared, to touch and kiss every part of her body, not stopping until she was pleading for him to enter her. The slow stroking quickly brought both of them to the edge, falling over at the same time, and collapsing together as they both tried to catch their breath. Again, Ken found himself automatically pulling Maddie in for a closeness he never dreamed he'd ever do. He wanted nothing more than to keep her in his arms, and as she snuggled he sensed that maybe she was feeling the same way. He could only take each day as it came, as she was asking him to do, and hope it would show her he cared enough to give her that space.

Chapter 16

Maddie could almost see her mother's condition deteriorating each day. The past couple of weeks had been very hard for her, and she felt so blessed to have Vanessa there to help guide her through the conflicting emotions of what she was seeing. She'd taken to calling Dan every day with an update, even shedding a few tears as they talked. He assured her that he could come at any moment she needed him, but she told him Vanessa was doing a wonderful job on all fronts and was spending all her time with her mother.

Somehow it had worked out, or maybe Ken had made sure of it, but he was helping Reed. At least that's what he told her. Reed was cleaning out the house of everything he didn't want. It was possible, she gathered, that Ken was just telling her that to keep her from feeling she needed to be with him, but then again it was also reasonable to assume that Reed was really getting rid of all of Ruth's stuff. Ken had told her Reed never did like her taste in furniture. Maddie could almost see all of it out on the lawn, waiting for some kind of charity pickup.

Apparently Reed was right. She'd moved that next weekend and took all her stuff to her new house on the Northern Neck, without the slightest whimper. Maddie could only shake her head. Reed was better off without her, for sure. Ken called her every night, checking on how she was doing and asking if there was anything he could do for them. They'd spend an hour or so on the phone, from their respective beds, nearly every night. With Thanksgiving only a week away Ken asked Maddie if she could join him at Reed's. His house was huge, and a chef would be cooking a massive turkey dinner. Drew, Trish, and families would be there, too, and he'd love to have her. He understood when she said she felt it was important for her to have Thanksgiving with Vanessa and her mother.

Thanksgiving was indeed a sorrowful day, and not one to be thankful for this year. Her mother was having difficulty eating and if it hadn't been for Vanessa, she would have broken down in tears. It was so hard to see her mother suffering. She forced herself to think about the nice dinner she was missing at Reed's. She would have loved seeing the entire family again. And Ken? She missed him so much it hurt. It literally hurt. It was clear she was more than a *might be* in love with him. She had fallen. She started clearing up the holiday table after Vanessa helped her mother back to bed.

"She's already half asleep." Vanessa cocked her head and looked at Maddie. "Are you doing alright, Miss Maddie?" Vanessa's eyes were filled with concern.

"I'm fine, Vanessa. Just lost in thought and worried about Mother."

"I'm going to call Dr. Foster tomorrow. I want to see if he might have information on any medicines that might help her. They are forever coming out with new protocols for MS, and he likely hasn't suggested them because your mother hasn't been all that reliable at taking the meds. Perhaps when I swear to him that we've made sure she's taking them he'll start her on something that will help with her appetite and attention span. Would it be alright with you if I call him tomorrow?"

"Absolutely, Vanessa."

Picking up a drying towel Vanessa moved next to Maddie and began wiping off the pots and pans as Maddie finished rinsing them. Speaking softly, "You haven't seen your young man, lately. Is he alright?"

"Oh, he's fine. He's helping his brother clear out his house. He tossed his wife to the Northern Neck and is now getting rid of all the stuff he hated."

"Goodness! That sounds horrible."

"Not really. Reed, that's his brother," she looked up from the soapy water, "was married to a very nasty lady, well, that is if you were beneath her social status. Most everyone fell into that category." Rinsing a pan she handed it to Vanessa, "Reed finally had his fill, showed her the prenup she'd signed, and off she went. Kinda comical in a way. For sure I'd never sign one of those things."

"Well, I don't mean to meddle, I just noticed you hadn't been going out is all, and worried something was wrong"

"I've also been worried about Mother and felt I should stay closer." Maddie sighed. "Maybe Dr. Foster will have some ideas."

"I'll find out. Meanwhile I want you to go somewhere tomorrow. You need a break."

"If anyone needs a break it's you, Vanessa."

"I'm used to it. Spent my life caring for people like your mom. Dr. Foster always knew where to send me when I needed some money after I retired. When my husband died it kind of left me in a bit of a bind, and he stepped right in with several suggestions. I made money, and even better than that I made friends and had a reason to get up in the morning."

"He's a smart man for sure. He sent you to us."

Vanessa just smiled and started to hum a tune. She paused, "Still, though, I'd like to meet that young man of yours. You always look so wistful when you speak of him, so he must be very special."

"Oh, he is that. His name is Ken. Ken Avery. It all seems so strange that after twelve years of no interest in another man, all of a sudden he falls out of the sky…sort of."

"Now I totally want to meet him."

"We've had our problems. He was lying to me, telling me he was in intelligence when he's actually a doctor. He was a Navy surgeon." She continued to fill Vanessa in on Ken, and how it was affecting her.

"Sometimes we just have to accept things the way they happen and move on." Vanessa folded her towel and replaced it on the rack, "and when you line up priorities it all tends to fix itself. If you really care about him, you'll find a way. I've learned in my job that life is way too short for making waves over things that really aren't that critical."

Maddie paused, then pulled the drain plug out of the sink, letting the water gurgle out. Vanessa had a point. Mark, then Mr. Avery and now her mother. Life was short. She wondered when the last time would be that she looked at Orion, and then…. dead. She shivered.

On Black Friday Vanessa insisted Maddy get out of the house. It wasn't important where she went, just go, and don't come back for most of the day. Go shopping, catch a movie, have lunch with your young man if he's nearby. Vanessa had to give her mother a bath and do her best to feed her, and she didn't want Maddie to have to go through all that.

"Alright, alright, I'll go. I'll feed the critters and go. Just promise me you'll call if anything goes wrong."

"Done. Now go."

Where to go? What to do? Shopping was not an option. She didn't need anything at all. She certainly didn't need to be entertained. The weather was nice as she drove away, so she rolled down the window for some fresh autumn air. She hadn't gotten any call at all from Ken the day before, which made Thanksgiving all the more depressing. Nothing so far today, either. As blue as she was feeling it was an odd thought that she could take the key to Ken's house, go inside, clean, do laundry, whatever she could think of... but he might not like that. Why hadn't she heard from him? A day and a half seemed like a century. It was becoming quite clear that she was indeed in love with him. Shaking her head, she managed a half smile. Yes it was true. She thought about him constantly. And just as suddenly she knew where she had to go.

It was a forty-five-minute drive, but the location was breathtaking. Well cared for, serene, and peaceful, the Albert G. Horton, Jr. Memorial Veteran's Cemetery in Suffolk was just as she remembered it from the day Mark was buried, with full honors. A lot had happened since that day, so many years ago. The cemetery had nearly doubled in size, and it took her a few minutes to find his grave. Those first few years she had come on their wedding anniversary, his birthday, and the date of his death, but after starting to care for her mother she didn't want to risk the long drive and amount of time necessary to continue her visits. If something were to happen to her, her mother would be left helpless.

She wished she had stopped for a couple of flowers to lay on his grave. It was a thoughtless omission. Sitting down on the grass, with her legs off to the side, she ran her fingers through the grass. The sun was warm on her face, and she looked up to see the small grave marker with his name, rank, dates of birth and death, and a small cross at the top.

"I'm sorry I haven't been here lately, Mark. I'm sure you know my mother is sick. She's very sick, and it's hard to leave her. But I have some news, and I want you to know about it. I think, after all this time, you'd approve. I'm pretty sure I've found someone who loves me, and I love him back. It's a strange feeling after all these years. I've missed you so, and now he's filling up a little bit of that huge hole in my heart from the day you left me. I don't know if you were awake or not at any point, but the doctor who tried to save your life... well, that's him. His name is Ken. Dr. Ken Avery. He did all he could to save you, but, well,... you know. Anyway, I want you to know about it. Somehow I know you want me to be happy and live the rest of my life as best I can. I promise to do that, Mark, and I'll never forget you. Not ever. Ken understands that. I'm not sure how it will all turn out, in the end, but he says he wants me to move in with him, and when my mother dies I might do that. Time will tell. I just don't think I want to live alone again. But I wanted you to know, Mark. I'll always love you and miss you. We'll meet again, someday."

She should have brought tissues out of the car. She sat there, calmly, tears streaming down her face, until she had to use the sleeve of her t-shirt to wipe them away. Finally standing she looked down one more time. "Rest in peace, Mark."

Slowing walking back to the car, she gathered her wits, picked up her phone and made a call.

"Tessa, Hi. It's Maddie. I'm in Suffolk running an errand and wondered if I could come visit for a little while."

"You just better git on up here. I'll get the coffee going and find one of those bags of critter peanuts for you."

Putting the address in her GPS, Maddie headed on up route 460 toward Richmond, finding their farm with ease.

"Gosh, Maddie, we missed you for Thanksgiving, but we sure understand. Ken told us your mama is not doin' as well as we hoped."

"It's true. I felt I should spend Thanksgiving Day with her. I'm glad I did, though I would have loved being with all of you at Reeds. That must have been some day with a huge house and chef doing all the hard work!"

"Loved it. I felt like a princess, being served all that incredible food. The chef and his crew actually served us, at a table, doin' the "course" thing... like seven courses or something. I lost track." She winked at Maddie.

With a hearty, laugh, "Sounds like we all need to convince Reed to keep the house for all future events."

"OH, good idea! I'll start a petition," she doubled over in laughter. "Now, you just git in here. Coffee is ready and I have some sugar cookies to munch on."

Following her into the house, "Where are Drew and the boys?"

"Believe it or not, Drew has them out in the field picking up little bits and pieces of peanuts and anything else Drew thinks needs to be cleaned up. He's gitten the fields semi ready for the April and May planting season. Teaches the kids about doin' work. With school out for the Thanksgiving weekend it also keeps them out of my hair!" she giggled.

"Well, from what I saw after Mr. Avery's funeral, all four of the children are well behaved, considerate young men."

"That they are. Would be nice we lived closer to Trish. That's a hike. It's almost an hour and a half drive between us, plus the fourteen bucks each way for the Chesapeake Bay Bridge Tunnel."

Maddie nodded in agreement, "I went over there a couple of times when the Wildlife Center of Virginia released a rehabilitated bald eagle. Just awesome, but yes, expensive. Gorgeous views though."

"It's the same for them as for us. His job is there and ours is here."

"But at least Reed and Ken are somewhat in the middle."

"Good thing, too"

Tessa put the coffee and sugar cookies down on the table, and Maddie helped herself to a cookie. "Did you bake these?"

"Sure did. Don't buy what I can make."

"Delicious. You spoil me."

Tessa smiled. "I like to spoil people. So, what brings you way out this way?"

It was a simple, innocent question, punctuated by Tessa smacking her hand on the table and smiling.

"Truth?"

"Hon, I don't mean to be nosey, thought you mighta gone to Belk's for Black Friday or something. It's the only Belk's round here. Good store, but closer to you than Williamsburg."

Rotating her coffee cup back and forth, "I went to visit Mark's grave at the Veteran's cemetery."

"Oh, Maddie," She swiftly sat back in her chair. "I don't mean to poke my nose into your private business."

"It's not a problem, Tessa. Really, it isn't. To be honest, I went to tell him about Ken. It's been twelve years since Mark died. It's been such a coincidence, what with Ken trying to save his life, and somehow I like to think Mark had a hand in us meeting. Maybe, anyway."

"I believe in angels in every way you can believe in them," Tessa locked eyes with Maddie. "Look what they did for me and Drew. I never would have believed I could snatch someone as kind and gentle as he is. And he took me for what I was. He's hasn't tried to change a hair on my head, but I sure fixed my ways in a hurry. Them angels did it. So, I'm guessin' they did it for you, too."

Quickly lifting her cup to her mouth, Maddie took a long gulp, doing her best to keep the tears at bay.

"And I'm tellin' you, Maddie, that guy's squirrely over you. All he does is rattle on about you. Every time his jaw moves your name comes out of his mouth," she pointed a finger at Maddie. "Yup, every time."

Maddie could only follow that with a jovial laugh. "Squirrely, huh?" Her laughing continued, and Tessa smiled from ear to ear.

"You're amazing, Tessa. Truly you are. Tell me, what does the name Tessa mean?"

"HA! You are gonna love this one! My name *is* Tessa, but for some it's just short for Theresa. Whatever! It comes from the Greek Therizo, meaning…. Are you ready for this?..... HARVESTER. Can you believe it? See, I was talkin' about them angels, and here I am, a harvester of peanuts. I just love thinking about that." She stood to refill the coffee cups. "To reap, to gather. Totally perfect, don't ya think?"

"In a way it's giving me chills. How you and Drew got together. How I met Ken, dragging a tree down the side of my house. Has to be angels at work for sure."

"Dragging a tree?"

Maddie giggled. "I was hauling a small tree I'd had cut down, to the curb, and Ken scared me half to death when he was suddenly behind me asking if he could help."

"Yup. Angel doin's for sure."

Finishing the second cup of coffee, Maddie regretted that she had to leave to get back to her mother. While she knew Vanessa was totally in control, it still was Maddie's responsibility, and she was extremely grateful for the time she'd been given that day to carry out what she wanted to do. And Tessa? That woman was a hoot. The last thing she did was haul a 50-pound bag of critter peanuts out to her car, "And these are better than any critter peanut you'd ever buy at some store," she huffed.

"Your mother slept most of the day and had a good lunch." Maddie hung up her jacket and could smell that dinner was in the oven. "Dinner will be ready in about an hour. Did you enjoy your day, Maddie?"

Maddie told Vanessa what she had done that day, ending with a grateful hug for having been given the opportunity.

"You did very well. I'm proud of you, Maddie. There are chapters that we have to savor, and then move past. It's all in the heart, and I'm so glad to hear you were able to turn that page."

Maddie nodded.

"I talked to Dr. Foster today, and he sent over a new med they have found useful. It's not a cure, of course, but has shown some improvements with appetite and movement. Not a lot, but even the smallest benefit is worth it. The only real side effect is drowsiness, but I'll watch for that."

Maddie nodded. "One step forward, then two steps back."

"Yes, that's the way of it sometimes. We do the best we can."

"I know that Vanessa. I thank the gods every day that we have you."

Just as dinner ended and her mother was taking her medicines, Maddie's phone rang. She stood to take the call in the family room.

"Hi, Maddie. I'm so sorry I didn't call you sooner. Reed has been busting my butt. He seriously has."

"I thought you were probably busy."

"We went out first thing this morning around all that stupid Black Friday traffic, to rent a truck. Seems Ruth wanted a pile of the furniture because her little three-thousand-square-feet cabin on the water didn't meet her specifications for proper living."

"She didn't know what was in that house?"

"Of course, she did. She was the one who had it decorated, but Reed figures she just wanted to push his buttons, and he was very happy to let her. He never liked her choices."

"Which were?" She was giggling.

"High French, or something. Reed wants something more eclectic."

Maddie couldn't help but burst out laughing.

"So, we hauled stuff into the rental van, then I had to drive of course, then unload, then drive back. I'm whupped!"

"It sounds like Reed will be fine once all the dust settles."

"Yes. And oddly, just as we were coming back he gets a phone call from Tessa. She says she's starting a petition to make him keep his current house so we all have a place, centrally located, to have our parties." He was hooting and slapping his legs the whole time he was talking to her. *"I do think Reed is one of us, finally."*

"What did he say?"

"He thinks she has a great idea."

"I was there today."

"Where? His house?"

"No. Tessa's."

"Really?"

"I wanted to tell you in private, but I can't leave the house now. I barely just got home."
"I was hoping you could come over."
"Not tonight." Taking a deep breath, she told Ken about visiting the cemetery and her trip up to see Tessa. *"It's all good,"* she said softly.

Ken was silent for a moment, then she heard him sigh. *"I'm glad you went there, Maddie. Maybe someday, in the future, we can both go. I'd like for him to know me... again."*
"I'd like that, Ken."
"See you tomorrow?"
"Yes. For sure."

Hanging up the phone and returning to the kitchen she half expected some kind of smart remark from her mother and was pleasantly surprised when she started talking about how good the dinner was. Maddie agreed.

Over the next couple of weeks her mother did actually seem to rally. She was eating better and seemed to handle her fork and spoon more easily. While she was nearly blind she could see just well enough to try feeding herself. When she faltered Vanessa was there to give her a hand. She'd been able to spend quite a bit of time with Ken, spending one or two nights a week in his bed. They had even set up a walking routine where she did the circuit with him, although admittedly he had to walk at a slower pace to accommodate her. Waking up one morning it was clear the mid-December weather had zoomed in overnight. She was freezing. Ken was not in bed, so she was about to get up when he came back in and quickly got back into bed with her.

"I'm freezing," she shuddered.

Pulling her into his arms, "I just turned the heat up. But I'll be glad to keep you warm in the meantime."

Snuggling close to him, "I think Mother is starting to fade again," she rubbed his chest gently with the palm of her hand. "I don't know what I'd do without Vanessa. She literally forces me out of the house sometimes, now that Mother sleeps all the time. I need to come up with something really nice for her, when… well, when…"

"You said her condo was all paid for and she's just saving money to go spend some time with her daughter in Hawaii, right?"

"Umm."

"We can set up a gift of up to $10,000.00 a year for her, without having any tax problems. That way she could go to Hawaii at least once a year, or more."

"We?"

Ken chuckled, "I think I have benefitted immensely from the generous care she is giving to your mother. You told me she's not even charging a normal rate and kicks you out the door every chance she gets."

"True."

"Both of us have more money than we know what to do with. Our houses are paid for. We both have lived simply all our lives. So, we could set up a transfer of ten grand a year for her for say, ten years. She won't need all that so it should last her until she dies. I'm sure I can have the bank automatically transfer that money to her on the first banking day of each new year. How does that sound?"

For a moment she went rigid. What he was saying was a commitment to her, in many different ways. To do what he suggested meant a life with him. That had been on her mind, of course, but this was a solid suggestion that told her he had no doubt they would get married. Was that what she wanted? Forever?

Lifting her face to look at him, "I've got something to tell you."

Partially rising, he shifted his eyes to look into hers, "What?" he said a little nervously.

"I love you."

His smile lit up the room, and his kisses took over until they were both lost in the throes of passion, loving each other to the point of ecstasy, then panting as they try to catch their breaths.

"It's hot in here," Maddie whispered.

Ken smacked her butt, laughing. "Then let's get up and go for that walk."

All he could think about was how lucky he was. He couldn't believe she had finally said the words he'd been longing to hear for weeks. They could move forward now, although he knew that he still had to bide his time and not apply any pressure. Her mother was still her first priority, and while she was able to get away for a couple nights a week, she spent most of her days at home. He agreed it should be that way. He'd taken the time to be with his dad, and he owed her that same consideration. As often as he'd declared a death each one affected him differently. Despite knowing how horribly her mother had treated her, all her life, he had to let her walk through to the end of the emotional highs and lows. He would be there when she needed him. But those three little words meant there was likely to be a future with her, and he couldn't be more excited.

Maddie walked into the guest bedroom to get into walking clothes. For some reason she would never understand it seemed it took longer for Ken to get dressed than for her to do the same.

She had the coffee and oatmeal ready when he came into the kitchen. Just as they finished eating, Ken's phone rang.

"Jerry, great to hear from you."
"You doing alright now?"
"I'm fine. How's it going?"
"Nice and slow, just how we like it."
"Oh, good. No 'go team' then."
"Nope. In fact, Donna and I were wondering if we could come down and collect on that steak dinner you owe us. I want to see for myself that you're okay."

Ken paused, rubbing his chin, *"Of course, sure. I'd love it. When?"*

"We thought we'd head down that way tomorrow, if that doesn't mess with anything you're doing."

"Tomorrow is perfect. I'll have the guest room ready."
"We'll see you then."

Pushing the red "end call" button and seeing Maddie knit her brow he was quick to explain. "That was Jerry Hepler. He's the man in charge of Doctors World Wide. We served together all through our Naval careers. He did me a huge favor when we were in Haiti, and I promised Jerry and his wife a steak dinner. Seems he's going to collect on that."

"You'll enjoy seeing them again, I know. Must have been some favor." Her half-smile and narrowing eyes belied her curiosity.

Ken put his finger to his mouth in thought, tapping his lips while eyeing Maddie. There was no way to keep Jerry from bringing up good old Nurse Nancy, so he told her the story.

Maddie could only laugh. "Such a horrible position for a handsome, rich, single physician to be in, having nurses chasing him all around the hospital."

He grabbed her and kissed her. "She dressed like a street walker. Nuff said."

"I really should spend the evening with Mother anyway."

"No, you don't. You're going to dinner with us." Escorting her to the door to start their walk, "I've never met his wife, Donna, so you can talk to her about whatever women talk about."

Maddie didn't talk much during their walk. "Nice weather," was about the extent of her conversation, as both were left with their thoughts. Ken was trying to figure out where to take them for the steak dinner. Maddie was trying to figure out how not to go with them. She wasn't sure exactly why she was having a problem with that. If it was one of Ken's best friends it almost went without question that he would be an outstanding man with an equally great wife. Still, there was something she couldn't put her finger on, so she switched her brain to worrying about her mother.

Finishing their walk, "I'll help you get the house ready for visitors?"

"It's fine, Maddie. They won't notice any dust."

"Men! Honestly! Especially 46-year-old bachelors."

"Huh?"

"The bed needs to be made, fresh towels in the bathroom, clean shower, toilet, and sink. Add a new bar of soap, dust and vacuum, then turn the vacuum on the family room rug…"

Ken held up his hands in a "stop" motion. "Good thing I have all day then. Holiday time is over, Reed is back to work, and I need to go," he turned on his heels and headed for the closet, "and get the vacuum out."

Chuckling, "I'll take care of the guest room and bath."

"Ah, another good reason to love you."

"Boo, hiss," was all she could manage.

Chapter 17

She was there when Jerry and Donna arrived. Ken had pouted to the point that she couldn't refuse any longer. She'd never seen him pout before, and it was so cute she couldn't stop laughing. Which only made his face get longer.

"You're gonna trip over that face, you know."

His response was to look at her with puppy dog eyes, so sad, so, so sad.

"Geeze, alright. I'll go to dinner."

He was in the middle of a long primal kiss with her when the doorbell rang. "Dang," he pulled away. "I was hoping for another hour."

Flashing him a sexy grin, "Answer the door, Kenneth. Your guests have arrived."

Ken was promptly grabbed into a huge man-hug, both men slapping each other on the back. Donna stood in the background as the hugging and slapping and handshaking continued, punctuated by laughs and "hey man," and "good to see you man" comments. Maddie had to smile as she looked at Donna, who was rolling her eyes, just as Maddie felt the urge to do so herself.

Finally coming through the open door, thank the gods the flies and mosquitos were gone for the year, all the introductions were made.

"I picked a good restaurant down on the ocean front. It's called Chix on the Beach and is right on the ocean. They have a varied menu, with all sorts of fish stuff, steaks, chicken, burgers, so you should be able to find something to spend my money on." It was obvious Ken was thrilled to have Jerry and his wife visiting.

Maddie and Donna again stood back while all the reunion shenanigans continued. Shaking her head she turned to Donna, "And they talk about women and our little get togethers! Those two are the very definition of BFF. I'm Maddie," she leaned in toward Donna.

"Hi, Maddie. I'm Donna. You know, I never thought about that. BFF seems to only be used in describing women, but who's to say men can't have best friends forever?"

Maddie just smiled in agreement.

"Does Ken have a mancave, too?"

"No, thank goodness. I suppose he could figure out how to make one in the future. He is getting more civilianized as time goes by."

"Come on, Donna. Let's get the suitcases unloaded in the bedroom." Jerry was wiggling his index finger at her in a come-hither motion.

"The master calls," she said sarcastically, but with a smile.

An unfortunate fact about Virginia Beach in mid-December is that it's cold. Highs don't get much above mid 50's and lows can get close to freezing. They settled for a table with a view of the ocean.

"We can walk outside after dinner, if you ladies would like," Ken offered. "Jerry and I have seen more ocean that we care to admit to, but we'll be glad to escort you guys."

"You're just too sweet for words," said Donna, pursing her lips in a flat line. "We'll just come back in the summer. I think Jerry said something about you owing him TWO dinners."

"Nurse Nancy must have been more active than I was told," snickered Maddie.

"You have no idea," said Jerry. "She won't be coming back with the teams again. The guy we set her up with…" he looked at Ken… "she's stalking him now. He's fit to be tied."

Ken slid back in his chair a bit as the server placed his food down. As she continued around the table Ken just sat there with his mouth hanging open. "Hope he has the cops on it."

"He does. He said he might even join the Navy!"

Ken laughed.

"The sad thing Jerry, is she's an outstanding surgical nurse. All the many times she was part of my team she was spot on with every move. She knew in advance what I'd need, and other surgeons agreed with that. It's just a shame her personal life is such a mess."

"Maybe they can get her some help." Adjusting his chair, "So," Jerry continued, "Are you well enough now to be put back on the go-team?"

"I'm fine, and still thinking about it, to be truthful." How could he explain, sitting at a dinner table in a restaurant, that he just wanted to stay with Maddie and not travel anymore?

"Well, keep thinking. You were one lucky dude that the bullet missed your artery by a quarter of an inch." Holding up his finger and thumb with a tiny space between them, his gaze shifting to Maddie, then back again to Ken, "That much closer and you'd be dead." He started to cut into his steak. "Scared me half to death, gotta tell you."

Ken looked over at Maddie, who had turned white.

"What did you say, Jerry?" Maddie's lips barely moved as she spoke.

"He had to be airlifted to Portsmouth for recovery to make sure there was no infection. Could have easily been bad what with the bullet staying in his chest and not going all the way through."

Ken let out an audible gasp, then watched the light fading from Maddie's eyes, her chest deflating and her shoulders dropping.

Suddenly aware of what had just happened, Donna reached over and put her hand over Maddie's.

Not only did Ken not have any idea what to do about the disaster occurring right in front of him, but Jerry had no idea what he had just unleashed, continuing to talk about how nice it was to have a respite from all the world's catastrophes and looking forward to Christmas.

"Steak alright, Jerry?" Ken needed to change the subject, his voice shaking with a visible tic in his jaw.

"Perfect. This is a nice place. How's the lump crab cakes, Donna?"

"Very good, with just the right seasonings." Her eyes stayed firmly glued to Maddie, aware there was something seriously amiss with what was being said about Ken's wound.

"Hey, Maddie. Is something wrong with your tuna? You've only eaten a bite!" Jerry was pointing his knife at her.

"What?" She shook her head, almost imperceptibly, "Ah, oh, it's fine. Really. I've just been, ah, enjoying the conversation." She quickly forked off another bite of tuna and ate it. "Really, good."

Her hands shaking, she did her best to cover that fact, turning to Donna. "How long are you staying in Virginia Beach?"

"Just the one night. We have to get back tomorrow. I do all the ordering of supplies and deploying of the go-teams, so I need to get back. We're a small non-profit company, so relying on donations keeps us hopping. This has been a wonderful outing for me."

Maddie could see the concern in her face but kept up chatter about the nicest places to go in the area, and how they should plan to return someday for a real visit.

"Good steak, Ken. Consider the bet paid off."

"Dessert anyone?" Ken chimed in. His eyes had never left Maddie's face, knowing that deep down she was hurting in the worst way possible.

Everyone nodded no, but Jerry looked over at Maddie, his face serious, "You barely ate any dinner, Maddie."

She folded her napkin, needing to think quickly. "I'm worried about my mother is all. She has MS and there's a nurse staying with us now. I should get back to her."

"I wasn't aware of that. I'm so sorry. Yes, of course. We understand completely."

Taking care of the check, Ken stood with Jerry and Donna. He had no idea what to do or say as Maddie stood. She followed behind them and was glad to be sitting next to Donna, in the back seat of the car.

"You said your mother has MS," Donna gently tapped Maddie's hand.

Speaking in a very low voice, "Yes, she's nearing death now. Totally bedridden. We've been lucky to have a wonderful nurse who stays with her all the time. But I like to be home to give her some relief, too. Even just giving her time to take a walk around the block is important. She's retired now but taking care of someone like my mother is stressful."

"What's her name, Maddie? I'll add her to my prayers."

Tears began to form in Maddie's eyes, but she managed to contain them. "Dori Rogers. Thank you. You're very kind."

Ken knew better than to ask or say anything. He pulled into Maddie's driveway, got out and opened the door for her.

"It was very nice meeting both of you," she slid out toward the door and waved back at them. Taking the hand Ken offered she stood on her feet, "Thank you for dinner, Ken." He nodded as she walked past him and into the house.

Back in the car Donna leaned forward. "You didn't tell her you were shot, did you?"

Ken shook his head. "She knew I was shot but I told her it was just a flesh wound, and nothing serious." Jerry's neck snapped to look at him, in shock! "Damn, Ken, why didn't you tell me that. I never would have said a word."

"It was so long ago, and we've talked about it on the phone several times so I just didn't think it would come up."

"I am so sorry. Is she really angry?"

"Probably more than that. She had an issue with me lying about my job in the Navy. I used the intelligence line, like most of us do. But she hadn't ever told me how her husband died, so in the end we figured it was a draw. The worst part was when she told me how he died." Ken swallowed hard and his hands were tight on the steering wheel. "He died on my table on the Ike, Jerry."

Donna slammed herself back into the seat, gasping. Jerry's mouth just hung open in disbelief. "Of all the operating rooms on all the carriers in all the world...."

"Exactly, Jerry, and I told her exactly how he died. It seemed to help her. When I got shot I didn't want her to worry about something like that. I guess I was wrong. Maybe I'm too out of practice with women to get married."

"Well, that's a crock, Ken." Donna sat forward again. "I've only known you for a few hours, but I know what Jerry has told me ever since you two met. You were practically joined at the hip from the time you both joined the Navy. I have a feeling it will all work out. Just give it some time."

Pulling into his garage, "Anyone for a nightcap? For once I think I need one."

"I think we all could use one," agreed Jerry.

Jerry and Ken opted for beers, while Donna requested the white wine. The first several minutes were spent in total silence, but Jerry was pacing.

"I'll call her, right now, and explain things, Ken. I just never, ever thought..."

"No. Don't call her. It won't do any good. It's as much my fault for not warning you. She had a serious trust issue with me when she found out I lied about my job. We managed to get past that, and even though I had promised to never lie to her *again*, the lie about the wound was an earlier one, so I thought I was safe. Turns out, not so. She'll never understand that I kept it secret because she'd already lost her husband tragically. I didn't want her to worry about my safety every time I went out on the go-team."

"Every minute of anyone's life is risk, Ken. As surgeons we know that better than anyone else. One second you're walking down the street and the next you're on the ground, either because of a heart attack or a car slammed into you and sent you flying, or someone shot you for some initiation rite. Whatever. They're on our operating table, and we fight like hell to save their lives. There's no such thing as life without risk. There isn't a single place in the world that you can live risk free. I've thought about this a *lot*, Ken. Tornados, hurricanes, flooding, wildfires, sinkholes, earthquakes, landslides, tsunamis, ice storms, volcanos, torrential rains and thunderstorms, ah, I think that's all of them... and someone dies in every one of those."

"He's memorized the list," Donna explained.

Pausing in thought, "You forgot blizzards and heavy snowfalls."

"Yes, shoveling snow. Frost bite and heart attacks. Thanks."

Ken flopped into a chair, "I hear what you're saying Jerry. And I'm all for taking any risk to get her back, but I don't see it happening."

"You do know," Donna interrupted, "that the *way* you die, or *how* you die, or even *when* you die, is not the problem here."

Both men looked at her with interest. "Obviously she's interested in you, Ken. If she wasn't she probably would have said she's afraid to commit again because she might lose you too soon. Has she said anything like that to you?"

Ken shook his head. "No, she hasn't."

"She's older. Her mother is dying. Your dad just died. She knows from personal experience that life is short, but that doesn't mean you can't find love, or she wouldn't be seeing you *at all*."

"She has a point," Jerry conceded.

"Never thought of it that way," admitted Ken.

"Well, obviously she feels betrayed, and you need to figure out how to overcome that. Somehow you'll have to convince her that the lie was an old one, before you made the promise, but that's sketchy at best, Ken. More importantly you need to tell her you were worried that her past experience with her husband dying so horribly would send her running if she knew you'd been seriously shot, so you didn't tell her because you didn't want her to worry. It was a one-time event and lessons were learned."

Ken's cheeks puffed as he let out a large breath. "I suppose I could try that approach with her. It's true, of course, but just finding the right words will be my challenge." A sigh escaped his nose as his chest deflated.

"Well, sleep on it, Ken." Donna leaned down and patted his hand. "Let us know what happens."

With Jerry and Donna on their way home the next morning, Ken hid behind his favorite spying tree and waited. He'd stand there for hours, if necessary, waiting for her to come feed the birds. With his back leaning against the tree, he pulled out his iPhone and started to play games. Glancing around he hoped no one thought he was some kind of nut, calling the cops to come check him out. That would be all he needed at this point. But it was only about twenty minutes later when he heard her garage door open. Quickly crossing the street as she came out with the scoops of peanuts in her hand, she saw him and stopped. Tossing the peanuts under the tree, she glared at him, "I'm very angry with you right now, Ken. You said no more lies and here's another lie. You were shot and I thought you just got a small scratch. SHOT, Ken. Bullets. A quarter inch from dying."

"But it's a PAST lie. I meant no more NEW lies., EVER. From that point on." He was so anxious it was hard to speak, making good use of his arms in a surrender motion.

"Splitting hairs, Ken. I am so angry with you right now."

"Please, Maddie. I understand your anger and you have a right to be upset, but I just didn't want you worrying. It was a once in a life-time thing. Lessons were learned. I could fall down a sinkhole later today."

She almost laughed but caught herself. She was just too upset to let him con her. "How much longer are you going to keep doing this dangerous stuff – off in disaster areas where there are tons of germs and desperate people willing to kill for a few bites of food? I mean, you're retired? Military can recall you forever? This isn't the military - another lie. Jerry's outfit is a private civilian operation according to Donna, and you told him last night you were thinking about going back to the go-team." She lowered her arms in frustration, tapping the empty scoops against her leg. "Look, you tried to save Mark, and I appreciate that fact. You told me how he died on the table and the Navy hid all those details from me. You tell me he didn't suffer at all and that had he lived he would have been quadriplegic." She brushed something off her face and turned to check one of the sunflower feeders.

Ken just stood there, his hands outstretched. "Please Maddie. I love you. I didn't want you worrying about me when you have so much on your plate with your mom. And I didn't lie about Jerry's charity being a non-profit. I never said anything about that."

"You said you were being recalled by the NAVY, Ken. To spy. Jerry is *not* the Navy."

Ken began running this fingers through his hair in frustration. "I'll give you that one. But again, those lies were before the promise, and I didn't think it mattered that much."

"I'm tired, Ken. Just tired." She slowly turned and walked back into the garage, closing the door behind her.

With the garage door closed she paused on the steps to the kitchen door, her hand on the handle and her head on that arm, trying to compose herself. She'd found out he was shot. ALMOST DIED. What else hasn't he told her? She was just so angry with him and at the same time extremely worried about her mother. Thank God, the care Vanessa was giving her was beyond outstanding, but it was agonizingly clear her mother was deteriorating. She was now being fed in bed by Vanessa's gentle hand. Maddie felt the pain of exhaustion and now was just fed up with Ken's pussy-footing around about the bullet wound. Let him go back to his little doctor job. She should have known it was too good to be true. She wished she could talk to Vanessa about it, but there was no way she would bother her when there was so much going on with her mother.

And calling Tessa wasn't in the cards either. While she would understand, and maybe help, Maddie was just too exhausted to go through it all again.

Time stood still for Ken. Christmas was two weeks away, and he sat on the bed they had shared, twisting a diamond engagement ring in his hand. He'd sent her messages for the past five days, and she never answered. His phone calls went to voice mail. There was no point in trying to ambush her again, she'd only turn and walk back into the house. He'd blown it. No doubt about it. He should have been honest with her. How would he feel if she had something wrong like breast cancer or some woman problem and she kept it from him? He'd be very hurt, that's what. All he could think to do was bide his time and hope she would answer something he had sent to her. But each day that saw dawn, and then dusk was another arrow missing the mark. It was one more day that let her get further away from him. All he could think to do was get busy. He hadn't stopped his walks. He refused to give that up, but he wasn't stopping or even slowing down, as he passed her house. If she waved, which he doubted, he didn't see it because he refused to look for it. He hadn't talked to any of his family since Jerry and Donna left, he didn't want to talk to them either. They had busy lives and didn't need his constant drama. To be truthful, he didn't need it either. Carefully putting the ring back into its case, he placed it in the back of his top drawer. If nothing changed, despite his daily messages begging her for forgiveness, he would return the ring the first week in January, rejoin the go-team, sell his house, and move on with his life. Or maybe sooner if his heart turned into a rock.

Every day, twice a day, one would be a text message and one would be voice. While the words changed, the theme did not. *"I'm sorry, please forgive me, please talk to me, I miss you, Maddie please, I'm begging, I love you,"* he said or wrote the last time. It didn't go unnoticed to her, though, that he was being sincere, and honest in his attempts to get her attention.

Still, she felt empty even as a new one would pop up on her screen. She had too much else occupying her mind. She called Dan daily, giving him complete reports and even putting Vanessa on the phone when she couldn't explain herself clearly enough. One odd thing that kept her going was a daily call from Tessa. Tessa always kept her comments brief, just wanting Maddie to know that Dori was in her prayers and to be sure to let her know if there was anything at all that she could do to help. She was humbled by Tessa's show of support. But the stress was splitting her in two directions. Her mother. Ken. She could actually feel her blood pressure rising in her head.

The doorbell rang, jerking Maddie back into the present. Opening the door, she saw her brother standing there, his downturned mouth showed obvious concern and sadness. Maddie fell into his arms, relieved to know he cared enough to be with her and their mom.

"Oh, Dan. Thank you for coming. I didn't want to interrupt your work schedule. I know you're always on the move."

"It's not a problem, Maddie. Honestly. Vanessa told me the time was getting near. She's been calling me with updates, too. Mother's heartbeat is slowing down and she's getting more and more unresponsive. Hopefully she'll wake up when I go in to see her."

"Please stay here, Dan. I know Vanessa has the spare bedroom, but the couch in the family room turns into a bed, and people have told us it's very comfortable. I'll even sleep on it, and you can have my bed."

"The one in the family room will be fine, Sis."

Maddie nodded. Her face relaxed. She was so grateful to have her brother there.

Walking into his mother's bedroom, "I'm Dan," he held out his hand to Vanessa. "Maddie tells me you're taking outstanding care of our mother, and I appreciate it." Nice, he thought. A very competent nurse who's also very pleasant to look at! He hadn't expected that.

"Nice to meet you as well, Dan. I'm Vanessa Cambridge. She's still asleep, I doubt she'll wake up again until tomorrow. She's been fairly alert in the morning hours. I'm so glad you decided to come. She'll be happy to see you."

"I'll be staying here. Maddie is setting up the couch/bed for me. I'll have to ask her about which bathroom I can use."

"That's not a problem, actually. You probably didn't get that far when you were here before, but there's a full bathroom with shower next to the laundry room. It's off the kitchen. We always keep the door closed to that area, but I'm sure you'll find it good enough."

"Nice! I had no idea. Then I'm all set. Just wanted you to know there will be a man in the house in case you like to get a glass of milk in the middle of the night." Bending down, conspiratorially, "so don't go running around naked."

Vanessa laughed. "Same goes for you, hot-shot!"

Leaning closer he kissed her on the cheek. "Get me if you need me for anything, Vanessa. Seriously, even middle of the night if something happens to Mother."

She nodded. Then she sighed. How many years had it been since she'd been kissed, even on the cheek? It made her smile.

Maddie almost had the bed made when he returned.

"I'll go get my suitcase. This is really nice. I hadn't had a chance to make any hotel reservation, and I'd rather be here."

"I hope it's comfortable enough for you," She plumped the pillows and settled them on top of the spread.

He laughed. "I've spent so many nights in so many different hotels I've lost count. Trust me. This will be fine. Vanessa told me about a third shower, so that will work out perfectly."

"Can I help you unpack?"

"No, I don't have much. Can I use the coat closet to hang my things?"

"Absolutely. And I think there's an empty shelf in the credenza. Feel free to use that. You can always store things in my bedroom, too."

"I'll be just fine, Maddie. And I told Vanessa not to walk around nude in the middle of the night, so that should go for you, too."

Giggling, she hit him in the chest with the back of her hand. "Can I get you something to eat?"

"I am a little hungry, but I can order something delivered."

"There's leftover fried chicken in the fridge."

"Perfect."

Sitting across from each other as he nibbled on a chicken leg, "Are you still seeing, ah, what was his name? Ken?"

Pursing her lips and squinting, "I'm afraid he lost my trust, so no."

Dan's mouth dropped open and his hand froze with the chicken leg pointing at her. "What happened, Sis?"

She filled him in on the lie about his job in intelligence, finishing with the bullet wound deception. Dan put the chicken leg back on the plate and wiped his hands off on the napkin. Wiping off his lips next, "Hmm. Let me ask you this. Do you love him?"

Maddie lowered her eyes and nodded. "Yes, I love him. I just feel so betrayed. He promised no more lies."

"But from what you just told me his lie about the wound was before he promised, right?"

"You're splitting hairs just like he did. He could have told me about that at the time he promised no more lies. You know, something like, 'Gee Maddie, I have one more lie to confess to before the no more lies promise goes into effect.'"

"Huh? Oh, okay, I see your point. But I think I see his, too."

Rolling her eyes, "How?" She leaned back in her chair, folding her arms in front of her chest.

"I'm just speaking from the male point of view..."

Maddie sat forward and opened her mouth to speak, but Dan put up his hand to stop her, "Just listen, okay?" He could see the anger in her eyes but ignored it. "I think maybe he was just trying to protect you, Maddie. Yes, he was shot and yes, he was lucky, but I can imagine he was thinking about what happened to your husband. Why give you reason to worry if it wasn't really necessary. It was a one in a million happening. I suspect there will be adequate security for that kind of scenario in the future. Right?"

"I suppose so, and he even said just that, but lightning can strike twice, you know."

Dan sucked in a deep breath, shaking his head, and trying hard not to grin at her odd analogy. "Maddie, Maddie, Maddie. Now I don't know the guy, but I think he might be going through one huge emotional upheaval right about now, especially since you tell me he's texting and calling every day. If he didn't care about you he'd just be on his way, for sure he wouldn't be texting and calling and wearing out his fingers on the phone trying to get through to you. Sounds to me like he loves you very much."

Maddie eyed him suspiciously, her eyes narrowing slightly. "He says that, but it could just be one more lie, you know!"

Slowly rubbing an open palm against the table, "I'm guessing he's in some form of panic, Maddie, judging by the number of attempts to contact you. He can't believe you don't, or won't, understand his motives. Now you gotta know just in case it matters... me being a guy and all and thinking like one...next he'll get angry, and eventually he'll accept that you don't want anything to do with him anymore and he'll move on in life. He's an intelligent man, Maddie, and he's lived his entire life alone. I know if it was me and I was thinking my woman was upset over something like that, refusing to even try to understand my overall motives and all, I'd probably just move on. There will come a point when he just quits trying."

Maddie took in a deep breath then leaned forward, putting both forearms on the table. "I appreciate what you've said, Dan. It's something I need to think about." She didn't want to start a fight with her brother, and it was hard to concede that he might have a point, so she just wanted to drop the subject for now.

Dan picked up his chicken and bit into it. "Good chicken."

"How about a beer chaser?"

"Perfect. I could use one about now."

"Help yourself to anything you need or want."

"Thanks, Sis."

"Do you need anything else before I go to bed?"

"Nope. I'm fine."

"Vanessa usually goes to bed very late, like around eleven, and gets up early. She'll be very quiet, but she does sleep with her door open in case Mother uses the horn beside her bed."

"No problem, Maddie. It will all be fine."

Giving him a peck on the cheek, Maddie headed down the hall to her own room.

Chapter 18

Maddie was up early for some reason. Tiptoeing into the kitchen she was surprised to see Dan already there, starting the coffee pot and looking for something to eat.

"Bad night?"

"Not at all," he replied. "The bed really is as comfortable as you've been told." He continued to open cabinets, unsure of what he would find.

"Bacon and eggs?" She opened the fridge and took both items out and put them on the counter.

"Sounds like heaven."

"Bread is in the middle drawer," she pointed to the island, "and jelly in fridge."

Finding both, Dan set the table then started the toaster. Sitting down to get out of her way he watched her as she put the bacon on paper towels and into the microwave, cracked the eggs into a skillet, and got the butter ready to swipe onto the toast. He realized he hadn't *really* looked at her before. She was a beautiful woman, even with the gray flowing through her brunette hair like the peaks on a waterfall. And, he noted, she was still one sexy looking broad, even if she was his sister. Figure was still perfect, and there were only minimal aging lines on her face. He didn't understand why but it was comforting being with her. Odd that it took their mother, reaching out in frustration and anger, to bring them back together after all those years. And this guy, Ken? He wanted to meet this unmarried doctor, Navy captain, perhaps to get the real view from the other side, as it were, kinda man-to-man sort of view. He watched Maddie effortlessly manage the routine of breakfast, taking the bacon out of the microwave, buttering the toast, flipping the eggs for 'over easy' and starting to plate.

"If you want some OJ, it's in the fridge."

He poured out two glasses worth as she set the plates down. He dove in with gusto. She couldn't help but smile.

With the dishes cleared Maddie sat back down to join her brother with a strong cup of coffee. They spent the next half hour chatting about his job and his life in Chicago. Dan missed being with his son, Andy, every day, but was thankful his divorce had been amicable. Sara was even dating a nice guy that he approved of, wishing them well on all levels.

"I guess that surprises me a bit," Maddie refilled the cups.

"We became two different people with two different goals when I got that new job. It just happened when we weren't looking, I guess. But we made sure that Andy understood right from the get-go that he had nothing to do with our getting a divorce, that it was just his mom and dad growing up in different ways, but both of us loving him always. He knew I'd been traveling and gone a lot, so he accepted it. Now he sees we were right. I actually see him *more* than I did when we were married. We make it a point to go to baseball and football games, and unless I'm out of town I go to all his events at school. He's looking at colleges now since he'll graduate next year. He'll be a fine young man."

"I'd like to meet him sometime. I am his aunt, you know!"

"Good point." He laughed. "You'd even like Sara."

They were interrupted when Vanessa came into the kitchen.

"Can I fix you some breakfast, Vanessa?"

She had stopped just past the doorway, "Your mother wants to see you, Maddie, please."

"Ah, okay," she slowly stood and followed Vanessa. Dan followed behind afraid that his mother might be dying at that minute and not aware that he was even there.

Hesitating as she walked behind, "Is she alright, Vanessa?"

"No, hon. I'm afraid not. She doesn't want any food and her vitals aren't good." Entering, Vanessa pointed to a chair for Maddie to use.

Gently taking her mother's hand, "You wanted to see me, Mother? Dan's here with us."

Dori gulped, and swallowed, giving a small nod as she gripped Maddie's hand. "So soli," Dori fought to look at her daughter, squinting her eyes trying to get the tiniest image of her, even a shadow. I love. Jerish. Dadd girl." She twisted her body in frustration. "Tools, no wan cook." She gasped in irritation.

"Mom," Maddie tried to understand, "Are you saying you were jealous because I was a daddy's girl?"

Dori nodded yes, tears beginning to well up in her eyes. "Yesh."

"Because Daddy taught me to use tools and I didn't care about cooking?"

Dori's head nodded up and down, a tear fell down her cheek, through her hair, and onto the pillow. "Jearish happy Mark."

Maddie grabbed a wad of tissues and began to dry the tears from her mother's face. "Oh, God, Mom, if only you could have told me. You liked Mark? You were jealous of him? If only I had understood."

Dori was gasping, fighting to catch her breath. "Yesh, Mark goot. Love you."

"You liked Mark?"

"Mark goot. Sad die."

Maddie burst into sobs, her heart had jumped up into her throat and she could barely breathe. "Oh, my god, Mom. All those beating because I used a screw driver instead of a spoon," she began hyperventilating. Vanessa quickly came up behind her and put both hands on her shoulders to help her calm down. Maddie was pale and shaking. "Maddie, breathe slowly, in from your nose and out your mouth. Very slowly. That's good, keep doing it, over and over."

Feeling Vanessa's hands on her shoulders she managed to force herself to breathe as Vanessa had instructed. Slowly her shoulders dropped and some of the shaking subsided.

"Soli, so soli love..." Dori started gasping

Vanessa jumped into action. "Call rescue, Maddie." Moving to the back of the bed she brought out the small oxygen generator she knew she would need eventually. Maddie let go of her mother's hand and quickly dialed 911, as Dan tried to help Vanessa place the oxygen mask on his mother.

Fifteen minutes later her mother was on the way to the hospital and she and Vanessa were following in her car. They needed to be there to help get her checked in quickly. Dan said he would follow as soon as he got dressed.

Standing in the bay as the doctors and nurses took over, her phone beeped. Ken's daily message. She wanted to ignore it, but it would only beep again in a few minutes. So, she looked down. It was from Dan. He was on his way. Checking her message list closely there were no other new ones added. Maybe a phone call and she'd been too busy to hear it ring? But her Recents page was empty as well. For a fleeting moment she wondered if Dan had been prophetic, and Ken had quit. What a horrible day, just horrible. Dan and his thoughts, her mother gasping for breath, Ken. It was so overwhelming she had to close her eyes and do Vanessa's breathing exercises.

He thought he'd start his morning walk a bit early. He knew no matter what he did he wouldn't see Maddie, so there was no point in trying to do so. It might be a good day to go over to Trish's. The kids were in school, Paul would be working... sounded like a good idea. Maybe he could help her put up some

Christmas decorations or something. He needed something to keep him busy. Turning the music up on his iPhone he headed out, slowly making his way down the street. As he automatically made the turn in front of Maddie's he was stunned to see a car in the driveway. It had to be Dan. Knowing Maddie as he did there was no way some other man was staying there. He knew of no other family, aunts, uncles, cousins. Maybe a doctor for her mother? He stopped as he watched a man come out of the house and lock the door. Quickly approaching the driveway, "Are you Dan?"

"Yes. I'm Dan."

"Is everything alright?"

"You are…"

"I'm Ken. I've been seeing…"

"I know who you are, Ken. She's told me about you."

He stiffened a bit. Was that hostility or anxiety in his voice. "I'd like to see her."

"Now's not the best time. She's at the hospital. Our mother is dying. She and Vanessa followed rescue. I need to get there, now."

Ken nodded and backed off. "Please tell her I'm so sorry to hear about her mother." Hopefully it was the anxiety that was in Dan's voice, and not some anger towards him.

Dan nodded as he got into the car and started it.

No point in sending her a bunch of messages anymore. She needed her time with her mother, and if she died, a bunch of useless messages interrupting her would only be irritating. She would have too many things to take care of. He'd had a ton of help with his dad's estate. She had Dan, for a little while, and maybe Vanessa, and that was all. Turning around he walked back home.

Leaning back against the wall, her eyes closed, she felt Vanessa get up and walk away. She watched her approach one of the doctors. Judging by her body language it seemed that things might be under control now. Dan came into the waiting room just as Vanessa sat back down.

"What's happening?" Dan pulled a chair up.

"She's comfortable now. They want to put her in a room and watch her carefully. If it happens again they want to be sure to get to her quickly."

"Do they know she has a DNR?" Maddie wanted to be sure her mother's wishes were followed.

"Yes, when they checked her in they saw that there was a copy on the hospital computer."

"I don't want her to suffer." Maddie caught the irony of her statement since all she had done all her life was suffer around her mother.

"She won't, assured Vanessa. They'll call in Hospice if it gets to that point."

"Let's all go get some coffee while they move her She'll be in room 314."

They returned to her room an hour later, seeing her laying there, so fragile, so small, no longer the holy terror with a cane. Her eyes were closed, and her breathing was shallow. Even Maddie could tell that. The monitor beeped a regular rhythm, itself soothing yet scary. She and Dan took opposite sides of the bed, sitting down, each holding one of their mother's hands. No one spoke, they just listened to the beeps and hisses, the harbingers of death. Vanessa had taken a seat at the foot of the bed, silently watching a scene she had seen so many times before. She had always cared deeply for her charges. This was no different. Maybe even much worse. The tug on her heart told her the time was near. She simply had to wait.

Maddie looked up at Dan, who was gently rubbing Dori's arm. His face was solemn as he looked down at her. He knew, despite her fight to see her children, Dori was now blind.

Then suddenly she opened her eyes and sat straight up in bed. She looked up, and in a voice as clear as it had ever been, "That's the most beautiful light I've ever seen." A smile of peace touched her face and drifting backwards, her head gently touched the pillow. With one last exhaled breath, she died, still holding Maddie's hand.

Suddenly convulsing in sobs, Maddie put her head down on her mother's chest, completely unable to process what had just happened. Her mother had sat up. Her words were clear, and could she actually *see*? Did she see a beautiful light? She was gone. Her mother was gone. She was an orphan. What an odd thing to think. She'd heard someone say that once… when your last parent died you couldn't call home anymore, and you were an orphan. Lifting her head for a moment, she saw Dan had simply pushed his chair back and was watching without any discernable expression on his face. She couldn't stop crying, as Vanessa came over from the chair she had been sitting in, gently lifting Maddie off her mother's chest.

"She's at peace, Maddie, and now she's left you in peace."

Maddie could only nod, trying to deal with the mixed feelings of relief, sorrow and knowing that her own life had just taken a dramatic shift.

Chapter 19

Even though they knew the hospital would contact the funeral home they wanted to make sure it was done as soon as possible. Dori's written wishes were to be cremated at once and placed in the Columbarium as soon as possible. Upon arrival they were asked if there was an obituary. While Dori had prepaid her funeral she had never given them an obituary. Escorting all three of them into a private room, Dan and Maddie tried to write something that honored their mother without going overboard. In the end it was a simple:

Dori Rogers, 68, died December 19. Born in Virginia Beach, VA, she was predeceased by her husband, William (Chicago) and is survived by a son Daniel, (Chicago), daughter Madeline Davis, (Virginia Beach), and two grandchildren. Cremains will be placed in the Columbarium at the Woodlawn Cemetery, Norfolk, at 10 A.M. on December 21. Memorial donations may be made to the Multiple Sclerosis Society.

There really wasn't much more they could add to that. Vanessa declined to have her name put into the obituary, and they honored her request.

Maddie had one more request of the funeral director. Handing him her mother's cane she asked that it be added to the cardboard coffin in which her mother would be cremated. She was assured that would be no problem at all.

"You brought her cane with you," Dan was surprised.

"No. It was one I kept in the car for when I took Mom to the doctor or drug store."

Dan nodded. "Yeah, then. It should go with her."

Handing over the obituary they were leaving just as Maddie's phone rang. Nope. Not Ken. It was Tessa, making her usual daily call, in support.

"Hi, Maddie. Just wanting to call and let you know I'm here for you"

"Oh, Tessa, hi," she choked back tears, *"Mom died this morning."*

"Oh, hon. I am so very sorry, Maddie. What can we do to help?"

"Nothing... really. We just left the funeral home and she'll be inurned on the 21st. Altmeyer's is handling the cremains, but there won't be any service. Those were her wishes. Just a small obituary in the paper."

"Keep me posted, alright. We're here for you."

"Thanks, Tessa. I'll be out to visit again one of these days."

"I certainly hope so. We miss you."

The following day she felt lost. Maddie had no idea which way to turn. Why hadn't she planned all this better. She knew it was going to happen, yet she dragged her feet on important things like the obituary. She wished she had more information about her mother. She was horrified to realize she had no idea what schools her mother had attended. Did she go to college? Even Dan had no idea. He just shrugged. There was nothing she could do about any of that. At least her mother was debt free, the house was paid for, but she still had to figure out all the insurance and paperwork details that had to be done, like notify the bank, change the name on the utilities, and she was suddenly overwhelmed.

"Maddie, honey," Vanessa knelt down next to her chair. "I can put your mother's clothing in boxes, unless you'd rather do it yourself. Some folks would rather wait awhile."

"That's so thoughtful of you, Vanessa. Please go ahead."

"I'll leave the jewelry box and other small mementoes for you to sift through."

Maddie nodded. Suddenly there was so much to do and no energy to do it. After 41 years of pain and suffering from her mother it still didn't seem to be over yet. She wondered if it ever would be. Could she climb out of the hole she'd been buried in since Mark's death. She laid her head back and thought about Ken. This was the second day she hadn't heard from him. She felt so empty at that moment. She'd give anything for a hug from him. Just one little hug. Hadn't she read somewhere that you needed four hugs a day for survival? She'd had one hug from her brother in the past couple of days. And before that? When had Ken last given her a hug? Or when had she last allowed it? The salty taste of tears slid through the corner of her mouth. She wanted to fall into his arms for comfort, feel his kisses and know his body. It was just that simple.

Rubbing her forehead, she heard her brother come into the room.

"You alright, kid?"

She managed just the smallest upturn of her lips for a moment. "I am, and I'm not."

Dan stood behind her chair and put his hands on both of her shoulders, kneading them. "You're very tight."

"That feels so good. I'm just a mess right now, I guess."

"Well, Mother won't be bothering you anymore and maybe you can get back to Ken."

She broke into a small smile, "You remember his name."

"He stopped me outside when I was on my way to the hospital."

He felt her body stiffen, her shoulders turning back into iron.

"You saw Ken?" Maybe he'd misidentified some other man as Ken.

"Oh, it was Ken. He asked me if I was Dan, and I told him yes. Said he wanted to see you, but I told him it wasn't a good time since Mother was in the hospital, dying, and that's where you were. He said to tell you he was sorry to hear about our mother."

"Anything else."

"No, I didn't give him a chance. I jumped in the car and headed here. It looked to me like he went back around the corner, but I wasn't paying all that much attention. But I have to say I think you need to give more consideration to all that bullet wound stuff. The poor guy looked beaten down when I saw him. If you really think you care about him you need to dive in and live Maddie."

Maddie stood, "I'll go help Vanessa. Sorting clothing really isn't her job."

"I ordered some food for the reception after we do the inurnment. Just in case neighbors come. Better safe than sorry."

"Thanks, Dan. I never even thought about that."

Walking into the master bedroom, "Your mother didn't really have much clothing, so it's in three boxes. We can deal with what to do with them later. I'll remake the bed and you can move in here or let Dan have it while he's here."

"Let Dan have it." She began stripping the bed while Vanessa retrieved clean sheets. Together they had the bed freshly made in just a few minutes. "I'll tell Dan to come on in here, and bring his shaving stuff, too."

"Good thinking, Maddie. We might need the guest bathroom if people stop by."

The three of them sat at the kitchen table. No one was particularly hungry, so they nibbled on leftover garlic bread and potato soup for dinner.

"I remember Mother making this soup when we were young." Dan stirred it with his spoon. "I'd forgotten all about it."

"One of her favorites. She demanded… ah…requested it at least twice a month. But I always liked it, too."

"Okay, Maddie. All that's over now. We need to get you back with Ken."

Vanessa managed to nod her head in agreement as she slurped her spoonful of soup.

"I'm thinking about what you said, Dan. Somehow stuff like those lies just start slipping into the background and don't have the same force anymore. It's like, why am I worried about it all? I do hear what you've been saying, really. Maybe after all this is over I can get my head on straight and be able to think clearly again. I also worry that I might not ever see you again, too, Dan."

"Not to worry." He laughed a good belly laugh. Sliding his chair back he put his soup dish in the sink. "You're stuck with me now. I've had jobs in Richmond and can always hop on down here and visit you. I will go back to Chicago for Christmas. Want to be with Andy. Why don't you come up there with me?"

"I'd love to meet him, but I think since Christmas is only a few days away I'll just try to catch up with my life and get some serious decisions made."

"Well, know you're always welcome."

Standing she gave him a kiss on the cheek then put her own bowl in the sink. "Meanwhile, I'll go feed my critters, then help you move back to the master bedroom, and then maybe I'll go take a nice, long bath and go to bed early."

On the morning of the inurnment, they plowed through some of the necessary paperwork, lining up what needed to be done and in what order. Not as easy as one would think, even when things like funerals and inurnment were totally taken care of already. A quick look at Dori's very short Last Will and Testament gave Maddie the house. At first she cringed. Dan should have part of it.

"I don't like that, Dan. You should have half the house – half of everything in fact."

"Kiddo, I have a gorgeous home in Chicago, and a few million in the bank. I honestly don't need anymore. Andy is taken care of, and I even pay Sara support money, and I don't have to do that. But I care for her. I always will. We just grew apart is all. I'm truly hoping she finds a wonderful man to spend the rest of her life with. I'm serious about that. No. You keep the house and everything else."

"You're sure?"

"Absolutely."

They received a call from Altmeyer's that everything was ready. They would pick them up and transport them to Woodlawn at 9:30.

It was a chilly day, and the ride to Woodlawn seemed to take hours. She just wanted to get it all over with. She sensed that Vanessa was concerned about her but getting used to the new way her life would change was going to take some time. Vanessa would go back to her condo, and she'd be alone. It had been years since she'd been alone. Maddie was shocked when they arrived at the Columbarium promptly at ten and she saw neighbors, and school teacher friends, including Elle and Joan quietly standing there. In the background, Ken, Reed, Tessa and Drew, Trish and Paul, and all four of the boys, dressed up in suits, quietly watching the happenings. Woodlawn had supplied enough chairs so they could all be seated, while a minister offered a prayer. It was simple, but beautiful, and something Maddie had not thought about doing. The funeral director then presented the urn, asking Dan and Maddie to stand as official witnesses as the funeral director placed the urn in the Columbarum. The facing was reattached and sealed. The cemetery would add her name, and dates of birth and death later. With a sigh, Dan and Maddie turned back to the group and invited them to the reception at their mother's home as a small thanks for them taking the time to be with them.

She was almost certain it was all Tessa's doing that brought their entire family to the cemetery. It was the last thing she expected to see that day. Mouthing a silent 'thanks' to Tessa, she saw Tessa turn her face to look at Ken. An obvious, but welcome, hint.

Back in the limo for the ride home, "Good thing you ordered all that food, Dan." She was smiling. It made her happy seeing the entire Avery family there. That meant a great deal to her. She felt a soothing comfort. They cared. They supported her, and more importantly they were there hoping that she would see how much they stood behind Ken. An unspoken solidarity. It gave her a warm feeling.

The house would be full for the first time in probably ever! Just before leaving they had set up a couple of card tables, and when the caterers arrived a few minutes later there was plenty of space for all the food. Appetizers and hors d'oeuvres galore.

Maddie was surprised when several of the neighbors arrived to offer condolences. Her mother, it seemed, had been very active in the neighborhood, interacting with many of her neighbors over the years. They had all backed off when told that her daughter would be coming to care for her, because the MS was preventing her from doing many of the things she liked doing. Maddie had always just assumed her mother had been as nasty to the neighbors as she was with her. That didn't seem to be the case at all.

"Your mother was such a good bridge player and loved bingo. When she got sick we really missed her," the next-door neighbor confessed.

"I wondered why no one visited," was Maddie's only reply.

"Oh, she told us not to. She was horribly upset because her eyes were starting to give her problems, and balance was an issue. So, we just abided by her wishes. Sometimes people don't want to be seen as weak, and we figured that was a fair description of your mother."

"You're probably right. It does sound like Mother. Thank you so much for coming today. I wish I had known. I might have been able to talk Mother into having all of you over for bridge, or just to chat. I'm so sorry you all felt dumped so suddenly."

"It wasn't a problem, dear. We understood. We're all elderly, too, and have various health problems that make us feel disconnected at times. We just wanted to say goodbye to her. She's been in our prayers."

As the neighbors moved away to speak to others, Maddie saw Vanessa head toward the door and shake the hands of a man whose back was turned to her. Approaching she was astonished to see Dr. Foster. It brought tears to her eyes, which she managed to blink away before extending her hand.

"Dr. Foster! How kind of you to come."

"I couldn't make the service but wanted you to know I thought about your mother a lot. Up until the very last she was always fun, energetic, and very conversational. I could see her decline the last three visits. Doctors always think they can fix everything and then find out they can't. I'm so sorry for your loss, Maddie."

"Thank you Doctor. I really appreciate you being here today. Please help yourself to the food. There's enough for an army I think."

Maddie managed to spend some time with Elle, Joan and the other teachers who'd come to express their condolences. When Elle took her hand, and squeezed it, she knew that all was well with her. She'd been paying off her debt, and in fact had only two more months left, since she had been more than doubling her payments. Maddie just sensed that she was truly going to be fine.

As tired as she was getting she was pleased to see that Dan was mingling with everyone and having a good time telling folks about the job he did. She noticed the Avery family also doing a fair amount of mingling themselves and now their family group was circled around Dan, listening to him, and asking questions. Somehow the day was brighter. Every single person in the room had come to share their love with her, the neighbors, the doctor, and especially the Avery family. They all took the time, out of their busy lives, to stop and care. Her breathing increased as she began to feel the warmth in the room. Suddenly overwhelmed she found a chair and sat down. She'd spoken to everyone except the ones who meant the most to her. They were giving her space and time – space to come to terms with her mother's death and time to understand that she belonged in their family group. Massaging her hands on the arms of the chair she saw Ken look over at her, mouthing 'I love you' and smiling. Her response was automatic. She mouthed the same words back to him. She meant every one of those words.

Slowly, the room emptied out and Vanessa was removing empty dishes and disposing of the paper and plastic into pop-up trash containers supplied by the catering company. Maddie had to smile as Tessa walked straight towards her and sat down on the arm of the chair. "How ya doin' hon?"

Maddie couldn't keep the tears from starting. Catching her breath, she patted Tessa's hand. "I'm hanging in there, Tessa."

"No more of them tears, now. You can cry all you want later. But now you need to git yourself up off that chair and come jaw with your new family." Standing she reached down and took Maddie's hand, pulling her up from the chair. "This is all your doing, isn't it?" she followed as Tessa pulled on her arm.

"Who, me? I mighta put a small bug in their ears about your momma, but they kinda took it from there on their own. Knew they would," she grinned like she'd won the lottery.

Dan and Vanessa joined the group and conversation turned light and happy.

"I'm trying to get Maddie to come on up to Chicago for a visit," Dan put his arm around her shoulders. She looked up and met his eyes, then put her head on his shoulder. "I will come for a visit, but I think I'll stay here," she patted his chest.

Trish went back to check on the kids and returned with a thumbs up. Dragging fold-up chairs into the kitchen all nine of them sat down, scrunched in around the table, as Vanessa started pouring coffee into cups. "There's still a lot to eat, folks. Before you leave we'll bundle it for you to take home. We'll never eat all of that."

Ken had seated himself next to Maddie, and while chit chat was going on all around him he turned to her, speaking softly, his blue eyes locking onto hers. "I'm so sorry, Maddie. I've missed you so much. I honestly just wanted to protect you. You had enough to worry about with your mom and you didn't need to stress over something that would never happen again. I'm truly sorry."

Smiling, she reached over and took his hand. In just those last few minutes she had made up her mind. No more hiding the truth. No more ducking what had caused her more pain than all her mother's beatings, or even Mark's death.

As Vanessa started pouring coffee and handing out cups, Maddie sat straight up in her chair. "When Vanessa has served all of us, I have something I need to say."

The room grew instantly silent, the only noise was the glugging of the coffee pot as the last cup was filled and distributed. Sugar, cream, and spoons were passed around, then all eyes turned to Maddie.

Breathing in the maximum amount of air, she slowly let it out and began..

"All of you but Vanessa know how Mark died, and how Ken tried to save him. And for Vanessa, he died when his plane crashed on the deck of an aircraft carrier. I found out very recently that Ken was the doctor on the ship and tried to save his life. What I have never shared is what happened next. Mark's body had been returned to me, of course, and is now at the Memorial cemetery in Suffolk, but it was six weeks after his funeral when I was told the squadron was returning. Did I want to be present when they arrived at Oceana? Air squadrons always fly off the carriers and land at the airfields to which they are attached. I called Mike's wife, Carol, and we agreed to go together. The men hadn't had a chance to express their condolences, and despite knowing we would be seeing husbands reunited with wives and children, we went. The Navy sent cars for us, so we didn't even have to drive."

Gulping, she reached down and slowly sipped her coffee, gathering the strength to continue. "Anyway, we were welcomed by the Commanding Officer of the air station and were all standing outside the hanger when they announced the squadron would be arriving in just a few moments. Everyone was standing outside and began looking upwards as the jet noise grew louder. The band started playing the Navy Hymn, and it took every ounce of strength I had to stay on my feet. It's a hugely haunting song. Carol and I were holding hands almost to the point of pain, but it didn't stop the tears. Then the planes were suddenly there, four of them coming across the sky, and just as they reached where we were standing one plane veered off to the side, to honor Mark and Mike. It's called the "Missing Man Formation." Everyone, and I mean *everyone,* was in tears. I didn't have enough tissues, but others did and shared. Their hearts broke with ours. Our husbands weren't forgotten. Children were even silent. It was magnificent and overwhelming. Pilots from other squadrons led us to chairs and told us we were welcome to stay for the reception. It was so carefully orchestrated. We could either watch the men come from their planes and see the hugs and kisses, or remain inside with the reception, where many others from the base were milling around. We stayed inside. Carol and I had a very difficult time, and after about ten minutes we asked to be taken home."

Ken took her hand and Trish grabbed a box of tissues, placing it next to her. She heard low mumbles of sorrow, seeing tears on their faces as well.

Vanessa sat there stunned. She'd never heard the back story about Mark, other than he had died. She couldn't help gasping, "Oh, my God, Maddie, I'm so sorry."

Maddie held up her hand. "Unfortunately, there's more." Swallowing and gripping Ken's hand, "When I got word of the deaths I was three months pregnant. I lost the baby."

There! She's said it all, and out loud at that. She hadn't spoken of it to anyone but her attending doctor. Not one single person on earth knew she'd ever been pregnant but him. It was like a bomb had exploded, blasting the bitter and painful bits of her memory into the air. She had no idea it would make her feel so good to get it all out.

The only sound was a gasp from Vanessa. Everyone else just looked at her, not sure what to say or what to do. Finally, Dan, visibly upset, put his hands up to his face, "Oh, God, Maddie, I should have been there for you. I just thought Mom didn't want me and you'd forgotten all about me. I am so sorry."

She smiled at him, a huge, smile of relief. "I love you, Dan. I am so glad Mother made that stupid phone call to you and I'll be eternally grateful that you took the time to come and see for yourself." She laughed loudly, "and I didn't even recognize you when I opened the door. Thought you were some kind of salesman."

Walking around the table he pulled Maddie to her feet. "Well, you're stuck with me now." Giving her a huge hug, she squealed in delight. "I can accept that. I guess I'll keep you."

By then the entire group was hugging Maddie and telling her how sorry they were for the losses she had suffered during her lifetime.

"Thanks, all of you for hearing me out. Those were my only other secrets, and they were deep and hard to talk about. All of you have been so kind to me," she reached out and put her arm around Ken's waist, "and I'm so glad there are no more hidden secrets, or lies," she looked up at Ken with narrow eyes and cocked head, "Right Ken?"

"Right…unless you want the down and dirty about nurse Nancy."

Everyone laughed. "That's okay," Maddie assured them. "From what he's told me already I don't have a thing to worry about."

"Well, I don't know about the rest of you guys," Trish took Paul's arm, "but I'm going to grab my two youngins and head for home."

"Grab mine, too, Trish. We need to head back as well."

Giving Maddie hugs and kisses as they left, she was surprised when Reed bent down and told her, making sure Ken heard, "You do know I'll be divorced soon, and if this brother of mine isn't up to standards, well…" smiling, he left it at that.

"Just remember," Ken interrupted, "I fix what comes in the ambulance. All you do is chase it."

They gave each other a brotherly hug.

Dan and Vanessa had divided most of the food between the families, keeping a little for themselves to snack on the next day. Everyone was obviously exhausted.

Approaching them both Maddie and Ken told them they were heading to Ken's house, and she didn't have any idea when she'd be home. Both Vanessa and Dan nodded, with Dan adding, "See you tomorrow, Sis."

Climbing into Ken's car Maddie noted, "Hmm, you do know both Vanessa and Dan have bedrooms in my house, don't you?"

"Then maybe we'd better make sure you don't go home tonight."

"Sounds good to me," she reached over and patted his thigh.

Chapter 20

"I don't want to get up," Maddie said, sleepily.

"Then we won't. We can stay here all day as far as I'm concerned." Ken leaned over and kissed her. "So cozy," she whispered, "so comfortable."

His kisses had already started down her neck and she groaned. "God, you are so good at that, Ken," she breathed. "Umm."

Gently bringing his fingers up to stroke the side of her breast, like a puff of soft air, making her squirm in anticipation. A light brushing of his finger tip against her nipple and she could only pull him closer, guiding him.

"You're so beautiful, Maddie. I've been going insane with worry."

She could only groan again, softly, and call out his name.

It only took a minute to get her ready, as he slowly filled her, saying her name over and over as they became one. This was love. This was beautiful and meaningful and far more than he had ever experienced before.

"I love you, Maddie." He pulled her into his arms as they lay together, both trying to calm their breathing.

Her response was to snuggle up as close to him as she could get, holding him close with a contented sigh. "But I guess to be fair I really should spend some time with Dan. You come, too."

"Yeah, I get it," he grinned. "I think we need to go grab both Dan and Vanessa and go out to a smashingly good dinner."

"Okay, I love that idea. And when we get to the house you can help me with something."

"What?"

"It will be a surprise."

They held each other without any further conversation when Ken realized Maddie had fallen asleep again. What a wonderful ending, to see her smile so contentedly. Getting up carefully he showered and dressed, walking into the kitchen to make her breakfast.

Maddie woke, the smell of bacon just too much to ignore. Grabbing her clothing from yesterday she dressed and headed into the kitchen.

"Look at you, making breakfast!"

"I think you'll like it. I'm not a half bad cook."

"Good to know," she smiled and sat down.

Ken was curious about Maddie's surprise but didn't want to bug her about it. Instead, he put a cup of coffee down in front of her and grimaced a bit.

"What?" Maddie scrunched up her face.

"We have to take care of Vanessa, like we planned."

"Absolutely, but why do I feel you've taken care of it already?"

Ken's eyes looked down, but she noticed his eyes blinking more than usual.

"Um, well maybe. I don't want you to be mad because I didn't... well, under the circumstances I couldn't... talk to you. I tried... anyway..."

Maddie started laughing a huge belly laugh. "You are so transparent. It's easy to tell you're feeling guilty. So, sit down and tell me what *we* did?"

Maddie was surprised to hear that not only had Ken set everything up perfectly, but that Dan was in for a one-third share. It really tugged on her heart strings to know that he'd gone to that much trouble for Vanessa.

It was almost noon when they finally got back to Maddie's. "I need a shower before we do *anything*." she had demanded.

"Well, look what the cat dragged in," kidded Dan. He shook hands with Ken, then hugged Maddie.

"Hush your mouth, brother, or we won't take you out for a smashing dinner."

"Actually, Vanessa and I were talking last night, and we have a much better idea. We have just enough time to accomplish it, too."

"I'm listening," Maddie looked at both of them with suspicion.

"Then pile into my car. Vanessa will navigate, I'll drive, and you two get blindfolded."

"What?"

"Try to keep up, here," Dan scolded, with a chuckle.

"Alright, but I need to change clothes. Give me five minutes, ten at the most."

"We can do that. Speed it up," Dan said, moving his arms forward and backward, "hustle, hustle."

"Well, I took a two-minute shower and here I am. What, eight minutes?"

"Close enough."

Vanessa stepped forward carrying two scarves. "Alright, you two. We'll blindfold you as we get into Dan's car. Then we have to trust that you'll not peek."

Maddie looked at Ken, who shrugged his shoulders. "Ooookay, then. Let's see what you have up your sleeve."

The car ride wasn't long, and Maddie tried desperately to keep up with Vanessa's 'turn left here', and 'turn right at the next light' stuff.

The car came to a stop and Dan and Vanessa helped Maddie and Dan out of the car.

"Okay, give it up." Maddie said.

"You can take the blindfolds off." Vanessa closed the car door as they both reached up and took off the blindfolds

"A Christmas tree lot!" Maddie was so excited she bent forward and backward like a child.

"We are decorating a tree in your new house, tonight," Dan and Vanessa, smiled. They were hoping she would take it as a thoughtful gift.

"When was the last time you decorated a tree, Maddie?" Dan asked.

"It was before coming to live with Mother. After Mark died I just put up a little two-foot tree on an end table. It was all I needed, and it never had any gifts under it."

Dan froze, "Are you saying the last time you got a Christmas gift was the Christmas before Mark was killed."

"Pretty much. The children always had small gifts for the teachers, and I got the coffee cups and a small gift card or something. It was all I needed."

"Let's go, before I start to cry," said a crestfallen Vanessa.

Maddie rushed forward, clapping her hands.

They all agreed on a four-foot-tall tree. Next Dan pointed them across the street to a store selling Christmas ornaments, a tree stand, and tree skirt. Despite Ken's attempts to pay part of the bill, Dan refused, "It's Vanessa's and my gift to her, Ken. She needs bright and cheery now, and lots and lots of blinking lights will do it. I remember as a kid she would stand for hours looking at the lights when they were blinking. And trust me, I can afford it."

Ken shook his hand. "Thanks, Dan. I'll make sure those twinkle lights are on 24/7 except when the house is empty, which won't be very often!" He gave Dan a sly smile.

Fully loaded they dragged everything into the house. "Dinner is still on me, guys," Ken announced. "Pizza or Chinese?"

Pizza won.

Admiring the job, they had done over the past couple of hours, Maddie couldn't contain herself. "Gosh this is wonderful. I never would have thought of it. Thanks so much you two," pointing at Dan and Vanessa. "I'll leave the lights on all night so if I get up in the middle of the night I can see them. So pretty." Her exuberance made them all laugh.

"She reminds me of when she was five," Dan said.

"Wait until it gets dark outside, and they'll really be pretty," Dan hung another ornament he found in the bag.

Turning, Maddie pointed, "Which reminds me of something. Ken, will you help me with that surprise I told you about?"

"Sure, what do you need?" Finally, he thought. This will be interesting.

"I want you to help me open the blinds."

"My pleasure," he grinned. "Absolutely my pleasure."

"Then they'll only be closed at night."

They walked around the rooms with the blinds down and made a ceremony of opening them, their laughs getting bigger with each one. When the last one was done she gave Ken a kiss, then led him back to where Dan and Vanessa were waiting.

"Listen, Sis. I'm going home Christmas eve, in the morning. I promised Andy I'd be there for him. So, I can spend tomorrow with you before leaving." Ah, he side-eyed and hooked a thumb towards Ken, "I trust I can leave you in Ken's hands?"

Ken nodded. "Won't let her out of my sight." Picking up his phone he punched in a favorites number and walked away to make the call. Returning, "What would you all think about going out to Suffolk tomorrow and seeing the peanut farm? Drew and Tessa would love it."

"I'd like that," Dan said.

Vanessa looked at each of them. "You want to include me?"

"Oh, Vanessa," Maddie gave her a stunned look. "You are a member of this family, whether you like it or not." Holding up a card, "And speaking of which, we all want to give you this for all the care and love you gave Mother, and the peace you gave to me."

Vanessa brought her hand up to her face, her index finger just touching her jaw, her lips pulled up a bit on one side. Slowly she reached out and took it. "Should I open it now?"

"Yes," Ken, Maddie, and Dan spoke at once, then grinned at her.

Her hands shaking, she looked at the papers inside the card, and as she moved one to the back to see the second she burst into tears. "I can't take all this," she was crying so hard Dan stepped up and put his arm around her.

"Trouble is, Vanessa, you don't have a choice," Ken's eyes were bright and had a sparkle to them. Maddie was almost jumping with glee. "Ken speaks the truth," she added.

"We called your daughter in Hawaii, and she's practically standing in the airport waiting for you to get there. So, we're sending you off day after tomorrow, Christmas eve, to be with them for Christmas."

Tears were flowing down Vanessa's face, and Dan grabbed some tissues for her.

"Unless, of course, if you'd rather not go, and just stay here, hang out in your cold, undecorated condo…"

"Oh, Ken, stuff it," Vanessa was so busy wiping tears off her face she could barely talk but managed those few words.

Ken and Maddie walked up to hug her.

"And a trust fund, guys, it's way over the top and far too much."

"Vanessa, really. Maddie, Dan and I all have more money to spend than we'll ever be able to do, so use it to visit your daughter wherever the military takes them. When they finally retire or he gets out of the service, buy a condo or house near them. It's the least we could do for all the comfort you gave to Maddie."

More tears, Vanessa nodded, "Thank you two, so very much. But you three are as much my family as is my daughter and hers. I'll be spending all my time convincing them to end up here, in Virginia Beach, when he gets out of the Navy."

"That sounds great," Maddie chimed in.

"Are you all in for peanuts tomorrow then?"

Everyone nodded their heads yes.

"Then meet us here tomorrow at 9, and we'll head on over. I suspect they'll have all the bells and whistles out for us. for Christmas Eve Eve!!"

The house was lit up from stem to stern. The four of them stood in front of it, amazed. "Imagine what it looks like at night!" Maddie was fascinated. While a few of the houses in her neighborhood did decorations and lights, it wasn't anything like this. Not that she ever went out looking of course. For years Christmas was just another day on the calendar, but it was a quieter one. There was no other movement when she would go out to feed the critters. No cars drove by, and no one was out walking their dogs, or for exercise. It was just eerily quiet. Of course, the critters weren't concerned that it was a holiday. They wanted their food, and she had that handled. Seeing Drew's home made her want to go see the boardwalk display, and then head to the Botanical Garden and drive through theirs as well. She honestly felt like a new person.

Drew and Tessa both loved talking about growing peanuts, raising two sons, living in the country, and seeing more stars at night than if they lived in the city.

"Farm's large enough for a wedding, too," he punched Ken in the arm.

"Yeah, with a reception of peanuts, huh?" Ken kidded back.

"Peanut pie, peanut butter sandwiches, peanut butter served with ice cream, throw in a banana, roast and caramelize them...."

"I would demand peanut brittle," Maddie bowed. "And when bride and groom leave the family throws peanuts instead of rice."

Everyone chuckled.

Tessa had a gigantic spread set up for lunch and all the growling stomachs were grateful.

"Well, Drew and I stay here for Christmas, naturally, and the boys always swamp the living room with all the stuff we give them."

"Yeah," Drew said sarcastically. "Paper everywhere."

Tessa shushed him. "What are all of you doing?"

Maddie spoke up first, "I'm staying home and watching the blinking lights on my tree. Dan and Vanessa gave me a tree and we decorated it and it's beautiful. No matter where my spirt had gone for all those years, that brought it right back into my life." She smiled broadly at Dan and Vanessa.

"Ken?" Tessa looked at him, "You're certainly welcome to come here and be with us."

"I'll stay with Maddie," he locked eyes with her, and pointed his chin in her direction.

"That's way better than coming over here," Drew surmised.

Ken just grinned right back at him, with a thumbs up.

"Vanessa?"

"I'm leaving tomorrow for Hawaii to spend as long as I can with my daughter's family."

"How wonderful," Tessa tapped the table with her hand. "And Dan?"

"I'll fly back to Chicago tomorrow to be with my son."

"Oh, good. We'll all be with family, one way or the other."

Making sure there was a fifty-pound bag of critter nuts in the trunk of Ken's car, Tessa and Drew waved goodbye to them.

"We need to get these two home, Maddie, so they have time to pack and prepare for their trips."

Pursing her lips, and turning to look at Vanessa and Dan, "I'm gonna miss you guys. Seriously." She took a deep breath to keep her tears from falling.

"I'll only be gone two weeks, Maddie, and that will give you and Ken time to figure everything out."

"I agree," piped in Dan. "And I'll be down here as often as I can, which will likely be so often I'll have to find a place to live. Maybe buy a small house or get a condo or something. A lot of what I do can be done remotely!"

Maddie turned on the radio to a Christmas music station and they all listened as Ken drove them home.

Both their flights were close enough together that Ken and Maddie took them both to the airport at the same time.

"Dan, will you do me a favor?"

"Sure."

"Will you buy some flowers and put them on Father's grave for me?"

Seeing the waterworks start, Dan pulled her into his chest and held her tight. "I'll be happy to do that. I'll send you a picture."

"Thanks," she whispered.

Handshaking and hugging over, both Dan and Vanessa entered the lobby. No point in Ken and Maddie going any further as the TSA Precheck line was just to the left. Waving one last time they got back into the car and drove away.

Ken rubbed his fingers over the steering wheel, "You think there's anything going on between Vanessa and Dan? I mean they were alone in the house together last night."

Maddie paused in thought. "I don't know. I don't think so. When I went in to change clothes her bed was still unmade, and Dan's shower was still damp. I went back real quick and the shower she uses was also damp. So, no. I don't think so. Would be kinda neat, though."

He nodded. "I'm guessing it's your house for Christmas?"

"You wouldn't dare make me miss all those shiny lights, twinkling on the tree." She reached over and put her hand on his thigh. "Would you?" her saucy voice said.

"Right. I'll pack a suitcase and be over soon."

Christmas Day was spent at Maddie's, relaxing, and enjoying each other. They talked about everything they could think about. What games they played as a child, what subjects were their favorites in school. What about religion, and where they were with politics. Maddie had to admit that a lot of those subjects weren't something she had given any thought to in the past ten years, but she had general ideas based on his questions. They were more alike than either of them thought possible.

Ken took hold of her hand, "I didn't get you anything for Christmas, and I'm sorry about that."

"Oh, Ken. You gave me YOU. I don't think you have any idea how happy I am right now. You are so handsome and caring. I'll never understand how I managed to catch your eye."

Kissing her, "Wasn't just my eye, sweetheart," He growled. "I see this incredibly gorgeous woman dragging a tree, backwards, and my heart flipped upside down."

"Best tree job I ever had done." She giggled.

Christmas Eve and Christmas night were spent in bed, door open, and twinkle lights on. They reflected on the hallway walls, making Maddie's eyes glow with wonder.

They both woke up to the ringing of Ken's cell phone. He groaned, then worried it might be Jerry. He was relieved to pick it up and see Trish's name.

"Hey, Ken. Happy day after Christmas! Why don't you and Maddie come over and celebrate New Year's Eve with us?"

"Happy day after Christmas to all of you, too. Can I call you back? Maddie's still asleep."

"Sure."

"Okay, bye."

"Love you, bye."

"I wasn't asleep," Maddie poked him.

"I know, but I wanted to give you time to decide if you want to go to the Eastern Shore for New Year's Eve. We'd end up spending the night."

"Yes. I can overfeed the critters, and not feel guilty. I'd love to go."

Chapter 21

Paul and Trish were excellent hosts. It was fascinating to hear about Paul's job. He was a conservation police officer, and as such came up against everything from poachers of big game to those who illegally harvested marine life. He also watched for habitat damages, evaluated wildlife, and educated the public on conservation.

They ate like royalty, and that evening Paul and Trish let the boys stay up to watch the Chincoteague Horseshoe Drop on television. As Trish had predicted, both boys were asleep on the couch by 10:30. Just before heading to bed they celebrated with the New Year's kiss. Trish then reached over to the counter and pulled a frame across. Handing it to Maddie, "It's a really great picture I took of you and Ken, at your mother's reception. I hope you like it."

Maddie looked at it, then showed Ken, finally clasping it to her chest. Her eyes misting, she hugged Trish. "I absolutely love it. Our first picture together. Thank you so much."

With a final toast everyone went to bed, Paul waking the two boys, and sending them off to their rooms.

"Oh, I am just so happy," Maddie said, as they entered the guest room. She was putting the picture on the dresser when she heard Ken cough.

"You alright?" She turned quickly to see him down on one knee. "Oh, my God," her hand went to her mouth in shock.

"Maddie, the first day I saw you, dragging that tree down the driveway, I knew you were so different I had to pay attention. Well, you've taken up so much more than that. My every waking moment has been thinking about you – loving you – and praying you'd forgive all my stupid mistakes. So, Madeline Rogers Davis, will you marry me?" His hands were shaking so hard he could barely flip open the box to reveal a beautiful one caret diamond solitaire ring.

"It's so beautiful," she stammered. "So, so, sparkly." She was lost in space just staring at the ring.

"Maddie?" He choked.

"What? Yes, oh, my gosh, yes."

Standing he put the ring on her finger. "Okay. now we can go to bed," he said, calmly.

"Why would I want to do that?" she countered, as cool as a cucumber, her hand held up, wiggling her fingers, her eyes fixated on the glint of the diamond.

All she heard before her body landed on the bed was a deep and forceful, "Grrr."

They planned a January 30th wedding. Neither one of them wanted to wait even that long, but some things took time. Tessa couldn't wait to start decorating, since both Ken and Maddie took them up on their offer of having the wedding at the peanut farm. Knowing it would be very cold outside they did opt for inside if the weather was as bad as it usually got in January. No snow was expected for the next three weeks. They had to count on that. Maddie was still wrestling with who would be her Matron of Honor. All her friends were married. She thought of Elle. She had to admit Elle had amazed her. She'd gotten help through a psychologist and had gained serious insight as to the causes of her behaviors. She was making solid ground on all the changes. But Elle was a stranger to everyone else. Vanessa was in Hawaii. Her one regret was that Vanessa wouldn't be there, but as was said about every major event, you could never make it onto everyone's schedule. She was pleased to know that one of Reed's partners knew of a man who could do a video feed of the wedding so Vanessa could watch. Reed said that was his gift to them, knowing they wanted for nothing. She smiled, recalling the gifts others had provided. Tessa and Drew gave her a lifetime supply certificate for critter peanuts, and not the bottom of the harvest either. Trish and Paul threw in camping gear and a tent for two. Surprisingly there was a gift from all four boys. It was a wedding time capsule - a tin container, decorated appropriately, where they could put all sorts of memory stuff from the time they met to the time they married, then seal it, and set it to reopen on a special day in the future, like a 25th anniversary. They were already coming up with ideas.

But back to the dilemma, that left Tessa and Trish, and she tapped her finger against her lips with a huge sigh. Trish was obviously adored by Ken. Tessa, though, had been the one to call her every day to make sure she was alright, offering any and all help that might be needed.

"How's the planning going?" Ken asked as he walked into the room, putting a cup of steaming hot coffee down next to her.

"Hmm. Well, the best part is knowing that Dan can come to walk me down the aisle." Her smile was broad and her eyes shining with happiness. "And, for the most part, everyone else took some part of the event to do, so all I have to do is get a dress!"

"I like simple. I really do. I do want to run something by you though."

She turned to watch him. "Go ahead."

"Well, I'd like to ask Jerry to be my Best Man, but I don't want to upset you. I'm planning to tell him I won't be coming back to Doctors World Wide. I don't want to give you any cause to worry, Maddie. Never again."

Taking his arm, she led him to the couch. "Sit."

She sat down beside him. "First, of course Jerry should be your Best Man. He's been your best friend forever."

Ken visibly relaxed. "I was afraid you'd worry about him bugging me."

"Ken, I'll be most disappointed in you if you quit working for Jerry. I know I went overboard about the bullet wound but calming down I realized that the chance of that happening again is zero, and I gather from now on there will be proper security for any medical deliveries."

"You won't mind if I leave for a week or two here and there?"

"Ken, I'm a Navy widow. I'm also absolutely positive I can take care of myself. I'd be shocked if you doubted that. Besides, Vanessa will be around most of the time, so I'll have plenty to keep myself occupied. Little trips to visit Tessa and Trish... goodness... I'll have tons of things to keep busy, including all my critters."

"You're absolutely, positively, totally, alright with it?"

"All of the above, dear. Now, ah, I have a small predicament of my own."

"Okay, go ahead." She was so beautiful; how could he not just sit and stare at her.

"I need to ask someone to be my Matron of Honor. I don't want to offend anyone or make them feel left out. I've narrowed it down to Tessa and Trish, and I love both of them deeply. I just don't want any hurt feelings."

"Maddie, whomever you choose is fine with me. Both are wonderful women, worthy of your choice. I honestly and truly have no favorite."

"You're sure."

"Absolutely, positively for sure."

"Okay, then. I'll go from there. But there is one other thing."

"Shoot."

"I'd like to ask the Davis' to attend." She lowered her eyes, folding her hands on her lap.

"Maddie, I have no problem with that," he took her hands in his. "I'm very serious about that. You told me Mark was their only child. It's been years, but maybe it's time you figured out how they are doing and what they are feeling. It can help you put the past back into the past, but it's also a way to caress the future. And if they are willing to come that speaks volumes about their acceptance of you as his wife."

"But they were so distant to me, especially at his funeral."

"Maddie, they had just lost their only child. It takes years to get over the shock, sometimes, and their son was so very young. I've seen so many things happen when a loved one dies. Surgeons get a lot of life's lessons when they have to tell families that their loved one has died. Give them a chance. And, if it means anything, and they can come, they can stay in my house. It's empty now. I live with you." He winked at her.

Tears welled in Maddie's eyes. "I thought about Dan living there, but he said he and his son want to stay with Drew. Andy is anxious to see what a peanut farm is."

"What about Jerry and Donna?"

Ken laughed. "You're going to throw me out of the house the night before the wedding, right?"

"Absolutely right."

"Jerry can come with me to Reeds, and maybe Donna could stay with you, here? You two seemed to hit it off at the dinner, ah, er, that crummy night."

She burst out laughing, barely able to swallow the sip of coffee before he said that."

"That's good. She can keep me calm. Meanwhile, you go ahead and go do whatever it is you need to do, and I'll write them a letter and see you for dinner."

She pushed him out the door. She needed the time. She'd found a beautiful cream-colored dress that fell just below her knees. It had short sleeves, a scoop neck, and was lace over satin. Perfect. It kept with the "semi-casual dress code" she had requested for everyone. Men didn't need suits, and sport jackets would be fine. But Maddie had one last thing she needed to take care of, and it wasn't going to be easy. Sitting down at her desk she picked up a pen and paper, took in a deep breath, let it out, and began to write:

Dear Mr. and Mrs. Davis:

I apologize for being so remiss these past several years. I was so depressed when we lost Mark, and then my mother got seriously sick, and I've had to spend the last several years caring for her. It's not an excuse, I know. She died recently, and I just wanted you to know that after all these years another man has come into my life.

I will never stop loving Mark. He was my everything, but I have found a wonderful man who understands completely that Mark will always have a piece of my heart. I want you to know that Ken was the doctor on board the U.S.S. Eisenhower, who tried to save Ken's life. He swore to me that Ken was so seriously hurt he never would have led a normal life. He died on his table, despite heroic efforts to save him. Ken and I will be married on January 30th, in Suffolk, at the peanut farm owned by one of his brothers. I would be honored if you could attend, and in the process I would love to take you to the cemetery when Mark is buried, not far from where we will be married. If you would like to come, please call me, or write to me, at the address and telephone number below for more information. You would be more than welcome to stay in Ken's home, just around the corner from mine, and would have the house to yourselves.

I sincerely hope you can make our small wedding.

Love, Maddie, adding her phone number and address.

Sealing the letter in an envelope she put it in the mailbox. It was one of the few times she was glad the carrier was late.

One last item to get off her check-off-list was to call Tessa first.

"Oh, Maddie, I am so very honored that you asked me to be your Matron of Honor, but please, please know that I will be extremely busy here making sure everything is ready for the big event. I'll be rushing to see the ceremony then rushing around while you get the pictures taken to be sure the caterers are doing what I want them to do... not that I'm a perfectionist or anything," she howled, "but I don't want a single mistake here."

Now she could only hope that Trish didn't say no... but Trish was thrilled to be asked.

"Just wear something simple, Trish. Don't go buy anything new."

"I have just the dress. Wore it at one of my friend's weddings, and it will be perfect."

Maddie wiped the sweat off her brow. All she had to do was done. Well, she hoped it was at least.

Her final action was to take the picture she had of Mark, next to her bed, and move it to the shelving next to the fireplace. Just as she finished she heard Ken return. "What's up?" he walked into the family room.

"I hope you don't mind. I moved the picture of Mark from my bedside to here," she pointed to the shelf.

"Of course, I don't mind, Maddie. I don't need every little, tiny corner of your heart to know you love me. You'll always have a place for him there. I would be upset if you didn't. It's wonderful to know you can care for someone so deeply. I want to secure my place in that heart of yours as well," he walked up and gave her a gentle kiss.

"I've often wondered," she softly placed her hand on his cheek, "what would have happened if you hadn't scared me half to death while I was dragging the tree out of the back yard."

"Hmm. I think it would have been the same. Every time I walked by your house I wondered who lived there and was bound and determined to find out somehow. It might have been a fluke that you were dragging that tree, but eventually I would have seen you out there loaded down with peanuts."

"Speaking of which, I'm going to have to get another fridge to store them in since Tessa can't seem to shove them at me fast enough!"

He patted her hand. "We can do that."

"Listen," she said softly. "I did write to Mark's parents and asked them if they would like to come to the wedding. I doubt they will, but I felt I should tell them about you, even that you were trying to save him."

His eyes looked over her head, as he pulled her head into his shoulder. "I think that's good. Maybe we can be of comfort to them. But you did what you needed to do, and time will tell. I'd love to meet them. Mark was their son. I can tell them anything they want to know."

"And Trish will be my Matron of Honor. She's thrilled"

Backing off and looking at her, "Want me to ask her to dress up in a way that our mother would have approved of with her appearance?"

"I double-dog-dare you, cause I'd be forced to call off the wedding when she showed up with one-inch fingernails and over-sprayed hair."

That made him laugh.

Charles and Darlene Davis did indeed come, arriving two days before the wedding. Maddie was thrilled, and hugs and tears were everywhere. Ken made sure they were settled in his home and sat down and answered all the questions they had about their son. They were so grateful they couldn't stop thanking him. With most of that day free they drove them out to the Albert G. Horton Memorial Cemetery to visit their son.

"Maddie," Darlene began, taking Maddie's hand. "You will always be our daughter. You know Mark was an only child, and life has been very difficult for us since we lost him, but if you'd let us we'd love to be part of your new family in some way."

"Absolutely. In fact, move down here and join the party! Ken will be selling his home soon. Special good deal for family! That would be so cool! Virginia Beach is way better than Baltimore."

She saw Darlene look at Charles, almost as if she wanted him to give that some serious thought.

For two nights it was a mix of people and dinners in restaurants. While the Davis family stayed in Ken's home, Dan and his son were with Drew. Andy couldn't wait to get to a peanut farm and see what that was all about, and he was close enough in age, at 16, to do well with both Roddy who was 13, and Sonny 11. Andy was an easy going kid and one that Dan was very proud of. That left just Jerry and Donna. With Maddie determined that Ken not see her on the day of the wedding, both he and his Best Man, Jerry, were shuffled off to slum it with Reed. Well, that was what Maddie had said. "Go slum it with your rich brother." Maddie had been a bit cautious, as Jerry seemed uncomfortable, as if he wasn't sure what to say or do. His fear was that Maddie would never really be able to forgive him for "letting the cat out of the bag" about Ken's wound, but she assured him, immediately, that it was probably a good thing to happen. It cleared the air, once and for all, and she was thrilled that he could stand with Ken.

Her wedding day began with a gorgeous sun, rising from the East and making the entire earth beautiful. Well, Maddie thought so anyway. Trish had arrived in a beautiful soft dress, teal colored with an A-line skirt stopping just below her knees, and long sleeve over-jacket. It was perfect. Everyone else had gone ahead, so she rode out with Paul, Trish, and the boys. She would change into her dress at Tessa's, who greeted her with a hug.

"Wow, Tessa, don't you look fantastic!" The soft yellow dress was perfect with her complexion.

"Thank you, Maddie. Just for you," she grinned. "Everything is on time. You have an hour to change, and the catering service just finished setting up. The food will arrive when the ceremony is over, and while the pictures are being taken."

Maddie walked into the bedroom, Trish right behind her, grinning oddly. "What's the grin for?"

"Oh, nothing Just anxious to get that handsome brother of mine settled down."

"Me, too," Maddie put her hand in prayer, rubbing them up and down, then she turned. "VANESSA! Oh, my gosh, Vanessa!" Maddie's hands came up to her cheeks and her eyes were opened wide. "What are you *doing* here?"

"Well, duh! Someone I know is getting married today, and nothing in the world would make me miss that."

"But you were visiting your daughter."

"For over a month, Maddie. And just to keep you up to date," she rolled her eyes up into her head, "I've come into a huge amount of money. Like I'm a CEO of something, so I can even charter a plane back to Hawaii if I want to."

Laughing at the obvious dig, "Oh, Vanessa, give me a hug."

"This is your day, hon. I wanted to be here."

"I want you in my wedding pictures. You're not that much older than me, but you've been like a mother, someone I could talk to when I was so down and confused."

"You're going to make me cry."

Now everything was perfect. Maddie didn't care if it poured down rain, there was nothing that could ruin this day.

"Oh, but we were going to do a live feed for you to watch the wedding in Hawaii." Maddie cringed.

"We know," Vanessa said. "We've talked to the video man, and he'll still send the video so my daughter can watch. She wants to see the family that means so much to me."

Could this day get any better? Only when that ring was on her finger.

Vanessa and Trish left just as Tessa came into the room. Maddie had finished dressing. "Oh, Maddie, you are a vision. Ken will need Jerry to be very strong to keep him standing. Drew says he's gonna love watching his baby brother cry when he sees you come down the aisle. I think he has his camera set on maximum closeup, so he doesn't miss that. In video." She laughed a good belly laugh. Pointing to the door, "Dan is just outside. Shall we?"

Pressing both her arms into her body, taking a large breath, and hunching her shoulders, Maddie's face broke into a wide smile, "We shall."

"Kiddo, you are absolutely breathtaking," Dan offered his arm and began the walk, suddenly turning to go outside.

Freezing in her steps for a moment, "Dan, where are we going?"

"You'll see."

Having no choice but to trust her brother, she walked carefully beside him as he led her towards a barn.

"A barn?"

"Um, hmm."

What in the world, she thought? What are they doing to us? Just then all five boys opened the doors and Trish entered ahead of her. They closed the doors briefly, to allow Dan to position themselves at the opening. As the strains of the Wedding March began the boys again opened the door. Maddie was shocked. The entire inside of the barn had been decorated in the most incredible wedding decorations. White streamers were hanging from the rafters, and large hanging baskets, filled with flowers, hung between each drape. Holding on to Dan's hand tightly she wasn't sure she could walk it was so amazing. Lights twinkled softly, flowers were all along the sides and at the front, the chairs were all covered with white fabric, and she was so overwhelmed Dan had to turn to her and speak softly. "Let's go, kiddo. I'm hungry."

Maddie exhaled the breath she'd been holding, let go of his hand and took his arm. Looking only at Ken, she started down the aisle. She saw him gasp, just a little, then gulp, and watched as Jerry put a hand on his shoulder to steady him.

There really were tears on his face as she reached him. Gently reaching up she pushed them away with her soft hands. He mouthed "I love you," to her, and she smiled. They barely heard their vows. All they could do was look into each other's eyes. It was magic.

As they kissed, the group went wild, clapping, hooting, whistling, and cheering. She was now Madeline Rogers Davis Avery. Ken had insisted she keep all those names, both in memory of her father, more than her mother, and Mark as well. But yes, she could shorten it to Madeline Avery, for legal stuff if she so desired.

The reception was indeed inside the house, and once Maddie and her entourage had all the pictures taken, courtesy of Reed and a wedding photographer he knew, they saw that the caterers had arrived during the ceremony and the food was ready to eat. Good thing, too, since Maddie reminded Dan he was hungry.

If she lived to be one hundred, nothing could outshine this day. It was a simple reception with food to satisfy even the pickiest eater.

The surprises never seemed to end. When most seemed to be done with eating, Tessa moseyed into the laundry room, coming back out pushing a wheeled cart with a beautifully decorated wedding cake on top. Maddie was so stunned she had to grab Ken's arm to keep from falling. "Oh, Tessa, how beautiful. You made it, didn't you?"

She nodded.

"Your talents astound me. Thank you, from the bottom of my heart." She gave Tessa a gentle hug.

Tessa handed her a knife to cut, and they all watched as Ken and Maddie shared the first slice. Then Trish and Vanessa took over the rest of the cake cutting, making sure to save the top layer for Ken and Maddie to put in the freezer for their first anniversary.

"Oh, and there's one more thing," Tessa cued the music. "You have to do the first dance. At least start it, then the rest of us lugs will join in!"

The strains of Elvis singing 'Can't Help Falling in Love with You' began as Ken took Maddie's hand and led her into the middle of the room.

"Our first dance," he whispered in her ear. "I don't ever want to stop dancing with you."

Chapter 22

It was no secret they were planning to go to Niagara Falls for their honeymoon. Maddie had loved visiting there as a child and was curious about seeing the falls partially frozen. She'd heard it was a beautiful sight. Ken had been around the world. Anywhere was fine with him. Vanessa would stay in her old room at Maddie's for that week as critter feeder. Heck, half her clothes were still there since they'd hustled her off to Hawaii so fast. This would also give her a chance to slowly move her things back to her own condo and spruce up the house for Maddie. She even enjoyed feeding the birds and squirrels. She felt so blessed that Maddie and Ken had come into her life. Dori wasn't so much a nasty old lady as one overtaken by jealousy. It was sad to know that she had wasted so many years of enjoying her daughter because of hatred and spite. Vanessa absolutely adored her own daughter, and now her son-in-law and grandson. The gift from Ken, Maddie and Dan meant everything in the world to her. She could visit her own family, on a whim, anywhere in the world at any time. Now that she was sure that Ken was moving in with Maddie, she wanted to do some small, nice things for them. While the bedspreads were in good order, she wanted fresh, new ones.

Replacing them was easy, and she put the older ones in plastic bags in the closet. A couple of new area rugs were in order now that there was no longer any reason to worry about Dori and tripping hazards. It wasn't much, but it helped brighten up the house. The week went quickly, and before she knew it Ken and Maddie were home.

"My gosh, you two, you look all wore out!"

Maddie looked at her, "I haven't walked or stood that much since I taught school, and that was in a galaxy far, far away."

Ken laughed. "She's not far off. We made use of every minute and I might have pushed her a bit too hard. I'm used to going for hours at a time in the operating room, without food even. I forget she's had an active life, and a ton of stress, but yeah, I overdid it."

"There's more to see than I would have suspected. Seeing the falls partially covered with ice, with the water still flowing underneath was amazing. Then there was an hour tour where we got to visit the Niagara observation deck. Then, of course, there was the journey behind the falls. And that included a bunch of tunnels directly behind the Horseshoe falls. And I got soaked!" She saw Ken raise his hand to cover a smile, and she smacked it. "Not funny, Ken. I had to do my hair all over again."

"Sorry," he burst out laughing again. "I have great pictures of that, Vanessa. You should see her with her hair all soaked…"

Maddie side-eyed him, complete with evil sparks. "Then there was the butterfly place, and the bird place, and the flower place." She let out her breath. "All that and we still had to get breakfast, lunch, and dinner. Non-stop and we didn't see all of it by any means."

"Show me all the pictures and tell what you liked the best." Vanessa had lunch ready for them. After they'd eaten, and showed everything to Vanessa, they gave her a Niagara Falls Christmas tree ornament, for all her future Christmases.

"This is a perfect yearly reminder for me to be so grateful for having you two in my life. Now, I think I have all of my stuff moved back to my own condo, so you should be ready to entertain guests now. So, I'm going to head on to my own condo and leave you two to your own devices. Call if you need anything or can't find something! Walking to her car, she turned back to them, "Oh, by the way, glad to have you guys home. I hear Reed is planning a huge welcome back party this weekend, so y'all might want to check on that. I think you're the main attraction."

All Maddie could do was groan. "You call Reed, Mr. Surgeon person. I'm tired and going to take a nap."

"Okay. You deserve it," he gave her a gentle kiss.

"What's up, Reed? Vanessa says something is planned for this weekend?"

"Yup. Everyone will be here. Even Dan can make it. We gotta welcome you guys back to the fold. Get all those pictures in order and we'll supply the food. Let's just hope it doesn't snow, but if it does I have lots of bedrooms for our foreign friends from Suffolk and the Eastern Shore."

"Alright. Send me the time and all by message so I can forward it to Maddie. She's sleeping. I ran her into the ground in Niagara Falls."

"Not a nice way to treat your new wife there, Kenneth, old boy."

Ken laughed. *"We'll be fine. Just hard to realize we're getting older and can't run around like we were twenty anymore."*

"Amen, brother. I'll send you the info. See ya then."

"Bye."

With night already coming across the Eastern horizon, Ken decided he'd take a shower and join his wife in bed. He was a bit tired, too.

Making their way through town on their way to Reed's, Maddie yawned, more than once.

"Keeping you up, am I?"

"I just need to catch up on my sleep. I spent twelve years doing absolutely nothing, every day, except cook and clean for Mother, and feed critters. Don't get me wrong, I loved everything we did, just maybe next time we only do 5 or 6 things a day instead of 15."

Ken laughed. "Fair enough. You should have said something, Maddie. I'm so used to going for hours at a time…"

"Hush. I love you."

She really did have a great time at the impromptu party – if impromptu was the right word. It was for them anyway. It was fun telling them all about their various adventures and showing all the pictures. Ken just put his memory stick into Reed's smart TV, and the show was on for all to see. It was so special of Dan to take time out of his busy schedule to be there, and even the four kids were having fun. None of them had been to Niagara Falls, but they were so excited they were begging their parents to take them there. Her energy was returning. That was good. She seriously needed to take an exercise class.

The weather was perfect, but cold. No snow, so everyone was able to head for home with no problem. Ken handed Dan the key to his house since he now lived in Maddie's. "How much you want for it?" Dan asked.

"Seriously?" Ken looked at him with interest.

"Yeah. Actually, yeah. I'm showing up here often enough that it would be nice to have my own place, and it's close to you guys. All I'd have to do is hire a yard cutting company, and you guys are close enough to keep minimal tabs on it. I'd put in a good security system. If things get ahead of me I can always hire someone to be caretaker, too."

"I'll figure out a fair price and let you know."

"Don't tell Maddie. Let's surprise her."

Ken just grinned. "I like that."

Life was returning to normal. She's spent the last couple of years so wrapped up in her mother's deteriorating condition that she seemed to be strung like a rubber band the entire time. Now she found it easy to relax and actually enjoy the small things that she and Ken did. It was early March when he was called back for a go-team. This time it was Hawaii, where heavy flooding had caused significant damage. Floods always involved injuries of every kind. Maddie sent him packing, knowing he'd be fine. Now she could get caught up on a few things that had been postponed multiple times because of caring for her mother. First was the dentist. As much as she dreaded it, she pulled her big-girl panties on and went for a regular cleaning. The whole time she was there she kept her fingers crossed that there were no new cavities. She was lucky. Next was her primary doctor for her routine bloodwork. She was way overdue for that, and this time invoked crossing her fingers *and* her toes. Her blood pressure was a little higher than the doctor was happy with, but once Maddie explained all that had happened to her, especially in the past couple of months, she understood and gave Maddie a six-month pass. If it wasn't back to normal by then she would consider medications. All that was left was the OB/GYN, and she'd never had a bad pap smear in her life so wasn't concerned about that either. Three home runs in the time Ken was gone was good. She went through her calendar to be sure she wasn't forgetting something. She'd been horribly remiss on house maintenance, so called the plumber to just clean out the pipes, the air conditioning/heating folks to do a routine check on her heat pump, change out the house filters, and just get everything done that could really mess up their winter if it failed. It was the perfect time to do all that with Ken in Hawaii. They managed to get some skype time almost every night, but the five-hour time difference made it a bit harder. He could be in surgery when she was fast asleep, so they did the best they could. It was the Hawaiian shirts that made her shake her head. "Not a fan, huh? he quizzed. She waved her hand, iffy. "I'll go pick a pineapple and bring it home to you then." That made her laugh.

Ken was only gone for ten days. He looked a little worse for wear when she picked him up at the airport.

"You need a haircut," she ran her fingers through his unruly hair.

"And sleep. They ran us ragged. Maddie, I see what you went through in Niagara Falls now. I'm whopped."

"Then I guess we'll just have to go right to bed when we get home, won't we?"

"Can I get something to eat first. A bag of peanuts on the plane isn't very filling."

"I just so happen to have some beef stew in the crock pot, waiting for you."

"I knew there was a reason I married you!" And boy was that the truth, he mused. Without her he'd be on his way to a cold house, with no food in the fridge, picking up some fast-food hamburger on the way. He put his head back on the headrest and dozed.

Maddie sent him off to bed while she cleaned up the kitchen and secured the house. Sliding gently in beside him she folded herself into his chest and listened to his breathing. She was so very glad to have him home. She was asleep in minutes. Tomorrow she would confess to all her medical and house maintenance doings, knowing he'd be glad she was healthy, and the house was ready for winter. Yes, thank God, all is well.

"Mind if we rest for a few days, Maddie?"

"No, it's a good idea, actually."

Ken smiled and she saw the devil in his eyes. "What have you been up to?" Her eyes narrowed.

"I have a surprise for you?"

"What?"

"Dan just bought my house."

"What?"

"Yep. Dan just bought my house. He plans to use it for a base, and still go back and forth to visit Andy. He'll even have Andy come here. Kid's almost 17, so it should be a good thing for both of them."

Maddie started crying.

"Hey, you alright? It's good, right?"

"It's perfect. I'll need all the help I can get."

His eyebrows sank, "Why?"

"I'm pregnant." Nothing like dropping the bomb like those idiots did with microphones.

Dead silence. Shock. Gasp. "What?" His head was cocked, and his eyebrows creased, as if he hasn't heard correctly.

"You're going to be a father."

"When? How?" Simple statements but didn't tell her anything about how he felt.

"Well, the how is the usual way, and the doctor and I figure the baby will be born around the middle of September. Best I can figure it was conceived when we were together just before Jerry's visit. I had been having trouble with my periods for a couple years but with all the stress of my mother, meeting my brother, the ups and down of some guy named Ken, plus getting married, I just figured it would all be fine now that everything had settled down and I wasn't so upset all the time. A doctor told me a couple years ago I might be starting through the change, so I gave up worrying about it. She watched him for any sign of panic, or that he might not want the baby. She held her hands together tightly to keep them from shaking.

"Is that why you were so tired, you think?" Clinical question, no sign of acceptance. She was getting very nervous.

"Probably part of it. I'm right around three months now... Ken, if you don't want the baby..."

"WHAT? Are you NUTS? Of course, I want the baby, I just never thought you could get pregnant anymore, or I assumed you were on the pill, and why would I ever assume that? That was an odd conclusion I made, and I know that after 35 pregnancy is a serious risk, especially for a first baby, but this wouldn't be your first baby, really, and I just never considered protection, and now I wonder why I never did, maybe subconsciously I wanted a baby, for sure with you, so I didn't...."

The only way to shut up his babbling was to reach over and kiss him. And he kissed her back with more passion than she believed possible.

"You are so beautiful and now you're going to give me a child, and from this minute on you'll be in bed, tended to minute by minute, we'll figure out the perfect diet, I'll hire Vanessa to care for you until the baby is born, and the family will all come to keep you occupied. I'll hire someone to cook and clean..."

"KEN!"

"What?"

"WOW! Okay. I do know I'll need to be very careful. And I'll cooperate with that. Rehiring Vanessa would be fabulous for me. I know my risk is higher not only because of my age, but because I've already lost one child. All I care about is knowing you want him or her."

"I'm going to be a dad! This is cuddle stuff. Let's go to bed."

Epilogue

It was possible to turn into a smush of jello, just laying around for nine months being pampered, coddled, and practically slobbered over.

"Oh, here, let me get that for you."
"I've made your favorite food for dinner."
"Take your vitamins now."
"Don't fall, I'll help you get to the bathroom."
"You need to sleep, Maddie."
"Please get lots of rest."
"Here, drink your water."
"I'll massage your feet."

Despite the heroic efforts of her dear, beloved, smiley faced husband, and the equally chipper nurse named Vanessa, she was bored. You can only watch so much television before you start gagging. Even the food channel could make her stomach roll over, so she quit watching that. Vanessa brought her books, which she did enjoy, and Tessa, God love her, brought her Peanut Butter Cookies, Fried Peanuts, Peanut Brittle, and Chocolate Covered Peanut Clusters.

"I'm having such fun finding all these new recipes online," she bragged.

Trish showed up at least once a week with a baby book or child's camping tent. All this stuff was on top of a huge baby shower where so much clothing and boxes of diapers were unwrapped she was sure her child would be six before she got through all of it.

Maddie even begged Reed and Drew to "take this man away from me." Honestly. She'd seen a lot of helicopter mothers when she taught school, but a helicopter father-to-be was insane. She would swear in court that he checked on her every fifteen minutes for the entire nine months. Absolutely grounds for divorce.

And when the labor pains started. Thank God there was only one kid in there. How in the world did a woman have two or three of them at the same time? Or more than one of them at all. Vanessa checked her out and declared it was time to go to the hospital.

It figured. Mr. Helicopter… Mr. Walk Around the Block…was frozen stiff. Bug-eyed.

"Kenneth Avery, if you don't put your detached doctor hat on and get that car ready I'll divorce you."

Vanessa squealed with laughter, then noticed the scowl on Maddie's face. "Sorry, not funny I guess."

Maddie screamed again and Ken flew through the door to the garage to back the car out and get her suitcase loaded.

William Martin Avery was born on Labor Day. How utterly appropriate, thought Maddie. But he was one healthy screamer and seeing Ken cry made every single labor pain worth it.

With his son's hand wrapped around his finger he bent down and kissed his wife. "Thank you, Maddie," he whispered.

Vanessa entered the room dragging Drew and Tessa with her. They were soon followed by Trish. Paul had to work since it was Labor Day and there were campers all over the Eastern Shore.

It wasn't long before the room was full as Elle and Joan stopped by to offer congratulations and a huge balloon. Right behind them a nurse's aide delivered flowers from Jerry and Donna. Maddie couldn't believe there would be a time again when she would be surrounded by so much love. This was so perfect. She couldn't imagine how all of them found out so quickly!

Most of them only stayed about fifteen minutes, knowing Maddie was tired and needed some rest. Left alone, Ken's beautiful blue eyes looked at his son, then to Maddie, back and forth in a silent smile. At that moment no words were needed.

A gentle tap on the door and it opened. Maddie was shocked to see Charles and Darlene enter.

"Oh, my gosh," a tear started down Maddie's face. "It's so wonderful to see you two."

"My dear, how could we miss this? We really do think of you as a daughter. You loved our son as much as we did, and we are so grateful for the years of happiness you gave him." She took her husband's hand. "Now, who have we got here?"

"This is William, for my father, Martin, for Ken's dad, Avery."

"So beautiful." She ran her hand over the slight bit of hair growing on his head. "He really is perfect." She stood and shuffled a bit and leaned into her husband, "Ah, Charles and I were wondering…"

Maddie and Ken looked up at them, and Ken nodded.

"Well, we understand that both of you have lost both parents, and we were wondering if you would consider allowing Charles and me to be sort of… like grandparents to William?" She was rubbing her lips together in her nervousness. "We know it's a lot to ask…"

Maddie looked at Ken and saw his smile.

"We think that's a wonderful idea, Darlene. William will love having grandparents. Every child should have a grandmother that bakes him cookies, and a grandfather to tell him about the good old days. This is a super idea!"

Darlene and Charles relaxed instantly. It was close to a 'woosh' coming from Charles.

"We are so happy now," Charles said. "We missed out on buying Ken's other house, but we found one just a mile away and are thinking of putting in a bid in on it."

"If that doesn't pan out," Ken looked at Charles, "Dan was thinking about hiring a caretaker for his house because he's gone so much. He would only be using it about a weekend a month or so. Maybe he'd agree to you two living there as caretakers. Let me call him when things settle down if you're interested."

"I think that's a great idea. We can at least discuss it with him, can't we Darlene?"

She nodded yes.

"Knowing my brother, he'll build a mother-in-law suite for you. His back yard is huge. It could work for sure." She held up her son to let Darlene hold him. "Hold your grandson, Mom!" She stopped and, "Oh, may I call you that instead of Darlene?"

"We are now mom and pop."

Oh, good grief, the only one who wasn't crying was William (henceforth to be known as Bill) Martin Avery.

THE END

Made in the USA
Middletown, DE
20 October 2021